Praise for the John Madden My

"Move over, Inspectors Alleyn, Dalgliesh, and Morse, and make room for John Madden in the pantheon of great, civilized English sleuths. With *The Dead of Winter*, Rennie Airth now carries us through the third of Madden's encounters with a killer sprung from a Europe at war with itself. It's safe to say that once you've read it, you will start longing for Madden's next case."
—Jane Kramer, *The New Yorker* (on *The Dead of Winter*)

"*The Reckoning* is about the comforts of redemption and forgiveness—and the impossibility of forgetting."
—Marilyn Stasio, *The New York Times Book Review*

"Airth writes with arresting authority and compassion. . . . A major talent." —*Chicago Tribune* (on *River of Darkness*)

"[*The Reckoning*] delivers all the suspense and twisty plot turns that readers have come to expect from this popular series." —*Booklist*

"Starts off as a genteel British whodunit but soon escalates into a suspense thriller. . . . However, Airth's novel has an added psychological assurance and a tension-packed elegance. It's up there with the works of P. D. James and Ruth Rendell. High praise indeed."
—*The Cleveland Plain Dealer* (on *River of Darkness*)

"Unnerving . . . From this richly textured background, Airth draws a vivid cast of full-bodied characters and a plot that satisfies."
—Marilyn Stasio, *The New York Times Book Review*
(on *The Blood-Dimmed Tide*)

"Enter John Madden, protagonist of three fine novels . . . Madden is seamlessly admirable. . . . In an era when our real-life heroes tend to have feet of thick, grubby clay, it can be bracing to spend time with a man who is naturally but not implausibly noble."
—*The Washington Post Book World* (on *The Dead of Winter*)

"An excellent and convincing evocation of wartime London."
—C. J. Sansom, author of the Matthew Shardlake mystery
series (on *The Dead of Winter*)

"One of the best mysteries in years."
—*The Boston Globe* (on *The Dead of Winter*)

"A spellbinding series of mysteries set in the bygone England of our imagination . . . *The Dead of Winter* is the latest gripping installment in what's becoming my favorite series of British crime novels."
—David Ignatius, columnist for *The Washington Post* and
author of *Body of Lies* (on *The Dead of Winter*)

ABOUT THE AUTHOR

Rennie Airth was born in South Africa and worked as a foreign correspondent for Reuters news service. The first novel in his John Madden mystery series, *River of Darkness*, won the Grand Prix de Littérature Policière for best international crime novel of 2000 and was nominated for Edgar, Anthony, and Macavity awards.

RENNIE AIRTH

THE
RECKONING

PENGUIN BOOKS

PENGUIN BOOKS
Published by the Penguin Group
Penguin Group (USA) LLC
375 Hudson Street
New York, New York 10014

USA | Canada | UK | Ireland | Australia | New Zealand | India | South Africa | China
penguin.com
A Penguin Random House Company

First published in Great Britain by Mantle, an imprint of Pan Macmillan, 2014
First published in the United States of America by Viking Penguin,
a member of Penguin Group (USA) LLC, 2014
Published in Penguin Books 2015

THE LIBRARY OF CONGRESS HAS CATALOGED
THE HARDCOVER EDITION AS FOLLOWS:
Airth, Rennie.
The reckoning : a novel / Rennie Airth.
pages cm
ISBN 978-0-670-78568-1 (hc.)
ISBN 978-0-14-312694-2 (pbk.)
1. Detectives—England—Fiction.   2. Serial murder investigation—England—Fiction.
I. Title.
PR9369.3.A47R44 2014
823'.914—dc23
2014004499

Printed in the United States of America
1   3   5   7   9   10   8   6   4   2

Set in Stempel Garamond LT Std

This is a work of fiction. Names, characters, places, and incidents either
are the product of the author's imagination or are used fictitiously, and
any resemblance to actual persons, living or dead, businesses,
companies, events, or locales is entirely coincidental.

For Jack Langguth

THE
RECKONING

PROLOGUE

Lewes, Sussex, 1947

As he was fitting a new fly to his hook, Oswald Gibson looked up and saw two figures on the ridge above, both of them carrying what looked like fishing gear over their shoulders, long, cylindrical cases of the kind that you could fit two sections of a rod in.

'Damn!'

They were coming over a saddle in the low green hills and, having spotted the grassy bank where Oswald was standing with his rod, were probably heading for that very spot. Upstream from a small pool where the trout paused, as though waiting for any tempting flies that might come their way, it was the best fishing site on the stream and one that Oswald had come to think of as his own.

And he knew what was going to happen next, almost as though it were fated. The men would turn up, they'd exchange polite greetings and then, after looking around and seeing that this was the place to be, they'd say, 'Mind if we join you?' and take out their rods, probably not even waiting for a reply.

And Oswald would say nothing. He'd make no complaint, not say that he *did* mind and would they kindly shove off and find somewhere else to do their angling. No, he'd stand there dumb and resentful, accepting – as he always had – his failure to stand up to others, unable to escape the vision he had of himself as one of life's doormats.

'For heaven's sake, Oswald! For once in your life *assert* yourself.' The words were inscribed in his memory as though on marble, which wasn't surprising, given the number of times he had heard them. 'Why do you let people walk all over you?'

He could hardly have replied that it was because he *was* a doormat (though he'd been tempted to, and more than once). Still, the whirligig of time brought in its revenges. (The saying was one of Oswald's favourites.) Fresh in his mind still was the memory of the morning a year ago when he had come upstairs with Mildred's breakfast tray and found her lying in bed, with her eyes staring and her mouth agape: stone-dead.

'Stiff as a rod,' he had murmured to himself in wonder as he'd touched his wife's hand for the last time.

Meanwhile the men had crossed the saddle in the ridge and were coming down the hillside, close to where a flock of sheep were grazing, watched over by a dog. They were on a path that would join the one that ran along the valley floor, which in turn would bring them to his doorstep. Oswald braced himself for the encounter he was sure was about to take place. He could at least be cool with them, he thought: he would let them see they were not welcome. Perhaps they would take the hint and depart. As he stood there, already uncertain in his resolve, knowing in his heart that he was simply unable to deal with confrontation, he heard a piercing whistle and saw the sheepdog, a border collie, rise from the grass and begin to circle the flock it was guarding, coaxing them into movement. He scanned the hillside for their shepherd, a man he knew by sight, but it was some moments before he spotted him standing at the edge of a small copse near the crest of the ridge, his familiar figure blending with the shadow cast by the trees. For some minutes the sheep continued to move across the hillside, urged on by the dog, until a final whistle, different in pitch, brought it to a halt and the flock settled down again.

Distracted by the spectacle, Oswald had half-forgotten the approaching threat, but when he turned his gaze on the fishermen again it was to discover that he'd had a reprieve. During the minute or so that he had spent watching the shepherd, the pair had reached the intersection of the two paths, but instead of coming upstream to join him, as he had feared they would, they had gone in the other direction; in fact he could hear the sound of their voices growing fainter as they moved away. His solitude was preserved.

'Well, thank heaven for that.'

With a sigh of satisfaction he turned back to face the stream and a moment later his line, with the fly attached, went soaring off in an arc to fall softly on the still surface of the pool. He felt better already.

Earlier that morning he had awoken from a fitful sleep still troubled by the memory of an uninvited visitor who had called on him the week before, a nosy intruder he'd never met or heard of, who had knocked on his front door and, without so much as a by-your-leave, had proceeded to question him, sharply at times, about some long-forgotten episode in his past. Names, dates, places – the questions had been fired at him like so many missiles, as if he could be expected to remember details of that kind after all this time; and when he had dared to object to the interrogation, he'd been assured that the enquiry had official backing – something he'd been unable to challenge, but suspected was true, as this new Labour government seemed to think it had the right to stick its nose into everything. Oswald had endured the ordeal sullenly. He had sensed the hostility of his questioner without being able to identify its source and for this reason had been as uncooperative as he dared.

In particular he'd neglected to mention the journals he had

kept as a young man, when he had still thought his experiences might have some value – that his life might amount to something – and which were gathering dust in a desk drawer. When his inquisitor had left at last, and without a word of thanks, he had dug them out and quickly found the volume that dealt with the events in question. Yes, there it was, the whole business faithfully reported in his own unique style, a mode of expression clear to him, but not to prying eyes (Mildred's, for example). And although Oswald had been surprised by the amount of information his tormentor possessed, at least he'd been given an avenue to pursue: one possible means of getting to the bottom of what had been an unusually disagreeable experience.

Among the names flung at him, most of which he had forgotten, was one that struck a special chord in Oswald's memory: not because it had seemed important at the time (on the contrary, he hadn't even bothered to record it in his journal), but because he remembered some remarks this individual had made that prompted him to wonder now if the fellow was still alive and whether he could track him down. He'd be just the chap to ask about this so-called investigation, Oswald told himself: he would know, if anyone did, what lay behind it all. Finding him had been the problem, however. The only way Oswald could think to do so was to write to the man's former employers on the off-chance they were still in contact with him. But although he had begun to pen the necessary letter, he had quickly lost heart and put it aside. What was he getting himself into? he had wondered. The truth was that he hadn't enjoyed having his past raked up – not that bit, anyway – and when he'd thought more about it, and about his strange and unsettling interview with his recent visitor, he'd been inclined to let the whole matter drop: to let sleeping dogs lie.

But for some reason the business had continued to bother him. When, a few days later, he had travelled to Hastings to spend a long weekend with an old friend of his who had retired to the seaside town, he had found himself still dogged by the memory of his impromptu interview and, even before he set out to return home, he had resolved to talk the matter over with his elder brother, Ned. Ned was the person he turned to most often for advice and, as luck would have it, Ned was coming down from London to spend the following weekend with him.

Oswald looked at his watch. It was after five. Mrs Gannet, his daily, was usually gone by half-past four and he would have to wait until tomorrow to have a word with her about his weekend guest and how to feed him. With rationing still in force – and that in spite of the war being over for two years now – food was perpetually in short supply; fortunately Edna Gannet was a resourceful woman (and a great relief to have about the house after thirty years of marriage to the relentless Mildred) and Oswald was sure that somehow she would make ends meet. For one thing, there were the trout, which continued to attach themselves obligingly to his hook and line, and which were at least beyond the ration man's reach. Only that afternoon he'd caught a fine specimen – it was still flopping in its death-throes on the grass bank behind him – and by Saturday, which was four days off, he might have caught more. The thought brought a grin to his lips as he sent his line winging over the water for the last time. Though something of a novice as an angler – he'd never had the time for it when he'd been married, Mildred had seen to that – he'd found he had an unexpected talent for the sport and, now that he was retired (and a widower to boot) and able to devote more hours to his hobby, he was reaping the rewards of his determination to master its finer points.

Reeling in his line, he heard the shepherd's whistle again, coming from the hillside behind him; this time he ignored it, continuing instead to gaze at the scene before him: at the willow trees on the far bank bending to touch the stream, and at the water itself, which still sparkled in the last of the sunlight. It had been a gem of an autumn day, with the October sun only now beginning to pale in the blue sky and the shadows starting to lengthen, and throughout the quiet afternoon Oswald had hummed contentedly to himself, as if in harmony with the chorus that came from a pair of ringdoves in the giant oak tree that overlooked the stream at that point, and whose spreading branches offered welcome shade. For many years he had been a member of the local choral society and for some weeks had been attending rehearsals for the concert of Gilbert and Sullivan favourites that the group planned to give at their annual autumn concert in a few weeks' time.

Oswald had been picked to sing one of the solo numbers and had been practising hard.

'*A wandering minstrel I . . .*'

As he bent down to collect his things from the grassy bank, stowing the trout in the old kitchen basket he used as a creel and gathering up the crumbs of his lunchtime sandwich to put in a piece of greaseproof paper, he broke into song.

'*A thing of shreds and patches . . .*'

He searched about him for his tin of flies; he knew he'd put it down on the grass somewhere.

'*Of ballads, songs and snatches, And dreamy lullaby . . .*'

Spying it some way up the bank, he began to move in that direction; but stopped when he saw a shadow fall across the tin.

Oswald looked up. Squinting against the setting sun, he saw the silhouette of a man on the bank above him. Dressed in hiking clothes – breeches of some kind – topped by a baggy sweater, he stood faceless in the shadow cast by his hat brim.

'Yes . . . ?'

Uncertain as ever, Oswald hesitated – and in that moment recognition dawned on him and he stared, open-mouthed, as the figure moved, coming down the bank towards him with unhurried steps.

'What in heaven's name—?'

The question died on his lips. He had been gaping in wonder

at the face beneath the hat brim. But then the glint of metal had caught his eye, and his heart had lurched.

'No—'

The word was his last. Struck dumb in the last minutes of his life, in the grip not only of terror but of sheer disbelief, he could only stay where he was, planted like a tree on the bank, crouched over his knees, until he felt the cold touch of steel on his neck.

And then nothing more.

PART ONE

PART ONE

I

'You keep thinking nothing will surprise you in this job. Then something like this comes along and all you can do is scratch your head.'

Vic Chivers took off his hat as if he was going to do just that, but mopped his brow instead. It was close to noon and the sun was high in the sky.

'First, this Gibson fellow gets murdered in broad daylight, with no explanation. Then the bloke who shoots him vanishes into thin air.'

Glancing at him, Billy Styles thought Vic hadn't changed all that much. Heavy-set, with a lantern jaw and dark, bushy eyebrows, he was pretty much the same chap he remembered from the days when they had learned their trade together as young detective-constables with the Metropolitan Police. Good-humoured, sharper than he looked and something of a wag, Vic had resigned from the Met in the late twenties after marrying a Brighton girl and had joined the Sussex county force. Now, like Billy, he was an inspector and the senior CID man stationed in the town of Lewes.

'And to top it all, we get a call from your lot telling us the Yard wants to stick its nose in.'

Vic had been at the station to meet Billy when he'd stepped

off the London train earlier that morning and had driven him to a village called Kingston, on the outskirts of Lewes, where they had left their car and set off on foot down a narrow lane that led from the hamlet into the surrounding countryside.

'So get off your high horse, old chum, and tell me what's going on?'

Billy chuckled. 'Before we get to that, there's something I need to know. I read in your report that Gibson was shot from close up. How close exactly?'

'From no more than six inches away, according to the pathologist. There were powder burns on the collar of his shirt and on the back of his neck, too. And in case you're wondering, the bullet was a nine-millimetre slug. We got the ballistics report this morning.'

'Just one other question then.' Billy kept pace with his colleague. 'The report I read said that Gibson was on his knees when he was shot? Are you certain of that?'

'As sure as I can be. I put it in the report, didn't I?' Vic winked at him. 'But I'm still waiting to hear why the Yard is so interested.'

He apparently didn't think it worth pointing out that normally Scotland Yard was only called in to cases outside the London area at the express request of a chief constable, and that in this case it was the Yard that had initiated the contact.

'Come on, Billy – what do you know that we don't?'

'Not that much; only that there was a murder like this up in Scotland last month. A man was killed in the same way: shot in the back of the head, at the base of the skull, actually. It was very precise. There's no obvious connection, but since the Scottish police haven't any leads, it was thought I ought to come down here and take a look at this. Tell you what: let's deal with your one first. Then I'll fill you in on the other.'

'Fair enough.'

Satisfied – for the moment at least – Vic strode on, with Billy at his heels now. They had left the village behind and the lane they'd been following had petered out into a dirt road, which in turn dwindled to a footpath that joined the course of a stream running through a valley. Lewes itself lay on the South Downs, and the green hillocks on either side of the town, gashed white with chalk, were part of the long chain of grassy uplands that stretched across much of southern England.

'It's downstream from here, the place where he was killed,' Chivers announced, talking over his shoulder as he led the way. Ahead of them Billy could see the narrow waterway meandering down the valley, shaded here and there by the odd tree and flanked by a tangle of low bushes. On either side of it the land rose in steep, grass-covered slopes topped by rounded hillocks. He had passed through the South Downs often enough on his way to Brighton with Elsie and the kids for a day by the seaside. But this was the first time he had paused long enough to take in the rolling green countryside.

'And, just to fill you in, Gibson was sixty-two: he was deputy manager of a bank in Lewes until he retired. He and his wife – late wife – both came from London originally, but they decided to settle here when he quit his job. She died a year ago, but he stayed on. And before you ask, he was a model citizen: no form, no questionable associates, no enemies. In fact, from all we've been able to learn, he seems to have spent his whole life trying not to offend people. But if that's the case, it doesn't seem to have worked.'

He shrugged.

'As for his movements, we know that before he was shot he went away for a few days to stay with an old colleague of his from the bank, who retired to Hastings. The fellow rang us up when he heard about the shooting. The day after Gibson got back – that would be the Tuesday of this week – he went out fishing. It's how he spent most of his time. He left his cottage around two o'clock. That's confirmed by his daily; she says it was his usual routine. He always fished from the same place, and we know he was killed just after five because the shot was heard by a couple of fishermen who were a little way downstream from him.'

Vic paused. He seemed to be considering his next words.

'What's hard to stomach about this, Billy – what really gets my goat – is that the killer was seen. We've got a description of him. What's more, he knew he'd been spotted. You must have read that in my report. But somehow he still managed to vanish.'

'So I noticed. It's something I want to talk to you about.'

'Good.' Vic spoke over his shoulder. 'Because I've got plenty to tell you. But let's wait till we get there. It'll be easier to explain.'

He continued his steady plod, Billy following in his wake, and after a few minutes they came to an open, grassy area sloping down to the stream, free of bushes and overhung by a giant oak tree. The space had been cordoned off with tape tied to metal posts and hung with a pair of police signs, warning the public to keep off.

'This is the place.'

As he spoke a uniformed constable stepped out of the shadow cast by the oak tree, touching his helmet as he did so.

'Morning, Boon.' Vic acknowledged his salute with a nod. 'This is Inspector Styles, from London.' To Billy he said, 'Boon was the first officer at the scene. I thought you might have some questions for him.'

Billy nodded a greeting to the young man. 'You can tell me where the body was, for a start,' he said.

'It was over here, sir.'

Boon moved down the slope closer to the water and pointed to the ground.

'He was lying face-down, with his rod and an old basket that he used as a creel on the grass next to him.'

'What made you think he was on his knees when he was shot?' Billy put the question to Chivers.

'Because our witness saw him kneeling. And that was just before he was killed.'

'What about this witness? I read he was a shepherd?'

'That's right: name of Hammond.' Vic turned round. 'He was up there by that copse, watching over his flock of sheep.' He pointed to the slope behind them and Billy saw the clump of trees he was indicating near the top of the ridge. 'He said he'd noticed Gibson fishing – he knew him by sight – and, shortly before he was killed, he saw a man walking up the path towards him.'

He pointed again, this time downstream from where they were standing.

'Hammond had plenty of time to take in his appearance. He said it was hard to judge how tall the man was from where he was standing up on the hill, but he seemed to be of average size and looked young, judging by the way he strode up the path. He was wearing tan-coloured trousers and a cherry-red sweater and had a hat on, and a knapsack on his back.' Chivers paused. 'And now comes the strange part. Hammond had decided to start moving the sheep back to his farm – it's some way down the valley – and he whistled to his dog. The man on the path, the killer, heard it. He looked up, Hammond said. He actually paused for a moment. But he didn't stop. He went on. It made me wonder if he was all there.'

He waited for Billy's reaction.

'Was there anyone else around?'

Chivers shook his head. 'Not according to Hammond. Earlier in the afternoon he'd seen some hikers go by on their way to the Downs. But they were in groups.'

'He didn't see anyone on his own?'

'That's correct, and certainly not this fellow. Hammond said he would have remembered the sweater. It was bright red. Later on he saw those two fishermen who heard the shot. They came over the ridge and he saw them disappear into the bushes. When I spoke to them the next day I realized they must have been about a hundred yards downstream from here.'

'Then the man Hammond saw walking up the path must have gone by them?'

'He must have. But they didn't see him. The bushes are quite thick at that point and most likely he didn't see them, either. Anyway, Hammond spotted this bloke, as I say, and watched as he walked up the path to where Gibson was fishing – here, in fact – and then stop and go down the bank to talk to him.'

'He could see they were speaking?' Billy interrupted.

'I'm not sure about that, and neither is Hammond, but it looked like it.' Chivers shrugged. 'Gibson had been bending down, getting his stuff together. He seemed to be on the point of leaving. Then this man appeared and Hammond saw them facing each other, as close as you are to me, and he watched as Gibson went down on his knees in front of the man. But then he turned away . . .'

'He turned *away*?' Billy scowled. '*Hammond* did? Why?'

'Because of his sheep.' Chivers shrugged. 'They were starting to move, and for the next few minutes he was busy with them. When he finally glanced down at the stream again he saw there was someone lying on the bank.'

'Hang on a minute,' Billy cut in. 'What about the shot? Didn't he hear it?'

'Yes and no.' Vic shrugged. 'He heard something, but didn't realize it was a shot until later, when he found the body. He was some way away, remember, up on the hill, whistling to his dog; besides that, he's an old boy and hard of hearing.'

'But he saw the body. He must have known something was wrong.'

'Well, he wasn't sure it was a dead body, not at first: just somebody lying there. But then he spotted the man in the sweater walking back down the path in the direction he'd come from. And just walking, mind you; not running, not hurrying. Just striding along, as cool as you please.'

He shook his head.

'By that time Hammond had decided he ought to do something and he went down to the stream. When he found Gibson lying there with a hole in the back of his head, he climbed back up to the path to see if he could spot the other chap. But he'd vanished. So Hammond did the next best thing and legged it as fast as he could into Kingston, which is where he ran into Boon.'

He turned to the young officer.

'All right, Constable. It's your turn now.'

Boon straightened.

'I'd just come off duty, sir.' He addressed himself to Billy. 'I live with my mum and dad in Kingston and, as I reached our gate, I saw Mr Hammond coming up the road towards me, half-running. He was out of breath and could hardly get his words out. When he told me about Mr Gibson being dead and described the man he'd seen with him, I rang Mr Chivers at once, and he told me to go back to the stream with Mr Hammond and wait by the body. But just as we were setting off I saw some hikers coming back from the Downs. I knew they must have been on the same path and I asked them if they had seen the body. They told me they hadn't, and when I got out to the stream I saw why. It was lying near the bottom of the bank; easy to miss. And, besides, it was getting dark.'

'What about the shooter?' Billy asked. 'Surely he was on that same path.'

'He was when Mr Hammond spotted him.' Boon nodded. 'But the hikers never saw him, so he must have got off it.'

'These hikers . . . Were they all together? Are you sure he wasn't one of them? Couldn't he have slipped past you that way?'

'No, sir, he couldn't have.' Boon spoke firmly. 'There were seven of them: two couples who'd been together, and three ladies who were walking on their own. As it happened, I recognized one of the couples by sight. They're members of a ramblers' club in Brighton and I've seen them up here before. The other couple were friends of theirs. Anyway, Mr Hammond said it wasn't either of the men. The bloke he'd seen was younger and dressed differently—'

'They've all been spoken to,' Chivers interrupted. 'The couples went back to Brighton as soon as they reached the station, but after Boon alerted me I arranged for them to be met and interviewed when they stepped off the train. The three women were staying in the same hotel in Lewes. I questioned them myself the next morning. They'd been on the Downs all afternoon, but none of them remembered seeing anyone like the man Hammond described.'

'So what happened to him?' Billy looked from one to the other.

'That's the question.' Vic looked rueful. 'And I wish I had an answer. It's pretty certain he never came into Lewes. He was going in the opposite direction when Hammond saw him, heading for the South Downs Way, which links up with a track called Jugg's Road that'll take you to the outskirts of Brighton.'

'Didn't you say it was getting dark?'

'Yes, but with a torch and an Ordnance Survey map he could have found his way easy enough. And he must have known he'd have to get off the Downs before daylight; that we'd have searchers out from early next morning, which we did. His description was circulated to every police station and village bobby in the area. If he'd still been out there, we'd have collared him, Billy. You can be sure of that.'

'So you reckon it had to be Brighton he was heading for?'

'It was the only place that made sense. He could have walked down to Newhaven, I suppose, but that would have taken him all night, and we had it covered. Unless he lived locally – which seemed unlikely then, and even more so now, given the enquiries we've been making – he would have been looking to leave the area, and I had the police in Brighton checking the trains and buses that night and for the next few days. There was no sign of him.'

'Could he have had a car?' Billy wondered. 'Could he have got out that way?'

'From the Downs? Not a chance.' Vic dismissed the idea. 'There just aren't the roads. Never mind petrol rationing.'

He shrugged.

'The truth is I can't explain how he disappeared. For my money, he's a blooming Houdini.'

'And that's only the half of it.'

Leaving the constable to continue his vigil, Billy and Vic had started back on the path to Kingston. But Vic wasn't done yet.

'It's bad enough that he was able to slip through our fingers so easily. But what brought him here in the first place? Did he come looking for Gibson in particular, or was he out to pot anyone? Is he a loony?'

Vic let the question hang there in the air between them for some moments. Then he shrugged.

'I think we can safely say Gibson wasn't expecting trouble or he wouldn't have gone wandering off on his own. But all that says is that he'd probably be just as surprised as the rest of us. If he wasn't dead, that is.'

He shot a glance at Billy.

'I don't suppose you can shed any light on all that?'

'I'm afraid not, Vic.'

'Then tell me what happened up in Scotland. Who was the lucky bloke there?'

'A doctor called Wallace Drummond, a GP in Ballater. That's in Aberdeenshire. It happened a month ago.'

They had reached the outskirts of the village and Billy paused beside a wooden bench placed conveniently under a chestnut tree at the edge of the lane.

'Why not?' Vic guessed his intention. 'I could do with a breather myself.' They sat down, but when Billy offered him a cigarette, Vic shook his head. 'I gave up during the war. They were starting to taste like sawdust.'

'They still do.' Billy drew in a lungful of smoke. 'As I said, this Drummond bloke was murdered in the same way as Gibson. A single bullet in the back of the head: nine-millimetre, same as yours. It happened in his surgery and he was made to kneel down, just like Gibson was.'

'How did they know that?'

'The poor chap wet himself before he was killed. He must have known what was coming. The urine ran down his thighs and his trousers were stained as far as his knees, but no further. So although he was found lying face-down, the police there reckoned he'd been kneeling when the bullet struck him.'

'Any witnesses?'

Billy shook his head. 'Drummond's rooms were above a shop: he lived out of town. It was late afternoon, but the shop was still open and the owner heard the sound of the shot from below. He didn't know what it was, but he was concerned enough to go up to the floor above and try the door to Drummond's rooms. It was locked, and after he had knocked on it and called out a couple of times, he concluded there was no one there and went back downstairs. It wasn't until later that evening that the body was found. After her husband failed to return home, Mrs Drummond rang the local police station and they went round to his rooms.'

'So the killer wasn't seen at any point?' Vic had been paying close attention.

'Apparently not. The shot was heard at about a quarter-past five, and soon after that the shopkeeper closed up for the day and went home. The shooter must have waited for a while until the street below had emptied. That's what the police thought, anyway.'

'A cool customer, in other words. Just like our bloke.' Chivers scowled.

'So the coppers up there were stumped. There seemed no reason why anyone should have shot the chap. He had no enemies, as far as they could tell. Nothing had been stolen from his surgery. The investigation was handled by the Aberdeen police. They sent their report to Edinburgh, who forwarded it to the Yard. They weren't asking us to do anything; they just thought they ought to bring it to our attention.'

'Kind of them.' Vic sniffed.

'After we heard about the shooting down here, we asked them to send us their bullet. It's on its way to London now. I'll have to take yours back with me when I go. We've cleared it with Brighton.'

'Fine by me.' Chivers shrugged. 'But it's hard to see any connection – other than the two men being used for target practice. A Scottish medico and a deputy bank manager? You're not going to tell me they were acquainted.'

'Not as far as we know.' Billy trod on his cigarette. 'That's all I've got to tell you. We're going to have to wait on ballistics now. But I've got a few questions still. Is there anyone around we could talk to – someone who knew Gibson well?'

'There's his brother, name of Edward. He lives in London, but he came down when he heard the news. And Gibson's daily, a

Mrs Gannet. I've spoken to both of them, but only briefly. Mrs Gannet was at Gibson's cottage the day he was killed: she was there when he went off fishing, but he hadn't returned by the time she left, so she didn't find out what had happened to him until the next morning. His brother's staying at the cottage. I told them both to expect us.'

'Then let's go and see them, shall we?'

2

'I KEEP HAVING TO pinch myself. I can still hardly believe this happened – and to Oswald, of all people . . .'

Edward Gibson shook his head helplessly. Stout, with pink cheeks and a fringe of hair like a monk's tonsure around his bald pate, he came across – admittedly on short acquaintance – as a cheerful type forced into a role that didn't suit him: that of a grieving brother. Or so Billy thought, as he listened to Edward sigh and watched as he stared out of the window, seemingly at a loss for words. A solicitor by profession, he had greeted them in shirtsleeves at the door when they knocked, and explained that he'd been busy going through his brother's papers.

'I've already told you he had no enemies, but it was more than that. Poor Ozzie – he'd do anything to avoid trouble. I used to tell him, right back from the time when we were boys, that he shouldn't let people push him around. But he was a timid soul.'

He had led the detectives into a small sitting room at the front of the cottage, where Billy's eye had been drawn to a framed photograph of two men – one of them Edward Gibson, the other his brother – standing on a table near the window. It was Billy's first glimpse of the man whose violent end they had been discussing and it came as no surprise, after what Vic had said, to discover that Oswald's appearance was unremarkable. The snapshot, taken in a garden, showed the brothers standing beside a fishpond: Edward, smiling, with a straw hat pushed back on his head and seeming to enjoy the moment, stood with his arms akimbo, while Oswald, shorter by a few inches and pale of face, looked up at his elder sibling with a wistful expression.

'He let people walk all over him – his wife in particular. It's not for me to judge, but they had a rotten marriage. He wouldn't stand up to her, and she despised him for it. When she died last year I think it came as a relief to poor Oswald. He was finally free of her. They were free of each other.'

He looked at them.

'That sounds harsh, I know, but the point I'm making is that Ozzie was a happy man after that, happier than he'd ever been. He had already retired from the bank. He had enough to get by on, and he set about trying to enjoy his life for the first time. He had his fishing – he loved that – and his stamp collection, and enough friends that he wasn't lonely. There was nothing in his life to distress him: if there had been, I'd have been the first to know about it. I've been going through his stuff all morning, hoping I could find something that might explain this – a clue even – but there's nothing, absolutely nothing.'

He waited, hoping for a response perhaps, but Billy stayed silent. It was better to let the man talk, he thought.

'There's no denying Ozzie found life a struggle. He was always expecting the worst, waiting for the next blow to fall. But he was my brother, and I loved him. And this – what happened to him . . . It's outrageous.'

His glance challenged them to deny the assertion. Billy acknowledged the word with a nod.

'That's just how it seems to us, sir. Outrageous. But we still have to look for an explanation, if there is one. It helps that you're a solicitor: you know how police inquiries proceed. We need to know if anything unusual happened to your brother lately, anything out of the ordinary. It might not have seemed important at the time, but—'

He broke off. He'd noticed a slight change of expression in the other man's face: a look not so much of puzzlement, as of indecision.

'Look, I don't know if this is significant . . .' Gibson seemed to gather himself. 'But there was something he wanted to discuss with me.'

Billy waited.

'I haven't mentioned it, but I was due to come down this weekend anyway. On my own, as it happened – my wife had other plans – and Oswald was pleased at the thought that we'd have some time together. He was going to have another go at turning me into a fisherman, he said.' Gibson smiled sadly. 'Some chance of that! But the point is that he also said, when we spoke on the phone, there was something he wanted my advice on.'

'Did he say what?'

Gibson shook his head. 'I asked him the same question, but he said he'd tell me when I came down. It was too complicated to explain on the telephone.'

'*Complicated?*' Chivers spoke up.

'That was the word he used.' Gibson frowned. 'But I could tell it wasn't serious, or urgent.' He looked at them both. 'I knew my brother well, believe me. In fact I was the person he usually turned to. I knew when he was worried or upset, and that wasn't the case. It was just something that he mentioned. I was struck by how cheerful he sounded – he was looking forward to our weekend together.'

He sat back. Billy waited until he was sure Gibson had finished.

'Well, thank you for telling us that,' he said. 'We'll keep it in mind.'

The solicitor turned his gaze on him. His eyes had narrowed slightly and his next words confirmed an impression Billy already had that his initial judgement of the man might have been wide of the mark: Gibson was a lot shrewder than he looked.

'Before we part, there's something I'd like to ask you, Inspector. How does Scotland Yard come to be involved in this? There must be a reason.' When Billy failed to reply at once, he added, 'As you said yourself, I'm a solicitor. I know the drill.'

Billy shrugged. 'I wouldn't say *involved* exactly. Not yet, at any rate. But we've had a report of a similar shooting in Ballater, in Scotland. It's possible the two cases are linked, which is why I'm here.'

'Ballater?' Gibson looked bemused. 'I think I can safely say Oswald had no connections north of the border, or any contacts that I was aware of. We were born in London, both of us, and he spent all of his working life in the south. He joined the bank when he was quite young, before the First World War, and stayed with them until he retired. I can give you a list of the places where he worked. They were all in the south.'

'That could be useful.'

Gibson rubbed his chin. 'Have you considered that this might be a tragic error? That Ozzie was mistaken for someone else?'

'What do you mean exactly, sir?'

'This man who shot him – the one who was seen walking off afterwards – doesn't his behaviour strike you as odd, almost unbalanced?' He looked at the two detectives. 'I mean, there was poor Ozzie, busy with his fishing and, as far as I can gather, this man simply walked up to him and shot him. Might he not be deranged?'

'Acting at random, you mean? Looking for anyone to shoot at?' Billy caught Chivers's eye. 'It's certainly a possibility. We've thought of that. Although it's true people like that generally utter threats in advance and act in irrational ways, it's not always the case. They don't necessarily seem disturbed, at least not to the casual eye.'

Billy paused deliberately.

'By the way, sir, I'd be grateful if you didn't mention any of this to the press; or what I said about Scotland. We don't want to stir them up.'

His words brought a tired smile to Edward Gibson's lips.

'They won't hear it from me, rest assured. But I should warn you, some of the newspapers have been on to me already, asking questions. It's not every day a man gets shot in broad daylight. It won't take much to get them going. I'm surprised they haven't picked up on that Scottish report yet.'

'They're bound to – and soon. But I'd rather not do their work for them.'

'Quite so.' Gibson made as if to get up. 'But fair's fair. Can I count on you to keep me informed about the investigation? I don't want to be left in the dark.'

'We'll stay in touch, I promise.'

'Then I'd better get back to those papers.' He heaved himself up. 'You wanted a word with Mrs Gannet, is that right? She's in the kitchen. I'll send her through.'

'What did I tell you, Billy? This is one of those cases. It's going to give us both grey hairs, you mark my words.'

Tilting his chair back, Vic hoisted his feet up on his desk. They had returned from Kingston a short while before and he had sent out to the nearest pub for a couple of sandwiches, which they were washing down with cups of tea before Billy caught his train back to London. The CID offices were situated on the first floor of Lewes police station, and on their way in Vic had introduced him to a detective-sergeant and two constables, who were busy sorting through statements collected from parties of hikers and ramblers who had been out on the Downs on the day Gibson had been murdered.

'We know the shooter didn't escape this way, via Lewes,' Vic said. 'I've been hoping he might have been spotted walking cross-country towards Brighton. But no luck so far, I'm afraid.'

'If Gibson was his target – if it wasn't a random killing – then he must have known he'd be fishing there.' Billy had been turning the problem over in his mind. 'He must have had some idea of his habits; that suggests he made some earlier visits to Lewes.'

He had been looking over the file compiled by the pathologist while he chewed on a cheese sandwich. The police photographs of Gibson's body lying face-down on the bank had added little to what his colleague had already told him. Other pictures taken at the mortuary later showed the effects of the bullet, which struck him at the base of the skull and exited through his jaw, leaving an ugly wound.

'The sawbones made an interesting point,' Chivers had told him. 'If you want to make a clean job of topping someone, that's the best spot to shoot them: it breaks the spinal cord, severs the brainstem. Death's instantaneous.'

'So he knew what he was about?'

'It looks that way.'

Billy put down the file. He took a sip from his tea.

'What I'd like to know is who that visitor was who got Oswald so upset. And did the letter he was writing have anything to do with this business?'

These facts, both new, had emerged in the course of the interview they had had with Gibson's daily, a spry old party named Edna Gannet, who had not only proved to be more observant than most, but could also put two and two together. As she'd been quick to point out.

'As soon as I saw the chair, I knew. He didn't have to say nothing. And I could tell he was put out. I'd heard him in the study going on about it, muttering to himself. "Some people," he was saying. "Some people . . . !"'

Small in stature, and with a face as brown and wrinkled as a prune, Mrs Gannet had seated herself on the sofa at Chivers's invitation and regarded them both with a steady, birdlike stare. Unprompted, she had given them a brief description of her late employer.

'He was a nice gentleman, very quiet, very polite. But he couldn't be doing with fuss. He hated being bothered. Fishing was what he liked best, I soon learned that. The first thing I'd do when I arrived was fix him his lunch – a sandwich, say, or a cold sausage with a piece of cheese – and he'd take it with him when he went off; and either I'd see him when he got back or I wouldn't, depending on how late he stayed out.'

Asked whether there'd been any change in Gibson's behaviour prior to his death, she had replied in the negative. But when Billy, remembering what Edward Gibson had told them, asked if she thought her employer had had something on his mind, she had surprised both detectives by giving the question what appeared to be long and serious thought.

'He did have that visitor,' she had ventured, finally.

'What visitor?' Chivers had been the quicker with his question.

'Don't know who it was.' Edna Gannet had shrugged. 'I never did see. But I heard the front door slam and Mr Gibson's footsteps when he walked back from the hall to his study. He was going on about something, talking to himself. In a rare state, he was.'

Further questions had elicited a more coherent account of the episode, which, it turned out, had occurred the previous week – on the Tuesday, Mrs Gannet thought it was. She had arrived at the cottage at her usual hour, which was midday, but via the backyard and the kitchen door, having looked in on a friend who was ailing and whose own cottage lay on the other side of a small orchard at the back of Gibson's house. As she had entered she had heard the front door slam and her employer returning to his study. Shortly afterwards, having also heard his subdued mutterings and overcome with curiosity, she had knocked on the door on the pretext of asking him what he wanted for his lunch and had found him sitting at his desk 'with a look on his face that'd turn milk sour'.

Later, when she'd returned with the Spam sandwich he'd requested wrapped in greaseproof paper, she had found him busy at the desk writing a letter. He had barely looked up, she said.

'Yes, but how do you know he'd had a visitor?' Billy had asked.

'By the chair, of course.' To Edna Gannet it had been obvious. 'See, he had this stamp collection and he kept it on a table in the corner with a chair next to it, so he could sit down there when he wanted to. But the chair had been moved: it was standing in front of the desk, so he must have had a visitor.' Her glance had been triumphant. 'Anyway, how did the front door come to slam, and who else could he have been talking about, muttering that way? "Some people . . . some people . . . "'

Before leaving, the two detectives had looked in at the study where Edward Gibson was at work, the desk in front of him awash with files and papers, to ask him if his brother had mentioned being upset by a visitor, when they had spoken on the phone.

'It's the first I've heard of it,' he had told them. 'Perhaps that was what he wanted to talk to me about.'

'Mrs Gannet saw him writing a letter afterwards.' Looking around, Billy had noted the position of the chair she had mentioned. It had been returned to its proper place beside a table in the corner, where a pile of stamp albums lay. On the wall above was a photograph of a young man in military uniform and it took Billy a moment or two before he recognized Oswald Gibson's features in the youthful image. 'We're wondering if the two were connected – the caller and the letter.'

In response Gibson had turned his hands palm upwards, showing them to be empty. 'I wish I could help,' he had said. 'But I'm as much at a loss as you are.'

The station clock at Waterloo was showing ten minutes past five when Billy got back to London. A journey that was supposed to have taken less than two hours had taken three instead. Along with the other passengers he had endured the delay philosophically, there being not much else one could do these days. The optimism felt in the country at large when the war had ended two years earlier had all but evaporated; the expectation that life would soon be back to normal now seemed a distant dream. Food was still rationed, clothing hard to come by, housing in short supply and petrol all but unobtainable. It seemed hardly reasonable in the circumstances to expect the trains to run on time; and they didn't.

'Grey hairs, Billy. Grey hairs . . .'

Vic Chivers's parting words as he had waved his colleague off were still echoing in Billy's mind as he left the station in a taxi. Although Gibson's murder remained a Sussex case, the two detectives had agreed to keep in touch and Vic had promised to let Billy know if the possible leads they had uncovered earlier that day led anywhere.

'We're going to have to talk to everyone in the village,' he had said. 'Maybe one of them caught a glimpse of Gibson's visitor. In a small place like that strangers are noticed. It'd be useful to get a description. And then there's that letter. Just who was he writing to? I wonder. At least we know it wasn't brother Edward.'

On the off-chance that the address on the envelope might have been noted, Vic had decided to return to Kingston to ask in the village shop, which also served as a post office. When Billy wondered aloud whether it was worth the trouble, his colleague had chuckled.

'You city lads don't know about village life. You wouldn't believe how nosy people are. I'd lay odds they'll be able to tell me whether or not Gibson posted a letter last week. The only question is: did someone take a peek at the address?'

But he'd been under no illusions.

'Odds-on it'll turn out to be a wild goose chase,' he'd predicted, pessimistically, as they waited on the platform together. 'Whatever the problem with this caller was – and just because it got Oswald in a state doesn't mean it was serious – we've no reason to think it had anything to do with him getting topped a week later. Same goes for the letter. The inquest's tomorrow and, as things stand, I've got sweet fanny to tell the coroner, and not much prospect of any improvement in that department. Grey hairs, Billy. Grey hairs . . .'

Given the hour, Billy would have liked to call it a day and go straight home to Clapham, where he lived. But he was carrying the bullet used to kill Oswald Gibson in an envelope in his pocket and he went instead to the Yard, so that he could leave it with the ballistics lab. The one recovered by the police in Scotland was on its way south and would arrive the following day. Before departing he looked in at his office and found a message on his desk to ring Detective-Inspector Chivers in Lewes.

'You won't believe what I've got to tell you . . .' By the sound of it, Vic's gloom had lifted at a stroke. 'Ozzie never posted that letter, never finished it even. His brother found it among the stuff in his desk, dated last Tuesday. He'd started writing it on a pad and it was still there: he hadn't torn the page out. He must have begun the letter, then changed his mind. But he didn't destroy it.'

Billy listened as Vic recounted how he'd gone first to the post office, only to discover that Gibson hadn't posted any letter there for some time, and had then called in at the cottage to see if Edward had found anything interesting among his brother's papers.

'He'd been trying to ring me at the station. He'd only just come across the pad.'

'Well, what about it, Vic?' Billy sensed that his old pal was enjoying drawing the story out. There'd better be a good punchline, he thought irritably. 'Who was he writing to?'

'The commissioner of Scotland Yard!'

There was a long pause.

'Crikey!' Billy breathed out the word. He was dumbstruck.

'And that's not all. He starts off by apologizing, saying how sorry he is to bother such a busy man, et cetera – this is Ozzie all over – but he's trying to get in touch with someone who worked at the Yard a long time ago and he wonders whether they might have knowledge of his whereabouts . . .'

'Yes, but who was it, for Christ's sake?' Billy's patience had run out.

'I thought you'd never ask. It turns out to be a bloke we both worked with. But you knew him a whole lot better than me.'

Vic chuckled.

'Does the name Madden ring a bell?'

3

MADDEN FILLED IN THE last form, signed it and then added it to a stack of papers, which he handed to George Burrows, his farm manager, who was standing beside him, looking over his shoulder.

'That's done,' he announced. 'You can send them off.'

'There's nothing but paperwork with this lot,' Burrows grumbled. 'They've got a form for everything.'

'Yes, but we mustn't complain.' Madden eased a stiff muscle in his back. 'Not when we're being treated like royalty.'

The word was one his wife had used, not without a touch of envy. Helen was a GP, the village doctor, and while a new National Health Scheme was in the wings, it was yet to pass through Parliament and no one knew how well it would work out for either patients or physicians. Farmers, on the other hand, were already the anointed (another of Helen's words). Under the terms of the recently passed Agricultural Act, they had acquired fresh status. Needing to feed the population while keeping down costly food imports, the new Labour government had acted to increase domestic production, promising farmers guaranteed prices and assured markets for most of their produce and, where necessary, showering them with subsidies.

'Royalty?' Burrows sampled the word suspiciously. 'Aye,

well, I'll believe it when I see it.' His face brightened. 'I've got the accounts for you to look at, sir. It's been a decent year.'

'Let's leave them till tomorrow, George.' Madden stretched. 'I should be getting home.'

With the last of the autumn ploughing just completed – the tractor had been busy until well into the afternoon – it had been a long day, but when they left the cobbled farmyard by its arched entrance Madden was able to feast his eyes on a broad vista of freshly turned soil stretching all the way to the stream at the bottom of his land, which ran the length of the valley and was overlooked by a long, wooded ridge called Upton Hanger. As he paused to take in the view he caught sight of the swaying backs of his dairy herd as they made their slow way up from the unploughed fields on a sunken track towards the cowshed for milking. The sound of a horse's hooves mingled with the squeak of wheels interrupted his reverie. He turned to see Fred Thorp, one of his farmhands, exiting the yard in a dog-cart loaded with bulging sacks.

'I'm delivering these vegetables to Mr Dobie,' he announced. Horace Dobie was the village grocer. 'I can give you a ride home, sir.'

'Thanks, Fred, but I have to water Mr Sinclair's roses. And I fancy a walk through the woods.'

The cottage, brick-built and well proportioned, was set back from the stream and, with his hand on the wooden gate, Madden paused to admire the neat garden in front, whose principal showpiece was a pair of rose beds planted on either side of the path leading up to the front door. Formerly occupied by a widow named Granny Meacham, a near-mythical figure thought by generations of village children to be a witch, it was now the home of a personage no less terrifying (or so Helen averred): none other than Angus Sinclair, lately a chief inspector with the

Metropolitan Police in London and a man with a string of notorious murder investigations behind him.

'Your name is spoken in whispers in the village, Angus,' Helen had teased him. 'You are held in awe. Wicked children are warned by their mothers that if they're not good, the chief inspector will come to call.'

A detective himself in his younger days, Madden had learned his trade under Sinclair's eye and, despite differences of age and rank – and even after he had left the force to become a farmer – the two had remained friends; so much so in fact that when the latter had retired from his post at the end of the war he had elected to make his home in Highfield and, at Helen's urging, had bought the vacant Meacham cottage, which was near to the Maddens' own house.

With its occupant away at the moment – he was spending three weeks with his sister in Aberdeen – Madden had volunteered to see that Sinclair's roses were kept watered and, after parting from George Burrows, he had walked down to the bottom of his land, crossed by a set of stepping stones the stream that ran there and continued along a path bordering the rivulet until he reached the cottage.

Ten minutes spent with a watering can were enough to see the job done and, having cast a quick eye on the shuttered windows of the cottage to see that all was in order there, Madden resumed his walk home, choosing a roundabout route, however, turning his back on the stream and climbing the ridge until he struck a familiar path, one he had walked many times, but so overgrown now that in parts he had to pick his way through the overhanging branches of bramble and holly. He was just negotiating one such barrier when a movement in the ferns clustered about the trees below him caught his eye and he froze; then he sank silently to his haunches. As he watched, the handsome red head of a fox appeared, ears pricked forward. It was a vixen whose presence in the woods he had noted previously.

She had a dead rabbit in her jaws and stood motionless, sniffing the air for long seconds, before emerging fully into the small clearing in front, followed by three cubs that tracked their mother, nose-to-tail, across the leaf-strewn ground. In a moment all four had vanished behind the thick trunk of a horse chestnut. Madden expelled his breath in a sigh and stood up. A countryman at heart, he had never felt at home in the city despite his years with the Met and, at moments such as these, with the last rays of the evening sun piercing the dark greenery above him like golden spears and the deep, rich scent of the woods filling his nostrils, he was not above counting his blessings, which seemed many to him.

Twilight had fallen by the time he unlatched the gate at the bottom of the garden, and as he walked up the long lawn from the orchard he was greeted by the baying notes of a basset hound; and, seconds later, by the beast itself as it came galloping down the lawn to meet him.

'For heaven's sake, Hamish – don't you know me yet?'

A chance acquisition, the animal had belonged to a patient of Helen's who had died the previous winter, childless and without close relations. Discovering that the dog was destined for the Guildford pound, Helen had decided to adopt it instead, and its good-natured, albeit noisy presence was now a fixture in their lives.

Stooping to fondle the silky head pressed against his knee, Madden saw his wife come out of the house onto the terrace above and, at the sight of her still-slender form silhouetted against the light behind her, his heart skipped a beat and in an instant he was transported back years, to an evening just such as this when, in gathering twilight, he had walked up to the house from the gate at the bottom of the garden and seen her for the first time.

'We thought you might be coming back this way.'

Helen smiled a greeting from the terrace as he climbed the steps to join her.

'I saw our vixen,' he told her. 'She's got a new litter. That's her third, by my count.'

'Don't you dare call her *our* vixen. She's yours, not mine.' She greeted him with a kiss. 'At this very moment she's probably off plundering some hen-coops. The woods have run wild – I hear about it from my patients all the time. They want me to speak to Violet when she gets back.'

She meant the daughter of the late Lord Stratton, Highfield's largest landowner who had died the previous year. A childhood friend of Helen's, Violet Tremayne, as she was now, was married to a diplomat currently posted to the British Embassy in Moscow.

'Are you expecting them?' Madden asked.

'Next week. I had a card from her today. Ian's got leave.'

Helen took her husband's arm.

'And I've got more news. I had a letter from Lucy today. She's coming home. She says she's penniless.'

'Penniless?'

Their twenty-year-old daughter had been in Paris for three months, learning French. Under new regulations introduced recently by the government, it had become impossible to send money abroad and Madden had been concerned about her, wondering how she was coping. Not so his wife.

'A relative term, where Lucy's concerned, my darling.' She kissed him. 'Our daughter is nothing if not resourceful. I shouldn't bother my head about it, if I were you. Just think how nice it will be to have her back. We never seem to see our children any more.'

Their son Rob, a naval officer currently serving on a destroyer in the Far East, had not been home for nearly a year.

'What you must do, though, is call Billy Styles at the Yard. He wants to talk to you.'

'Now?' Madden glanced at his watch.

'He said to tell you he'd wait for your call, even if you were late back. It must be something important.'

'Do you mean to say he went out fishing and somebody *shot* him? Why, for heaven's sake?' Helen gave her husband the glass of whisky she had poured for him. He had made his call from the study and then joined her in the sitting room.

'The Sussex police have no idea. Billy was down in Lewes today. He's only just heard about the letter.'

'And your name was in it?'

'Apparently. Or at any rate the name Madden. But the man who wrote it – the man who was shot – said he knew this Madden had worked at the Yard years ago, so it must be me.'

'And they don't know why he wanted to get in touch with you, or why he didn't send the letter?'

'They haven't the first notion. His brother doesn't know, either. It's a mystery.' Madden shook his head. 'Of course, that doesn't necessarily mean it's got anything to do with him being killed a few days later. He had a visitor, this Oswald Gibson, before he was shot – some person who upset him. It was after that that he began to write the letter.'

He paused, biting his lip.

'And that's not all. According to Billy, something similar happened up in Scotland a month ago. A doctor, a GP, was shot in his surgery in exactly the same manner.'

'So both men could have been killed by the same person?'

'It's possible. The bullets used have been retrieved and they'll be tested shortly. If they match . . . well, then it becomes a different matter. I've told Billy I'd be happy to look at a photograph of Gibson, if he can get hold of one. Perhaps it'll ring a bell.'

They stood in silence. Then Helen spoke.

'And you're sure you've never met him?' She was still having difficulty believing what she had just heard.

'As sure as I can be.' Madden shrugged. 'I haven't the faintest recollection of an Oswald Gibson. The only Gibson I knew was a boy at school called Henry. He was our cricket team's leg-spinner.'

Helen regarded her husband fondly. Madden's memory was legendary.

'You can remember that Henry was a leg-spinner, but you don't remember Oswald at all. It's obvious there's been a mistake. I don't believe you ever met.'

'Neither do I.' Madden looked at her. 'But if I can't remember his name, how is it that he knows mine?'

4

'HAVE YOU FIXED AN appointment?' Madden asked. 'Is Gibson's brother expecting us?'

'Any time this morning, he said. He's got some photographs to show you.'

Billy had been waiting at Waterloo station to greet Madden when his train pulled in.

'He offered to send them to the Yard, but I thought it would be quicker if we did it this way. Besides, you might have some questions for him.'

There was no need for him to explain the need for urgency that lay behind his decision, least of all to the man who had taught him his trade, or the better part of it, as Billy liked to say. As an old investigator himself, Madden knew how important it was to resolve murder cases quickly – how trails tended to go cold after a few days – and the shooting of Oswald Gibson had now taken on a critical importance, thanks to the news Madden had received from Billy the evening before.

'It didn't take the lab boys long. The slugs were in good shape, better than they expected.'

The call had come half an hour after Madden had got back from the farm. Billy had stayed late at the Yard waiting for the results of the ballistics examination of the two bullets.

'The reason for that was that both had iron cores.'

'Say that again.' Madden wondered if he'd misheard.

'Well, bullets are made of lead usually. But these had iron cores coated in lead, which was why they kept their shape so well. According to the lab technicians, they must have been made in Germany during the last war.'

'In *Germany*?'

'Apparently the Jerries started producing them when they ran short of lead. I'm trying to get more on that.'

Madden absorbed the information in silence.

'But there's no doubt about your lab's findings?' he asked finally.

'None at all. The bullets were fired from the same pistol.'

'Time's become an important factor now,' Madden had explained to Helen later, when he told her he had decided to go up to London the following day. 'The murder in Scotland happened a month ago, and the police still have no lead in either case. I've no idea whether Gibson mentioning my name in that letter is significant or not. But there's just a chance that if I can remember him – his face, at any rate – it might give the police a starting point for their investigation.'

Greeting Madden on the platform now, Billy told him he had a police car outside that would take them up to St Pancras, where Edward Gibson's office was located.

'He's as keen as we are to get this question cleared up. Then I'm going to have to go down to Lewes again to talk to Vic Chivers. It's odds-on this will become a Yard case now, with the Sussex police taking the lead, at least for the present. But it'll all have to be sorted out and the chief constable informed.'

Glancing at his companion as they walked briskly out of the station concourse, Billy felt the tidal pull of the past. Although it was many years since they had worked together, he had never forgotten those days. The occasion had been a murder case that had held the nation in thrall, the slaughter of an entire household in Highfield, and despite his youth and inexperience Billy had found himself pitchforked into an investigation led by Chief Inspector Sinclair, in which Madden had played a leading role and in which he himself had come of age (or so he had always believed). Now, as they strode side-by-side out of the station deep in discussion, it seemed that nothing had changed.

'We still don't know much about the medico who was shot – his history, I mean, or whether he had any tie to Gibson, though that seems unlikely. But there's no doubt now that we're looking for a solo killer.'

When they got to the car Billy handed Madden a transcript of the half-written letter salvaged from Gibson's desk. Sitting in the back seat, Madden scanned the few lines it contained, quoting from the text: '". . . I would very much like to get in touch with a person who I know worked at Scotland Yard many years ago. His name was Madden. He was a detective. I realize this is an imposition, but I would be very grateful if you could tell me whether he is still employed there and, if not, how I might get in contact with him . . . "'

Madden weighed the piece of paper in his hand.

'I still find it strange that he knows my name.'

Billy shrugged. 'He might have read it in the papers years ago. I'm thinking of that Melling Lodge business,' he added, referring to the case on which they had worked together a quarter of a century before and which was known simply by the name of the house in Highfield where the murders had occurred.

'Yes, but that was years ago.' Madden shook his head. 'Why bring it up now?' He gnawed at his lip. 'There must be a reason for it. I wonder why he didn't finish the letter.'

'Changed his mind?' Billy suggested.

'Or lost his nerve?' Madden pondered the problem. 'And the wording's strange. "I would very much like to get in touch with a person who I know worked at Scotland Yard . . ." I was thinking we might have met in the course of some other investigation, but now I'm not so sure. It doesn't sound like it. Have you checked the files?'

Billy nodded. 'We've found nothing. No mention of Gibson's name, though that's not surprising. One of the problems is he doesn't seem to have been the sort of chap who was ever in trouble, and particularly not with the police. And if he was just a minor figure in some inquiry that you were involved in – a casual witness – there might have been no reason to make a note of his name.'

The firm of solicitors where Edward Gibson was a partner was situated in Gray's Inn Road and to get there they drove through streets scarred by wartime bombing, a wilderness of broken walls and shattered foundations, where little had been done as yet to mend the damage.

'They keep saying they're going to make a start on all this.' Billy gestured with his hand. 'But then something new comes up, some financial crisis or other, and they call a halt. It's the same with these new towns they're supposed to be building. The plans have been drawn up, but that's as far as they've got.'

The building that housed Gibson's office, when they reached it, proved to be untouched, though the house beside it had taken what looked like a direct hit. With neither a roof nor an upper floor, it had been reduced to a walled shell, above which a single staircase could be glimpsed climbing into empty air.

'A buzz-bomb did that,' Edward Gibson told them when they were shown into his office a few minutes later. 'It was one of the last to hit London – in late '44. I was in the basement digging out some records when it landed, and I thought the whole building – ours, I mean – was going to come down on my head. But the damage turned out to be minor. The fortunes of war, I suppose.'

Without a jacket, and wearing his shirtsleeves rolled up at

the cuffs, he had risen from behind his desk to greet them and, on hearing Madden's name, had eyed his visitor's tall figure with open curiosity.

'I must say I've been wondering who it was poor Ozzie wanted to get in touch with. Do you recall meeting him, by any chance?'

'I'm afraid not.' Madden shook his head. 'Not by name, at any rate. But I'm hoping I'll have more luck with a photograph.'

In response, Gibson opened a drawer in his desk and drew out a pair of glossy prints. He passed one of them across to Madden, who was seated beside Billy in a chair.

'That was taken just before the war began, when he was made deputy manager of the bank in Lewes.' Gibson's smile was wistful. 'Poor Ozzie. He didn't have many triumphs to celebrate, but this was one of them. At least he thought so. He used to have the photograph hanging in his office.'

Madden studied it in silence. Clearly a studio portrait, it showed the head and shoulders of a man whose thinning hair had been carefully combed to cover a growing bald spot. Dressed in a business suit, he stared back at the camera with a solemn expression.

'I don't recognize him.'

Wordlessly Gibson took the photograph back and handed the other across his desk.

'This was taken a few years earlier. That's his wife with him. They came with us on a family outing to Henley.'

Less formal than the first picture, the snapshot showed the same man, noticeably younger – his hair hadn't started to thin yet – looking up from the cushioned deck of a punt with a hesitant smile. He was dressed in white flannels and an open-necked shirt. Beside him, but looking away across the river in what seemed a deliberate attempt to distance herself from the scene, was a middle-aged woman whose heavy-featured face was scored by lines of discontent.

'As you might guess from that, they didn't get on, Ozzie and Mildred. In the end it wore them out. But I was surprised Mildred went first. I always thought she'd live to bury him.'

Edward Gibson's gaze remained fixed on Madden's face as he waited to hear his reaction.

'I'm sorry, Mr Gibson.' Billy heard the regret in his old chief's voice. 'I wish there was something I could say. I've simply no recollection of your brother.'

He handed the photograph back.

'Are you sure?'

'Quite sure.'

'When you were with the police, perhaps?' Gibson's tone had a pleading note.

'I don't think so. Inspector Styles and I have gone over that. It's really not likely.'

'Even though Oswald refers to it in his letter?'

'Even so.'

'But from what Ozzie wrote, it sounds as though at the very least there was some kind of encounter between you.'

'Not necessarily.' Madden spoke gently. 'All he said was that he knew that I had worked as a detective at Scotland Yard. He didn't say we were acquainted.'

'Yes, but . . .' Gibson bowed his head. For a moment he seemed lost for words. 'I was at the inquest on Friday.' Looking up, he directed his gaze at Billy, who had been sitting silent beside Madden. 'I don't wish to sound critical, but it didn't seem to me that the police down there had got very far with their case. There was no mention made of that murder in Scotland, I noticed. And that was after the coroner had asked if there were any leads in the investigation.'

'That's because we still didn't know if the cases were connected or not, sir. And, as we agreed before, we don't want to get the press going without good reason.'

Billy hesitated. Madden saw he was in two minds whether to go on.

'I said I'd keep you up to date with the investigation, and I mean to, provided you agree to treat everything I tell you as confidential.'

'That's understood, Inspector.' Gibson's voice had grown tense.

'We now know that the bullets that killed your brother and that doctor in Scotland were fired from the same weapon . . .'

Gibson turned pale at his words. He stared at Billy.

'. . . which means we're looking for a single killer, and that changes the whole aspect of the investigation. However, as far as we can tell, there was no connection between the two victims, so what we need to find out is why were they singled out? *If* they were singled out, that is. We've not ruled out the possibility that the killings were random. I know you've been going through your brother's stuff, his papers, looking for any clue to what happened, but you might bear this new development in mind while you're doing that. In case you don't know, the name of the doctor murdered in Scotland was Drummond.'

'Thank you, Inspector.' Gibson had recovered from his shock. 'I don't know the name myself, and I can tell you now that I've seen no mention of it in my brother's papers.'

He nodded towards a stack of files that rested on a table behind his desk. Beside them was a pile of leather-bound notebooks and he pointed to them.

'Those are Ozzie's diaries. He kept one from the time he was a boy. I'm going to go through them, and I'll keep an eye peeled for any mention of a Drummond, or any reference to Scotland.'

'Thank you, sir. That could be useful.'

Billy caught Madden's eye and they rose to leave.

'I glanced at them when I was down at Lewes.' Gibson picked up one of the books and riffled through the pages. 'The early ones are full of Ozzie's thoughts about life and his plans for the future. It made me sad to read them. Once upon a time he had dreams, poor fellow, but those died when he was still quite young, and after that it became just a record of his daily doings – quite cryptic at times, as though he'd lost all interest in life. Still, who could have imagined it would end this way?'

'Billy, I'm sorry. I've wasted your time.' Madden's chagrin was plain to see.

'Not a bit of it, sir. We had to find out if you recognized the bloke, and this was the quickest way of doing it. But it's more of a puzzle than ever now. How on earth did Ozzie get hold of your name?'

They were back in the police car, heading towards the Embankment. Billy, in front beside the driver, was sitting half-turned in his seat so that he could speak to Madden.

'I can't explain it. But there must be an answer.' Madden stared out of the window. 'Did you say you were driving to Lewes now?' he asked.

Billy nodded. 'I need to talk this over with Vic Chivers. They've run into a brick wall down there. There's still no trace of the man they're looking for, and they've got no other leads. But I can easily drop you off at Waterloo. It's no problem.'

'I thought I might come with you.'

'To Lewes?' Billy was startled. 'There's no need for that, sir. I'll keep you informed about any developments.'

'I know you will. But this is something I can only do myself.' Madden continued to gaze out of the window. 'I've been thinking . . . How long had Gibson been living at Lewes? Do you know?'

'Since well before the war, I was told. He was a teller in the bank at first and in time he became chief teller; then deputy manager. That was as far as he got.' Billy eyed his old mentor. 'Why do you ask, sir?'

'Because Helen and I used to go there regularly. It was before the war. They started putting on operas at a house called Glyndebourne, near Lewes, and we went with friends of ours from London, often for the weekend. I wondered if it was then that I ran into Gibson.'

'At the opera, do you mean?' Billy thought about it. 'It's possible. He liked music, Ozzie did. Vic told me he sang with the local choral society.' He frowned. 'But you say you don't remember him.'

'And I don't.'

'Still, that doesn't mean you weren't introduced, during the interval at the opera, say, or in a restaurant. You might have shaken hands, nothing more.'

'But would he have remembered my name?' Madden didn't think so. 'And how could he have known that I'd once worked at the Yard?'

Billy pondered the riddle. His face brightened.

'Could it have been those friends of yours who told him?'

'I've thought of that.' Madden sighed. 'They were a couple called Forrest. But, sadly, they can't help us. They were both killed in the Blitz. Their house was hit by a bomb.'

He shook his head.

'No, the only thing I can do – the only thing that might help – is if I go down there myself and wander around a bit. I can do that while you and Chivers are having your chat. It might just jog my memory.'

5

MADDEN PEERED ABOUT HIM. The view from where he stood, atop the battlements of Lewes Castle, was a striking one and, despite the lingering autumn mist that tended to blur the outlines of distant objects, he could see a large swathe of the Downs spread out below him, part of the meandering course of the River Ouse and a glimpse of red roofs, away to his right, which his companion assured him were those of Kingston, the village where Oswald Gibson had resided.

'It's less than fifteen minutes' walk away.' Constable Boon eased the strap on his helmet and patted his pink, down-covered cheeks with a handkerchief. The ascent to the castle keep had been steep. 'And then another fifteen or so further on, to the spot where the gentleman was shot.'

Assigned to accompany Madden on his walk around Lewes, the young officer had been assiduous in showing him the sights of the town and filling him in on its history, unaware that his charge was listening with only half an ear to his spirited account of the Battle of Lewes (1264) and the burning of Protestant martyrs some centuries later; that he was more intent on trying to place the man whose face he had been shown that morning and who, given his long association with the town, must have strolled these same narrow streets day after day. Before climbing the stone steps they had walked the length of the high street, and Madden had seen the hotel where he and Helen had stayed on two occasions, and the pubs and restaurants where they had eaten and drunk with their friends, but to none had he been able to attach the elusive image of Oswald Gibson.

Earlier he had received a warm welcome from Vic Chivers when he and Billy had arrived at the Lewes police station.

'It's been a long time, sir, but I must say you're looking well.'

Madden remembered the burly detective from the years after the end of the First World War, when he had returned from the trenches to find the Yard full of new faces – Billy's among them.

Told the reason for his visit, Chivers had offered the services of one of his men to show Madden around.

'Billy and I will be caught up here for the next hour at least. There's a chief inspector coming up from Brighton to talk about this. He'll want his hand held. But Boon's a bright young copper. As it happens, he was first man at the murder scene and, if you like, he could take you out there later so that you can see the place.'

Thanking him, Madden had made a further request. 'I should have mentioned it to Edward Gibson, but from the way Oswald phrased that letter, it seems that if we met at all, it was some time ago. The two photographs his brother showed me were both quite recent: Oswald was already middle-aged. I'd like to see some of him when he was younger, if that's possible, and I wondered if there were any at his cottage.'

'I can't say for sure.' Chivers was dubious. 'His brother took some stuff back to London with him. He left me a key, though, and when Billy and I are done we could meet in Kingston. You'll already have had a chance to see where Gibson was killed, and I'd be interested to hear any views you might have on the subject: any ideas at all.'

Grimacing, he had pointed to a stack of interview forms lying on his desk.

'We've spoken to everyone we can think of: to townspeople and villagers, and to every hiker or rambler who was out on the Downs that day, but so far we've drawn a blank. No one seems to have spotted the man Hammond saw. But there is one line of enquiry we can pursue, and I'm hoping you can help us there, sir.'

He had paused to eye Madden meaningfully.

'We still don't know what prompted Ozzie to sit down and start writing that letter to the commissioner with your name in it. But now that it's clear he and that fellow in Scotland were killed by the same man, we have to look hard at that visitor he had a few days before he was shot – the one who upset him. It's only a guess, but if these murders aren't random, he could be the man we're looking for. If we can only establish a link between these various things – between Ozzie's visitor and the letter he almost wrote and him wanting to get in touch with you – we might begin to understand what this is all about.

'As things stand, though, we're no closer to finding a motive for Gibson's murder than we were on the day he was shot. In fact, based on what we know about him now, it's hard to think of anyone less likely to get himself topped. But somehow Ozzie managed it.'

With that gloomy prospect weighing on his mind, Madden had spent the next two hours wandering about the town with his assiduous guide, whose eagerness to be of help made him an agreeable companion and from whose lips he received a detailed account of the shooting and of the subsequent search for the killer.

'What nobody understands is why he wasn't spotted,' Boon told him, echoing the words of his superior. 'I mean, both before and after Mr Hammond saw him walk off. It's as if he suddenly appeared and then disappeared . . . like . . . like . . .'

The young officer struggled to find the right image.

'Like a genie into a bottle?' Madden offered.

'Yes, sir, just like that.' Boon beamed. 'And the amazing thing is there must have been lots of walkers out on the Downs that day – there always are at this time of year – and there's nowhere to hide. It's all open country.'

They had reached the village of Kingston, where Boon had paused to point out Gibson's cottage, and as if to underline his words they were overtaken just then by a party of ramblers. At least a dozen in number, and of both sexes, the men were dressed in twill or corduroy trousers, the women for the most part in tweed skirts and sensible shoes. Armed with staffs and walking sticks – and each with a knapsack – they strode on in determined manner, one or two of them calling out a greeting as they went by.

Madden watched them pass without comment. But the sight gave him food for thought, as he remarked to Billy later when they met up again.

'The killer can't have known Gibson would be fishing that day. Didn't you say he was away for a few days before he was shot? So either the killer came on him by chance or he already knew Gibson's habits, which means he'd been here before and was waiting for him to come back. It all boils down to the same question: was Gibson deliberately chosen as a victim, or was it just blind chance?'

Billy had been waiting for him outside Gibson's cottage with the news that Chivers was still busy with his visitor, but that he'd been lent the key. They could go in and look around. Madden thanked Boon and, telling his young guide he needn't linger, followed Billy inside.

'Vic's praying you'll find a picture in here that you recognize,' he murmured to Madden as they went through a small entrance hall, where a raincoat hung from a peg, and a pair of waders like the legs of an otherwise invisible man rested on the paved floor, into the silent house beyond. 'To quote him, he's hoping you'll pull a rabbit from the hat.'

The hope proved a vain one. Although all of the pictures in the house, whether paintings or photographs, had been removed from the walls, they were found to have been stacked in wooden crates collected in the study ready for shipping to London, or whatever other destination Edward Gibson had in mind for them. One of them held what seemed to be family photographs – some in frames, others collected in albums – but after the two men had spent half an hour going through them, Madden was forced to admit that he was no closer to recognizing Gibson's face than before.

He had looked hard at two in particular, both of them studio portraits of Oswald as a young man. In one he was pictured sitting in an affected pose with his legs pushed to one side, while his face and the top half of his body were turned to face the camera. Two locks of his lank, dark hair had been carefully combed to frame his temples. His expression was contemplative.

Billy had chuckled on unearthing it from a stack of framed photographs already gathering dust in one of the crates.

'I remember seeing that one when I was here before,' he said. 'It was on the wall by the desk. I thought for a moment it was that bloke – what's his name – Oscar Wilde? But it's Ozzie all right.'

Madden said nothing. He simply shook his head.

The last photograph was the study that Billy had seen hanging above the table where Gibson kept his stamp albums, and showed him in the uniform of a First World War officer. Seated with his cap clamped under one arm, he stared back at the camera with a solemn expression. The long locks had vanished: his hair was cut short and he wore a moustache.

Madden studied it for a long moment. But again he shook his head.

'They all looked like that when they came out to France,' he said. 'Those young men . . . they were so determined to do their duty. They had no idea what was waiting for them.' He glanced at Billy. 'I'm sorry. It's no good. We never met.'

Billy squinted at the photograph. 'Knowing what we do about Ozzie, I can't help thinking it was a mistake to put him in uniform. He wasn't exactly cut out to be a soldier, was he?'

Madden shrugged. 'He was the right age, and that was all that counted then. Anyway that's an Army Service Corps badge on his cap. He was a supply officer. It's doubtful he saw any action.'

'So much for pulling a rabbit from the hat. All things considered, I doubt if I've ever spent a more useless day. I achieved absolutely nothing.'

Madden held out his cup to Helen and she filled it from the teapot. It was after midnight and they were sitting together at the kitchen table while Madden ate a long-delayed supper. Despite getting to Waterloo at what had seemed like a reasonable hour after his return from Lewes, he had had to wait a further hour before his train left and then spend an even longer period sitting in the station at Guildford while their own locomotive – which, according to an announcement broadcast on the loudspeaker, had developed 'brake trouble' – was detached from the carriages and replaced by another. It was not until a few minutes after eleven o'clock that they had finally rolled into a deserted Highfield station.

Expecting to find Helen in bed, he had instead discovered her in pyjamas and dressing gown curled up in a chair in front of the dying fire with a book on her lap, fast asleep. Or so he had thought until he bent to kiss her and she opened her eyes.

'I couldn't think what had happened to you.' She had circled his neck with her arms and drawn him down to her. 'So you had no recollection at all of him?' she asked now.

'Absolutely none. Lewes didn't jog my memory at all, and neither did Gibson's face. I'm just where I was. It's a complete mystery how he came up with my name.'

He fell silent, peering into his cup. As his wife watched, he put a hand to his brow, touching a scar that showed there near the hairline. It was a legacy of his time in the trenches.

She studied his face.

'Are you worried about this?' she asked.

'Not really,' he began, then checked himself as he found her eyes fixed on his. (They were dark blue, and Madden had always felt she had the power to see into him: that she could read his innermost thoughts.) 'Well, yes, to be truthful. All we know for certain is that a few days before he was killed Gibson had a visitor and that directly afterwards he started to write that letter to the commissioner with my name in it. It's hard not to think the two must be linked. But what the police are wondering – and so am I – is whether that visitor was the same man who shot Gibson a few days later.'

'What do you think?'

'He could be.' Madden gnawed at his lip. 'But I'm hoping he's not.'

'Because then you wouldn't be involved.'

'Exactly.'

'Is there any way of finding out?'

'There might be. What I need to know is whether that doctor up in Scotland had an experience similar to Gibson's. Did someone call on him in advance? Was he threatened or given some kind of warning? If so, it suggests that Gibson's letter might well be connected to his murder; and that somehow I'm involved in it too, though I can't for the life of me think how.'

Madden frowned.

'The trouble with that idea is that it doesn't quite fit the facts. If his visitor had frightened him, Gibson would have rung the Lewes police. He was a timid soul. His reason for writing that letter – or starting it, at any rate – seems to have been to get in touch with me; nothing more. But why is a mystery. And just as puzzling is how he knew I had once worked at the Yard.'

Smothering a yawn, he looked at his watch.

'No, we can't go to bed yet.' She took hold of his hand. 'You haven't told me how you mean to find out about the doctor in Scotland, and whether or not he had a visitor like Mr Gibson did – whether the pattern was repeated.'

'Oh, that . . .' He smiled. 'Well, Billy can certainly help by asking the police up there to enquire, but that might take a while. I want to get this cleared up as quickly as possible, and I've thought of a shortcut.' His smile widened. 'I'm going to put Angus to work.'

'Angus . . . !'

'He's sitting up there in Aberdeen with his sister, twiddling his thumbs, probably bored stiff. Ballater's not that far away: a couple of hours at most. I looked it up on the map. Chances are he knows some of the local police. And they'll certainly know him – by reputation at least. He ought to be able to ask a few questions without upsetting anyone. I should think he'd jump at the chance.'

6

Rising later than usual next morning, Madden came downstairs to discover that Helen had already had her breakfast and was preparing to leave the house.

'I'm sorry, darling, I couldn't wait. I've got to drive into Guildford later this morning. I've got two patients in the hospital there and I really must look in and see how they're doing.'

As a doctor, Helen was one of the privileged few with a petrol allowance.

'By the way, Violet rang yesterday. She and Ian are back from Moscow. He has to stay up in London for the time being – he's needed at the Foreign Office – but she's coming down at the weekend. I asked her to lunch on Sunday, but she insists that we go to the Hall. They're going to have to put the place in order, she and her brother, and she wants our advice.'

Madden helped her into her coat at the front door. She kissed him.

'When you ring Angus ask him how his cold is. He was coughing and sneezing when he left home, and I was a bit worried about the long train journey that he had ahead of him. Give him my love.'

A short while later, after he had breakfasted, Madden rang the number Angus Sinclair had left with him and, after a lengthy wait while the call went through several exchanges, found himself talking to a terse lady with an accent even more clipped than the chief inspector's, who told him she was Sinclair's sister, Bridget, and that her brother had gone for a walk and would not be back for at least an hour. Aware that his former colleague had a testy relationship with his sibling – both were widowed and, in the course of time, their reunions, never easy, had become trials by ordeal, at least in the telling – Madden contented himself with enquiring after Sinclair's health, and on being told it was excellent, left a message to say that he would ring again later in the day.

In fact, the chief inspector – for so he was still referred to by many, in spite of his retirement – had enjoyed a new lease on life since abandoning London for the quiet of the countryside, losing the grey, harried look he had worn during his last years at the Yard, when wartime restrictions on staffing and recruitment had placed an ever-increasing burden on him. Attached to his cottage and garden now – in particular to his roses – he had even contrived to shed the gout that had afflicted him at the end of his career, a cure that he was inclined to view as miraculous, although his doctor took a more prosaic view of it.

'He's finally accepted my advice,' Helen had reported, 'even if it wasn't entirely voluntary. At last he's eating sensibly and cutting down on alcohol. If he wants to send up a prayer of thanks, it ought to be to the rationing board. A monkish diet is just what Angus needed. Sadly, it won't last. Things will improve and, when they do, I expect to see him limping into my surgery again.'

Thanks to the delay in getting in touch with his old chief, Madden had time to review the revelations of the past few days, with their disturbing intimation that he might be connected, however unknowingly, with the death of Oswald Gibson. He went over in his mind the interview he and Billy had had with the murdered man's brother and their subsequent visit to Lewes. The case was so strange, and its link to the shooting in Scotland so inexplicable, that as the day wore on (and in spite of his confident assertion to Helen) he found himself wondering if he wasn't being too hasty in taking his old colleague's cooperation for granted. The mantle of retirement had settled comfortably on Angus Sinclair's shoulders: there was no reason to suppose he would want to shed it.

But the need he felt to resolve the question – if for no other reason than his own peace of mind – would not allow him to sit idle, and as soon as he returned home from the farm that afternoon he placed another call to Aberdeen.

'Two murders – both apparent executions: that presupposes the same killer in each case. But what's still not clear is whether the victims were chosen.'

It was Sinclair himself who had answered the phone, with the welcome news that his sister had gone out to play bridge and consequently their conversation would be undisturbed.

'That's the question, Angus. Were they deliberately targeted?'

'Because of who they were, you mean? But isn't it possible they might also have been handy victims? This man Gibson went fishing regularly, you say, which suggests that he was out in the fields on his own for long spells. What we don't know is whether the doctor was also an easy mark.'

One of the fruits of their long friendship – and of the investigations they had worked on together – was the appreciation each had gained of the other's qualities. Once his fears had been settled on the score of his former colleague's reaction, Madden had known that Sinclair's sharp, retentive mind would be turned like a searchlight on the puzzle presented to him.

'So you think he might be deranged? He's not particular who he kills?'

'It's a bizarre idea, I grant you, but the lack of any connection between the two victims and the geographic distance between the crimes rather points to a man travelling about the realm with murder on his mind.' The chief inspector paused. 'Unless there is a connection, of course.'

'That's what bothers me.' Madden fell silent himself. Through the open window of the study he saw Hamish gallop heavily across the lawn in pursuit of a crow that had alighted on the grass a moment before, and which now rose with a bad-tempered caw, easily evading the dog's ponderous challenge. 'That and the possibility that somehow I'm mixed up in this.'

'You're thinking of that visitor Gibson had?'

'And the letter he started writing with my name in it. They could be connected.'

'So if that visitor was the same man who killed Gibson later, you've reason to be concerned. I quite understand.'

Listening to his old chief, Madden smiled. He had yet to explain his idea, but the chief inspector seemed to have grasped it already.

'What you need to know is whether the doctor up here received a similar visitation. Did he have an unpleasant encounter with a stranger? Was the tenor of his life upset in any way?'

'Yes, it's possible he had some sort of warning of what was about to happen, even if he didn't recognize it as such.'

Madden paused.

'Now I'm sure the Scottish police will get on to that aspect of the investigation. But they'll have to coordinate with the authorities here and it may take a while. I don't want to wait that long. I'd like to know the answer as soon as possible. Are you acquainted with the police up there?'

Sinclair's response was a dry chuckle, which reached him clearly over the line.

'Now I see what you're up to. Well, you'll be pleased to hear I've made a habit of looking in on the Aberdeen constabulary. The current head of the CID is a man called Murray, a superintendent.

We're on good terms. He'll certainly be familiar with the Drummond investigation; he may even have been involved in it to some degree. I'll ask. I might even slip over to Ballater, if I get the chance.'

'I don't want you to put yourself out, Angus,' Madden began, but was cut short by a fresh cackle.

'Set your mind at rest. There's no question of that. As a matter of fact, you'll be doing me a favour. I shall be home by the weekend, but at present that seems a long way off. A day away is just what I need, and I'm sure Bridget would agree. It's been a long three weeks for us both.'

He chuckled again.

'Don't misunderstand me, John. I love my sister dearly, but we seem to bring out the worst in each other: her prolixity, my lack of patience. She'll be glad to see the back of me, if only for a few hours.'

7

Late on friday, having received no word from the chief
inspector, Madden rang Billy Styles at the Yard to discover that
the investigation was temporarily at a standstill.

'It's a question of how we go about it,' Billy explained. 'Is
this a Scottish inquiry, or should we take charge of it? Where is
this man based? Is he from down here or north of the border?
That's still not known.'

He said he had been in touch with Edward Gibson, who had
told him he was slowly working his way through his brother's
diaries to see if they contained any hint of past trouble: with no
result as yet.

'I had Vic on the phone, too, from Lewes. He's extended his
investigation to farms and villages in the area, some of them
miles away, hoping this man might have stayed at one of them,
or at least been spotted. But it's the same story: there's no trace
of him anywhere.'

Madden told Billy about the approach he had made to the
chief inspector.

'I hope we're not stepping on anyone's toes,' he said. 'But I
want to get this settled. Either Gibson had something important
to tell me, or that letter is a red herring. As it happens, Mr Sinclair is up there at present, staying in Aberdeen. I spoke to him

yesterday and asked him if he could find out anything about the doctor that might be useful. He seems to think he can talk to the police there without upsetting anyone.'

Billy received the news with a dry chuckle.

'I'd better let the chief super know that,' he said. 'He gets back next week: he's been in hospital.' He was referring to his superior at the Yard, the man who had stepped into Angus Sinclair's shoes, Detective Chief Superintendent Chubb – someone Madden himself had known well in the past when they were both young detectives learning their trade the hard way, under Sinclair's unforgiving eye.

Madden promised to pass on to Billy whatever he learned, but when Saturday passed without a phone call from Aberdeen, he resigned himself to the fact that he would have to wait until his friend's return to discover what, if anything, he had discovered.

In the circumstances, the lunch to which he and Helen had been invited on Sunday was a welcome distraction, as was the sight of Violet Tremayne standing beneath the portrait of one of her ancestors in the drawing room at Stratton Hall wearing a fur hat perched on her dark curls and waving a red flag emblazoned with the hammer and sickle.

'A gift from one of the comrades,' she announced as she greeted them with a kiss. 'Some of them are dears when you get to know them. Mind you, they say the same thing of Uncle Joe, and I'm not so sure about him.'

A slip of a girl in the photographs Helen had of their youth, Violet had become more matronly with the years, but her dark eyes retained a mischievous glint.

'We used to fight like cats when we were little girls,' Helen had told her husband on the way over. 'I lost count of the number of times I was sent home from the Hall in disgrace. It's a wonder we ended up friends.'

Over a glass of sherry in the drawing room Violet told them

she was there on behalf of her elder brother, the new earl, who was in Delhi serving on the staff of Lord Mountbatten in his capacity as the first Governor-General of an independent India.

'I have to make an inspection. Everything's gone to rack and ruin since Daddy died. Peter wants to hang on to the ancestral seat, but it'll cost a fortune to keep up and the only answer seems to be to hand it over to the National Trust. The trouble is, now that the Labour Party is in power I'm afraid they'll just use it as an excuse to grab other people's property.'

'Grab other people's . . . Honestly, Violet.' Helen couldn't contain herself. 'I don't know where you get your ideas. For your information, the National Trust is run exclusively by Old Etonians, and although it was originally set up to protect the countryside, its only purpose now seems to be to preserve the aristocracy.'

'Well, bless them, if it's true.' Lady Violet was defiant. 'But I've heard differently. And you can't deny that this new government, which I know you voted for – and shame on you, Helen – is after our blood. Taxation . . . death-duties . . . there's no end to it.'

'Oh, you poor darling.' Helen contrived to appear grief-stricken. 'But never fear. When the tumbrels arrive, you can come and seek refuge with us. We'll look after you.'

'Joke about it all you like, but one of these days you'll see the red flag flying over Stratton Hall, and then you'll be sorry.'

Before going in to lunch Violet led them over to the window and together they looked down at the sad sight of the extensive gardens now reduced to a wilderness of overgrown borders and uncut hedges. The handsome lawns surrounding a lily pond choked with weeds, once the realm of strutting peacocks, had become little more than muddy strips where the grass tried vainly to recover from the war years when the Hall had been converted into a convalescent home for wounded servicemen and the young officers had used them for their football games.

'We're going to have to put all this in order, and the house as well, before we approach the Trust. Peter's asked me to make a start.'

She took Helen's arm in hers.

'Do you remember the parties we used to have before the war – the first war, I mean – and all those young men we danced with? Then they went away, and so few of them came back.'

Later, as they were leaving, she came out with them to the stable yard where they had parked their car and showed them the coach house, now the repository of junk that had accumulated over the decades: a tractor with its innards exposed, a dog-cart missing a wheel; cracked mirrors and chairs without legs. In one corner was a giant cage, once home to a pair of exotic parrots, which Helen remembered from her childhood, and beside it a claw-footed bath piled high with moth-eaten rugs and carpets.

'I'm going to have to get rid of it all.' Violet sighed. 'I can't bear looking at it. It reminds me too much of the past.'

As Madden opened the front door, the sound of Hamish's trumpeting bay came from the other side of the house, and when they went through the sitting room to the terrace they saw the spruce figure of Angus Sinclair, dapper in tweeds, walking up the lawn from the bottom of the garden twirling a walking stick in his hand and with the basset hound trotting at his heels. He hailed them from the foot of the steps.

'Tell me: does Cerberus greet everyone this way? Or am I singled out for special attention?'

'Angus!' Helen greeted him with a kiss. 'How are you? How is that awful cold you had?'

'It went of its own accord. I won't say the Scottish air cured it, though Bridget might. She still can't believe that I actually chose to spend my life south of the border with the auld enemy. And before you ask, my dear, my toe is in capital shape. I haven't felt a twinge of gout.'

He caught Madden's eye. Helen sensed, rather than saw, the silent communication passing between them.

'We've just been to lunch with Violet Tremayne at the Hall. Most amusing, but exhausting too, so I'll leave John to tell you all about it while I go upstairs and rest.'

Her glance went from one to the other.

'And I rather think you have something to tell him too,' she added.

'Drummond was fifty-eight, a little younger than that fellow in Sussex, but the same generation. He studied medicine at St Andrews and, from what I could gather, spent his whole working life in Scotland, first as a junior partner in a practice in Edinburgh and later with his own practice in Ballater. That's where he came from, by the way, so he was well known in the community, and well liked, too.'

The chief inspector moved his chair a little so that the late-afternoon sun no longer shone in his eyes. They were sitting on the terrace side-by-side looking out over the long lawn and, beyond it, to the great wooded ridge of Upton Hanger rising like a wave, golden and flame-coloured in the full glory of autumn. Stretched out at their feet, Hamish's long body lay motionless in sleep.

'His connection with England seems to have been minimal. His receptionist remembers him making two or three trips to London, including once for a medical conference. And he had a cousin in Cumberland whom he would visit from time to time.

But he had no links with the south of England – she was almost ready to swear he had never been near Lewes – and the name Gibson meant nothing to her. Neither did yours, incidentally.'

Madden stirred.

'It's the period before he was shot that I'm interested in, Angus.'

'Yes, I know, John.' Sinclair smiled. 'But bear with me. I thought it as well to give you the whole picture: you'll see why. But let's deal with your questions first. You wanted to know if Drummond had received an unexpected visitor before his death; and whether anyone – any stranger – had been observed checking on his movements. The answer to both questions is "No" as far as I'm aware, though of course he may have kept it to himself. I say that because your man in Lewes didn't exactly broadcast the news of *his* visitor, did he? The police only learned about it thanks to his daily.'

The chief inspector paused, as though to give his listener time to digest what he had said. Then he resumed.

'I was right in thinking the Aberdeen police might have been involved in the Drummond shooting. Murray told me he had assigned a detective from the city force to oversee the investigation. Of course they already knew about the two bullets being matched, but the news of Gibson's visitor hadn't reached them yet, so he was more than interested to hear what I had to tell him. The upshot was that he decided to send the same man, a sergeant called Baillie, back to interview some of the witnesses again and allowed me to accompany him. And before you start to thank me, let me say it proved to be the high point of my holiday. It's years since I did any honest-to-God investigative work. The experience was refreshing.'

He beamed.

'Now, to put you in the picture, Ballater's a small town where everyone knows everyone, and after a morning spent walking around talking to Drummond's friends and acquaintances I can say with some assurance that there were no dark secrets where his life was concerned. No one we spoke to could come up with an explanation for the killing, and the only suggestion put forward was that he must have been murdered by mistake. Either that, or it was the work of a madman. We weren't able to talk to Drummond's widow – the poor woman still hadn't come to terms with his death and had gone to stay with a sister in Dundee – or with their two children, both of them grown-up and neither of them living in Ballater. But Baillie said he'd spoken to all of them in the aftermath of the shooting, and none had been able to shed any light on the crime or to think of any reason why Drummond should have found himself a murder victim.'

The chief inspector paused for breath.

'However, we managed to have a long conversation with the person who probably knew him best after his wife: his secretary-receptionist, a Miss McRae. She had worked for him for more than fifteen years and was clearly devoted to the man. We found her at home – she lives with her mother – and interestingly, from our point of view at least, she still had all the doctor's files in her possession, ready for handing over to Mrs Drummond when she returns from Dundee. With her help we were able to piece together the last fortnight of Drummond's professional life – the patients he saw, in particular – which may or may not provide you with a lead.'

'How so, Angus?' Madden was listening closely.

'You're interested in who might have called on Drummond: or any visitors he might have had. Well, as I said, we drew a blank on that. But he did have patients who came to his rooms, and some of them were strangers. Ballater's a tourist centre. It's next door to the Cairngorms and, rather like Lewes, it's something of a magnet for ramblers and the like. During those two weeks, apart from his regulars, Drummond saw a total of six patients who Miss McRae said were previously unknown to him: four men and two women. They were all tourists of one sort or another. Four were Scottish – two men from Edinburgh, and a couple from Inverness – and two English: a man from Manchester and a woman from Ipswich. They all left their names and addresses with Miss McRae, who also had notes on their various complaints in the doctor's handwriting in her files. Would you like to know what those were?'

'Yes, I would.'

'Two of the men had sprained ankles and one had fallen over and cut his hand. The Scottish couple were suffering from a stomach upset, and the doctor had made a note of the hotel they were staying at. Perhaps he planned to have a word with the management. The woman from Ipswich complained of menstrual cramps. She was given a prescription.' Sinclair frowned. 'Needless to say, Miss McRae was present at her desk in the waiting room when these patients were admitted to the doctor's surgery. While she had no idea of what went on inside, none of them gave the sense of anything having gone amiss when they left and Drummond himself had nothing special to say about any of them. As for the description you passed on to me, Miss McRae said that to the best of her recollection two of the men were youngish, in their thirties at any rate. They hadn't struck her as being particularly slight in build, but she cautioned us that her memory of the occasions was hazy.'

The chief inspector shrugged.

'Be that as it may, I made a note of all their names and addresses in case you might want them.' He removed a sheet of paper from the pocket of his jacket and handed it to Madden. 'The CID in Aberdeen has the same list, of course, and may choose to send it on. But to be on the safe side you might as well give it to the Yard.'

He waited in silence while his companion scanned the list.

'I can't thank you enough, Angus.' Madden looked up with a smile. 'Billy will see that the Lewes police are informed. They might get a match to one of the men's names.'

'Let us hope so.' The chief inspector stretched in his chair. 'Well, so much for events leading up to the murder. Now let me tell you about the shooting itself. To start with, there was nothing unusual about that day, nothing out of the ordinary so far as Drummond was concerned. We have that from Miss McRae. He followed the same routine he always did. He spent the morning at his surgery seeing patients. This went on until one o'clock, when both he and his secretary went home for lunch. In the afternoon he made his rounds while Miss McRae went back to her office to attend to secretarial work. It was understood between them that she would leave at half-past four on the dot. This was because her mother liked to have her tea equally punctually at five. As a result, and depending on how long the doctor spent on his rounds, he would either see his secretary just before she left for home, or not until the following morning. He himself always returned to his surgery before going home in case there had been a call from a patient while he was out, or some other message left for him by Miss McRae.

'In fact, that day he returned quite late. The shopkeeper who heard the shot and whose hardware shop was beneath the doctor's rooms saw Drummond walk past his window at ten past five. A few minutes later he heard the gun go off, though he didn't know what it was, and went upstairs to the doctor's rooms to investigate. The door from the street was always left open during the day – Drummond himself would lock it when he went home – and the shopkeeper was able to go up to the first floor and try the door to his suite. It was locked and, after he had knocked a few times without response, he assumed that when he'd seen the doctor go by earlier he must have been on other business. Shortly afterwards he shut up shop for the day and went home, and it wasn't until later that evening after Mrs Drummond had raised the alarm that the local police went round with her to her husband's surgery and found his body.'

He paused to take a breath.

'I haven't described Drummond's surgery yet. Baillie showed it to me. It was still unoccupied and the furniture was left as it was. Miss McRae had lent us the key. Basically it consisted of two rooms: a waiting room where Miss McRae sat at her desk, and the doctor's surgery, which was reached by an inner door and which overlooked the street. This was furnished as you might expect with a desk, an examination table, a screen . . .' Sinclair gestured. 'There was a carpet in front of the desk and Drummond's body was found lying on it, face-down. You know about the urine-stained trousers. It seems clear that he was made to kneel down facing the desk and was shot once through the back of the head from close range.'

The chief inspector frowned.

'Normally one might wonder how the killer gained access, but in this case it would have presented no problem. Given that he had some prior knowledge of the doctor's routine, he need only have watched for Miss McRae's departure before going up to the first floor and waiting there for Drummond to return from his rounds. We don't know whether they had met before, but even if they hadn't, he could have posed as a patient in urgent need of medical help, in which case Drummond would have invited him in.'

Sinclair tugged at an earlobe; he looked reflective.

'What struck me most about the whole business was the speed with which the killer acted. Only a few minutes elapsed between the moment the shopkeeper saw Drummond walk past and the second he was shot. There can't have been time for much talk between them. Yet Drummond knew he was going to be killed: the trousers tell us that. But was he told why?'

The chief inspector paused to allow his listener to comment if he wished. But Madden could only shrug. In the silence that ensued he got to his feet and began to pace up and down.

'What are the Aberdeen police doing now?' he asked.

'Not a great deal, I fancy.' Sinclair frowned. 'The description of the man seen by the shepherd had reached Murray through the normal channels, and he was having all hotels and boarding houses in Ballater checked, to see if anyone could recall having had a guest who matched it. Earlier the CID up there had given some thought to the possibility that the assassin might be a local man, but the murder of Gibson and the linking of the two cases have pretty well ruled that out.'

The chief inspector sighed.

'Other than that, I dare say the Edinburgh and Inverness police will check up on those three men – the Scottish tourists who consulted Drummond – to make sure they are who they say they are. But beyond that there's not much they can do. I'm afraid my efforts were largely wasted.'

'Not at all, Angus.' Madden paused in his pacing. He looked down at his old friend with affection. 'You've done heroic work. They'll all be agog at the Yard when they hear you're back in harness.'

'Will they . . . I wonder.' The chief inspector looked dubious. 'Somehow I can't see Charlie Chubb rejoicing at the news. And not so much of the "back in harness", if you don't mind. You see before you a man content to cultivate his garden.'

He stretched luxuriously and rose to his feet.

'But I wish I could have been of more help, John. It's still not clear whether you're involved in this. All I can tell you is that the answer doesn't lie in Scotland.'

They descended the steps from the terrace together and, with Hamish trotting at their heels, walked down the lawn in step with their lengthening shadows. When they reached the gate Madden paused with his hand on the latch.

'There was something you said earlier . . . about why you were giving me so much background on Drummond. You said you had a reason. What did you mean?'

Sinclair grunted. 'I'd forgotten about that. I was trying to underline how unlikely Drummond's murder seemed to me: how hard it was to imagine why anyone should have wanted to kill him. I believe you felt the same about Gibson.'

Madden nodded. 'That's why they seem random victims.'

'So you don't think they shared a guilty secret?'

'A Scottish doctor and an English bank official who had never met? I'd be amazed if they did. What's more, neither of them was expecting trouble. While it's true Gibson began writing that letter, he never finished it; and nothing in his behaviour suggested he was worried or concerned for his own safety.'

'What are you going to do now?' Sinclair asked.

'Ring Billy this evening and tell him what you've told me. Murray's report may not have reached the Yard yet.'

'So you think the matter's urgent?'

'I don't know.' Madden shrugged. 'But it may be. If this man's really bent on a killing spree, is there any reason to think he'll stop?'

8

'COME ALONG, SANDY.'

Tom Singleton tugged impatiently at the lead, but the Sealy-ham resisted. It had found something interesting to investigate in a pile of autumn leaves that had gathered beneath the straggly bushes lining the towpath, and Tom knew that his efforts to shift it before it was willing to move would be useless, short of strangulation; and although Sandy was more Nell's pet than his, he was still fond of the little brute.

'Do get a move on.'

He gave another sharp jerk, but to no effect. Their walk that day had taken them to Port Meadow, a flat, watery expanse lit-tle more than half a mile from the house in north Oxford that he and Nell had bought on his retirement. Although the weather had been fine all day, offering up the same cloudless sky and mild sunshine they had enjoyed for the past fortnight, the sun was sinking rapidly: in another hour darkness would fall, and with it the temperature. As if in tune with the thought, Tom began to cough, and then to wheeze as his lungs laboured to draw in enough air, while his face grew red and his eyes began to water. Cursed from boyhood with a weak chest, he had suf-fered the further handicap of being gassed in the First World War and the damage done then had lingered in the form of a persistent cough and a rattle in his chest when he breathed too hard.

'Damn and blast!'

The incident had occurred during the Battle of Loos in 1915 and Tom had been inclined to make light of it, particularly when it turned out that it was his own side that was to blame: the whiff of chlorine gas that he'd inhaled had come from shells fired at the German defences, when a change in the wind had blown some of the poisonous cloud back over the British lines.

'There I was, sitting in a dugout on a nice sunny day, minding my own business . . .' was how he would begin his account of the episode, adding further piquant details as time went by, mainly for the benefit of the schoolboys he had taught for three decades, who had relished the tales of life in the trenches that Tom would introduce into his history lessons as an antidote to wearisome details of the feudal system and the tedium of the Corn Laws.

In fact he still had a clear memory of that autumn morning when he and the other members of his battalion had watched, from the seeming safety of their lines, as the shells exploded around the German redoubt they were soon to assault; how the white cloud, pale as mist, had hung over the ground for long minutes and then begun to drift slowly back towards them. He had been lucky: he'd barely taken a lungful before someone had slapped a wet towel over his face and told him to hold it there. But he had never forgotten the sight of the Tommies on either side of him choking and retching; of the bodies convulsing on the duckboards at the bottom of the trench.

It wouldn't have done to tell the boys that; or about the men cut down like wheat stalks in the deadly cross enfilading fire of the German machine-guns; or of the thousands – the tens of thousands – of bodies that still lay hidden in the rich soil of France, unburied, and recorded only as names carved on stone.

Better to amuse them with tales of the whizz-bangs the Jerries sent over, hissing like firecrackers, which you could see coming and could dodge, if you were quick enough. Or, better still, with accounts of visits made to the battalion bathhouse for delousing.

'Yes, you grubby lot, delousing – and I've half a mind to give you a taste of it.'

Above all, what he could never bring himself to tell them was the deeper truth: that what they thought of as the civilized world – the one he had taught them about, the world that had risen out of the darkness and superstition of the Middle Ages into the dawn of the Enlightenment – had engaged in a war more terrible than any other before or since, and for reasons that even now he could not satisfactorily explain, either to himself or to them, let alone justify.

As to why he and so many others had answered the call of their country when it was clear they were being used as little more than cannon-fodder, he had tried to be truthful.

'It was a question of duty, you see. It had to be done. It's a hard thing to describe, duty. But you know it when you see it.'

At that point Tom had always paused, so that the new faces looking up at him, the ones who had not heard his answer before, could take in the importance of what he was about to tell them.

'At least you think you do . . . But you can be wrong. So remember: don't always believe what everyone else believes, even when it seems obvious. Don't always listen to what people tell you. Make up your own minds. Decide for yourselves.'

These words had a purpose. He hoped they would leave at least the residue of doubt in the minds of his young listeners; and that perhaps one day when they were faced with a decision requiring moral courage in the face of overwhelming opposition, they would remember them. His own moment of truth, if he could put it that way, had come many years before and could never be redeemed. Although he'd survived the war unwounded, apart from the damage to his lungs, his joy on his return home had been marred by a shadow, a stain on his character, on his very image of himself, which he had known, to his sorrow – even as it was incurred – would last a lifetime.

'Oh, for heaven's sake, Sandy!'

Lost for some minutes in the pain of remembering, Tom came to his senses abruptly and, losing patience, gave an even harder yank on the lead, dislodging the terrier from its chosen spot and dragging it after him along the path. Sandy had been particularly difficult that afternoon, running off as soon as they reached the meadow, where Tom had let him off his lead to pester a pair of French poodles trotting peacefully along behind their mistress and wanting nothing to do with the irritating presence that had suddenly appeared, snapping at their heels. Tom had been forced to hurry after them faster than he would have liked, in order to collar the terrier and attach him to his lead again: all this under the irritated glance of the poodles' mistress, who had made her annoyance plain. As a consequence he had been overcome by a fit of coughing, which had kept him immobile for minutes, red in the face and with tears streaming from his eyes.

The walk that followed – Tom had elected to circle the wide pond that occupied the middle of the meadow and cross the River Isis near Fiddler's Island – had calmed them both and by the time he led Sandy off the bridge and onto the towpath, the terrier had quieted down and was trotting along obediently at his side. Such walkers as were still out – the sun was low in the sky – were headed towards the city, and Tom went the other way, up the towpath, until he came to a bench bordering the track, where he stopped to let Sandy off his lead. There was a clump of bushes behind the seat and, knowing from experience that the terrier would be happy to nose around in them for a few minutes, Tom sat down on the bench for a breather.

He looked about him. Across the river there were still people walking through Port Meadow, either on their way home or simply enjoying the last of the sunlight, unseasonable for early November though it was, but welcome just the same. The last school he had taught at had been near Oxford, and on his retirement two years earlier he and Nell had decided to make the city their home. They had met during his convalescence after he'd been gassed. Nell had been a nurse at the hospital where he was treated, a job she had quit when they got married, and although Tom had always dreamed of having a son to carry on his name, he had been more than consoled by the three daughters Nell had borne him; and when war broke out again he had blessed the good fortune that had denied him a boy, whose fate it would have been to follow in his father's footsteps and perhaps not return.

Remembering the train of his thoughts earlier, he sighed. It wasn't often now that his memory went back to the years he had spent in uniform: a time already fading into history, and in any case overtaken in the public mind by the more recent triumph of arms, which – unlike the exhaustion that had marked the end of the terrible death-struggle earlier in the century – had been celebrated throughout the land. Yet perhaps it was not so surprising. In a few days the country would be marking Remembrance Day, when the fallen of both wars would be remembered at a ceremony in Whitehall. Wreaths would be laid, veterans wearing their medals would march again and although Tom had never felt drawn to attend the event, it was a time of year when the pull of the past was strongest, when the winds of memory blew coldest.

He shivered and looked at his watch. The light was beginning to fail: it was time to go home.

He whistled to Sandy and then, as he was about to turn round to look for him in the bushes, noticed that there was a college boat crew out practising some way downstream. An old oarsman himself (he had rowed for his school), he paused to watch as the flashing oars sent the arrow-shaped craft speeding upriver towards him.

As he called to the dog by name, he heard a noise in the bushes behind him and looked round.

'Hello! I didn't know there was anyone there.'

A figure wearing a dark coat and cap had emerged quietly from the shadow of the tangled greenery behind him. Tom narrowed his eyes, trying to make out the face beneath the peak. Then his gaze dropped and he stared in disbelief at the dull metal shape gripped in the gloved hand. It was pointed at him.

'Don't move.' The quiet voice when he heard it was yet another shock. 'Do as I say. Face the front.'

Speechless, Tom obeyed. He felt the cold touch of steel on his neck.

'There's something you need to know before you die.' The voice had a terrible calmness. 'Something you need to hear. Listen now.'

Tom tried to speak, but the enormity of what was happening – of what was about to happen – robbed him of all words. Instead he sat rigid as the voice murmured in his ear. Through tear-filled eyes he saw that the boat was drawing closer. He heard the splash of the oars in the water, the cry of the cox, yet none of it seemed real. There was only the voice in his ear . . . the terrible words.

'Do you believe in God?'

The finality of the question pierced him like an arrow.

' . . . Yes . . .' It was all he could do to utter the single word.

'Then make your peace with him.'

He heard a metallic click behind him. The sound was repeated. In desperation he tried to act, half-rising to his feet, thinking perhaps to throw himself to one side, to make one final effort, but he had hardly moved when a white light exploded in his head and all was lost.

9

'THERE – UP THE PATH where that crowd is. That's where it happened.'

They had just crossed the river onto a towpath that ran alongside it and Morgan pointed ahead of them. A detective inspector with Oxford CID, he was in his late thirties, about Billy's age, with dark-red hair and foxlike features.

'Singleton was sitting on a bench. He was shot from behind through the back of the neck. It was starting to get dark and nobody saw it happen – or no one we've found as yet. But a couple of people heard the shot.'

They had already spoken that day. On instructions from his chief constable, Morgan had rung the Yard first thing in the morning to notify them of the killing, and shortly afterwards Billy had been on his way to Oxford. With the roads mercifully free of traffic, thanks to the petrol restrictions, he had reached the city before midday to find Morgan awaiting him at the central police station.

'I hope this isn't a wasted journey, boyo.' Morgan's Welsh accent had a musical lilt. 'But we live a quiet life down here. We don't go around blowing each other's heads off; not as a rule. I'd lay odds this is your man.' He handed Billy a sealed envelope. 'Here's the slug we recovered: if ballistics can match it to the two you've got in London, then Bingo, I say! Oh, and by the way, he left us a *billet-doux* this time, your shooter.'

'A what . . . ?' Billy was weighing the envelope in his hand.

By way of an answer, and with a conjuror's flourish, Morgan had produced a small object from his pocket, which proved, on examination, to be an unexpended bullet, but one whose copper jacket had been painted black.

'It's a nine-millimetre all right. I've had it dusted for prints, but it was clean.'

'Where did you find it?'

'On the ground behind the bench. I'll show you when we get out there.'

'Why is it painted black?' Billy was examining the object. 'I've never seen that before.'

'Neither have I.'

'What does it mean?'

'Search me. You Yard fellows are supposed to be the experts.'

'How did he come to lose it?'

'Now that's a question I can answer.' Morgan winked. 'At least I think so. It hasn't been tested yet, but I'll bet you now it's a dud. My guess is the killer hit on it with his first try and had to eject the cartridge and fire again. He's a cool customer, all right, but not so cool that he remembered to pick up the bullet afterwards. It could be his first mistake.'

He had shown Billy photographs of Singleton's body lying on its side on the towpath, curled into a near-foetal position.

'Looks to me as though he might have tried to get up just as he was shot, and fell forward and to the side.'

Other pictures taken at the morgue showed a blackened hole at the base of the victim's skull.

'According to the pathologist, the gun was only inches away when the shot was fired. It struck the base of the skull, severing the spinal cord. We won't have the full post-mortem results until this afternoon, but he said it must have been carefully aimed. Death would have been instantaneous.'

When Billy offered to give the bullet back to Morgan, he shook his head.

'You keep it. This is going to be a Yard case: I feel it in my bones. But if I were you, I'd get my ballistics boys to have a look at that.'

They had driven out to Port Meadow in Billy's car. On the way Morgan had filled him in on the events of the previous afternoon.

'It was getting on for five o'clock when Singleton got out there. He walked the dog every day – his wife told us that – and they generally went to Port Meadow.'

'So it was a fixed routine?'

'Pretty much so. He was as regular as clockwork.'

After they had parked, Morgan had led his colleague down a narrow lane and after they had crossed the railway line Billy had seen a wide expanse of grass ahead of them with a pond in the middle of it. Other than some cows that were grazing near the water, the meadow was largely deserted and the two men had walked across it to the towpath.

Now, as they approached the murder site – and the small crowd gathered around it – three men carrying notebooks and pencils separated themselves from the group and hurried towards them.

'I forgot to mention it,' Morgan murmured in Billy's ear. 'But the press are on to this. My phone started ringing first thing this morning. They know about the Sussex shooting, but they haven't tied it to that business in Scotland yet, so far as I'm aware.'

As the three men came nearer he spoke to them.

'Not now, lads. I'll have a word with you later at the station.'

Ignoring their protests, he shouldered his way past. Billy followed and they made their way through the ring of spectators and joined two plain-clothes men and a pair of uniformed officers who were standing watch over a cartoon figure in outline that had been marked out with white tape pegged to the ground. Beside it was a wooden bench, to which Morgan pointed.

'As far as we can gather, he was sitting there, and whoever shot him must have come out of those bushes.'

He pointed again – this time to a clump of laurel bushes that were growing a few paces behind the bench.

'It seems Singleton had let the dog off the lead. We haven't found anyone yet who saw him sitting on the bench – the towpath was more or less deserted; it was getting late – but there was a boat out on the river with a college crew, and their cox heard the shot as they went by.'

Morgan turned to face the river and Billy turned with him.

'They were coming upstream and the cox was yelling out the stroke through a megaphone. Just as they passed he heard a sound that he later realized must have been a shot and he glanced round for a moment – only a moment, mind you, for he was guiding the boat – and saw the figure of a man wearing a cap, standing here behind the bench, and something lying on the ground in front of it. That must have been Singleton's body, but he didn't recognize it as such. It was just a shape to him.'

'What about the man behind the bench? Could he describe him?'

'Hardly.' Morgan grimaced. 'He only glanced that way. All he could say was that the fellow was wearing a coat and a cloth cap. It was starting to get dark.'

'And nobody saw him afterwards?' Billy received the news with a frown.

'Not that we know, as yet. Like I say, there weren't many people around. But we'll be making an appeal through the newspapers and the radio for anyone who was on the towpath that evening to get in touch with us. Something may come of it. The people who found the body were a couple called Blake.

They were walking back into town and they told us they hadn't met anyone coming in the opposite direction, so it looks as though the killer made his escape into Oxford. The couple stopped by the bench long enough to make sure Singleton was dead, then legged it as fast as they could down to the bridge and across Port Meadow to Jericho, where they knocked on the first door they came to and rang the police. It was another fifteen minutes before the first uniformed officer got here.'

'Plenty of time for the shooter to get away.'

'I would say so.' Morgan shrugged. He bent to pick up a stick from the ground. 'This Singleton was a schoolmaster, by the way; a history teacher. He and his wife came to live here a couple of years ago after he retired. From all we've been able to learn, he didn't have any enemies; in fact, quite the reverse. Everyone we've spoken to seems to have liked him. As soon as I heard about the shooting I thought of that advisory that you fellows sent out last week. It sounded like the same chap to me, and nothing I've learned since has changed my opinion.'

He tossed the stick into the river and watched as it was swept away by the current.

'And, to tell the truth, I'm praying I'm right. Otherwise I'll be up duck creek with no paddle to speak of.'

'I'm sorry, Mrs Singleton. I know how difficult this must be for you. Just a few minutes and then we'll be done.'

Morgan paused. He'd been doing all the questioning up till now, and under his gentle probing the dead man's widow, a woman in her sixties with white hair and eyes the colour of cornflowers, had told them all she could, little though it was. There was no hidden undercurrent to her late husband's life, no secret that could explain what had occurred. He had been in good spirits when he had left the house to take their dog for its afternoon walk, and her first intimation that all was not well had come when the animal had returned alone and she had heard it scratching at the door.

'She came to the mortuary last night to identify the body,' Morgan had told Billy on the way over. 'She used to be a nurse, so it wasn't the first corpse she'd seen. But you could tell it hit her hard. From what we've learned, they were a close couple.'

The two detectives had driven up from Port Meadow to the Banbury Road, a wide thoroughfare lined with handsome villas, and then turned off it into a narrower street, which had led, after several turns, to the small semi-detached house where the dead man and his wife lived. Before knocking on the door they had sat in the car for a few minutes deciding on their strategy.

'I'm here to collect information,' Billy had told his colleague. 'Yard case or not, this is still your inquiry and, considering the way these shootings are spread around the country, I can't see us being able to do more than coordinate the investigations. But I do have a couple of questions to put to Mrs Singleton when you're done.'

'No problem there.' Morgan had flashed his foxy grin.

'And it might be as well if you tread carefully when you speak to the press. They'll have guessed by now that the Yard is involved and that this murder is connected to the Lewes one. But they haven't made the link with Scotland yet, and if they ask you about that you'd better play dumb. Or, better still, point them in our direction. It's not for me to say, but I reckon we'll be issuing a statement soon.'

Now, as they sat in the Singletons' sitting room and he waited to put his own questions to the murdered man's widow, Billy let his gaze wander over to a table in the corner where a collection of family photographs rested. He recognized Single-ton from the mortuary pictures as the young man in a black scholar's gown with a mortar board on his head. Beside it was another photograph, dating from the First World War, in which – dressed in an officer's uniform – he had been snapped emerging from what looked like a dugout into a muddy trench, with a broad smile on his face. There were also pictures of their children (three daughters, Morgan had told Billy). One of them was there when they arrived. A young woman with her mother's fine features and soft blue eyes, she had come over that morning from Reading, where she lived with her husband, to be with her mother. The two had sat side-by-side on a sofa with the detectives facing them across the small room.

Morgan caught Billy's eye. It was his cue to speak.

'As Mr Morgan told you, I've been sent down from London, and the reason is we think there may be a link between what happened here yesterday and a shooting that occurred near Lewes, in Sussex, a few weeks ago.'

'I read about that.' It was the daughter who responded. She glanced at her mother.

'What I'd like to ask you, Mrs Singleton, is whether you've had any surprise visitors in the past week or two – callers, I should say; people you weren't expecting; possibly someone who might have upset your husband?'

'Upset him . . . callers?' Consternation showed on her face. 'Oh no, I'm sure he didn't . . . we didn't. Since Tom retired he's been at home, so if anyone came to see him it would have been here and I would have known, or he would have told me. We kept nothing from each other.'

Tears came to her eyes as she spoke these last words, and her daughter reached for her hand. She shot Billy an imploring glance and he realized that the older woman had been struggling throughout the interview to keep her grief in check. Seeing her stricken face, he was reminded of the war years, of the Blitz, when death falling from the skies had had the power to shatter whole worlds; and of how so many dawns had left the survivors wandering the streets of the capital, white-faced as ghosts. Here it had taken only one bullet.

'Just one more question. Have you noticed anyone keeping

an eye on the house?' Billy hesitated. He didn't want to say too much. 'We're interested in talking to a young, slightly built man. It's not much of a description, I know, and I'm not suggesting he was the one who shot your husband. We'd just like to know if you've seen anyone like that in the neighbourhood.'

She shook her head mutely.

'Thank you, Mrs Singleton.'

Billy nodded to Morgan. He was done.

'And just what was that all about, boyo?' Morgan had had to wait until they were outside to fire his question at Billy. 'You gave us a description of the fellow; you didn't say he might have been hanging around here and calling at the house.'

'I'm sorry. I should have done.' Billy was quick to apologize. 'It's just that if Singleton was deliberately targeted, rather than a victim chosen at random, the shooter had to have learned about his habits somehow – that he took the dog to Port Meadow most afternoons – and it's hard to see how else he could have found out about that, except by keeping an eye on the place. The other stuff comes from the Lewes case, and I didn't put it in the advisory we sent out because it just wasn't strong enough. Look, I'll explain.'

He fished out his cigarettes and offered them to Morgan. The Oxford inspector took one with a grin, as if to show he didn't harbour grudges. They lit up and Billy went on.

'The chap who was shot near Lewes – Gibson – had a visitor a few days before he was killed, someone who bothered him enough that he sat down and started writing a letter to the commissioner.'

'Go on!' Morgan's jaw had dropped.

'He said he wanted to get in touch with a man who had worked at Scotland Yard years before, an inspector called Madden, who quit the force in the twenties. He didn't say why and he never finished the letter. Just put it away in his desk and got on with his life – what was left of it.'

Billy drew on his fag.

'But what we don't know is whether whoever called on Gibson had anything to do with the shooting, or if it was coincidental, which is why I didn't include it in that notice.'

'How about the bloke in Scotland? Drummond? Did he have a visitor?'

'Not that we know of. And now it seems that Singleton didn't, either. So maybe that's a dead end.'

Billy took a last puff on his cigarette and tossed it into the gutter.

'But we're still not sure. I'm going to call Mr Madden when I get back to London and try Singleton's name on him; see if it means anything to him. He's been helping us with this. As it happens, I worked under him when I was getting started in CID – it was that Melling Lodge case years ago – and we've never lost touch.'

'Melling Lodge, eh?' Morgan was impressed. 'I remember that. Nasty business.' He eyed his colleague. 'So you rate this Madden highly?'

'Oh, yes.' Billy chuckled. 'You could say that. But he's as much in the dark about this as we are.'

He trod on the burning stub.

'And now I've got to go back to London and report to my chief super. He's been in hospital having his appendix out – he only got back this morning – and I can tell you now, this isn't going to make him feel any better.'

10

'CRIKEY, STYLES . . . IS THAT all you've got to show me?'

Detective Chief Superintendent Chubb was aggrieved.

'Three murders, and hardly a lead to speak of. It's unnatural. What's going on here?'

His scowl suggested he was expecting an immediate answer; but having got back from Oxford less than an hour earlier and hurried to compile his report, Billy was in no condition to supply it and, seeing this, Chubb sank back into his chair with a sigh, wincing as he did so and feeling his side.

'Ever had your appendix out?' he asked.

'When I was a lad.'

'Did it hurt?'

Billy shrugged. 'I don't remember, really.'

'You don't remember . . .'

Chubb glared at him. Billy grinned back. He had a soft spot for the chief super, as did most of his colleagues, their affection deriving in part from his appearance, which had made him the butt of endless jokes. Sagging cheeks and a pendulous jowl – physical characteristics that, in memory at least, seemed to have developed when he was still a young man – had inevitably led to comparisons with a bloodhound, as well as to the nickname of Cheerful Charlie, still in use, but now only heard behind his back. Billy himself had worked under Chubb on a number of cases stretching back years and knew that he was a first-class detective, diligent and meticulous, qualities that he was quite ready to admit he had acquired under the stern regime of his immediate predecessor, Angus Sinclair.

'And what's this I see?' Chubb jabbed his finger at the file lying on the blotter in front of him, which contained not only Billy's report from that day, but a summary of all the information he had been able to collect on the shootings. 'Are you telling me His Nibs has been sticking his nose into this?'

Billy coughed. 'Do you mean Mr Sinclair, sir?'

'Who do you think I mean?' Charlie glowered.

'Well, he happened to be up in Aberdeen, and Mr Madden thought it might help if he asked a few questions.'

'Happened to be . . .' The chief super's laugh was mirthless.

'That's where he comes from. I know it for a fact. He was born there.'

His remark brought a snort of disbelief from Chubb. It was followed by a fruity chuckle.

'And there I was, thinking we'd seen the last of the old so-and-so.'

Billy grinned. 'It could turn out to be useful,' he said. 'Mr Sinclair got hold of the names of some patients who consulted that doctor before he was killed. Not ones on his regular panel. Tourists. Strangers. Four of them were men, and as well as passing on their names to Vic Chivers in Lewes, I'm going to have them checked out, just to be on the safe side.'

The chief super's grunt was non-committal. A frown settled on his brow. 'Right, how do we stand now? Is there any way forward, or do we just have to wait until he tops someone else?'

'Well, on the face of it we still haven't much, apart from the description we got at Lewes.' Billy had been wrestling with the same question. 'The Oxford police are still looking for any more witnesses who might have been on the towpath that evening. Then there's the slug they recovered. I sent it up to ballistics. We should have a result by tomorrow and, once we know for certain it's the same bloke, I'll update the advisory we sent out.'

'What about this other bullet? The one painted black?'

'That's with the lab boys too. Morgan reckons it's a dud, and I've asked them to check that. But they've already told me they don't know what the colour means: whether there's any significance to it.'

Billy hesitated.

'And something else you ought to know – there were reporters at the scene. They'll have made the link with the Lewes shooting. My guess is the papers will be full of it tomorrow. If we're going to issue a statement, maybe we should include something about the Scottish case.'

'Otherwise the clever clogs will think they've discovered it themselves and try to make us look stupid.' The chief super bared his teeth. 'Good point. We'll be issuing a statement later. I'll say we're looking for a man, and I'll give them the description we got from that shepherd. This is a Yard case now, by the way. It's official. I got Cradock to agree to that. He's talked to both chief constables involved, and the Sussex and Oxfordshire police are being instructed accordingly. I'll give Aberdeen a ring later and clear it with them. Anything else?'

Billy pursed his lips.

'I'm hoping Mr Madden might be able to help with the investigation. We still don't know yet if his name being in that letter of Gibson's means anything, but it might. I rang him after I got back from Oxford. He'd heard about the shooting: it was on the lunchtime news. I was hoping the name Singleton might mean something to him, but it didn't.'

Billy paused. 'I told him Singleton had been in the war – the first war, that is – same as Oswald Gibson was, though *he* wouldn't have seen much action, if any. It was just a thought. If we're looking for a connection, then Mr Madden served in it too.'

Chubb grunted. 'Good bloke, John Madden. Good copper too, in his day.'

'He told me he was coming up to London again this week. I was wondering . . . I could ask him to drop in, if you like?'

The chief super's face brightened.

'That's a good idea,' he said. 'We were pals in the old days, John and I. Tell him I'd like to see him, if he can spare the time. Say I'd appreciate the chance for a chat.'

He paused to smile – at some memory, perhaps. Then he collected himself.

'That'll do for now. I'll leave this in your hands, but don't let me down. If there's another shooting, I want you on the spot as soon as possible. It's too early to think of setting up a team – we'll have to wait and see how this develops – but you'll need some help. I can spare you a detective. Who do you want?'

It was a question Billy had thought would probably be raised and he had already considered his response.

'Poole,' he said after a moment and, as expected, he saw the startled look on Chubb's face. The chief super was regarding him narrowly. Although his eyes, with their heavy bags underneath, sometimes had a sorrowful aspect, at this moment they were fixed on Billy in a penetrating gaze.

'Why?'

'I want someone who's prepared to do more than just go through the ropes.' Billy had his reply ready. 'Someone with imagination and a sharp eye. Someone with a bit of passion for the job.'

'Passion, eh?' Chubb was surprised. 'And you reckon Poole can offer that?'

'I do, sir.'

A long pause followed. Then Chubb shrugged.

'All right. Poole it is. But get cracking, the pair of you.'

Relieved to have got that over with, Billy climbed the stairs to the office he shared with a fellow inspector but had to himself just then, his colleague being away on leave. He'd taken a chance with the chief super, but he felt all the better for it now. A call on the internal line was enough to set the wheels in motion. Soon he heard quick footsteps in the uncarpeted corridor outside. There was a tap on the door.

'Come in, Lil,' he called out.

Detective-Constable Lily Poole crossed the room to his desk. Smartly turned out in a skirt and blouse, topped by a man's blue jacket, she took the chair he pointed to.

'What are you up to at the moment?'

'Not much, guv. I've been working for Mr Strickland.'

'Forgery case, is it? Petrol coupons printed abroad – Belgium or somewhere?'

'That's the one.'

'What are you doing exactly?'

'Not a lot. Paperwork mostly.' Lily Poole looked him straight in the eye. Her expression didn't change.

And making tea for the lads, Billy guessed. It wasn't written down, but as far as most of his colleagues were concerned, women were still second-class citizens, good for only two things, and one of them was making tea. Even now there were only a handful in plain clothes and mostly they were restricted to domestic cases. But since he'd been one of the ones instrumental in getting Lily Poole transferred from the uniform branch to CID, and since she just happened to be several times brighter than the average heavy breather fleshing out the Met's roster of detectives, he wasn't about to stand by and watch her being put in her place by a mentality better suited to the Stone Age.

'Well, I've got something else for you to do,' he told her. 'More interesting, I reckon. It's this shooter.'

Lily blinked. It was her only reaction. She continued to look straight at Billy.

'I'll be working the case, and I need someone with me. Would you like the job?'

'Would I ever.'

Like sunlight falling on barren rock, the smile that lit up her face had the effect of transforming it. No beauty at the best of times, in repose Lily's features were marked by a steely jaw, testimony to the character and determination that had brought her this far. Now, for just a moment, she looked like a young woman who had been handed a bouquet. The effect was short-lived. After only a moment she scowled.

'But what about Mr Strickland?' she asked.

'Don't worry about him. Your job now is to go through this.' He pushed his file across the desk to her. 'I want you to read it carefully.'

Lily picked up the folder. 'More paperwork, is it, guv?'

Billy looked at her. She flushed under his gaze. They had met on a murder case a couple of years earlier when she had been a uniformed officer stationed at Bow Street. As luck would have it, she had played a notable part in hunting down a ruthless killer, and from the first Billy had admired her single-mindedness together with her refusal to kowtow to superiors: her insistence on standing up for herself. But there were limits.

'Now listen to me, Detective,' he said. 'There's a man out there with a pistol who's already topped three people and, as things stand, we've no real leads apart from an iffy description. In the circumstances you should do what you're asked to do and assume there's a good reason for it.' He paused to let that sink in; then he continued: 'Facts have a way of accumulating in an investigation. Statements get made and filed away, things get missed. That's why it pays to have someone look at them with a fresh pair of eyes. Do you get my drift?'

'Yes, guv.' She had turned redder under his gaze.

Billy smiled.

'Besides, you might find something there to interest you: Mr Sinclair's name, for one.'

'Strewth!' Caught off-guard, Lily burst out. It had been the chief inspector more than anyone who had brought about her transfer to CID. The recommendation that Sinclair had sent to the commissioner had been one of his last official acts before retiring. 'Is he back on the force?'

'No such luck. But he's a friend of Mr Madden's . . . You've heard that name, I fancy?'

Lily nodded.

'Well, if you read that file you'll see how they're both involved in this, and why there's no explanation yet for any of these killings. Have a good look through it and let me know if anything strikes you.'

Billy paused so as to underline his next words. He looked her straight in the eye.

'And don't hang about, Lil. We haven't a clue as to what this bloke's up to – why he's killing people – but there's a good chance he isn't done yet.'

II

Vivid? Visible? Visit?

Sally Abbot stared hard at the pencilled squiggle on her shorthand pad, as if somehow, by doing so, she could decipher its meaning.

Vindicate? Vilify?

The 'V' sign was clear enough, but there was no strategically placed stroke or dot, as decreed by Pitman's, to indicate what followed. Oh dear, her mind must have been wandering again. And none of the words she had thought of so far made any sense in the context of the paragraph.

'Vee,' she murmured to herself – and then all at once, like a bolt of lightning, the answer came to her.

'*Vimy*,' she said aloud.

It was the ridge he'd been going on about all morning – Vimy Ridge – which the Canadians had attacked so brilliantly in 1917. Just why Sir Horace wanted to include it in his memoirs – he wasn't Canadian and he'd played no part in the battle – was a mystery. But he seemed to take pleasure in describing war (even if he hadn't played much of a hand in it, having done most of his observing from well in the rear). 'Hard slogging' was frequently the order of the day in his accounts; divisions tended to get 'knocked about'. But although there were times when they suffered 'rather severe casualties', it was surprising – to Sally at least – how often, having gone through a day or two or three of this kind of thing, the men who survived the shells and bullets had remained in 'good heart'.

Once, out of curiosity, she had gone to a library in Winchester and looked up some of the battles that Sir Horace was describing in an official history and had stared in horror at the numbers of dead and wounded printed there. Ten thousand, twenty thousand . . . The figures had lost all meaning when you thought of them as individuals: as men with families, loved ones, children even. On one occasion more than fifty thousand had fallen in a single day. Leaving those who had survived the slaughter in 'good heart'?

Not for the first time Sally had wondered whether General Sir Horace Canning, Rtd, Knight Commander of the Order of the British Empire and currently Lord Lieutenant of the County of Hampshire, had a screw loose.

She looked at her watch and sighed. He was due to address the Winchester Rotary Club that afternoon and luckily the occasion would be preceded by a lunch, so he'd be out of her hair for several hours. She had only taken the job as a way of filling in time before her marriage, which was due to take place the following spring, but the three months she had spent with Sir Horace felt like a lifetime and she had recently told him she couldn't continue working for him beyond the end of the year. He had not been best pleased.

'Bad show, Miss Abbot. Thought I could count on you. Thought we had an understanding. Yes?'

He had that peculiar way of speaking. Barking, Sally called it. He barked at her and he barked at Mrs Watts, the housekeeper. He barked at Greig, his chauffeur, and at the maids and the gardeners. He was like a bad-tempered pug.

The bell on her desk rang. She rose and went into the next room.

Her employer was at the French windows, gazing out over the well-tended gardens fronting the old stone manor, standing with his hands locked behind his back and his chest thrust out, in a pose Sally supposed was military and which was reflected in nearly all of the photographs of his past career decorating the walls of the study. There he was as a younger man in an old-fashioned uniform astride a horse, but somehow managing to project the stiff, forward-thrusting pose. In the background was a flat expanse of grassland fading into the distance, and beneath the picture was a penned caption that read: *En route to Mafeking, 1900.* Seeing it, Sally imagined him barking at the Boers.

The most recent photographs dated from the First World War, in which, as Sally knew from the memoir she was helping him to compile, he had attained the rank of general. One picture showed him standing by an artillery piece, swagger stick clamped tightly under his arm; in another he was bent down in a trench, peering through a periscope. Pride of place in the collection was given to a print larger than the rest, which was placed in a commanding spot in the middle of the wall facing his desk. It pictured him striding along beside another senior officer, both grim-faced, both staring straight ahead. The caption beneath the photograph read: *With Field Marshal Haig, Arras, 1917.*

'Butcher Haig,' Aunt Millicent had remarked when Sally mentioned the photo to her. 'That's what people used to call him. Imagine sending all those young men to their deaths time after time. Mind you, if it hadn't been him, I expect it would have been someone else. Once the war started, no one knew how to stop it.'

They had reached a point in Sir Horace's memoirs when he had just been appointed 'corps commander' – obviously a big thing – and only the day before Sally had typed out a passage that recounted the summons he had received to attend the field marshal at his headquarters, where he had learned of his promotion.

'He wasn't much of a general by all accounts, our Sir Horace; it's a wonder he got where he did.' Aunt Millicent knew a surprising amount about the war. Her younger brother had been killed early on at the Battle of Mons and she had also lost two cousins later in the conflict. 'Most likely he was one of Haig's yes-men, someone who didn't question his tactics, no matter what they cost in terms of lives lost. He retired quite early – I think he realized he wouldn't be offered another command – but he was taken out of mothballs during the last war and given some job in the Home Guard. And now he's the Lord Lieutenant, if you can believe it. Not that that counts for much. Mostly he presents prizes at agricultural fairs and makes boring speeches.'

It was Uncle Guy who had suggested to Sally that she might like to work for Sir Horace for a few months before she got married. She had given up her job in London at the start of the summer in order to spend time with her mother, recently widowed and not long returned from India, where Sally's father had worked in the colonial administration, and to see her settled in Feltham, the Hampshire village where Uncle Guy was the vicar.

'Sir Horace has been lonely since his wife died, poor old boy, stuck up there alone at the Manor,' Guy had told her. Bascombe Manor, situated a mile or so outside the village, had been the seat of the Canning family for generations. Sally gathered that Sir Horace had inherited the estate following the death of his elder brother, who had expired leaving no heirs. 'He mentioned to me that he was working on his memoirs and asked if I knew of anyone with secretarial experience who could help.'

The Lord Lieutenant had shown no sign of having heard her come in now. He remained staring out of the French windows. Finally he turned and fixed his blue, slightly bulbous eyes on her. Sally had been taken aback by his gaze the first time they met. It was more like a glare, and she had thought something must have upset him. He had seemed to tremble on the brink of outrage. It was only later that she learned it was his normal look – the face he showed to the world – and with it had come a further realization.

'His glaring and barking are all a great front,' she'd declared to Tony, her fiancé, when she had told him about Sir Horace. 'I think he's afraid.'

'Of being found out, do you mean?' They had gone for a walk in the woods behind Feltham and were strolling hand-in-hand. 'Then I know how he feels. During the war we used to put up a terrific front. You wouldn't have thought we were the least bit scared.' Tony had been a pilot in the Battle of Britain and had won a Distinguished Flying Cross. 'But I know that every time I went up I was terrified. I kept wondering if that day would be my last. But I never showed it. Or at least I don't think I did, and the same was true of the other chaps.'

'Yes, but that was different . . .' It pleased Sally that, unlike some of his friends who were unable to put the war behind them, her fiancé never tried to play the hero. 'And with him it's not a passing thing. I bet you he's always been like that.'

'Pretending to be someone he's not?' Tony had ruminated on her words. 'Then I feel sorry for him. It means his whole life has been a fraud.'

Sir Horace was still glaring at her now.

'My speech, Miss Abbot?' His protuberant eyes were accusing.

'It's in that folder on your desk.'

Where I put it. Where you saw me put it.

Giving no sign that he had heard her, he went to the folder, glanced at the clipped pages inside, folded them neatly in half and slipped them into the inner pocket of his jacket.

'I shall be back by four. You've enough to keep you busy? Yes?'

'Quite enough, Sir Horace.'

'Good.'

Turning on his heel, he strode to the door. She heard his footsteps echoing on the uncarpeted, flagged corridor outside. The noise receded. Sally breathed a sigh of relief. As soon as she heard the front door close and the sound of the car starting she went out through the windows onto the terrace and lit a cigarette. Tony wanted her to stop smoking, and she'd promised to before they were married. But she felt she had earned a fag that morning and she stood at the balustrade looking down at the garden below. Laid out in the Italian style, its neat, symmetrical beds and gravel paths were contained at the far end by another balustrade, beneath which the parkland stretched away for a quarter-mile or more to a wooded knoll.

Leaning against the stone rail, enjoying the mild sunshine – and the taste of the tobacco, forbidden fruit as it was – Sally saw something move in the distant grove of trees. The Bascombe estate covered more than a hundred acres and extended for a mile or so beyond the wooded knoll. Again she caught sight of movement in the undergrowth, and this time a figure appeared at the very edge of the wood. Shadowed by overhanging branches, it was impossible to make out in any detail, but presently Sally caught sight of the glint of sunlight on glass – two glints, to be precise – and she realized that someone was studying the Manor through a pair of field glasses.

She giggled. It was lucky Sir Horace wasn't home. He had an intense dislike of trespassers. Once, when a party of ramblers had strayed into the park, she had seen him walk all the way across the garden shaking his stick at them (and barking like mad, Sally was sure).

Tempted to wave to the distant watcher, Sally trod on her

cigarette instead (dutifully picking up the stub, which Sir Horace's eagle eye would certainly have spotted). Turning away, she went back inside. There was still all that morning's dictation to be typed up. Before that, though, she would join Mrs Watts in the kitchen for a sandwich and a good gossip.

Then, sad to say, it would be back to the trenches.

12

In the days when he had had the ear of the assistant commissioner and been effectively in charge of all criminal investigations, Angus Sinclair had worked from an office on the second floor at Scotland Yard with a view of the Thames and the tree-lined Embankment, and it was into these same agreeable quarters that Madden was ushered later that week, with Billy in tow, to be greeted by the new incumbent.

'Ah! John Madden. It's about time you showed your face. What have you got to say for yourself?'

Detective Chief Superintendent Chubb rose with a scowl from behind his desk.

'Hello, Charlie.' Madden greeted him with a grin. 'You're looking well.'

'No, I'm not. I'm in pain. What do you expect? First they yank out my appendix and then, when I come out of hospital, I find some fellow's gone barmy, knocking off people left and right. And somehow *your* name's mixed up in it.'

He pointed an accusing finger.

'Don't look at me. I'm as baffled as you are.'

'Baffled? Yes, that's the word.'

Beaming now, the chief super leaned over his desk to shake

hands with his visitor. He gestured to Madden and Billy to take the chairs in front of his desk.

'It's the word being thrown around these days.' He lowered his bulk carefully into his own seat. 'Especially by the newspapers, in case you hadn't noticed. Did you see the *Daily Mirror* today?'

'I'm afraid I did.' Madden was regretful. '*Yard clueless*. Not very kind of them, I thought.'

'I'll tell the editor you said so.' Charlie chuckled. 'And before we get down to business, what's this I hear about Angus playing detective up in Scotland?' His eyes narrowed. 'Not toying with the idea of a comeback, is he?'

'Heaven forbid! He's more interested in his roses.'

Chubb's look was incredulous.

'It's true,' Madden assured him. 'He's grown some beauties. And by the way, he sends his warm regards.'

'Roses . . . warm regards? Don't tell me he's gone soft in the head.' The chief super's tone was wistful. 'My word, that man made me suffer.'

'You weren't the only one,' Madden reminded him. 'I had it worse than you did.'

'That's because you were his favourite. He used to stand over you.'

'How well I remember it. But don't worry, Charlie. He's mellowed with age. You wouldn't know him.'

'Wouldn't I, though?' Chubb's eyes glittered. 'Look, I don't mind you giving him *my* regards back. But just warn him not to come the King Lear with me, or there'll be ructions. And you can stop grinning, Styles. Count yourself lucky you've only got me to make your life a misery.'

He cleared his throat.

'Well, what about it, John?' His expression changed. 'What do you make of this business? I don't like the sound of it. I'd be happier if I thought this bloke doing the killing was an out-and-out loony: that way we'd catch him quicker. But I've a feeling he's not. He may be disturbed, but he still seems to be working to a plan.'

'I agree.' Madden nodded. He, too, had turned serious. 'He's too controlled; too careful.'

'Careful, yes . . . but not above making the odd slip. Now you've probably heard from Styles that the slug recovered at Oxford matches the other two. But did he tell you about the bullet they found near the body?'

'The black one? Billy said it's most likely a dud.'

'That's been confirmed by ballistics.' Chubb nodded. 'What's more, it's got an iron core, same as the others. Our lab didn't know what the colour meant, until someone had the bright idea of ringing Aldershot and getting hold of an ammunition expert. According to him, when the Jerries began producing these iron-cored bullets during the war they painted them black to distinguish them from ordinary ones with copper-coloured jackets. They were used mainly for side-arms; Lugers in fact.'

'Then that could very well be the weapon your shooter's using.'

The swiftness of Madden's response caused Chubb's eyebrows to shoot up.

'Why, necessarily? Those nine-millimetres are standard size.'

'Because it's odds-on the bullets came with the gun.' Madden explained, 'Lugers have always been prized souvenirs, Charlie. In my time there was nothing a Tommy liked better than to get his hands on one, and I don't imagine it was any different in the last war. And since as a rule they were taken off dead or captured enemy soldiers, the chances are that they were loaded at the time. In fact it's hard to imagine how else those particular bullets could have found their way to England.'

'Which suggests we could be looking for an ex-serviceman.' The chief super had taken the point. 'Some bloke who helped himself to a Luger in the last war.'

'And someone with experience, too,' Madden pointed out. 'When I heard about the first shootings from Billy, how the victims had been made to kneel, I wondered if there was an element of ritual in the murders. But the man murdered in Oxford was sitting on a bench, which made it different in one respect, though not in another.'

'Meaning what, exactly?' Chubb had become a rapt listener.

'They were all clean kills: one bullet for each in the back of the head, guaranteed to be lethal. To be sure of that, the killer had to have them stationary in front of him, and with his first two victims, kneeling was the best option. You can't move easily in that position. But seated, as the man in Oxford was, worked just as well. All the killer had to do was put the gun to his head.'

'And what did you deduce from that?'

'That it's possible the men were simply executed – and in the most practical way. It's obvious the killer knew what he was doing. I'd go further. I'd even hazard a guess that he might have had special training.'

'Special in what way?' The chief super's face darkened. 'Are you suggesting he could have been a commando . . . something of that sort?'

'Your guess is as good as mine. But one of the things you learn in a war, Charlie, is how to kill, and it sounds to me as though this man has either had experience in the art or been taught how to do it most efficiently. And assuming for the moment that he saw action, it's also possible he returned damaged in some way.'

'Mentally, do you mean?' Chubb scowled.

'It's only a supposition.' Madden shrugged.

His words brought a rumble from the other man. Chubb's brow knitted in a frown.

'Look, John, I don't want to drag you into this, particularly as it's not clear yet whether you're involved. The letter Gibson began writing . . . Does it have anything to do with the case? We still don't know. But if you've got any more ideas, I'd like to hear them. Right now we're treading water: all we have is a description that could fit any number of men. It still looks to me as though the victims were chosen at random. But let's suppose for a moment they weren't – that they were picked for a reason. Have you any thoughts on that?'

He eyed his visitor hopefully. Watching them, Billy saw his old chief put a hand to the scar on his forehead, a sure sign that his mind was engaged with the problem.

'Well, if the killings weren't casual, then they're probably linked in some way.' Madden spoke after a long pause. 'But that raises a difficulty that has to do with generations.'

'Come again.' Chubb blinked.

'The man who shot Gibson at Lewes – and presumably the other two as well – was younger than his victim. The shepherd who saw him said he walked briskly along the path; that he moved like a young man. Both Gibson and Singleton were in their sixties, Drummond in his late fifties, and while it's possible the killer knew one of them personally, it hardly seems likely he was acquainted with all three, particularly given where they lived and the fact that there was no apparent connection between them. So how did he know them?'

Madden looked at Chubb.

'I mean, how did he know who to kill?'

'He might have had their names.' It was Billy who spoke.

'Their names, yes. But he'd still have to be sure he was killing the right people. We're assuming now that there *was* a reason for the murders. I've been thinking about it, and it struck me that whoever called on Gibson that day might have gone there to determine his identity?'

'Prior to topping him, you mean?' Chubb sat forward in his chair.

'Exactly. Now it's clear that Gibson wasn't threatened. Otherwise he would have rung the police afterwards. But whatever was said was enough to make him sit down and start writing that letter to the commissioner. It's only an idea, but what if he'd just been asked some awkward questions – the kind he didn't want to answer; or perhaps dealing with something he didn't want dragged up? The reason I say that is because in the end he decided *not* to finish the letter, not to send it, and that sounds to me like the act of a man who has just had second thoughts. Mind you, that assumes that the caller was also his killer, and that Gibson's murder wasn't done on the spur of the moment: that it was carefully planned.'

He waited for his listeners' reaction.

'The doctor up in Scotland didn't have an unexpected visitor, and neither did Singleton, as far as we know.' Again it was Billy who spoke.

'No, but Drummond saw some patients, holidaymakers, who weren't on his list. Have the names of the men been checked?'

Billy nodded. 'They've all been cleared. There's no reason to think any of them is the person we're looking for.'

Madden's grunt signalled his disappointment. He sat brooding. Looking up, he caught Chubb's eye.

'Well, I've only got one other suggestion, Charlie, but I imagine it's something you've already thought of.'

'And what might that be?' The chief super lifted an eyebrow.

'I've no idea what's behind these killings, but if they're not random, I've got a feeling the answer must lie in the past. Although these men seem not to have known each other, logic suggests their paths must have crossed at some point.'

'You're thinking about the war, aren't you?' Chubb grunted. He had been listening intently. 'The First World War, that is. We did wonder about that, Styles and I, but we couldn't see any obvious connection.'

'Perhaps not, but it still seems to me to be the only event in recent history that could have brought them together, bearing in mind that they lived far apart and had different lives.' Madden frowned. 'And they were all the right age to have served, remember.'

Billy stirred. 'Singleton was in it – that's for certain. I saw a photograph of him taken in the trenches. And we found one of Ozzie Gibson in uniform at Lewes. Do you remember, sir? You saw the badge on his cap and said he must have been a supply officer.'

Madden nodded.

'But Drummond doesn't seem to fit the pattern.' Billy scratched his head. 'He was a doctor. Surely he wouldn't have been called up.'

'No, but he could easily have served in the Medical Corps. If you think this is worth following up, ask the RAMC to check their records. You need to find out if there was a moment when those three were in the same place at the same time; or even in the same general area.'

Chubb had listened to them in silence. Now he spoke.

'But hang on – this bloke who's been doing the killing, he's a lot younger. Like you said, he's a different generation. How could he be caught up in something that happened – if it happened at all – more than thirty years ago? Tell me that.'

'I only wish I could, Charlie.' Madden rose to his feet with a sigh. 'But I'm afraid I can't. Not without a crystal ball.'

'A crystal ball! I knew there was something I needed. Get on to it, Styles.'

Conscious that he'd started a wild hare running with no certainty of where it might lead, Madden left the Yard in a taxi that took him north through drab streets where the buildings, unpainted for many years, rubbed shoulders with bomb sites: craters that had once been home to cellars or basements, but were now empty pits.

Though the sight called to mind the bombs that had rained

on the capital only a few years before, it was not of the war just past that he was thinking as they drove by Regent's Park, but of the one fought earlier in the century in which he had played a part. The idea he'd put forward had been in his mind for some days, but he'd been slow to advance it, given the lack of supporting evidence, and he wondered now if he wouldn't have done better to have held his tongue. Precious time might be wasted on what could prove to be a fruitless search of old records; the trail of the killer – already cold – might vanish altogether.

However, the suggestion had been made and it was too late now to take it back. Meantime he had other business to attend to. He had come up to town in response to an appeal from Helen's aunt, Maud Collingwood, a perennial survivor, now in her nineties (but as fit as a flea, according to her niece), who dwelt in a house in St John's Wood from which she refused to move, and where she continued to flourish safe in the knowledge that help was at hand should she need it. Her latest request, conveyed by telephone the week before, had been for Madden to get himself up to London as soon as possible in order to clean out the gutters of her house before the winter rains set in.

'Her gutters? Her *gutters*?' Helen had been speechless. 'Is she out of her mind? Can't she pay someone to do these things? Lord knows, she's not short of money.'

She herself had more than once offered to take in her aged relative; or, failing that, to arrange for her to move into smaller, more manageable quarters; or even into an old-age home, if that seemed best. But her suggestions had been dismissed.

'I intend to die in my bed,' Aunt Maud had announced, and with that the subject had been declared closed.

Arriving at St John's Wood soon after one, Madden learned that the mistress of the house had not yet risen, the news being conveyed to him by Alice, Aunt Maud's maid and loyal companion for the past forty years. Fortified with a sandwich and a glass of beer, he settled down to work at once with ladder and broom and, having completed his labours by late afternoon, joined Alice for a cup of tea in the kitchen, only to be told that there were one or two other problems in the house that might bear looking at, since he was there. A brief inspection was enough to put the matter in its true light and, when he went upstairs a short time later to drink a glass of sherry with his hostess, it was as the bearer of bad news.

'I'm sorry to say it looks serious, Maud. I'll have to get some workmen in. And I'd better do it quickly.'

'Whatever you say, John, dear.'

Thin and brittle-looking as a twig, clad in a dressing gown of faded silk, and with her cheeks lightly rouged, Maud Collingwood sat with her hands folded in her lap in a posture thought suitable for young ladies a century earlier.

'I put myself in your hands.' Feared by all in Helen's family for her sharp eye and even sharper tongue, she had always treated Madden with an indulgence denied her own kin. 'I was sure I could count on you.'

'I'll get someone to come in tomorrow and give an estimate,' Madden told her. 'If he rounds up a crew, they can start work next week. I'll come up again myself and make sure things are running smoothly.'

'What a treasure you are, my dear.' Her needle-like glance glowed with affection. 'Helen's so lucky to have you.'

Later, after Alice had served him supper, he rang his wife to give her the news: 'The house is in worse shape than I thought. The kitchen sink's blocked and there's rising damp in the cellar. But the wiring's the real problem. It's falling to bits. It's a wonder they haven't electrocuted themselves, or burned the place down.'

'I might have guessed it. She's inveigled you up there and now she's got you in her clutches.'

'Darling, she's ninety-three.' Madden laughed. 'She can't be

expected to cope with this herself and neither can Alice. Someone has to organize the workmen and see that they do a proper
job. If Lucy were here, we could send her up. But she's not, so
it'll have to be me.'

'I suppose it will.'

'Oh, and by the way, I'm a treasure and you're lucky to
have me.'

'That woman!'

By noon the next day, having acquired the services of a local
builder, shown him over the house from roof to cellar and obtained from him not only an estimate of the cost of the repairs,
but an assurance that he could assemble a crew and begin work
by the start of the following week, Madden was ready to depart.

'Do be careful switching anything on,' he warned Alice.
'And make sure Miss Collingwood knows, too. Say goodbye to
her for me' – the lady of the house had not yet risen from her
bed – 'and tell her I'll be back next week to get things started.'

Before ringing for a taxi to take him to Waterloo station he
called Billy at the Yard.

'I had a thought last night. It's to do with that idea I put to
you and Charlie. Why not ring Edward Gibson and get him to
have another look at his brother's diaries? If there *is* a link between this business and the first war, he might find some reference to it.'

Billy chuckled. 'I'm ahead of you there, sir. I had the same
idea. In fact, after you left, I tried to ring him at his office. At
the very least we could find out if Ozzie was ever in France, like
you and Singleton were – in the same area, I mean; and if so,
when. But unfortunately he's gone away for a few days on business. He's in Bath for a court case. I got hold of the number of
the hotel where he's staying and rang him last night. He'd read
about Singleton's murder and realized it must have been the

same bloke who shot Ozzie. I had to tell him we're still in the dark. He hasn't got the diaries with him. He left them in London. But he promised to look at them again as soon as he gets back at the end of the week.'

'Then we'll just have to wait till then.'

13

Now that the evenings were drawing in, Sally didn't like staying late at the Manor. It meant she would have to cycle back to the village in near-darkness and, though Tony had recently fitted a headlamp to her bike, it wasn't something she enjoyed doing. The narrow lane was full of holes and unexpected bumps, and you never knew what you might run into, as she had found out only the other evening when she had collided head-on with a pig, of all things.

'What it was doing there I don't know, but it must have wandered into the middle of the road, and if I hadn't been wobbling along slowly I'd most probably have fallen off,' she told Aunt Millicent later. 'As it was, I hit it amidships and it was simply furious. It turned and snorted at me.'

Later it was discovered that the pig had escaped from a sty close to the road – somehow it had squeezed out between two broken slats – but Sally wasn't mollified.

'The evenings are getting so misty now. You can't see things clearly, even with a lamp. All you see are shapes and shadows. I've told Sir Horace several times that I like to get away in good time, but he always finds something for me to do at the last moment.'

That day was no exception, and what particularly annoyed

Sally was that she shouldn't really have been working, since it was a Saturday. But she had let herself be bullied into coming in, to make up for a day she had taken off earlier in the week to accompany her mother up to London on a shopping expedition. Sir Horace had also managed to imply that she owed him this extra effort, in view of her decision to terminate her employment at the end of the year and thus leave him in the lurch. Having spent a long afternoon typing up the morning's dictation and then retyping the pages he had corrected, she had been on the point of leaving when he had put a spoke in her wheel once more, reminding her that she hadn't yet typed the speech he would be giving at a civic luncheon in Winchester the following day.

'I can't imagine how you could have forgotten, Miss Abbot.' His blue eyes had bulged in disbelief when she had stuck her head into his study to announce her departure. 'It's a day of national mourning. What I have to say will be most important.'

Well, he might think so, Sally told herself crossly as she sat down at her typewriter again, but she doubted that anyone else would. What mattered was the Remembrance Day service in Winchester Cathedral that would precede it, along with all the other services that would be held that day, including one in Feltham, which her own Uncle Guy would conduct and which she would attend along with her mother and Tony. As far as she could tell, Sir Horace's words prepared for the luncheon afterwards were just a lot of hot air. Did the world – or, to be more accurate, the burgesses of Winchester, who would have to listen to it – really want to be told that the 'terrible price in blood' paid by all those young men who had died in the First World War had not been in vain?

And was that even true?

Would they feel reassured to learn that 'the flower of our youth' lay in 'hallowed graves' and that their sacrifice would never be forgotten? Especially since it had been Sir Horace and his lot who had sent them over the top and stumbling across no-man's-land to their deaths?

Her mood had not been improved by the latest chapter of his memoirs, which she had taken down and typed earlier that afternoon. They had reached the summer of 1917 and Sir Horace had held forth at some length on a subject that, as it happened, Sally knew something about, having heard Aunt Millicent speak of it: a battle called Passchendaele, fought near the Belgian city of Ypres in pouring rain. Shelled over and over again, the ground had become a morass of mud into which the bodies of men, dead and wounded alike, had vanished without trace. Aunt Millicent's two cousins had been among the casualties and their remains had never been found. The only record of their deaths was on a memorial in France, where the names of seventy thousand men killed during the war, but with no known grave, were inscribed in stone.

To listen to Sir Horace Canning, KBE, going on about the 'stern but necessary decisions' taken by 'our unflinching commander-in-chief' (he meant 'Butcher' Haig) and 'the heavy burdens laid on those with the responsibility of leadership' (he meant himself) had come close to turning Sally's stomach. Especially when it became clear once again that he had played no part in the fighting himself – his own corps had been stationed some way to the south – and, as far as she could tell, had simply wanted to associate his name with a battle that was already legendary. As for the losses suffered by the Allied side, Sir Horace had seemed to take them in his stride, speaking in that blind, unfeeling way that she was familiar with now, about 'the inevitable cost in human lives of great military undertakings'.

As she finished the last page and pulled the sheet of paper out of her machine she thought of Tony and how he never talked about the war, although he had been called on to risk his life in the air, day after day. All he had ever said to her was: 'War is terrible, Sal. It's the worst thing in the world, and don't let anyone ever tell you otherwise.'

The door to her office opened. The Lord Lieutenant thrust his head in.

'I've finished typing your speech, Sir Horace.' She spoke before he could. 'I can give it to you now.'

'Just leave it on my desk, would you? I have to go upstairs and change. I'll wish you goodnight.'

With a brisk nod he withdrew his head and shut the door. A moment later she heard the click of his footsteps receding down the corridor.

'And the same to you, with knobs on.'

Sally collected the typed pages, clipped them together, slipped the cover over her typewriter and then rose and put on her coat. Not a word of thanks; no apology for having kept her later than she wanted, yet again. He could see as well as she could that the fog was starting to thicken outside. She wondered if he was altogether human – if he was a whole man, or just a part of one: the part that had once strutted about in a uniform barking out orders; the part that no longer knew what to do with itself.

She slipped through the door and deposited the typed pages on his desk. Ready to leave now, she paused and then, acting on impulse, went out through the French windows onto the terrace. The early-morning mist had lifted for a while during the day, but now it was back, lapping at the balustrade and blanketing the garden below. Lost in thought, she wandered along the terrace. Tony was coming down from London by train later and, if the weather cleared, even for a few hours, they would go out for a picnic tomorrow after the service. They would take a blanket with them and after lunch they would lie in each other's arms and talk about the future: the long years rolling out before them, which Sally had already peopled with the children she would bear, their faces not yet known, but their presence vivid in her imagination. Although she was still a virgin, it was not from prudishness; she would happily have given herself to the man she loved. But, as if by common consent, they continued to postpone the moment, and this sense of hesitating on the brink had brought a feeling of excitement to their engagement, just as it brought a flush to her cheeks now.

Smiling to herself, she reached the end of the terrace and, rather than return the way she'd come through the swirling wreaths of mist, went down the steps at the side, joining a path that led past the kitchen garden to the back of the house, where her bicycle was parked in the yard. Seeing the light on in the kitchen, she went in for a moment to say goodnight to Mrs Watts.

'Oh, there you are, my dear. I was hoping you'd have gone home by now.'

A family retainer of the kind dying out in England now, Agnes Watts had worked at the Manor for close on thirty years, starting as a kitchen maid and climbing up the ladder of domestic service to her present rank of housekeeper. A plump, motherly woman, she treated Sally as she might one of her own children.

'I ought to have left ages ago.' They knew each other well enough that Sally could speak her mind. 'He knows I hate riding home in the dark.'

'I heard him go upstairs just a few minutes ago, probably to change. He's dining out.' She smiled up at Sally from the table where she was sitting with a book open. 'Cook's gone off for the weekend, and so have the maids. I'll be minding the shop. If I were you, I should get away smartly.'

Mrs Watts always referred to Sir Horace as 'he', never by his name. It was the only indication she ever gave of her feelings towards her employer. She smiled again.

'Is your young man coming down from London?' she asked. Sally had brought Tony to the Manor once, when Sir Horace was away, to meet her.

'I'm expecting him later this evening. We've got all sorts of plans for the weekend.' She glanced at her watch. 'You're right, I must run . . .'

But then, as she turned to go, she remembered.

'Oh, dash it. I left my handbag in the office. I'll just go and fetch it.'

At that moment, however, they heard the sound of footsteps coming down the stairs and then the measured click of heels receding down the corridor.

'He's gone back to the study.' Mrs Watts eyed her. 'You'd best be quiet now or he'll find something else for you to do.'

The warning wasn't necessary. With a smile to the house-keeper – and putting a finger to her lips – Sally slipped out of the door and began to tiptoe down the now-empty passage. The long stretch of stone-flagged floor produced audible echoes and she took pains to move silently along it until she reached the cubbyhole that served as her office. Slipping inside, she was about to switch on the light when she stopped herself. Sir Hor-ace might see it come on under the door linking the two rooms and, if he did, he was sure to summon her. He had probably thought of some changes he wanted to make in his speech and had come downstairs in the hope of intercepting her. Well, if so, he was in for a disappointment. She would quietly remove her handbag from the back of the chair where it was hanging and steal away.

She began to tiptoe across the floor, feeling her way in the darkness, but before she had reached her chair the sound of Sir Horace's voice brought her stealthy movement to a halt. The distinctive barking note was pitched higher than usual.

'*What?*' she heard him say. '*What the blazes . . . ?*' The words were sharp with anger. '*Now just a moment—*'

He stopped in mid-sentence: cut off as though by a knife, so sudden was the silence that followed. Sally wondered if he was talking on the phone, but then remembered that there wasn't one in the study any longer. He'd had it banished to the hall.

There was someone in there with him.

But *who*?

His last words had made her uneasy. When he had said, '*Now just a moment—*' she had detected what she thought was a note of alarm in his voice. Had some intruder found his way into the house?

The doors to the terrace were unlocked. She knew, because she'd gone out that way herself. Paralysed by indecision, she stood there in the darkness wondering whether she ought to knock on the door, or create some other disturbance. As she hesitated, a second voice made itself heard. Pitched low, it was impossible to hear what was being said. But the voice was soft and the tone even, and since there was no response from Sir Horace – no indication that he was still upset (if indeed he had been) – Sally decided to continue with her original plan of retrieving her bag silently and slipping away.

However, just as she was about to take a further and final step towards the chair where it hung, she heard a sound that made the hairs on the back of her neck stand up in terror. A hoarse, unintelligible cry, it was followed by a sob so clear that, without pausing to think, she turned instinctively to the inner door. Fumbling for the handle, she flung it open . . . And stopped, frozen in the doorway by the sight that met her eyes.

Directly in front of her was the slumped shape of a man. Although he was on his knees and his face was in shadow, she recognized the balding head of her employer. Immediately behind him a dark-clad figure stood, holding a pistol close to his head. Before Sally could speak or utter a sound there was a deafening report and the back of Sir Horace's head exploded in a spray of blood and bone. At the same instant a gaping hole appeared in his forehead and his body toppled over and fell face-down on the carpet. Unable to move, paralysed by shock, Sally lifted her gaze past the still-smoking gun to the figure behind. The face of the assassin was covered by a black bala-clava. All that was visible through the narrow slit in the close-fitting hood were two eyes. They were fixed on her.

The gun moved.

Steady in the killer's hand, it shifted to point at Sally's chest, and in that last, agonizing second the lovely future she had dreamed of – her marriage . . . Tony . . . her children . . . all the years ahead – poured through her mind in a torrent and were gone, leaving only the present moment, which was shrinking to a pinpoint, telescoping inwards with the speed of a comet, until there was only this single instant of time, this moment, *now* . . .

14

WITH THE MIST THAT had blanketed the countryside all day growing thicker now, Madden set out from the farm in good time to walk home, striding down through the ploughed fields to the stream at the bottom of his land and then following the path that ran alongside it, at this season ankle-deep in fallen leaves and all but invisible to the naked eye.

'Come along, Hamish.'

Lagging behind him, the basset was making heavy weather of the walk. Used to spending his mornings snoozing peacefully under Helen's desk in her surgery, and his afternoons lying on the back seat of her car as she made her rounds, that day he had received a rude awakening.

'He's getting fat and lazy,' Helen had announced at the lunch table, meanwhile stroking the heavy head resting on her foot. 'The only exercise he gets is digging up my flower beds. It's time he exerted himself. If you really are going over to the farm this afternoon, you might take Hamish with you.'

Although it was a Sunday, when he usually stayed home, Madden had earlier announced his intention of spending an hour or two attending to business.

'I'm falling behind with the paperwork and, since I've got to go up to London again tomorrow to see to Aunt Maud's house, I'd better get up to date before I leave.'

'You better had.' Helen had appeared to take his resolve seriously. 'Especially since there's no knowing when you'll be back.'

'It won't be more than a few days,' Madden promised her. 'I'll be home by the end of the week.'

'So you say.' Helen finished her coffee. 'But the siren of St John's Wood may have other plans for you.'

Madden was laughing.

'Do you really want the house to fall down about your poor old aunt's ears?'

'Must I answer that question?'

Rising from the table then, she had bent to kiss him.

'I'm off myself. I promised to look in on the Dawson clan. The whole family's down with flu. And then I'm going to pass by the Hall. Violet's busy cleaning out the butler's pantry. She's bought herself a pair of dungarees and says she's joined the working classes and doesn't know why they make such a fuss about it. Manual labour is perfectly healthy, she says, and good exercise too. I've told her if she carries on this way, she'll be lynched.'

Madden had accompanied her outside to the garage, only a few steps from the front door, but still half-hidden by the mist.

'I hate this weather.' Helen shivered.

'It reminds me of France.' Madden had looked about him. 'Sometimes it lasted for days, but we thought it a blessing. Nothing much could happen as long as we couldn't see the Germans and they couldn't see us. We used to pray it would go on.'

She had lifted a hand to his cheek and then, with no need for words or explanation, they had held each other in a long embrace.

'I'll be back in time for tea.'

Although they had made no mention of the fact, it was a day

special to them both – Remembrance Sunday – and that morning they had attended a service in the village church honouring the dead not only of the war just past, but of the earlier one as well, in which Helen had lost two much-loved brothers, and her husband a host of comrades-in-arms. But if the fallen were seldom far from Madden's mind that day, the anniversary had a further significance for him. Despite surviving the carnage he had returned home scarred in body and mind, numbed by what he had experienced and unable to feel any more; or so he had thought, until fate had led him to this quiet corner of the English countryside and to a love that had brought him his own peace at last.

Later, recounting his time in the trenches to Helen, he had told her of the shame he had felt at his own survival.

'I would see these young men arrive at the front thinking they were on some great adventure, and then I would see them die, and the ones who came after – they would die, too – and in the end it seemed there was only death to look forward to, so I shut my mind to it all. I stopped caring. I simply waited for my own time to come, but it never did.'

No longer trapped in an existence that had lost all meaning for him, he had found the courage to speak of things he had kept hidden, even from himself, and in return had received from Helen the assurance that the deadening of all emotion, of which he talked with such remorse, was simply the mind's way of protecting itself from unbearable truths; and that now that he had opened himself once more to the pain, healing would follow.

And so it had proved. With the passing of the years those memories had grown dim and, thinking back now as he walked beneath the eaves of the still, silent woods, it was not the images evoked by the anniversary that occupied his mind, but rather the continuing mystery of the murder investigation into which he'd been drawn. His suggestion of a possible link to the Great

War had not been made lightly. Although there was no evidence that the three murdered men had ever met, they were part of a whole generation that had been called to the colours – just as he had – and, try as he might, Madden had been unable to think of any other circumstance that might have united them.

But beyond that idea he could find no further clue to resolving the mystery, no event that might explain the killing of three seemingly unconnected individuals; and, aware that the alternative solution of a trio of purely random murders made just as much sense, he worried that he might have urged his idea too strongly, and resolved then and there to stress the point to Billy when he spoke to him next.

The thought had no sooner come into his mind when he heard the sound of voices and, as Hamish gave tongue behind him, a figure took shape in the mist ahead. To Madden's astonishment, the very person he was thinking of materialized out of the billowing cloud of grey.

'Billy!' He stopped dead. 'What are you doing here?'

'I was coming to see you, sir.'

As the younger man halted on the path a second form appeared out of the fog. It was Angus Sinclair, wrapped in a Burberry coat and scarf. A young woman was following in his tracks.

'I saw you pass by the cottage a while ago,' the chief inspector called out to Madden. 'I said we'd most likely find you at the farm.'

'We were on our way back from Winchester.' Billy blew on his fingers. Madden saw he was rumpled and unshaven. 'This is Lily Poole, by the way.' He gestured towards the young woman who had advanced to join them. 'Detective Poole, I should say.'

'How do you do, Miss Poole.'

Lily flushed as she shook the hand Madden held out to her. His was a name well known to her. He had once been on the force – she knew that – and there were those, Styles among them, who reckoned he was one of the best detectives who had ever held a warrant card.

'Highfield wasn't that far off our route back to London,' Billy was explaining, 'I thought we'd look in on the off-chance.'

'And I'm very pleased you did. But why?' Madden was still baffled by their presence.

Billy lowered his fingers. For a long moment he held Madden's gaze.

'You haven't heard then, sir?'

'You mean she actually saw him shot?'

'He was on his knees when she came into the room. It happened before her eyes. The killer even turned his gun on her, and the poor girl thought she was done for. But he didn't pull the trigger.'

As though his words called for a moment's silence, Billy paused.

'He was wearing a balaclava. She couldn't see his face. Maybe that's why he let her live. But she witnessed the murder all right, and he must have known that would be enough to put his head in a noose one day.'

He shook his head in wonder.

The four of them had repaired to the chief inspector's cottage, where Madden learned that Billy had called first at the house before going in search of Sinclair, who had just heard about the shooting on the lunchtime news and was considering walking over to the farm himself in order to inform his erstwhile partner of it. The two detectives, both pale with exhaustion, had driven down to Hampshire late the previous afternoon and had ended up spending a sleepless night at Winchester police headquarters. They had been happy to accept their host's offer of a cold leg of chicken and a sandwich by way of a late lunch, and were sitting now in his living room, a snug parlour lined with bookshelves and warmed by a fire burning brightly in the grate.

'Start at the beginning,' Madden said. 'Tell me about the girl. What happened to her? Did she call for help?'

'No, she fainted, passed out cold, and only woke up when the housekeeper found her lying by the body.' Billy lowered the glass of beer he was holding in order to reply, but then nodded to Poole, who was sitting beside him. 'I sent Lil over to her aunt's house to speak to the girl. She can tell you more.'

Lily opened her notebook. She wanted to appear calm, as if this was just another job. But there were people she wanted to impress here. Not just this Madden bloke, but Chief Inspector Sinclair – ex-chief inspector maybe, but still the man who had given her her chance in CID, and to whom she felt a debt of gratitude.

'She'd been put to bed and given a sedative by the time I arrived,' Lily began. 'But I went back to the house and spoke to her this morning. Sally Abbot's her name. She had her fiancé there with her. They're getting married next summer.' Lily shook her head ruefully. 'I reckon she knows how lucky she was. She told me she'd been working for Canning for a couple of months, helping with his memoirs. She didn't say so, but I got the impression she hadn't cared for him.'

'Still, he was the Lord Lieutenant . . .' Billy rolled his eyes in silent comment on the fact.

Sinclair grunted. 'It's not as grand as it sounds,' he remarked. 'But that won't stop the press from making the most of it.'

'So it was the housekeeper who raised the alarm?' Madden wanted to press on.

'She and the chauffeur.' Billy took a sip of his beer. 'They were the only ones on duty. They rang the police in Winchester, and they were on the scene in less than half an hour, but even so it was too late. The man had vanished. But they think they know how he got out there, and also how he got away. Earlier that day a van used for delivering newspapers was reported stolen. It disappeared from a depot in the city and this morning it was found parked near the station. One like it was spotted by a farmer a mile or so from the Manor late yesterday. It had been left in a lane.'

'That tells us something.' A scowl had appeared on Madden's forehead as he listened. 'It means he had to have planned it well in advance.'

'That's what I thought.' Billy nodded. 'And it clears up one question at least.'

'You mean Canning was his chosen target? There's no question of him being a random victim.'

'None at all, I reckon. There's evidence, too, that this man was watching the house a few days ago. We'll tell you about that in a moment.'

'Yes, go back to the van. It was found parked near the station, you say. Could he have left Winchester by train?'

'It's possible.' Billy took another sip of his beer. 'The murder occurred at about half-past five and there was a train leaving for London at a quarter-past seven. The police weren't slow off the mark. As soon as they'd heard Miss Abbot's story, officers were sent to the station and the bus terminal to check on the passengers, men travelling on their own. Unfortunately they didn't have much to go on in the way of a description.'

'The girl couldn't help there?'

'Apart from the balaclava, all she could remember was that he was dressed in dark clothing, possibly a coat of some kind. So, once he'd taken off his mask, he would have looked like anyone else.'

Billy drained his glass.

'In fact, the more I think about it, the more I reckon he's a quick-change artist.'

'Oh? Why?' Ever alert, the chief inspector pounced on the remark.

'Well, going back to Lewes, sir' – Billy turned to him – 'if you recall, the shepherd who witnessed the murder had a good view of him. He was wearing tan trousers and a red sweater. But nobody looking anything like that was spotted afterwards: not in Lewes, or on the Downs. And not in Brighton, either, which he could have walked to. It was the same at Oxford. The cox on the river saw a man wearing a coat and a cloth cap standing right behind the bench where Singleton was sitting. I rang the inspector in charge there the other day. He told me they'd had a good response to their request for people who were out on Port Meadow that afternoon, or on the towpath, to get in touch with them. But none of them were able to help: there were no sightings of the man they were looking for or anyone resembling him. He seems to have vanished, and that made me think he probably changed his appearance. There were some bushes behind the bench. He could easily have slipped in there and come out looking quite different.'

The chief inspector made no comment, but he seemed satisfied with the explanation.

'You said he might have been watching the house?'

Madden put the question, and again Billy turned to his young colleague.

'Go ahead,' he said.

Lily cleared her throat.

'That came up when I asked Miss Abbot whether Canning had a surprise visitor in the days before he was shot,' she said. 'I was thinking of Oswald Gibson. But she said no, not as far as she knew.'

'Still, in his case it might not have been necessary.' Madden frowned. 'Canning was a public figure: there was no danger of mistaking him for anyone else.'

'What she did remember, though, was spotting someone with a pair of field glasses lurking in a wood near the house.' Lily frowned. 'It could have been our shooter. He may have decided that the best way to get at Canning was in his home. It's an old stone manor with a terrace in front. He probably came in through the garden. It was already dark by that time and, being a Saturday, there was no one around. And, though it was foggy, he could have seen Canning in his study through the lighted windows. Nobody saw the killer leave, but I reckon it's likely he went out the same way he came in. That would have been safest.'

Lily was reading from her notes. When she looked up she caught Sinclair's eye and saw his approving nod.

'And obvious that he'd worked out a route.' Madden spoke again.

'Like a military operation.' Billy nodded. 'I remember you saying he might have had special training.'

'What happened to the slug that killed Canning?'

'It went clean through his head. We found it on the carpet. I'm taking it back to London.' Billy patted his jacket pocket. 'I noticed it was bent out of shape, so it's probably not like the others – iron-cored. Maybe the killer learned his lesson at Oxford. Maybe he thinks some more of those old Jerry bullets might be duds. Whatever else, he's no madman, this bloke; he's got his head screwed on.'

Yawning, he put his empty plate aside and then looked at his watch.

'Just one more thing, then we'd better be going.' He turned once more to Madden. 'It's that link you suggested with the First World War. It's come up again. I don't know if you're aware of it, but Canning was a retired general . . .'

'I know.' Madden nodded. 'I remember the name. In fact, he was our corps commander for a while. But I have to tell you, I never set eyes on him. What's in your mind, Billy?'

'I was wondering if revenge could be the motive. You'd know better than me, but isn't it a fact that a lot of those generals – Haig and the rest – are still thought to have blood on their hands?'

Madden was slow to reply. He was reminded of his earlier train of thought: his reluctance to push the idea that he had put forward too far.

'It's a tempting idea,' he said finally. 'But I doubt you can tar Canning with that particular brush. As a commander he was ineffectual. He had the reputation of being one of Haig's lapdogs. And he didn't last very long. He was replaced after only a few months.'

Billy rose to his feet. Putting her notebook away, Lily followed suit.

'Well, it's still the only possible connection we've come up with so far. I haven't told you yet, but I got in touch with the RAMC and they confirmed that a Wallace Drummond served in the Medical Corps for three years. He was posted to France for two of them. So that means all the victims were there at some point.'

'But was it at the same time?' Madden peered up at him. 'And were they ever together? And was I anywhere in the vicinity? It's still only a guess. I wouldn't place too much faith in it.'

'Billy, you and Miss Poole can't possibly drive back to London in this fog. Stay the night, both of you. You can leave first thing in the morning.'

Helen put a hand on his arm.

'I only wish I could. There's nothing I'd like more.' Billy grinned. 'But we have to get going. I talked to the chief super earlier today. He'd had the press on to him at home, and the commissioner, too. He's going to issue another statement in the morning and wants to discuss it with me first. And then there's Elsie and the kids to think of. It was Jack's birthday yesterday.' He was referring to his elder son. 'He was twelve, and his mum had been saving up ration points and what-have-you for weeks so as to make him a real chocolate cake. And then, right in the middle of his party, the call came from the Yard and I had to leave. I just had time to watch him blow out the candles.' He shook his head regretfully. 'A copper's life . . .'

He turned to Sinclair.

'Thank you for the bite of lunch, sir. It was more than welcome.'

The chief inspector had walked up from his cottage with the others. They had been standing in front of the house when they heard the sound of Helen's car approaching up the drive. When introduced to Lily, she greeted the young woman warmly.

'Lily Poole. I know that name well. Mr Sinclair has often spoken of you.'

Helen's smile on seeing the blush that her words brought to Lily's cheeks had quickly faded when she learned the reason for their presence and, on hearing that Billy planned to return to London at once, she had tried, unsuccessfully, to dissuade him from leaving.

'When all this is over, you must bring Elsie and the children down for a weekend.' Seeing that he could not be shifted, she had given in. 'Lucy's coming back from Paris soon. She'd love to see you all.'

'Now there's something to look forward to.'

Billy went to his car. Lily had already climbed into the passenger seat.

'And don't forget, I'll be in London myself next week,' Madden called after him. 'I'm going up first thing tomorrow. I'll be staying at Aunt Maud's house in St John's Wood. You've got the number there. Call me if anything comes up.'

'I hadn't forgotten, sir. In fact I may take you up on that offer.' Billy opened the car door. 'There are still those diaries of Ozzie Gibson's. Brother Edward will be back from Bath by now. He promised to look at the wartime entries again. Who knows – there may be something there.'

15

THE SOUND OF HAMMERING coming from the cellar was so loud that Madden didn't hear the phone ring. He had taken an early train up to London in order to get to the house well in advance of the crew of workmen he had engaged, but somewhat to his surprise they had knocked on the door at half-past eight, only minutes after his arrival from Waterloo station in a taxi. Three in number, they had included a foreman by the name of Milligan who, accompanied by Madden, had carried out an inspection of the cellar before announcing that the work on the rising damp in the back wall would take several days to complete.

'First we'll have to dig her out,' he'd explained. 'Then there'll be the brickwork and plastering to do. But once we've cleared the cellar we can start on the rewiring. That's a big job, and it'll cause some disturbance in the house. I understand there's an old lady living here?' His bushy eyebrows had gone up like question marks.

'A very old lady, Mr Milligan. She's ninety-three, and spends most of her time in bed. She'll have to be moved to another room when you rewire hers. I'll see to it that she's warned in advance.'

Shortly afterwards the hammering in the basement had begun and Madden had dispatched Alice upstairs to enquire whether her mistress was awake yet and, if so, to inform her that unfortunately the noise would continue all morning, and possibly into the afternoon. Alice had returned with the news that Aunt Maud was awake and in sufficiently good spirits to have asked for a cup of tea and some toast to be brought up to her. Shortly afterwards Alice had returned upstairs, this time with a tray, leaving Madden to sit in the kitchen and wonder whether his presence was really necessary or whether he could slip out of the house for an hour. Helen had given him a shopping list to work through while he was in London. Above the sound of the hammering he heard the phone ring, but before he had time to rise from his chair Alice appeared in the doorway.

'I was coming downstairs, sir.' She had to raise her voice. 'It's a Mr Styles. He's asking for you.'

'Billy?' The noise out in the hall was almost as bad. 'So you got back safely?' Pressing the receiver to one ear, Madden blocked the other with his finger. 'Helen was worried about you. How are things going this morning? Has Charlie issued a statement yet?'

'He had the press in half an hour ago. He gave them the stuff about the girl, and the bloke being masked. They lapped it up.' Billy sounded scornful. 'I called about something else, sir. I've just been talking to Edward Gibson. He's found something.'

'In the *diaries*?' Madden had to strain to hear. The hammering below had risen to a new pitch.

'That's what he said. But he doesn't know what it means. Ozzie had this cryptic way of writing. That's how Edward put it. He can't decipher all the entries, but he thinks they might be of interest to us.'

'Do they date from the war?'

'From 1917. Ozzie was called up the year before and served mostly in this country. But there was a spell of three months when he was posted to France, and it was then he made these particular entries. Edward has suggested that I go over to his office and have a look at them.' Billy hesitated. 'How are you placed today, sir?'

Madden considered the question. Though the noise was unpleasant, he felt it would be unfair to Aunt Maud and Alice to abandon them so soon.

'This morning's difficult, Billy. I ought to keep an eye on things here. Can we make it this afternoon?'

'Gibson's busy with clients at the moment. But he said he could see me at two.'

'I'll meet you then.'

'He'd seen the papers this morning. He knows about Canning's murder. He's in a state, I can tell you.'

Billy had been waiting outside the solicitor's office in Gray's Inn Road when Madden's tall figure appeared striding along the pavement towards him. Unable to find a taxi, he had travelled down from St John's Wood by tube.

'What has Gibson found in the diaries?' he asked as they climbed the stairs to the second-floor office. 'Did he give you any idea?'

'Not really. Only that there was something strange about some of the entries.' Billy was puffing before they reached the top and he noticed with envy that his older companion seemed to be making light of the steep stairs. 'He said he hadn't looked closely at the war years before: he thought it was too long ago to have any bearing. But he went through them again during the weekend after he got back from Bath.'

'These entries he's talking about – were they written in France?'

Madden paused when he reached the landing. Plodding behind him, Billy nodded.

'Ozzie's unit was stationed at Boulogne. But he was sent to some other place for a while, and that's where he was when he wrote them.'

Shown into the solicitor's office a few moments later, they found him standing behind his desk staring out of the window.

'At last!' He whirled to face them. 'Inspector . . . Mr Madden . . .'

Gesturing to the two chairs placed in front of his desk, he took his own seat.

'This is turning into a nightmare.' He fired the words at Billy. 'The man's on a rampage. How many more people will he kill?'

He gestured to the newspaper lying on his blotter. It was a copy of the *Daily Telegraph* – the same paper, as it happened, that Madden had read on the train coming up from Highfield. Although the headlines were upside down he remembered them: *Killer strikes again: Lord Lieutenant murdered. Yard at a loss.*

'Is there no way of stopping him?'

'We're doing all we can, sir.' Billy kept his voice calm. 'But, to be frank, we still don't know who he is, or why he's doing this. I'm hoping you can help.'

Edward Gibson shook his head in frustration. He pushed the newspaper aside, revealing one of the leather-bound diaries that he had shown them on their earlier visit.

'It's all in there,' he said. 'The stuff I told you about. But God knows what it means. Ozzie had his own way of expressing himself.'

'Can you tell us first where your brother was when he wrote these entries?' Madden spoke for the first time.

'At a supply depot near Arras.' Gibson took a moment to reply. It seemed he was trying to compose himself. 'Does the name mean anything to you?'

'Certainly. It was an important military centre during the war, one of the main Allied supply depots, which probably explains why your brother was there.' Madden spoke in the same even tone Billy had employed. 'He was in the Army Service Corps, wasn't he?'

'Do you mean that you remember him now?' Gibson's face lit up.

'No, I'm afraid not. I went down to Lewes with Inspector Styles. We saw a photograph of him in uniform. I recognized the badge on his cap.'

Gibson grunted. His disappointment was plain. 'Were you ever there yourself?' he asked.

'In Arras? Several times. There were rest areas for units withdrawn from the line nearby. But, as I say, I've no recollection of having met your brother.' He frowned. 'These entries you mentioned?'

'Ah, yes . . .' Gibson lowered his gaze to the diary in front of him. He opened it at a place that he had marked with a strip of paper. 'This one covers the year 1917 and the entries are all for the month of June. Ozzie's unit crossed the Channel in April of that year; they were stationed at Boulogne. But towards the end of May he was posted to Arras, where he remained for two months before being invalided home.'

'He was wounded?' Madden was surprised.

'Oh, no. Nothing of that sort.' Gibson smiled wistfully. 'I think the closest Ozzie came to any action was hearing the sound of shellfire. The front was only a few miles off. No, he picked up an eye infection, which the army doctors couldn't cure, so in the end they sent him back to a hospital in England and, when he got better, he was posted to a depot in Folkestone. He never went back to France.'

He picked up the diary.

'You can look at this, of course, but you won't make much sense of it unless I do some explaining first. Long before he went to France, Ozzie had got into the habit of using his own kind of shorthand in the diaries, partly because in the course of time they became more like aides-memoires than anything else, and partly to frustrate his wife, who I'm sorry to say had no scruples about invading his privacy. Luckily I can understand some of it, because we used to send postcards to each other in the same kind of language when we were boys. NG – no good. NBG – no bloody good. That sort of thing. You'll see what I mean.'

Gibson paused. He squinted down at the book.

'There's really nothing in the Boulogne entries to interest you, so I'll pick it up when he gets to Arras. He'd been there for about a fortnight – we're at 3 June now – when he makes an entry I don't understand at all: *BS*. That was Ozzie's term for a bombshell. *Stuck with FGCM. Bloody hell! Why me?*'

He glanced questioningly at Madden, who nodded.

'Go on.'

'There was nothing further for a few days, then on 8 June he writes: *Off to Sandybags tomorrow, but how? Transport? I'll be NBG and they'll know it. Keep thinking someone's made a mistake.* There was nothing the following day, but it sounds as though he may have been travelling. Then, on the 10th: *Oh, hell. Even worse than I expected. GG running show.*' Gibson looked up again. 'The GG was our name for the piano teacher our parents inflicted on us one summer when we were boys. She used to whack our hands with a cane when we made mistakes. We called her the gargoyle, GG for short, and later on it came to mean almost anyone Ozzie took a dislike to – his first bank manager, for example.' Turning back to the diary, he continued: '*GG read riot act. Huge row. Fire and brimstone. Told no option, so that was that. Oh, hell!* The day after that he's back in Arras and his only entry reads: *Feeling rotten. Nothing to be done.* Then there's a gap of three weeks with no relevant entries. But on 2 July he writes: *Just heard re Sandybags. It's the CCCBBB, as expected. Damned shame. Rotten business all round.*'

He laid the diary back on the desk and then, almost as an afterthought, slid it across the blotter to Billy, who reached for it.

'*CCCBBB*?' Billy peered at the page with a frown.

'Oh, that?' Gibson put a hand to his brow. 'It's from *The Mikado*. Gilbert and Sullivan. Ozzie knew all the lyrics. "The cheap and chippy chopper . . ."?'

He saw Billy's look of bafflement.

'"Awaiting the sensation of a short, sharp shock from a cheap and chippy chopper on a big, black block." *CCCBBB*. It was Ozzie's way of saying something was over and done with.'

He shifted his gaze to Madden.

'You see the problem? It's plain he was bothered about *something*. But how to make any sense of what he wrote . . .'

Glancing at Madden just then, Billy had a shock. His old chief's face had paled. He was staring at nothing. It took the sudden loud bray of a car's hooter in the street below to bring him out of his trance, and only then did he turn his head to look at Gibson.

'Did your brother never tell you he served on a court martial?' he asked.

'*A court martial?*' The solicitor's astonishment was unfeigned. 'No, he never said a word about it. Is that what all this means?'

'*FGCM*. Field General Court Martial. They could be held anywhere: in a schoolroom, or a farmhouse, or a Nissen hut – any place that was handy. The name "Sandybags" refers to a village called Saint-Bertrand in the Arras region. The troops used to make up their own names for towns and villages. Like "Wipers" for Ypres.'

He spoke in a dead voice.

'I'm not surprised your brother felt a mistake had been made in naming him to the board. It wasn't usual for an officer from a support unit to serve on a court martial.'

'What about all that other stuff, though? *Huge row . . . Fire and brimstone . . . Told no option*? What does it all mean?'

Madden put a hand to the scar on his forehead. 'Well, as you say, your brother was simply making notes. He was giving some kind of account of the proceedings, at least as they had struck him. He seems to have felt bad about the whole business, particularly the outcome.'

'The outcome?'

'The accused man was found guilty and sentenced to death.'

Gibson reddened. 'I see no mention of that.'

'It's implied, though. When your brother says there's no option, he means that he had to go along with the guilty verdict. And then, a few weeks later, he hears the news and it prompts him to say it's a rotten shame and a bad business all round.'

'What news?'

'That the man had been executed: shot by firing squad.'

The bluntness of his words seemed to shake Gibson. Unable to speak, he sat with his gaze fixed on Madden.

'*CCCBBB*. It was all over, you see. Finished and done with.'

Still wordless, the solicitor held out a hand to Billy, who passed the diary back to him. He stared blindly at the open page.

'I see how it reads . . . or could read.' He spoke finally. 'But you can't be sure, can you? It's only your interpretation, after all.'

'No, it's more than that.' Madden's voice was heavy with regret. 'I happen to know that the man they shot was named Ballard. James Ballard. He was in my company.'

He saw the light of comprehension come into Gibson's eyes and nodded.

'Yes, I was there too.'

'But what are you suggesting? That whoever shot Ozzie, and these other men, is somehow connected to the soldier who was found guilty at that court martial?'

Edward Gibson sat blinking in his chair. The blood had drained from his normally pink cheeks.

'I believe that to be the case. It's the only explanation.'

It had taken Madden some moments to compose his reply, and Billy saw that the revelation had left him as shaken as it had the man he was addressing. Nevertheless he managed to continue speaking in a reasoned tone.

'He's very likely a blood relative, someone with a close tie to Ballard.'

'For pity's sake! We're talking of something that happened thirty years ago.'

'Yes, but it's only *that* that makes it seem incredible.'

'What on earth do you mean?' the solicitor challenged him.

Billy saw his old chief hesitate.

'Let me put it like this,' he began. 'Considering the way many of those courts martial were conducted, it wouldn't have been surprising if some member of an executed man's family had sought revenge at the time, for what might have seemed a gross injustice. I'm not saying it would have been a balanced or even a justified reaction; but I can see how he might have fixed on the members of the court martial as being guilty of judicial murder.'

Madden paused, frowning.

'What I don't understand is how the killer got hold of the names of his victims. The records of those courts martial – the ones that resulted in executions – have been sealed since the end of the war.'

'And you think this is what happened with Ozzie?' Gibson seemed not to have heard Madden's last words. His eyes were glazed and his breathing had grown short. 'That some lunatic has decided to settle old scores, decades later?'

'It would seem so, yes.' Aware of the other man's distress, Madden kept his voice calm. 'As you know, we've been trying to find a motive for your brother's murder and at the same time search for any connection between him and me – something that could explain that letter he began writing with my name in it. Now it seems we've found both.'

Again he hesitated.

'You say Oswald had an eye infection?'

Gibson nodded.

'The president of that particular court martial was a major. He had two junior officers with him, and I remember one of them had an eye-patch. That may be why I didn't recognize Oswald from the photographs you showed me. As it happened, I didn't pay much attention to him. He was silent throughout the proceedings.'

'What about the third officer?' It was Billy who put the question. 'Was that Singleton?'

'It must have been.' Madden turned to him. 'I saw a picture of him in one of the papers after he was shot, but it didn't ring a bell. Mind you, it was blurred and he had a mortar board on his head. It looked like an old school photograph.'

'How does Drummond fit in?'

'One of the witnesses at the trial was a young medico called by the prosecution. He testified to having examined Ballard and found him fit to stand trial: this in spite of the fact that Ballard hadn't said a word throughout the proceedings and seemed barely aware of what was happening. I can't swear that the doctor was Drummond. I don't remember the name and I've never seen a photograph of him. But it seems likely now that it was.'

'And what were *you* doing there?' Gibson found his tongue at last. He had been sitting silent, seemingly stunned by what he had heard. 'I take it you weren't part of this court?'

'No, I was what was called "the prisoner's friend" – his defence counsel, if you like. Ballard was charged with desertion, a court-martial offence. I was a lieutenant at the time and it was the normal practice to give the job of defending an accused man to a junior officer from his own company or battalion.'

Breathing heavily still, Gibson stared at him. He seemed unable to grasp what he'd heard.

'Judicial murder, you said. Is that really a fair description? And could Ozzie have possibly been held responsible for it?'

'I'll stand by those words, particularly with regard to that court martial.' Madden looked steadily at him. 'But as far as your brother was concerned – no, I don't hold him to blame for what happened.'

'There's no need to spare my feelings, Mr Madden.' The solicitor's tone was bitter. 'He was part of the court, wasn't he? He was one of the judges.'

'True. But a junior officer, under the thumb of a man who came there determined to get a guilty verdict.'

'You mean the court president?'

Madden nodded grimly. 'He was a major in the Royal Artillery, a brute and a bully. He ran the proceedings like a kangaroo court. I discovered that early on when I tried to cross-question one of the prosecution witnesses and he cut me off, on the grounds of irrelevance.'

'But surely he had no right to do that.' Gibson scowled. 'I would remind you that I'm a solicitor. I'm perfectly familiar with court procedure.'

'Unfortunately he had every right.' It was Madden's turn to sound bitter. 'Or, rather, there was nothing to stop him – no higher authority present and no qualified officer in attendance who might have pulled him up on points of law. The trial was entirely in his hands.'

He saw the look of disbelief on Gibson's face.

'I know this is hard for you to grasp. Again, let me try and explain.' He got to his feet and began to pace up and down. 'First, you have to understand how these so-called field courts martial differed from peacetime, when there would have been a legally trained officer, a judge-advocate as he was called, present to advise the court. During the war, trials could take place with as few as three officers sitting, and none with any legal training. It was the president of the court, the senior officer, who ran the proceedings from start to finish.

'Now, according to the rules of procedure, every accused had the right to prepare his defence and call witnesses, but in practice this right was often ignored, to the point where a plea of extenuating circumstances was the only recourse left to him and it was seldom accepted. Ballard himself was unable to make a statement during the court martial. He was suffering from shell-shock – his nerves were shattered – but in those days the condition was barely recognized and was often attributed to funk. In the end it was left to me to make a statement in mitigation of sentence, after it became clear that he had been found guilty. I mention this because it must be why your brother remembered me as having been present and, more important, how he knew that I had once worked for Scotland Yard.'

'How was that, sir?' Billy spoke.

'When I rose to make the statement, the court president – this major – tried to rule me out of order (we'd already crossed swords) and make out that I was overstepping the bounds of my role as defending officer, due to my ignorance of court procedure. That gave a chance to hit back. I revealed that I'd been a Scotland Yard inspector in civilian life, and that in fact I had wide experience of trials and how they should be conducted.'

Madden paused in his pacing to frown.

'I may even have implied that I knew more than he did, which was probably a mistake. In any event he took it badly and, when the court rose, he warned me that he would be sending a report to my commanding officer with a recommendation that I be punished for insubordination. Nothing came of that, but it does help to explain why Oswald mentioned my name in that letter.'

He turned to Gibson.

'I put an idea to Mr Styles earlier. I thought it possible that your brother's visitor that day called on him in order to confirm his identity. If so, it's likely that he brought up the subject of the court martial, which in turn must have prompted Oswald to start on that letter. He remembered what I'd said at the trial: that before the war I had worked at the Yard. He may well have thought I was someone who could explain why this skeleton from his past, which he'd hoped was dead and buried, was being dug up.'

The solicitor received Madden's words in silence. When he finally spoke, it was only after a long pause.

'All right, I can see that makes some kind of sense. But to go back to the court martial – it seems to have been a travesty of justice by any standards. Surely the accused man had the right of appeal?'

'Unfortunately not.' Madden's tone was grim. 'There was no appeal against these decisions. But the sentence of death wasn't automatic. It had to be confirmed by the proper authority, which in the case of capital offences was the commander-in-chief.'

'Do you mean Field Marshal Haig?' Gibson was astonished.

'Yes, Haig would have been the senior officer who confirmed the sentence. The file would have been sent to him. But prior to that there was a procedure that had to be followed. After the accused had been found guilty, all papers concerning his case were sent to his commanding officer and then in turn to his brigade, division and corps commanders, for their opinion as to whether the sentence should be commuted or confirmed. I took some pains to find out what happened with Ballard's case and I discovered that right up to division level the recommendations made were all for mercy. They were based on our own company commander's view, expressed in the clearest terms, that although Ballard had committed a capital offence, he had been a good soldier up to that point and deserved better than a firing squad. It's clear to me now that the file must have gone to Canning next. He was our corps commander at the time and he must have recommended that the sentence be carried out. Why else would he have been on the killer's list?'

As though struck by a bullet himself at that moment, Madden stopped suddenly in his tracks. He stood scowling.

'But the killer could only know that if he'd seen the court-martial record, Ballard's file. And that's not possible. I told you – all those records are sealed.'

He shook his head in bafflement.

'I've no explanation for that. Where was I? Yes, at that point I was wounded.' He touched the scar on his brow. 'It wasn't particularly serious, but it got me sent to a base hospital, and during that time Ballard's case reached Haig's desk and the sentence was confirmed. He was executed a few days later.'

'Hold on a second.' Gibson broke in. 'You said all those recommendations were for mercy. Surely Haig would have taken them into account.'

'Would he?' Madden's shrug seemed to suggest otherwise. 'Well, it's not a question anyone can answer now: not even Haig, since he's no longer with us. But what I can tell you is that it was far from being the only instance of its kind and, if you want my opinion, I doubt that the question of mercy played any great part in his decision. It became clear in the course of the war that some of the most senior officers in the British Army believed that the only sure way of ensuring discipline in the ranks was to make the threat of executions a real one, particularly for anything that smacked of desertion or cowardice. They were meant to set an example to the other men and to serve as a warning. It was a line of thinking that was fairly general, but in Ballard's case there may have been a further reason for putting him before a firing squad, one that could have swayed Haig's mind more than any considerations of fairness.'

'And what was that?'

'The condition of the French Army at the time.'

'The *French* Army?' Gibson's jaw dropped. 'What had that got to do with it?'

Madden turned to him.

'Many people have forgotten, but for some months in 1917 the discipline in the French Army on the Western Front came close to breaking down completely. They'd suffered terrible losses, first at Verdun and later at the Chemin des Dames. The men had lost confidence in their generals and there were cases of entire units refusing to go into battle. Pétain sorted it out in the end, mostly by improving conditions for the men. But he also set about weeding out the ringleaders among the mutineers, and four hundred or so were sentenced to death and more than fifty eventually executed. Of course the British commanders were well aware of what was going on and were probably terrified of the same thing happening among our troops, though they needn't have worried. We had very little contact with the French and there was never any question of the contagion spreading. But the fear was there and it may have contributed to what happened. There was never any doubt in my mind that the officer I spoke of – that major – had orders to find Ballard guilty, and the more I thought about it afterwards, the more convinced I was that at some level it had been decided to make an example of him.'

He paused before going on. His gaze was fixed on the solicitor.

'It's no consolation, I know, but for what it's worth, I believe your brother was desperately unlucky to have been named to that court. I gather, from what you've told us, that he wasn't a forceful character.'

'Ozzie?' Gibson smiled sadly. 'Anything but, I fear . . .'

'Then he may have been chosen for that reason. It's quite possible the word was put out discreetly for a junior officer from a support unit, one with no experience of action, who would follow whatever lead was given. You see, no accused man could be sentenced to death unless the verdict was unanimous. Your brother and the other officer, Singleton, were both young men, and one can only imagine what kind of pressure they were subjected to. It's clear from Oswald's diary that he felt tainted by the proceedings and the fact that he never told you about it supports that conclusion. I don't know whether it helps to say so, but he should never have been placed in that position.'

Madden fell silent. He caught Billy's eye. They waited for Gibson to speak.

For some while the solicitor said nothing. His gaze was held by the diary lying open in front of him and, as the seconds ticked by, he continued to stare at it.

Finally he looked up.

'Thank you, Mr Madden . . . and you, too, Inspector.' He put a hand to his head. 'Poor Ozzie . . . But that was the story of his life, I'm afraid. He always tried to avoid trouble. Right to the end he thought everything would be all right so long as he did as he was told.'

With a sigh he closed the book.

'You'll want to know the name of the officer who presided at Ballard's court martial, but I'm afraid I can't help you there.' Madden sat frowning. 'It's possible I took note of it at the time. But if I did, it's gone from my memory now.'

His words came as a shock to Billy. Accustomed as he was to his old chief's powers of recall, he had felt confident that Madden would supply him with the necessary information. Following their meeting with Gibson they had sought refuge in a nearby pub and were sitting at a table in a corner of the crowded lounge bar.

'But you'll have to find him as soon as possible,' Madden went on. 'Assuming he survived the war, he must be at risk. The quickest way will be to get hold of the record of the trial, but that could be a problem. As I said, all those cases were put under seal thirty years ago, and although there have been several attempts to get them released, mainly by the families of the men who were executed, none has ever succeeded. Every government since the war has taken the same position, and most likely they'll dig in their heels again. If you have any trouble, get hold of the adjutant at the Royal Artillery barracks at Woolwich. He should be able to help.'

Madden broke off, biting his lip. Billy waited. It was plain to him that his old chief was still feeling the effects of the shock he had suffered in Edward Gibson's office: the realization of what lay behind the string of killings, and his own connection to it.

'As for Ballard himself, I can't claim to have known him well. He wasn't one of the original men in our company. After the Somme there weren't many of those left. He came over with a draft of replacements in the autumn of 1916. But the one thing I can tell you about him is that he was married and had a daughter.'

'Are you sure, sir?' Billy pulled a face. 'I was hoping it might have been a son.'

'I know you were, and I can see why.' Madden's tone was grim. 'But it's something I'm certain of. When I was assigned to defend him one of the first things I did was find out whether he had a family, because if he was convicted I meant to use that in mitigation. Since I couldn't get a word out of him – he'd gone silent – I turned to his closest friends in the company and they told me he had a baby daughter. He had shown them photographs of her.'

'What about his own kin then? Did he have a brother by any chance?'

'I've no idea.'

Madden shook his head hopelessly.

'If he did, though, it couldn't have been the same person spotted at Lewes. He moved like a young man. But you're right – the killer must surely be someone with a close tie to him, and a blood relation seems the most likely answer. You'd best speak to his widow when you find her, or his daughter. They might be able to point you in the right direction. You'll be looking for someone who feels so strongly about what happened thirty years ago that he's willing to offer up his life to avenge an injustice. That's extraordinary in itself – unheard of, I would say – but just as puzzling is why.'

'Why?'

'Why now . . . after all this time?' Madden stared at him. 'It's inexplicable.'

As Billy watched he put a hand to his head. Again Billy waited for a few moments before speaking.

'What about Ballard himself?' he asked. 'What do you remember about him?'

'Not much.' Madden shrugged. 'I was promoted from the ranks shortly before he arrived. I'd become an officer, so I never got to know him well. But I recall he was highly strung. He'd been a painter before the war, an artist. He used to sketch in his spare time. The men would offer to buy his drawings, but he wouldn't accept any money for them. The ones he didn't keep he gave away. The men took his execution badly. They knew it was unjust.'

'Still, he was highly strung, you say?'

'He had a vivid imagination – an artist's sensitivity, if you like – but that's the last thing a soldier wants to be burdened with when he goes into battle. I thought his sketching was a way of dealing with his fears – the fears we all had; of reducing them to pencil strokes on paper. I could see his nerves were stretched to the limit, but he never shirked his duty, and I thought him a brave man for that reason.'

'Until he cracked?'

'Until he cracked.'

Billy caught the change in his old chief's tone.

'He'd been wounded shortly before. It wasn't much – just a gash caused by a shell splinter – but it got him a sort stay in base hospital at Boulogne and a few days' leave afterwards. It wasn't long enough to go home, and he told me when he got back that he'd used the time to go to Paris to look at some paintings. He thought it might be his only chance to see them. Later I wondered if there hadn't been more to his words than I'd realized.'

'Are you saying he didn't expect to live much longer?' Billy leaned closer.

'It could have been that. I had seen it happen to others. The fear . . . the expectation of death was very strong in those days. It affected all of us and it could easily harden into a certainty. All I can say for sure is that he was much quieter when he came back, more withdrawn, and I worried that he might be thinking too much. I knew by then it was the worst thing one could do. It was best to take each day as it came and to blank out all thoughts of the future.'

Madden stared at the glass-topped table.

'The Germans had been shelling our lines off and on for a week or more and Ballard had the bad luck to be in a dugout that was hit several times and caved in. When we pulled out the men inside, we found two of them had suffocated and another had had his head crushed. Ballard was unhurt, but strangely silent, and I told his sergeant to keep an eye on him. However, in the confusion he wandered off and we discovered later that he had made his way to the rear. I'm not sure to this day whether he knew what he was doing. I believe he was shell-shocked. What's certain is that he didn't try to escape: he didn't make a run for it. He found a ruined barn not far away and simply lay down and went to sleep. The MPs came across him two days later, half-starved. When they tried to question him he stayed mute. In fact, I'm not sure he ever said another word. He'd reached his limit, you see. He couldn't go on.'

Madden's gaze had lost focus while he was speaking. To Billy it seemed that he was miles away. Or was it years?

'I was appointed to defend him at his court martial and initially I had hopes of getting him off. It was plain, to me at least, that Ballard wasn't fit to stand trial: that the proper place for him was a hospital. But it was a lost cause from the start. We know how Oswald Gibson reacted. He made that clear in his diary. Perhaps the others felt the same: Singleton and that Scottish doctor. I know it left a mark on me. I felt soiled afterwards, as if I'd been made to play a part in a squalid charade whose outcome was never in doubt. It's the only explanation I can give for why I never connected it to these murders, why I can't even recall that officer's name, even though I knew I was somehow involved in this business; even though I'd guessed it might have a link to the war.'

Madden's dark eyes were filled with pain.

'It was something I didn't want to remember.'

16

'WE'RE MAKING PROGRESS, SIR, but it's slow going. And I'd better warn you now: there's good news and bad news.'

With a grunt Billy slid into a chair in front of Chubb's desk. It was late in the afternoon and through the windows at the back of the office he could see the last of the sunlight glowing on the coppery surface of the Thames. Less than forty-eight hours had passed since the revelations contained in Oswald Gibson's diary had come to light, and he and Lily Poole had been hard at work ever since chasing up whatever slender leads there were to pursue.

'Give me the good news first.' The chief super scowled.

Billy had found him sitting with his jacket slung over the back of his chair and his tie loose, a breach of sartorial etiquette unthinkable in the days when Angus Sinclair had held sway and a sight that had made him smile.

'We've traced Ballard's widow. She was living practically on our doorstep, just down the road in Richmond.'

'What's the bad news?'

'She died this June.'

'Damn and blast!' Chubb glowered. 'What about the daughter then? I trust she's still in the land of the living.'

'As far as we know.' Billy shrugged. 'But she's left the

country. She's gone to Canada. According to their family solicitor, she was planning to emigrate even before her mother died.
She went over there at the end of July.'

'Canada!' Charlie was indignant. 'What she want to go there
for?'

'I couldn't say, sir.' Billy scratched his head. 'But a lot of people seem to have the same idea these days. Canada, Australia,
South Africa . . .'

He was referring to a rash of recent newspaper stories detail-
ing the growing tide of emigration from Britain's shores. Fed up
with the never-ending restrictions and lured by the prospect of
greener pastures abroad, families were leaving in the thousands,
the reports said.

Chubb sighed. 'What else?'

'Poole and I have been digging and we've come up with a lot
of stuff about Ballard himself. For a start, we got hold of his
enlistment details from the War Office. He gave St Ives, in Cornwall, as his home town and his wife, Hazel, as next of kin. At
that stage they had no children, but six months later Mrs Ballard
gave birth to their daughter. Her name's Alma: Alma Rose.'

'You got that from the War Office?' Chubb was surprised.

'No, from a lady called Eve Selby. She's lived in St Ives for
the past forty years. She's a painter, like Ballard was. They were
part of an artists' colony down there. The local police put me on
to her. When I mentioned Hazel Ballard's name, she asked me
at once where she was living and if she was all right. They had
been friends, she told me, but she hadn't seen or heard from her
for thirty years, not since Hazel received word of her husband's
death. But what's interesting is that, as far as Eve Selby or anyone else in St Ives knew, James Ballard simply died in action.'

'You mean Hazel never mentioned the court martial?'

'She never breathed a word about it. Mind you, that wasn't
unusual, and she wouldn't have been the first to behave that
way. According to Mr Madden, the normal practice then was to

inform the man's widow or next of kin of his trial and execution, but not to publicize the fact in any way. Eve Selby was shocked when I told her the truth. She said a few days after receiving the letter from the War Office, Hazel upped sticks and left, taking the baby with her. Selby was expecting her to return, but instead she got a letter from Hazel saying she couldn't face living in St Ives any longer. It held too many memories for her. She was going to settle elsewhere and would contact her later on. But Miss Selby never heard from her again.'

Billy paused. A scowl had appeared on Chubb's face.

'That doesn't sound right. It's not how people behave. After a while they get in touch with old friends again.'

'Well, Hazel Ballard didn't. Like I say, she just vanished. But Selby did tell me something interesting. It wasn't a lead exactly, but it does help to explain how Hazel managed her disappearing act. It seems she had money of her own, enough so that she and her husband were able to live comfortably while James was trying to make his name as an artist. According to Miss Selby, Hazel adored him. There was nothing she wouldn't do for him. But as far as the money was concerned, it meant she could take off at a moment's notice and go . . . well, anywhere.'

Billy spread his hands.

'Where did the money come from?' Charlie's interest had been aroused.

'Her grandfather, originally. The family hailed from Gloucester, but he went to London when he was a young man and set up as a wine merchant. The business did well and was carried on by his son, Hazel's father. But when *he* died – and his wife soon after him – the firm was sold and the money divided between their two children. Hazel had an elder brother, but he was killed early in the war, so in the end it all came to her. She wasn't exactly wealthy, Selby said, but she was certainly well off.'

Billy bent over his notebook.

'Selby also knew something of Ballard's own family

background. His mother was a maid who was working in a Plymouth hotel when she got in the family way. James was the result. The girl died in childbirth and, since her family didn't want to cope with the baby, he was adopted by an elderly couple named Ballard who gave him an education and sent him to art school. After they died he was offered a job as an apprentice in an artist's studio in St Ives, which was where he met Hazel, who was there on holiday. She was a few years older than him, but according to Selby, it was a case of love at first sight – on her side at least. Hazel had lost her parents a few years earlier and the rest of her family was opposed to the match. For one thing, she was older than him by a couple of years; for another, it seems they didn't fancy the idea of her marrying a bastard. But it didn't stop her and they got hitched.'

Billy paused for a breather. He could see that Chubb was digesting the information he'd been given. The chief super was doodling with his pencil on a piece of paper.

'Are you trying to tell me Ballard may have some relatives that no one knows about; that somewhere there might be a bloke who's a little wrong in the head and wants to avenge his long-lost kinsman?'

'It's a thought, sir.' Billy grinned. 'Anyway, I've asked the Plymouth police to get on to it and see if they can track down any members of the maid's family. There's just a chance one of them might know the name of James's real father.'

'You'll pardon me if I don't hold my breath.' The chief super eyed him askance. 'About Ballard's widow, though – how did you get on to her?'

'Through the national register of births and deaths at Somerset House. Her death was recorded there along with her address.'

'What about the daughter – Alma? How much do we know about her?'

'Not a lot as yet; only what I've got from that solicitor, a chap called Royston. The Richmond police gave me his name and I rang him yesterday. He didn't know Hazel well – she was just a client to him – but after her death he had several meetings with Alma to do with her mother's will. It was he who told me she had gone to Canada.'

'Does he know her address?'

'She was staying in Toronto until quite recently. But she said in a letter that she didn't want to settle there and was going to travel across the country on the Canadian Pacific to Vancouver. She gave him the names of a couple of cities where she planned to stop, and said she'd check for letters left poste restante in case he needed to get in touch with her urgently.' Billy hesitated. 'We could ask the Mounties to trace her for us, if you like.'

Chubb grunted. 'It's something to consider.' He made a note with his pencil. 'Did this Royston bloke know about the court martial?' he asked.

'I don't think so. I asked him about Hazel's husband and he said he'd been killed in the First World War, but nothing more. Maybe he thought it was none of our business: he was starting to get shirty; wanted to know why I was asking all these questions. But I don't think he knew. It's possible she never told anyone.'

Billy chewed his lip thoughtfully.

'After we'd got her address I rang the police in Richmond and they sent a man round to her old house. It was empty and up for sale, but he talked to one or two people in the neighbourhood, who told him Hazel had been living there with her daughter since the summer of 1930.'

'And before that?'

'None of them knew. I had the impression Hazel Ballard kept pretty much to herself. But her daughter could tell us that. She wasn't living at home when her mother fell ill – she was in London – but she came back to Richmond to nurse her and was there when Mrs Ballard died. Soon afterwards she put the house up for sale and word got about that she was planning to emigrate.'

Billy closed his notebook and looked up in time to see his superior give an approving nod.

'You've been a busy bee. Now I'll tell you what I've been up to.'

Chubb stifled a yawn. It had grown dark while they were talking, and Billy could see the lights coming on in the buildings across the river.

'John was right in saying that we might have a problem getting our hands on that court-martial record. But I think I've sorted it out.'

When Billy had repeated Madden's warning about the obstacles they might encounter, the chief super had volunteered to tackle the matter himself.

'I talked to a chap called Cunningham today. He's an undersecretary at the War Office. He told me straight off the bat they wouldn't allow the records to be opened under any pretext, or used in a trial, unless we could persuade them that we had an airtight case: that we could tie these murders to that particular court martial.'

'Which we can't . . . not yet . . . not without more evidence.'

'Exactly. So I pointed out that the only way we could be certain was by seeing the papers. We had to be sure that the men who've been shot figured in that trial. And we needed to confirm the name of the presiding officer, since he'd almost certainly be next on the list. Cunningham hemmed and hawed and then said he'd put the matter before the minister. Apparently he's the only one who can give permission for the records to be unsealed. But Cunningham warned me not to get my hopes up. They're dead-set against doing it.'

A glint had appeared in Chubb's eye.

'I said I quite understood. But then I warned him that the press were hot on the trail, and it was hard to see how the ministry wouldn't be seen as blocking a murder investigation if word of that court martial got out, as it was bound to. After all, it wasn't every day a Lord Lieutenant got topped.'

'But it won't, will it?' Billy was surprised. 'Get out, I mean. I thought you'd decided to keep quiet about it, at least for the moment.'

'Yes, but they're not to know that, are they?' The glint was replaced by a twinkle. 'Let 'em fear the worst, I say.'

Chubb covered the yawn he'd been trying to keep in check.

'Remembering what John told you, I also asked Cunningham if there was any way our killer could have found out the names of those officers on the court-martial board without seeing the file, and he swore there wasn't. There were no other records of those proceedings kept anywhere. So that's still a riddle, unless the shooter works at the Public Record Office, where the papers are stored. Even then he shouldn't have been able to get his hands on them. They're kept under lock and key apparently.'

Chubb shrugged.

'Anyhow, as regards being allowed to see the record ourselves, I think I put the wind up Mr Cunningham. He said he'd get back to me as soon as possible.'

He mused for a moment.

'I gather you've been keeping Madden informed?' Chubb said.

Billy nodded.

'He asked me to. This business is weighing on him. He seems to think it's his responsibility somehow.'

'Well, it's not.' Chubb scowled. 'That court martial took place thirty years ago, and he wasn't to blame for how it turned out. Didn't he do everything he could for the poor chap?'

'That and more, I should think.' Billy spoke with assurance: he knew his man. 'But he sees things differently, Mr Madden does. He always has. He feels guilty about not being able to recall that officer's name. But if you ask me, he blocked it out of his memory. He wanted to forget the whole business. And I'll tell you something else: he won't let go of this now. He'll see it through to the end.'

'Then let's make the most of that. How long is he staying in London?'

'He's going home for the weekend, but he'll be back on Monday. There's still work to be done on that house.'

Chubb signalled his satisfaction with a grunt. He glanced at his watch.

'It won't have escaped your notice that the press have got their teeth into this.'

Billy confined his response to a grimace. The biggest-selling paper, the *Daily Mirror* – it claimed to have more than three million readers – had been going to town on the story. Having earlier toyed with the term 'mystery gunman' in its headlines, it had switched following the murder of Canning to the more picturesque 'faceless killer', while its main rival, the *Daily Express*, had stuck loyally to its own invention, 'silent stalker'.

Like all the papers, they had been asking why. Why these particular men had been chosen as victims? What was the motive behind the killings? But none had come up with an answer yet, other than to suggest that there might be a lunatic on the loose.

'With any luck we'll be given a stay of grace. Chances are they'll be busy for the next few days with this royal shindig.'

The chief super was referring to the forthcoming wedding between the heir to the throne, Princess Elizabeth, and Prince Philip of Greece, due to take place at Westminster Abbey later that month.

'But it won't last. They'll soon turn their attention our way again. And on that happy note I'll take my leave of you. It's time I went home.'

He moved to fasten the stud on his collar.

'Unless you've got something more to tell me?'

Billy hesitated.

'It's a long shot, sir, but while we're waiting to see that court-martial file I thought I'd pursue the question of whether the shooter called on his victims in advance. As Mr Madden says, he can't have been acquainted with them all personally and, except in the case of Canning, he had to be sure who he was killing. Just their names wouldn't have been enough. Now we know Ozzie Gibson had a visitor, and it could well have been the same bloke who shot him later. As far as Drummond is concerned, we haven't been able to make that link. The identities of the men who called at his consulting rooms prior to his murder – people not on his regular roster of patients – have all been checked. But that still leaves Mrs Singleton . . .'

'The Oxford lady?'

'I didn't get a chance to interview her properly when I was down there. She was too upset. But it's been more than a week now and I want her questioned again. I just can't believe this bloke put a bullet in her husband's head without being sure he had the right man. They must have had some kind of contact beforehand and, even if Mrs Singleton wasn't present, it's odds-on her husband talked to her about it later. They were a close couple. She said herself they kept nothing from each other.'

'What will you do – get the local plod to talk to her?'

Billy shook his head. 'I'd rather we handled it ourselves. I want to see if we can draw her out, get her talking.'

'And you think *you're* the man to do that?'

The look of sheer disbelief on the chief super's homely features made Billy laugh out loud.

'Not really, sir. In fact, I reckon it's more a job for a woman.'

'A *woman*?' Charlie was bemused.

'That's why I'm sending Poole. She's going down to Oxford tomorrow.'

17

'A SALESMAN?' LILY ASKED. 'What sort? What was he selling?'

'Vacuum cleaners,' Mrs Singleton said. 'Door-to-door. He looked exhausted, poor man, so I invited him in for a cup of tea and let him show me his cleaner. It did a perfectly good job on the living-room carpet. But I had to tell him we didn't want one and he looked so disappointed.'

'Was Mr Singleton here?' A moment ago Lily had come alert: now she was trying to keep her excitement in check. It was the first anyone had heard of this 'salesman'. There'd been no mention of him in the file she'd been given to read.

'Oh, yes. He was retired, you know. He was usually at home.'

'Did they meet? Did the salesman talk to him at all?'

'Oh dear, I can't remember.' Mrs Singleton frowned. 'Perhaps. Tom was here in the sitting room when the man demonstrated his cleaner. I had to ask him to move his feet. Why are you asking these questions?' She looked curiously at Lily.

'No special reason. We're just trying to find out if anything unusual, to do with your husband, happened before . . . before . . .' Lily lost her tongue for a moment.

'Before he was shot?' Mrs Singleton patted her hand. 'It's all right, my dear. I've had to get used to saying that. Well, I suppose that salesman coming to the house was a little out of the ordinary – we don't get many – but I doubt there was anything sinister about his visit.'

They had been sitting at opposite ends of the small sofa in the living room for close to half an hour, and up to now the older woman had provided little in the way of information. All of which had only served to increase Lily's frustration. She'd been waiting for a chance to show her mettle ever since she'd been picked to work on the case and, while she had done well enough up to now – the interview she had had with Sally Abbot during their hurried visit to Winchester had earned her a pat on the back from Styles – she felt she was yet to make any real mark on the investigation. Like all recruits to the Metropolitan Police she had had to serve her time in the uniformed branch, where her attempts to join CID had been consistently thwarted for no reason she could see, other than the fact that she was a woman. It had required the intervention first of Styles and, later and more crucially, of Chief Inspector Sinclair before she had finally been given the chance. But even that hadn't marked the end of her struggle to assert herself. The assignments she'd been given up to now had been mundane, most of them concerned with minor complaints or bureaucratic drudgery, the kind thought suitable for one of her sex (or so Lily believed). But now she had been given an opportunity to shine and she was deter-mined to make the most of it.

The recent introduction of a new element into the investiga-tion – its seeming link to the First World War – had caught her imagination. As it happened, her own father had died in the conflict, and images of the flickering figures stumbling across cratered battlefields, as captured by old newsreels, were etched in her memory. But the orders she'd received from Styles had been clear.

'Whatever you do, don't ask her about that court martial. We're keeping quiet about it for now. The records will tell us whether or not her husband was present. If you mention the subject, she's bound to talk to others about it and word will get out. Stick to the question of any visitors that Singleton might have had. That's what we want to know about.'

Confined to this single aspect of the investigation, Lily's hopes had been further dented before the interview began when she had called at the central police station in Oxford following her arrival by train and had met the officer in charge of the inquiry, Inspector Morgan.

'I've asked Mrs Singleton several times if anything happened in the days leading up to her husband's murder that might be linked to it – anything at all – but she insists there wasn't,' he had told her. 'I believe her, too. I mean I believe *she* believes it. You'll have a hard time convincing her otherwise.'

At least the red-haired inspector's greeting had been friendly enough, which as far as Lily was concerned made a pleasant change from the thinly disguised hostility she was used to encountering from so many of her male colleagues. She knew that most of them held it as an article of faith that there was no place for women in the force, and she'd developed a thick skin as far as the looks and the sniggers she heard behind her back were concerned.

'So your guv'nor thinks this job needs a woman's touch.' Morgan had risen from his desk to shake her by the hand when she'd been shown into his office. His Welsh accent lent a musical lilt to his words. 'That's fine by me, but I'm still not sure what he's hoping to find out. If I didn't know better, I'd say he was clutching at straws. But maybe you'll prove me wrong. Let's hope so.'

'About this salesman – is there anything more you can tell me about him? Can you describe him to me?'

Lily tried to keep her voice calm, her excitement under control. It was the first hint Mrs Singleton had given that there might be something here worth following up: that her journey to Oxford hadn't been wasted. Before that they had been chatting in an informal way, with Lily taking care not to act the policewoman. Instead, she had allowed the older woman to treat her in a motherly fashion, taking advantage of the brief exchange they had had the previous afternoon when she had rung to arrange the interview.

'Oh, I see – you're a *detective*, are you?' Mrs Singleton had sounded surprised when Lily had identified herself. 'I didn't know there were any – women detectives, I mean. What a good idea.'

The friendly note having been struck, Lily had worked hard to maintain it since her arrival at the house, a small semi-detached dwelling in north Oxford, where she had been dropped by a police driver after her meeting with Morgan. Walking up the short path from the gate, she had heard the sound of a dog barking inside. Before she'd had time to lift the brass knocker the door had opened.

'Detective-Constable Poole?'

Lily had found herself looking into a pair of eyes as blue as her own, but with a weight of sadness in them that remained unchanged in spite of the smile of welcome being offered to her. Grey-haired, but with her good looks still intact, thanks to the kind of bone structure that Lily would have given her right arm for, Eleanor Singleton was in her late fifties, or thereabouts.

'Don't mind Sandy. He always barks at visitors.' The Sealy-ham had been sniffing at Lily's ankles. 'I can't break him of the habit, and he's too old now to learn any new tricks.'

Instead of showing her visitor into the sitting room, as Lily had expected, she had taken her instead to the kitchen at the back of the house, where she had busied herself making tea for them and where, seemingly anxious to postpone the business of the interview, she had peppered her guest with questions.

'Did you apply to be a detective? Did you have to pass an

exam? Was there any opposition to your joining the police force? I ask because when I was a nurse – it was during the first war – the medical profession was quite hostile to the idea of women doctors. Now, of course, it's quite different.'

When the tea was ready they had gone into the small sitting room at the front of the house and, after settling her visitor on the sofa and taking up her own position at the other end of it, she had turned her gentle gaze on Lily.

'I've been racking my brains since we spoke on the telephone yesterday, trying to remember if there was anything Tom ever said to me that might be of help. But truly there was nothing. We've lived very quietly since he retired.'

Discouraged at the outset, Lily had introduced the subject of visitors to the house, in particular callers who might have turned up unexpectedly. But even there the knowledge gleaned had been scanty.

'Well, let me think.' Mrs Singleton's white brow had furrowed. 'We do get callers, of course. The vicar drops in unannounced from time to time and various neighbours and tradesmen, but you don't mean them. We had one of those lovely French onion-sellers knock on the door only a day or two before Tom was . . . before he died. They disappeared during the war, but now they're back. He was a sweet old man. Then there was a lady who came by collecting money for Armistice Day – Remembrance Day, they call it now – and handing out poppies. Tom gave her something, naturally. He always did, every year. And then there was the rag-and-bone man . . .' Her voice trailed off. 'I'm sorry, this isn't helping at all. No, there's been no one – no one you could say was a surprise caller, and certainly nobody who upset Tom.'

It was at this point that she had suddenly remembered.

'But wait a minute – there *was* someone else. A salesman. He came by that same week. I'd forgotten all about him.'

Now, with something to bite on at last, Lily pressed on.

'Can you describe him to me?'

'Oh dear . . . not very well, I fear.' Mrs Singleton put a hand to her temple. 'He was quite a young man – in his early thirties, I'd say.'

'How tall was he? Do you remember? And his build? Was he light or heavy?'

'How *tall*?' She seemed thrown by the question. 'Oh, of average height, or perhaps a little shorter than that: not as tall as my husband, for example.' She caught her breath and a tear shone in the corner of her eye. She brushed it away. 'He wasn't a big man; he was on the thin side.' She shook her head. 'Really he was quite ordinary; very obliging, in the way salesmen can be, not pushy at all. I think he was disappointed when I didn't place an order for one of his cleaners. I may have encouraged him too much.'

She eyed Lily.

'You surely don't think he had anything to do with it?'

'Oh no. I mean I don't think anything at all.' Lily revealed nothing of her thoughts. 'All I'm doing now is gathering information: facts. That's what we do mostly. Then later on, when I go back to London, I'll sit down with my guv'nor and see what we can make of them.'

'Your guv'nor . . .' Mrs Singleton seemed to take pleasure in the word, as though it were new to her. 'That sounds very sensible.'

She sighed then and Lily saw that, in spite of her friendly manner, she was exhausted, most likely from the strain of the interview; from having to keep up a front. The pain was still there in the soft blue eyes. It hadn't diminished.

'Just one more question. You don't happen to remember his name by any chance?'

It was a million-to-one shot, and Lily couldn't believe her luck when, after only the briefest of pauses, her hostess gave a crisp nod.

'Not his name, no. But he did leave a card. He gave it to my husband. Now where did Tom put it?'

For an agonizing moment she seemed unable to recall, her gaze swivelling around the sitting room as if the object might suddenly materialize in front of them. Then she snapped her fingers.

'Now I remember. He gave it to us as he was leaving.'

She rose to her feet and Lily followed suit. They went out into the entrance hall, where a small table stood. Mrs Singleton pulled out the only drawer and peered inside.

'There it is.'

She took out a small piece of pasteboard and squinted at it in the manner of one accustomed to using reading glasses.

'It's a company card,' she announced. 'He works for Hoover. They must have a branch here. There's an Oxford address. Oh, but look – he wrote his name on it, too.'

She handed the card to Lily, pointing to the pencilled scrawl.

'Do you see? He's a Mr Leonard Barker.'

Leonard Barker.

As she waved goodbye to Mrs Singleton, who was standing in the doorway, Lily glanced at the card again. She knew from experience that people using aliases often chose a name not unlike their own, and Ballard and Barker were close enough to make her wonder. Could this 'Barker' be a relative of James Ballard, one they didn't know about?

Granted there had been nothing suspicious about the man's behaviour – Mrs Singleton had been unyielding on that point – but the fact that he'd turned up only days prior to her husband's murder couldn't be ignored. Before leaving, Lily had made a last attempt to jog her hostess's memory and had learned that there had been a period of several minutes when Mrs Singleton had gone into the kitchen to make the cup of tea she had offered their visitor, leaving him alone in the sitting room with her husband, when presumably some words might have been exchanged.

But about what?

If Barker's purpose had been to identify Singleton as the man he was looking for, what sort of information would he have been after? Given that he obviously hadn't asked Singleton point-blank about the court martial (or Mrs Singleton would have known about it from her husband and reported the fact), might it not still have had something to do with the First World War? Perhaps he had pointed to one of the photographs standing on a table in the corner of the room, a picture Lily had spotted that showed Singleton in uniform climbing out of a dugout, and said something like, 'I see you were in the war, sir, the Great War. So was my father.'

Nothing more than that, and hardly the sort of thing Singleton would have thought worth reporting to his wife afterwards. But enough to tell the killer – after Singleton had confirmed that he, too, had fought in the trenches – that he had found the man he was looking for.

After that it would have been simply a question of opportunity: of waiting for the right moment. Perhaps Barker had kept watch on the house. He might have seen Singleton setting off for his afternoon walk a few days later and seized his chance.

As for the card and the vacuum cleaner – well, it would be easy enough to get hold of a business card and scribble a name on it; no problem to buy a Hoover machine and pretend it was a demonstration model.

Lily caught her breath. She knew she was in danger of jumping to conclusions. But the urge to pursue the idea was irresistible, and as it happened there was a simple test she could carry out. She could easily find out from the Hoover branch in Oxford whether they had a salesman named Leonard Barker in their employ. A phone call would suffice.

And if it turned out that they had no employee of that name on their books . . . !

Lily's cheeks went hot at the thought. She quickened her pace, heading for the Banbury Road, where she knew she could catch a bus that would take her back to the city centre, and to a public telephone.

The odds were against it: she had no illusions on that score. But it was possible – just *possible* – that she might have cracked the case at a single stroke.

'Yes, I see . . . *North* Oxford, you say? No, there's no message. I'll ring again tomorrow. Yes, I understand . . . before ten. Thank you. Goodbye.'

Lily put the phone back in its cradle.

'Bugger!'

Giving vent to her feelings, she backed out of the kiosk to make way for a woman with a shopping bag in each hand, who had been waiting while the conversation she'd been having with the bloke whom the Hoover switchboard had put her through to (and who had identified himself as the sales director) had come to its unsatisfactory end.

Yes, they had a salesman named Leonard Barker in their employ, but he was out of the office just then on his usual rounds and wouldn't be in again until late afternoon. Would madam like to leave a message?

Further questioning on Lily's part had elicited the fact that Barker's area included much of north Oxford, which was just where the Singletons' house was located.

Bugger again!

It had been a guess at best, but all the same Lily's hopes had been high, and now there was nothing for her to do but return to London empty-handed. She was only relieved she wouldn't have to admit as much to Morgan. The Oxford inspector had told her he would be in court all day.

What was it he had said about clutching at straws?

Buttoning her coat with a scowl, she set off for the station. Reaching it with a few minutes to spare before the next train departed for London, she slipped into the ladies' lavatory. As she stood in front of a mirror there, the scowl that she saw on her face brought a smile to her lips in its place. She was reminded of something Aunt Betty used to say to her when she was a child: 'Don't pull a face. It'll stay that way.'

It was her aunt who had raised Lily, following the death of her mother in the great flu epidemic that had swept the globe after the First World War. Betty's husband, Lily's Uncle Fred, was a uniformed constable stationed at Paddington – thirty years in the force and still going strong, as he liked to say – and Lily always maintained it was the sight of him going off to work each day in his blue uniform that had moved her to follow in his footsteps.

Thinking of them now, she remembered another saying from her childhood, one of Uncle Fred's favourites: 'When it's not your day, it's not your day.'

Well, this certainly hadn't been one of hers, she thought as she checked her appearance in the mirror and saw to her surprise that the Remembrance Day poppy she'd acquired more than a week ago, from one of the legion of women patrolling the streets of London armed with collection tins, was still pinned to her lapel. The anniversary was past: it was time to remove it.

Reaching up to unfasten the emblem, she winced as the pin pricked her finger and a drop of blood appeared. It rose like a tiny bubble on the end of her finger, redder than the paper bloom she was holding, and she regarded them both with a wry smile. *When it wasn't your day, it wasn't your day . . .*

Lily continued to stare at them.

Later that week, when she went to have supper with her aunt and uncle, something she did on a regular basis since she thought of them as her true parents, she would tell them that she still didn't know where the idea had come from: whether it was a case of real inspiration – this said with a broad wink – or simply an association of ideas. But it seemed to pop into her head from nowhere, as if by magic.

'Bloody hell!'

'I beg your pardon.' The old biddy at the next basin was outraged.

'Sorry, luv. It just popped out.'

Lily gave her a pat on the hand and a smile by way of an apology and then, without waiting to see the result, dashed out of the lavatory onto the platform, where her train was just drawing in. Only it wasn't her train any longer.

What she needed now was a taxi.

18

'Yes, guv. Right away.'

Billy put down the phone.

'Poole should be back any time now. If she's got anything worth reporting, give me a ring. I'll be with the chief super.'

Joe Grace looked up from the file he was leafing through.

'The lads are all scratching their heads,' he said. 'They can't understand why you picked her for this job.'

A veteran detective-sergeant, he was the latest addition to their squad, which Chubb had decided needed reinforcing, and Billy had set him the preliminary chore of reading the cumulative file.

'How about you, Joe?' he asked. 'How do you feel about it?'

Grace grinned. Thin, with a pockmarked face – and with a record showing as many commendations as reprimands on it – he was every bit as tough as he looked: one of those coppers who trod a thin line, usually managing to stay just inside the law, but sometimes overstepping the mark, which was one of the reasons he'd been stuck in his present rank for close on a dozen years and was unlikely ever to rise above it. Aware of the dangers he presented as a partner – Joe's bloody-minded approach to authority was a byword at the Yard – Billy had picked him for his sharpness and his hunter's instinct.

'I've nothing against the lass. Mind you, I took her for a budgie.' It was Joe's name for an officer confined to desk jobs. A caged bird, in other words.

'That seems to be the general idea. But I think she's better than that. I want you to keep an eye on her.' He saw a scowl begin to gather on Grace's hatchet face. 'Don't worry. She won't be a burden to you. She catches on quick.'

'If you say so.' But he sounded less than convinced.

Descending the stairs to Chubb's office, Billy had time to wonder why he'd been summoned. He had talked to the chief super less than an hour before, and only to inform him that there were no further developments to report.

'We've received a photograph of Ballard and his wife from the St Ives police,' he had told Chubb. 'I asked Miss Selby if she could let us have one.'

Billy had handed him the faded snapshot, with its dabs of glue on the reverse side showing where it had been removed from a photograph album. Taken on a beach, it showed the two of them – she in a flowered frock, he in white flannels – standing hand-in-hand at the sea's edge with the sunlight falling on their faces.

'He was a good-looking bloke, all right.' Billy had been struck by the figure of the tall, dark-haired young man pictured in the snapshot. 'You can see she thinks so too.'

Fair-haired and fair-skinned – and clearly somewhat older than the young man beside her – Hazel Ballard was gazing up at her husband with a look that wasn't far short of adoring (or so Billy thought).

'And since we're still waiting to hear from the War Office about the court-martial record, I did what Mr Madden suggested – I rang the artillery depot at Woolwich and asked the adjutant if he could get me the names of the officers commanding batteries in the Arras sector around the time of Ballard's trial. One of them is likely to be the bloke who presided at the court martial. He said it would take a few days to dig out the records, but he promised to get back to me.'

Now, as Billy opened the door to the chief super's office, he stopped in his tracks. Chubb was glaring at him from behind his desk. He had a face like thunder.

'I've just been speaking to a man called Bannister. He's the director of the Public Record Office. Before I tell you what he said, you'd better sit down.'

Wonderingly Billy obeyed.

'The record of Ballard's trial has gone missing.'

'*What?*' Billy jumped to his feet. 'What do you mean missing?'

'I mean it's been lifted. Stolen. At least that's my opinion, though Bannister claims otherwise. They've only just found out. Wait till you've heard the whole story, though. See what you think.'

Speechless, Billy resumed his seat.

'According to this Bannister bloke, towards the end of August they had an intruder who managed to get into a part of the building where they keep restricted material. It's a large room furnished with stacks where documents classified under the thirty-year rule are stored. Some of them had been rifled. Papers were found strewn about the floor and some documents were missing.'

The chief super's tone was derisive.

'No need to tell you what a state that put them in. It was panic stations all round. They called in Special Branch and, since some of the documents originated with the Foreign Office, MI6 as well. God knows what they were so worked up about: not a lot, if you ask me; probably the fear of leaving some politician with egg on his face. But word of it never leaked out – they made sure of that – and more to the point as far as we're concerned, they never bothered to check the court-martial records. They're not kept in the stacks, they're stored separately in a cupboard – no one ever looks at them, apparently – and as the cupboard was locked and didn't seem to have been tampered with, they didn't think it worth the trouble to check the files individually. They just took a peek inside, saw nothing was disturbed and let it go at that. As far as I can gather, the cupboard wasn't opened again until this morning, when someone was sent to get the Ballard file out for us to look at.'

Chubb sighed.

'If there's one group of people I hate dealing with it's civil servants,' he said. 'They've always got an answer, but it's never a straight one. At first Bannister tried to sell me on the idea that it was probably a clerical error: that the papers in the Ballard folder had somehow got mixed up with another file and it would just be a matter of sorting through them. When I told him, politely, to pull the other one, he finally came clean about that business three months ago. They never did get to the bottom of it. But as it turned out that the documents taken from the stacks didn't amount to much, they decided to let the matter drop. If you ask me, the whole business was staged. The theft of those documents was just a blind: it was meant to lead us in the wrong direction.'

'What about the intruder, though? How did he get in?' Billy had listened raptly.

'They couldn't say for sure. But as there was no evidence of a break-in, they concluded in the end that he must have hidden somewhere in the building and waited until everyone had gone home. I don't know how much you know about the place, but it's a glorified library. Originally it was set up to store Chancery Court records, but some time in the last century it was expanded into a national archive open to the general public. Anyone can walk in there and, provided you follow the drill, you can consult the documents you want to see in their reading room, so long as they're not on the classified list. You can spend all day there if you like. They reckoned that whoever got into the restricted area must have found a spot to lie up in – a cleaner's cubbyhole, maybe, or even the Gents – and then come out when the coast was clear. He could have done the same thing the next morning: waited until there were people about and then slipped out.'

Charlie was grinning now.

'To be fair, I don't suppose security was ever Bannister's first worry. It's not as though he's guarding the Crown Jewels. He probably never imagined anything like this could happen. I might have felt the same, in his shoes. Even now he can't believe that someone went to all that trouble just to steal the record of a court martial that took place thirty years ago. He's got his people going through all the files now. He's sure the Ballard papers will turn up. As for the other stuff stolen from the stacks, he says Special Branch thought it might be the work of a political malcontent, some bloke who wasn't quite right in the head. I'll have to have a word with them.'

He chuckled.

'But wait – I'm not done yet. I've saved the best till last. Before I spoke to Bannister I had a call from Mr Cunningham to tell me that permission had been granted for us to see the file. I'd hardly had time to thank him when he added that the minister hoped we wouldn't try to tie the murders to that court martial "prematurely". I was still wondering what he meant by that when the phone rang again, and this time it was our esteemed AC, Mr Cradock no less.'

Billy grinned. It was an open secret in CID that the chief super's relations with his superior were far from ideal. A recent appointment, Eustace Cradock had spent most of his career at the Yard in the traffic and budgetary departments, and the reasons behind his elevation to the prestigious post of Assistant Commissioner, Crime, were reckoned by many to be a mystery beyond even the powers of a Sherlock Holmes to unravel. Charlie's response had been to keep his AC in relative ignorance about the day-to-day workings of his department, a policy that Billy for one feared might one day backfire on their chief.

'He asked if it was true we were going to publicly link the shootings to the Ballard proceedings and, if so, why he hadn't been informed? I told him I had made no such decision, to which he responded that it was just as well, since I'd be in hot water if I had, and that I wasn't to take any action in the matter without consulting him first. He added that there could be no question of connecting the investigation to the court martial without "cast-iron proof".'

Billy whistled. 'He's been got at.'

'Done up like a kipper, if you ask me.' Chubb's snort was contemptuous. 'Still, I suppose from the point of view of the powers that be, this could look like the thin end of the wedge. If one court martial can be made public, why not others? Why not the whole lot?' He shrugged. 'But that's where we stand. As far as anything you might say to the press is concerned, we're looking for a man who may be unbalanced, but nothing more.'

He cocked an eye at Billy.

'You're keeping very quiet, Inspector.'

'I'm just thinking it through.' Billy tugged at an earlobe. 'Assuming it was our bloke who took those papers, at least it solves one mystery: how he managed to get hold of the men's names. But he still had to find out if they were still alive and, if so, where they lived. He's been at this for some time.'

'I wouldn't disagree.' The chief super sniffed. 'And he's not short of nerve either, sitting it out there all night, waiting until morning to leave. He's a cool customer all right. And he seems to know things you wouldn't associate with the average law-abiding citizen. Like how to open the lock on that cupboard without leaving a mark on it.'

His scowl reappeared.

'You don't think he's a villain, do you?'

'A professional? No, he's not that.' Billy was surprised by his own certainty. 'I don't know what he is. I can't make him out. He's a mystery to me. All I know for sure is he's a killer and that's—'

He broke off as the door behind him opened and Joe Grace stuck his head into the room.

'Sorry to butt in, but Poole's back.' He was grinning. 'She arrived soon after you stepped out. She's got something to tell you.'

'Can't it wait?' Billy frowned. 'We're almost done here.'

'I'm afraid not, guv.' Joe's grin widened. 'In fact it's something you both need to hear, and right away.'

Stepping to one side, he ushered the young woman into the room.

'Not to put too fine a point on it, it looks like we've been barking up the wrong tree.'

'Now wait a minute, Detective. Don't go making wild assertions. What sort of evidence have you got? She was probably engaged in fraud: collecting money under false pretences. That's an offence all right, but not one that concerns us; not at this moment.'

Chubb showed his disapproval with a scowl. He had listened in silence as Lily began her story, but under his steady glare she had lost the thread of her tale and had begun to skip back and forth, trying to explain first this and then that, until finally, in exasperation, Charlie had let fly.

Billy intervened.

'Take a moment, Lil.' He spoke in a quiet voice. 'Have a look at your notes.'

They were sitting side-by-side in front of the chief super's desk, Lily with her pad on her knee. Flushed and excited when she'd arrived, she now found herself faced by an audience of three – Joe Grace was perched on the windowsill behind Chubb's desk – all showing by their expressions at least a degree of scepticism at what they were hearing. As a result she had quickly become tongue-tied, her thoughts in a muddle.

'There's no hurry,' Billy told her. 'Start at the beginning.'

Lily bent over her pad. She took a deep breath.

'I didn't see it at first,' she confessed. 'I missed it. When I spoke to Mrs Singleton I asked her about any visitors they might have had before her husband was shot, and she mentioned this woman who had come by collecting for Remembrance Day. But she also told me about a vacuum-cleaner salesman who had knocked on their door – a bloke we'd never heard of before – and I was thinking so much about him that I forgot about the woman.'

'A salesman?' Chubb frowned. 'What salesman?'

'He worked for Hoover, guv, and I thought it might be our bloke, who was using that as a cover. But he turned out to be real. I rang the company's office in Oxford and they confirmed it. After that the only thing left to do was go back to London, but while I was at the station waiting for my train I went into the ladies' loo and that's when I realized.'

'The ladies' *loo*?' The chief super was lost.

'I was looking at myself in the mirror,' Lily explained. 'I saw I still had my poppy on, from when I'd got it in London a few days before. It was pinned to my lapel. I decided to take it off, but while I was doing that I pricked my finger and that's when it hit me.'

'*Hit* you?'

'I suddenly realized. They don't do that – the women who collect money at this time of year. They don't go to people's houses. They stand on street corners, and outside hotels and railway stations and big shops. They have those red tins and they shake them, so you know why they're there—'

'Yes, yes, all right.' Chubb cut her off. 'We get the picture. So what did you do about it?'

'I went back.'

'Back where?'

'To north Oxford, to speak to Mrs Singleton again. I told her we needed to know more about this woman, in case she was involved in some way. I asked her to tell me everything she could remember about her visit, starting with her description. Mrs Singleton said that, as best she could recall, the woman was in her late twenties or early thirties with dark hair, and was dressed in a smart coat with a silk scarf and a hat. She said she was well spoken – that was the word she used. She didn't say so, but I think she meant she was a lady.'

Lily paused to wet her lips. There was no need to hurry now. She had their attention.

'She turned up one afternoon, telling them she was collecting for Remembrance Day and that going round to people's houses was a new policy they had.' Lily looked up. 'I reckon that was in case they thought it strange. Mrs Singleton said she must be tired after all that walking and offered her a cup of tea.' Lily smiled. 'She's a nice lady. She gives everyone a cup of tea. While she was in the kitchen she heard them talking, her husband and this woman, and when she came back she found that he was showing her a photograph of himself taken when he was in the trenches in the first war. I'd noticed it myself when I was there. After the woman had gone, she asked him what they were talking about, and Mr Singleton said the woman had told him that an uncle of hers had fought in the First World War and she wondered if they had served in the same sector. It turned out that they had.'

'And whereabouts was that?' Billy asked.

'Near a place called Arras.'

The silence that followed was broken by a whistle. It came from the lips of Joe Grace. The sergeant still had a grin on his face, but he was eyeing Lily with interest now.

The chief super, too, had his gaze fixed on her.

'Well, that's very interesting, Detective,' he said. 'But aren't you jumping to conclusions? Can you be sure what this woman was doing – going round to people's houses with a collection tin – was out of order? She might have been telling the truth. Perhaps it is a new policy of theirs.'

'Yes, I know, guv.' Lily nodded eagerly. 'I had to be certain.'

'Certain?'

'After we'd said goodbye, I walked up and down her street, and along a couple of the side streets, too, knocking on every door and, if anyone was home, I asked them if they remembered a woman like the one Mrs Singleton described coming round to collect money a few weeks earlier.'

Lily paused. She was enjoying the moment.

'They didn't, guv. Not one of them. The only house she called at was the Singletons'.'

This time the silence lasted only for a second, and it was Chubb who broke it.

'Hell and damnation!' He struck the desk with his fist. 'Don't tell me there are *two* of them.'

19

'*Two?*' MADDEN SCOWLED. 'THAT can't be.'

'I know what you're thinking, John.' Chubb raised a hand. 'I had the same reaction. But facts are facts.'

'It's hard enough trying to imagine *one* person engaged in a vendetta of this kind. But *two*! It beggars belief.'

He looked at Billy, who was sitting beside him.

'Are you sure this woman isn't the daughter – Alma Ballard?'

'As sure as we can be.' Billy shrugged. 'We haven't actually made contact with her yet, but she's in Canada all right. It's been confirmed.'

Madden shook his head. It was late on Friday. About to set off from St John's Wood for Waterloo station to return home for the weekend, he had been diverted by a call from Billy and had stopped off at the Yard to lend whatever support he could to his old colleagues, faced as they were now by a fresh set of challenges.

'We did wonder if we'd been given some wrong information,' Billy went on. 'About her emigrating, I mean. But when we checked we found that she'd taken passage on a Cunard liner to Halifax at the end of July. I also rang the Canadian High Commission here in London, and they confirmed she'd gone through the necessary immigration formalities. She didn't ask for an assisted passage, but we know she's got money of her own. She was her mother's only heir.'

'What if she came back, though?' Madden was unconvinced.

'I thought of that, sir.' Billy grimaced. 'I rang that solicitor I told you about – Royston's his name – and he confirmed that the last letter he'd had from Alma before she set off by train for Vancouver was sent from Toronto on 18 September, which was just two days before Wallace Drummond was shot in Ballater. I haven't had a chance to tell you this yet, but we've good reason to believe that the woman who visited Mrs Singleton in Oxford also called on Drummond at his rooms a day or so before he was killed. It can't have been Alma Ballard. She couldn't have been in two places at once.'

Chubb stirred in his seat.

'I know how you feel, John. We thought it had to be Alma – it was the only answer that made sense. But like it or not, we have to face the fact we're looking for two people: a man and a woman. It looks like *he's* doing the killing and *she's* his accomplice.'

'But who could they possibly be?' Madden was lost for words.

'I can't answer that.' The chief super scowled. 'Not yet. But what I can tell you is that we're looking into James Ballard's family background. There may be something there. You know he was born out of wedlock?'

Madden nodded.

'Well, at first that looked like a dead end. But then Styles phoned Eve Selby again – that woman in St Ives who knew them – and she told us a little more about him.'

He gestured to Billy.

'Go ahead.'

Billy cleared his throat. 'According to Selby, James wanted to find out who his father was. He knew from his adoptive parents that his mother had died in childbirth, but he was able to learn from her relatives that his real father lived in Exeter and had a family of his own. They even knew his name, and Ballard went to see the bloke.'

'With what result?'

'Eve Selby didn't know. She only ever heard the story from Hazel, and that was after the war began and Ballard had been posted to France. She didn't tell her the man's name.'

'But Hazel might have known it.' Madden frowned. 'That's what you're thinking?'

'And so might her daughter. That's one of the reasons we need to get in touch with her. I sent a telegram to the Canadian police today, asking them to trace her. She gave this solicitor the names of the places she was planning to stop at on her way west, and I've passed them on to the Mounties. If possible, we'd like to talk to her by phone ourselves. Failing that, we'll get them to question her for us. It isn't only that name we want. We'd also like to know where her mother lived after she left St Ives; how she spent the years before she settled in Richmond; and who she might have known or had contact with. Anything Alma can tell us about her father and his background could be useful, too. Of course, she never knew him – she was only a baby when he died – but there's no telling what she might have learned from her mother's lips.'

'What about *her* family – Hazel's?' Madden's scowl had stayed fixed. 'Didn't you say she came from Gloucester? She must have had some relatives there. One of them might know the answer.'

'She did,' Billy answered. 'But they hadn't seen her for years when she died. I got that from the Gloucester police. I'd asked them to check up on her background and they found a cousin of hers who knew the whole story. There'd been a rift in the family, she said. It all went back to Hazel's decision to marry Ballard, when the rest of her kin were against it. By the time James died she was no longer on speaking terms with them, and I expect the court martial put a cap on things. She told them what she told others – that he had died in action – and said she was leaving St Ives for good and never wanted to see any of them again.'

'That was an extreme reaction.'

'But understandable, I reckon,' Billy said. 'It would have been difficult, if not impossible, to keep the truth about her husband from getting out, once she'd made peace with her family. They were bound to find out sooner or later. The safest thing would have been to cut all ties with them.'

He hesitated as another thought struck him.

'Did she even tell her daughter? I wonder. Does Alma know?'

'That's something else we can ask her,' Chubb growled.

'Going back to this woman who called on Mrs Singleton ...' Madden rubbed the scar on his forehead, a sure sign to Billy of his preoccupation. 'It sounds, from what you said, that you know something about her?'

'That's right, sir. There's fresh information. It only reached us this morning.'

Billy opened the file on his lap.

'It applies to at least three of the killings.' He sifted through the stack of papers and selected one. 'In particular it throws a light on Ozzie Gibson's murder and on the testimony given by that shepherd. He was on the hillside above where Gibson was fishing, and he saw the killer walking up the path towards him. The man was wearing a red sweater that was particularly noticeable, and he knew he'd been spotted. He looked up when Hammond whistled to his dog.'

'I remember.' Madden nodded. 'He didn't seem bothered, if I recall.'

'That's right. He just carried on to where Ozzie was gathering up his fishing gear and did what he came to do.' Billy paused. 'I spoke to Vic Chivers this morning. On the day of Ozzie's murder that young constable who took you around ran into a party of hikers coming back from the Downs. It included three women. Vic interviewed them the next day. Two of them were sisters, but the third told him she was there on her own.'

'What was her name?'

'Horton . . .' Billy checked the piece of paper in his hand. 'Emily Horton. The name she went under, at any rate. When Vic looked at his notes he found that she had given him a home address in Colchester. I got Joe Grace to ring the police there. They told him there was an Emily Horton living in the town all right, but she was a young woman who worked in a dress shop and hadn't been away all year.'

'What did the woman Chivers spoke to look like?'

'Well, she had dark hair, same as the lady who called on Mrs Singleton in Oxford, but otherwise they didn't seem to resemble each other much. "Dowdy and spinsterish" were the words Vic used to describe her.'

'Perhaps she changed her appearance.' Madden pursed his lips. 'She might have guessed you'd get on to her sooner or later and didn't want to leave any clear trail to follow.'

'She told Vic she had been in Lewes for a fortnight. She said she was a rambler. Now a fortnight was about right. It would have given her more than enough time to locate Gibson and confirm that he was the man she was looking for. We never did find out the sex of his visitor, the one who upset him, but I'm willing to bet it was her. Gibson went away for the weekend after that to stay with friends, so she would have had to wait a few days. But once he'd returned, they would have had him in their sights.'

'*They?* She and the man you think she's working with?'

Billy nodded. He slipped the piece of paper he had in his hand back into the folder and took out another.

'We know for a fact she was out on the Downs that afternoon, and I'm guessing she had a change of clothes with her. She was carrying a knapsack – that was confirmed by the constable who spoke to her. This is the statement taken from the shepherd.' He tapped the piece of paper in his hand. 'According to him, Ozzie Gibson's killer walked back down the path after he'd done the business and then disappeared. It would have been quite possible for this woman to have met him by arrangement somewhere in the bushes by the stream, so that he could change his clothes, get rid of that red sweater in particular. After that he could have disappeared into the Downs, while she would have joined up with those two other ladies and made her way back into Lewes. She might even have taken the gun with her, in case he was stopped and searched.'

'Could I see that?'

Billy handed him the statement. Madden got to his feet abruptly. He began to walk about the office, scanning it as he went. Familiar with his old chief's habits, Billy watched with a smile.

'What about the other killings?' Madden had stopped by the window. It was dark outside now and his reflection showed in the windowpane, along with an image of the lamp-lit office behind him. 'How does she fit in with them?'

'There's no obvious connection between her and Canning. But as you said yourself, she wouldn't have needed to confirm his identity. He was a public figure.' Billy spoke to Madden's back. 'However, we know she called on Singleton, and we can place her in Scotland too. One of the visitors who called at Drummond's surgery a few days before he was shot was an Englishwoman. She gave her name as Mary Oakes and provided the doctor's secretary with a home address in Ipswich. We checked with the Suffolk police today and found that both the name and address belonged to a thirty-year-old housewife who has never been north of the border.'

'How did she get hold of those two names?'

'We think we know the answer to that. Both of them lost

their identity cards not long ago, either mislaid or stolen. The woman Vic spoke to used a card in the name of Horton at Lewes – there's a record of it in the hotel register – and although we haven't yet had a chance to confirm it, it's likely she did the same thing at Ballater, only this time using the name Oakes. It seems she's in possession of at least two cards.'

'Are they difficult to come by?'

'Stolen or forged cards? Not if you know where to ask.'

Chubb shifted in his chair. He had been listening in silence, elbows on the desk, chin cupped in his hands.

'So that's where we stand, John. We've no clue to the shooter's identity yet, and we can only speculate on how he and the woman got together. It may turn out they're related. I told you we were looking into Ballard's background; the Plymouth police are helping us. It's possible these two are connected to Ballard on his father's side. Anything's possible. We're hoping Hazel Ballard might have been acquainted with them. She knew where her husband came from, after all. She may even have known the name of his father, and the same is true of Alma. As for the shooter himself, we've felt from the start that he's probably an ex-serviceman, someone used to handling firearms, and with other skills as well, the sort you only acquire through special training. Whoever stole the court-martial papers not only had the nerve to sit it out all night in the Public Record Office, but the know-how to open that cupboard without leaving a mark on it. But there's no use us scratching our heads wondering who he might be. We have to focus on her. It looks like she's doing the preliminary work, checking on the victims' identities, studying their movements. She's managed to leave a trail behind her, too, which we've been lucky enough to pick up. My feeling is that if we catch her, we'll catch him.'

He shifted in his chair.

'Now to put you in the picture: Oxford CID sent a police artist round to Mrs Singleton today, to see if she can remember the face of the woman who called on her well enough to make a sketch. Chivers is doing the same. If the two of them match, we'll know we're on the right track. At present, we're focusing on those identity cards. We want to know who sold them and to whom. Was it to the man or to the woman? Our snouts have been told to keep their ears open. And we've circulated those two names – Emily Horton and Mary Oakes – and the name Ballard as well. For the rest, we still don't know the name of that officer who presided at the court martial, though we're hoping the Royal Artillery will be able to help us. Styles took your advice and rang them. But the clock's ticking . . .'

He paused, weighing his next words.

'I said at the start I'd welcome any idea you might have to offer, John.' He eyed the other man meaningfully. 'I'm still in the market.'

Madden's response was to glance at his watch. Returning the statement he'd been reading to Billy, he went to the clothes rack by the door to collect his coat.

'There's not much I can offer in the way of suggestions, Charlie. I'm still having trouble convincing myself there are two of them. It doesn't make sense. Either they had the same idea together, which hardly seems likely, or one talked the other into it, which is equally incredible. Leaving that aside, however, there is one thing. I can't help feeling that Hazel Ballard's death is somehow connected to this.'

'To the *shootings*?' Chubb was surprised. 'But how? Surely you don't think she had a hand in them, prior to her death, I mean?'

'No, I wasn't thinking of that.' Madden shook his head. 'She was a sick woman. But not long after she died this plan was set in motion. First the court-martial record was stolen and then the killings began. The coincidence is too strong to ignore.'

'We can't exclude the fact that these two might have had some contact with her, though.' Billy spoke. 'They might even have visited her in Richmond. It's something we can ask her daughter when we catch up with her. In the meantime we've found someone else who might be able to help: Hazel's next-door neighbour. I got her name from that solicitor. He told me she not only witnessed Hazel's will, but also helped Alma clear out the house after her mother's death. I haven't had a chance to speak to her yet – she's been away for a few days – but I managed to get hold of her daily, who said she'd be back on Sunday. I'm going to ring her over the weekend and arrange to go down and see her.'

Madden grunted. He donned his coat.

'Well, I've only one other suggestion, Charlie,' he said. 'But I'm sure you've already thought of it. I mean making use of the newspapers. It might be time to tell them you think the killings are linked to the court martial. At the very least it might prompt that officer to come forward.'

His words brought a gleam to the chief super's eye.

'I've been waiting for you to say that. I was wondering when you'd get round to it.'

'Have I touched on a sensitive subject?' Madden smiled for the first time.

'You could put it that way. Do you know who I mean by Cradock?'

'Your new assistant commissioner?'

'That's the fellow. He's being leaned on from on high at the moment, and it's not a pretty sight. We had a session with him this morning as it happens, Styles and I, and we did just what you said. We told him it was time to come clean about the court martial. That way we could clear the air and get down to the business of tracing this woman.'

'And what was his reply?'

'You tell him, Inspector.' Chubb nodded to Billy. 'And you can wipe that smile off your face,' he added, turning back to their visitor. 'Just wait till you hear what he had to say about you.'

'About *me*?' Madden's jaw dropped.

'He said he couldn't allow us to go to the newspapers with this.' Billy took up the tale with a smile. For reasons best known to the assistant commissioner, he'd been summoned to the meeting along with Chubb and had observed the confrontation that followed. 'He'd read the report Mr Chubb sent him and reckoned our case was based solely on assumptions.'

'Assumptions . . . Can you credit that?' Charlie shook his head in wonder.

'And the first was that these murders were somehow associated with the court martial simply because one of the victims, Oswald Gibson, had referred to it in his diary. He said there was no proof that either Drummond or Singleton had ever been present at the trial, or that Sir Horace Canning had put his signature to the sentence; no evidence, either, that the woman who turned up in Oxford had any connection to the case. All of which happens to be true, unfortunately. We did get the Oxford police to ask Mrs Singleton if she knew her husband had sat on a court-martial board, but apparently she didn't. They may have been close, but he never told her that.'

Billy paused.

'Go on. Don't stop there.' A grin had appeared on the chief super's face.

'He said that as far as he could see, the only reason we'd come up with this explanation was because a former colleague of ours had suggested it – a man who had resigned his position at the Yard many years before . . .'

'. . . and whose credentials as an investigator must surely now be called into question.'

Chubb let out a guffaw.

Lost for words, Madden could only stare at him. But then he, too, burst out laughing. 'Well, he's right, isn't he?'

'Now don't you start.' The chief super shook an admonishing finger. 'This isn't a joke. I asked Cradock then how he could explain the theft of the record. Surely he didn't think it was a coincidence? Do you know what he came back with?'

Charlie struck a pose.

'*Theft*, Mr Chubb? I've already been informed that according to the director of the Public Record Office, those papers have simply gone missing. He contests your interpretation of the facts. He maintains there is no evidence to suggest that the cupboard containing the records was ever broken into. So unless you can present me with proof to the contrary, I strongly urge you to abandon this line of enquiry and return to your search for a killer who is not only armed and dangerous, but very likely disturbed in his mind.'

The chief super shook his head in despair.

'He was kind enough to remind me then – in case it had slipped my mind – that there would be a royal wedding at Westminster Abbey in a week or so, and the last thing people wanted to read about in their newspapers was some sordid account of a court martial that had taken place many years ago and, given its unhappy outcome, was hardly likely to chime with the country's mood.'

'"Chime with the country's mood . . ." He actually said that?'

'Those were his very words.' Chubb groaned. 'And they wonder why coppers take to the bottle.'

A few minutes later, waiting in the lobby downstairs for his taxi to arrive, Madden was still chuckling.

'I'd forgotten what a card Charlie is. I'm sorry we lost touch. I must ask Helen to invite him down for a weekend when this is over. They'll get on well.'

'Mr Sinclair could show him his roses. Charlie thinks you made those up.'

Billy was pleased to see his old chief in better spirits. They had spoken several times on the phone and he knew that Madden's anxiety hadn't diminished in the days that had passed since their meeting with Edward Gibson.

About to leave, Madden paused by the entrance.

'You mentioned something about going down to Richmond?'

'That's right, sir. I want to talk to this friend of Hazel Ballard's. Miss Dauncey is her name. Amanda Dauncey.'

'Would you mind if I came with you?'

'To *Richmond*? Of course not.' Billy smiled. 'There's nothing I'd like more. But are you sure you want to? Chances are it'll come to nothing.'

'Never mind that. But can you fix to see her on Monday morning? I'm due back at St John's Wood after lunch. I promised Aunt Maud I'd be there.'

'I'll do my best.' Billy saw Madden's taxi drawing up in the courtyard outside. 'Before you go, there's something I want to show you,' he said. 'It's a picture of Ballard lent us by Miss Selby.'

He drew the photograph from his file. Madden took it over to the porter's desk where a lamp was burning. He held it to the light.

'That's Jim Ballard all right.' It was a while before he spoke. 'I remember him well. He looks so young there. But he aged quickly. They all did. I remember how worn and tired he seemed at the trial. He had that look you sometimes see in the eyes of old men – that emptiness – as though they've reached the end of the road.'

He shook his head sadly.

'Is that his wife with him?'

Billy nodded. 'You can see she thought the world of him. You can tell by the look on her face.' He squinted at the snapshot. 'According to Miss Selby, she was already planning how they were going to live after the war. She was going to set him up in his own studio: she was sure he was going to be a great artist one day. Poor woman – it must have seemed like the end of her life, too, when he was shot.'

Madden's reply was slow in coming. He continued to gaze at the photo. Finally, with a sigh, he handed it back.

'But it wasn't, was it?'

20

ABOUT TO LEAVE FOR the day – he had his finger on the lift button – Lenny Loomis heard the phone on his desk ring. Office hours at Apollo Investments were nine till half-past five. It was ten minutes past the hour now, but with his boss, Sir Percival Blount, away, he had planned to slip off early that Friday afternoon. Blount was in the United States. He had crossed the Atlantic on the *Queen Mary* six weeks earlier on a combined business and holiday trip, and Lenny had got used to having his time as his own. But now he hesitated. There was just a chance it might be his employer calling from New York, and if he found his personal assistant had left the office early there'd be hell to pay.

With a scowl Lenny returned to his desk. He picked up the phone.

'Loomis speaking.'

'Raikes here. There's a young lady standing in front of me says she's got something for Sir Percival. Can I send her up?'

Lenny looked at his watch. He didn't want to be delayed. He had plans that evening. He was supposed to be meeting some pals at the Feathers for a drink, after which they were off to the Hammersmith Palais to see what they could pick up in the way of female companionship.

'Can't you just sign for it?'

'She says she has to deliver it to you in person.'

Raikes was the commissionaire. An old soldier with a chestful of medals, he'd never troubled to hide his contempt for Lenny after he'd discovered that he had spent the war in the Ordnance Corps as a quartermaster; or his disapproval of Lenny's elevation to the post of personal assistant to the chairman of Apollo, which he reckoned Lenny had somehow fiddled.

'Ask her who she works for.' Lenny looked at his watch again. He clicked his tongue with impatience.

There was a pause. He could hear the mutter of voices.

'She's from Mecklin Brothers. She says Lord Ackroyd gave her strict orders to put the letter in your hands.'

'He mentioned me by name?' Lenny didn't believe it. He'd never met Lord Ackroyd, though he knew who he was all right: head of Mecklin's and one of the City's leading merchant bankers; and probably a pal of Sir Percival's as well.

Again he heard muttering.

'She says no, not by name. She was told to give it to his personal assistant, into his hands.'

'All right, send her up.'

There was no getting round it. Lenny knew he couldn't afford to put a foot wrong. He'd only been in the job three months and still wasn't sure whether Sir Percival meant to keep him on as his PA. His predecessor had been fired without ceremony after ballsing up arrangements for a board of directors meeting – or so the story went – and Lenny had found himself plucked out of the obscurity of the clerks' department and sent upstairs to the chairman's wood-panelled office to be interviewed for the post.

'I'm told you've got your wits about you.'

It was the first time Lenny had met the big cheese in person. Heavy-set, balding and with the cold, blue gaze of a man accustomed to having his own way (and trampling on anyone who tried to prevent it), Sir Percival had taken his time, running his eyes over Lenny, examining him from top to toe.

'And that you don't need to be told things twice.'

Lenny had felt like an insect under a microscope.

'If that's not the case, I'll find out soon enough – and so will you.'

It hadn't taken him long to realize that what people said about Sir Percival was true: he was a bastard. Impossible to please, he offered neither praise nor thanks. Lenny had quickly been given to understand that his only reason for existing was to keep his employer's business life running smoothly. Human contact didn't enter into it. Most of the time Sir Percival looked right through him. But Lenny had refused to be thrown by his churlish manner. He'd started off life selling fruit from a barrow in Stepney and had dealt with enough rough characters in his time – hard men who wouldn't let you sell so much as an apple on their patch – not to be put off by scare tactics. Now that he'd got his foot in the door, he meant to keep it there. A year or two as Sir Percival Blount's PA was just the sort of entry he needed for his curriculum vitae. After that he'd be on his way. And when he quit Apollo, which he would, he'd take pleasure in giving the mean-spirited old sod a royal two-fingered salute.

He heard the lift arrive and saw the doors open. A woman stepped out. She wore a brown overcoat that matched the colour of her hair and had a large Manila envelope in her hands. She looked about her.

'Over here,' Lenny called out. He wondered why she hadn't seen him standing there behind his desk outside the door to Sir Percival's office. It wasn't as though there was anyone else in the reception area, just a couple of chairs and a sofa on either side of a low table with some magazines spread out on it.

She crossed the room without haste to his desk and handed him the envelope. It was addressed to Sir Percival by name and bore the words PERSONAL and BY HAND printed in large capitals.

'Will you see that he gets it?' she asked.

Lenny had assumed she'd be younger. As a rule, running errands was a job for the newest recruit to the typing pool. But she was thirty if she was a day, he reckoned, and sure of herself too, judging by the way she glanced about her, taking everything in.

'Do I need to sign for it?'

He tried to catch her eye, but she had turned to look at the nearly life-sized photograph of Sir Percival mounted on the wall above one of the chairs in the reception area. He'd been snapped sitting with his hands folded behind a highly polished table staring back at the camera with no trace of a smile on his ugly mug.

'Is that him?' she asked.

'I beg your pardon.'

It was her cool self-assurance that got Lenny's goat. She wasn't behaving like a messenger should, and when she did finally look at him, he got a nasty shock. There was something disturbing about her gaze. She had taken him in all right – he felt he'd been weighed and measured in a moment – but also dismissed; judged to be of no account.

'Sir Percival?' She nodded towards the photo. 'Your boss? Is that him?'

Lenny took his time replying. He was trying to compose himself.

'Yes, that's him,' he said, finally. 'And I asked you if I needed to sign for this?'

He tapped the letter.

'Nobody said so.' She shrugged. 'I was supposed to put it in your hands.'

'Not in Sir Percival's?'

'I was told he was in New York.' She was looking around her again.

'By Lord Ackroyd?'

'Not him personally. By his secretary.'

'What's her name?'

'I'm sorry ...'

'Lord Ackroyd's secretary – what's her name?'

Lenny had managed to startle her, at least, and now he gave the woman a hard stare, hoping it would further unsettle her. But she simply shrugged.

'I don't know ... she didn't say ... She just gave me the letter and told me what to do. I've only just started working there.' She glanced at her wristwatch. 'Look, I've got to go. Will you see he gets it?'

Without waiting for a reply, she turned and headed off in the direction of the lift. Lenny wasn't surprised when she didn't stop to press the button, but took the stairs instead. She'd done whatever it was she came to do. She didn't want to answer any more questions.

He weighed the letter in his hand. It was light. He had half a mind to break the wax seal and find out what was inside, but the word PERSONAL deterred him. What he could do, though, was ring Lord Ackroyd's secretary on Monday and find out if she knew anything about it. He had a feeling she wouldn't.

He wished that he'd asked the woman what *her* name was, but she had skipped off before he had the chance.

One thing was certain, though. She was a wrong 'un. He could spot them a mile off. It went back to the days when he'd been flogging fruit off his barrow.

Lips pursed, Lenny slipped the letter into the top drawer of his desk. He spoke his next thought aloud.

'Yes, but what are you up to, sweetheart? What's your game?'

PART TWO

PART TWO

21

'So you plan to move her this afternoon, do you?'

Helen glanced at her husband.

'I take it everything's arranged? The troops have their orders?'

'Everyone's standing by.' Madden smiled. 'The spare room's been prepared. Most of Maud's things have been moved there. The rewiring in the rest of the house has been completed. There's only her room to be done now, and it'll start as soon as she's settled. But it rather depends on how she reacts. She didn't take kindly on Friday to the idea of being moved. According to Alice, she came over all queer.'

'I have patients who do that, and it's usually because they've spent too much time in the pub. That can hardly be Maud's problem. No, I'm afraid it's just as I thought. She's plotting to keep you there. If this goes on much longer I shall come up to London myself and tell her I want my husband back.'

She caught his eye and smiled in turn. It was short of eight o'clock, but Madden had an early appointment in London and Helen was driving him to the station. The day was misty, the cloud cover low; at breakfast a little earlier they had heard a forecast on the wireless that warned of heavy fog later in the week.

'It won't take long now to finish the work,' he said. 'And if there are any more delays, we can send Lucy up to London. She and Maud are as thick as thieves.'

The Maddens' daughter had finally announced via a telephone call from Paris the day before that her return was now imminent, prompting Helen to wonder how she might best be occupied when she got home. The answer seemed obvious, and she had rung Violet Tremayne at once to suggest that Lucy help her in clearing up the Hall.

'It should keep her busy for weeks,' Helen had told her husband, though I'm beginning to regret the impulse. The first thing Violet said was, "Ooh, we must have a party for her. I'll invite some suitable young men down from London." I told her if there was one thing in life my daughter didn't lack, it was young men – suitable or otherwise. And that I'd much rather see her down on her knees at the Hall, scrubbing a floor. I don't think Violet was listening.'

Tempted to ask his wife how she herself had behaved at that age, Madden wisely held his tongue. Having bequeathed her beauty to her daughter, Helen had seemingly forgotten the time when she too had a string of admirers. Or so the late Lord Stratton had once assured Madden, with a twinkle in his eye. 'When she and Violet were girls, they went to every party in London and there was no end to the trail of broken hearts that Helen left behind her. Some of these young men used to come down here in search of her, and it was left to Violet to explain to the poor wretches that their journey had been in vain. Then, all of a sudden, Helen decided to chuck the social whirl and settled down to study medicine. Violet never got over it. She said it was worse than finding religion.'

Seeing her husband smile now, Helen was pleased. Aware of the burden of worry that he bore, she had been trying to distract him with other matters. The winding lane they were driving along was cloaked with early morning mist and her concentration had been on the road. But as they entered the village, where the lights in some shops were already switched on, she took his hand in hers.

'I do wish this business was over. I feel dogged by it. I thought we'd put that war and all its horrors behind us. Now I wonder if there'll ever be an end to it.'

There was little Madden could do except press her hand in response: the same sense of a lingering curse had been with him since the day Oswald Gibson's diary had yielded up its secrets and he had been drawn back into a past all but consigned to the vaults of memory. Although he knew he bore no responsibility for the fate that had overtaken James Ballard, there was a sense in which he could never forgive himself for his failure to save the unlucky soldier's life.

If Ballard's death had been fore-ordained, he had still been forced to play the role of cat's paw – a helpless witness to the ritual slaying of a young man who had never failed in courage, but whose mind had simply relinquished the struggle. He had tried to explain his reaction to Helen. He felt as if fate had stretched out its hand and touched him on the shoulder, he told her. 'This time do better,' it seemed to say.

'But do what?' she had asked. They had talked the matter over late into the night on the evening Madden had returned from London. 'You can't right a wrong. Not now. Not after all these years.'

'I know. It's far too late for that.'

'Well then?'

'I just want the killing to stop.'

He could think of no other answer.

Nor was it the last discussion he had had on the subject. On Saturday evening Angus Sinclair had walked up from his cottage to have supper with them, and to receive from Madden's lips a first-hand account of the latest developments. The news that a woman, yet to be identified, was now known to be involved in the case had stirred the chief inspector's memory.

'Thinking back to my trip to Ballater, I can see now how she found out what she needed to, when she visited Drummond in his rooms. There was a photograph of him and some other men in military uniform, hanging on the wall of his surgery. I didn't mention it at the time because it didn't seem relevant. But it occurs to me now that it would have given her the opportunity to bring up the subject of the war with him.'

'She used the same excuse with Singleton.' Madden had listened to his old colleague with a frown. 'But it was different with Gibson. Although he also had a picture of himself up, it was at the other end of his study and, since she was probably facing him at the desk, she wouldn't have seen it. She had to question him – at least that's what it sounded like – and whatever she said obviously upset him so much that he started to write that letter to the commissioner. But what part she's playing in all this is still a mystery to me. Chubb and Billy believe she's working with the killer. But, if so, how did that come about? Charlie thinks they might both be related to Ballard. But that's only a guess at best.'

The puzzle had continued to trouble him all weekend, but he had come no closer to solving it.

Late on Sunday, after an afternoon spent at the farm catching up on business, he had returned home to find that Billy had called with the news that their appointment for the following day was set.

'With yet another spinster lady, I gather. You'd better not mention it to Maud. She might get jealous,' Helen had teased him. 'Billy said he'd done what you asked and fixed it for first thing in the morning, so you'll have to leave at the crack of dawn.'

22

'I DIDN'T TELL HER much when we spoke. I just said Hazel Ballard's was one of the names that had come up in an investigation that the Yard was conducting. I didn't say anything about the court martial. I thought it would be better to wait and see if she refers to it herself.'

Billy kept pace with his companion's longer stride as they walked up the crowded platform together. Madden's train had been on time for once and Waterloo station was busy with commuters arriving from the suburbs.

'Judging by what we know of her, I'd be surprised if Hazel told her about it. But you never know.'

'How did you explain my presence?' Madden glanced at him.

'I told her the inquiry went back many years and that you used to work at the Yard. I said your name had come up in a curious context, and that you were trying to help us get to the bottom of it.'

'You didn't say I'd once known Ballard: that he was in my company?'

Billy shook his head. 'I thought it better not to, sir. I'd rather wait and see how the interview plays out.'

'How did she react?'

'She was surprised when I rang, naturally. She couldn't

imagine why the police should be interested in Hazel. But she said she'd help if she could.'

They had emerged from the concourse into the early morning bustle of taxicabs and buses. Billy looked around for his car and driver.

'By the way, Mr Sinclair sends his regards,' Madden said. 'He came to supper yesterday and we talked about the case. He wondered how you were going about finding this mystery woman.'

'We're doing what we can, but it's not much. We've circulated the description we got from Mrs Singleton, along with the names Horton and Oakes and copies of those two sketches we told you about, the ones made at Oxford and Lewes. They reached the Yard on Saturday.'

Catching sight of their car parked across the forecourt, Billy signalled to the driver.

'I'm going to show them to Miss Dauncey.' He pulled out two sheets of paper from his pocket and handed them to Madden. 'The trouble is they don't really match. If it was the same person, she obviously went to some trouble to change her looks.'

Madden studied the drawings. Neither of the faces pictured was remarkable, nor were they much alike, at least to his eyes. The woman in the Oxford sketch wore a smart cloche-type hat, which (together with her plucked eyebrows) hinted at a degree of sophistication. The other, by contrast, seemed careless of her appearance. Her dark hair looked uncombed and the glasses she was wearing sat awkwardly on the bridge of her nose.

'Based on those, I reckon we'll be lucky if we get a bite.'

Their car had drawn up while he was talking.

'And she may not look like either of them now. I think if we catch up with her at all, it'll be through the names. She doesn't know we're on to her yet, and I'm hoping she's still using those cards. Joe Grace has been busy chasing up our snouts to see if we can find the bloke who sold them to her. We don't know where she's holed up, but it could be London, and the chief super has ordered a check to be made on all hotels and boarding houses in the metropolitan area.'

'Any word yet on that officer – the major I told you about?' Madden looked at him.

Billy shook his head. 'I'm still waiting to hear back from Woolwich.'

'I'm consumed with curiosity, Inspector. I was going to say this was the first time I had ever had any dealings with the police, but that's not strictly true. When I taught art at St Mary's, here in Richmond, we had a burglary one summer term and I gave a statement to a detective. But I can't imagine why you want to talk to me now – and particularly about poor Hazel.'

Amanda Dauncey offered them a sunny smile. Well into middle age, she was a large woman with a friendly face, somewhat weathered, and thick grey hair cut in a bob. To reach her house, a bungalow overlooking the mist-shrouded Thames, they had had to drive through the town of Richmond (now a suburb of London) almost to its outskirts, and had found her dressed in rough clothes and working in her terraced garden. Pausing only to rinse her hands under a tap, she had led them inside, pointing to the adjoining house as she did so.

'That's where Hazel lived. She arrived here in 1930, so we were neighbours for more than fifteen years. And good friends, too, I should add.'

Guiding her visitors to a living room carelessly furnished and hung with a variety of paintings, old and new, including some canvases so amateurish it seemed they could only have come from the brushes of her former pupils, she had seated them together on a settee before taking her own place in a well-worn armchair facing them.

'Before we begin, I would like to know a little more about

the reason for your visit.' She directed the question at Billy. 'You have said you want to ask me some questions about Hazel. Could you be more specific?'

'I'll do my best.' Billy smiled. 'Unfortunately my hands are tied to some extent. This is an unusually sensitive inquiry – it involves matters of state – and I'm under orders not to reveal too much about it.'

'Matters of state?' Their hostess looked uneasy. 'Oh dear, that does sound ominous.'

'I'd ask you to accept that, without further elaboration, and also my assurance that although Mrs Ballard's name has come up in this investigation, it doesn't mean we suspect her of any wrongdoing: quite the reverse, in fact.'

Billy had given some thought to his opening remarks.

'She's only involved indirectly. We're trying to trace two people, a man and a woman, who may have been known to her. We have reason to think they might be related to her husband, James Ballard, or have some other connection to him.'

'James Ballard!' Miss Dauncey's eyes opened wide in surprise. 'But the poor man's been dead for years.'

'We're aware of that. Nevertheless, it seems this investigation we're engaged in may be linked to him in some way, just as it is to Mr Madden, who used to work at Scotland Yard and has offered to help us in this inquiry. Before we go any further I'd like you to look at these two drawings to see if you recognize either face. They were made by police artists, from descriptions given to them.'

While he was speaking Billy had taken the sketches from his pocket and he handed them to their hostess. She studied the pencilled portraits, frowning.

'In a funny sort of way they're almost familiar. The one on the left with the plucked eyebrows, for example – she looks a bit like a niece of mine; and I saw a woman very like the other one in a bookshop the other day.'

She continued to examine them, peering first at one, then the other.

'I can see it's the same person.'

'Can you?' Madden spoke for the first time. 'That's interesting. I couldn't spot the resemblance myself.'

She looked up to meet his glance. She had made no comment when Billy had introduced them earlier. Now she seemed to take him in for the first time.

'It's the shape of the face,' she explained. 'The way the cheekbones are set. I mean no offence, but I don't think your artists have caught it very well, though that's not surprising. I should tell you that I taught art for many years, and facial structure is a subject I'm familiar with. This is the kind of face that's particularly hard to get right, hence the problem your witnesses must have had in describing it – and the artists in getting it down on paper. It lacks distinctive characteristics. It could fit, or *seem* to fit, any number of women.'

'But you definitely don't recognize her?'

'I'm afraid not.' She handed the drawings back. 'Even if she walked into the room now, I might not know her from these. All I can tell you is she probably has features that don't leave a strong impression.'

She smiled.

'That wasn't much help, I know, but I should add that, to the best of my knowledge, Hazel had very few visitors other than people she knew locally, and not many of those were what you would call close friends. She was a solitary soul, but that was by choice.'

She paused for a moment.

'We were friends, as I said, but I wouldn't want you to think that I knew all her secrets.'

'She had secrets then?' Madden was quick to seize on the word.

'Oh, dear . . .' Their hostess looked unhappy. 'That wasn't

well put. What I should have said was that we were never truly intimate. Hazel was a naturally reserved person. She didn't find it easy to speak openly about herself or her feelings. But she was a dear soul, and I miss her.'

Billy waited to see if his old chief had anything to add. When Madden stayed silent he took up the questioning again.

'On another matter, do you happen to know where Mrs Ballard resided before she came to Richmond?'

'Oh, there I can help you.' Miss Dauncey's face brightened. 'She was living in France, in a village near Bordeaux. She went there soon after the first war ended, early in 1919 I think, taking Alma with her, of course. They stayed for ten years. I met her for the first time in 1930 when she returned to England.'

'Do you know why she went abroad?'

'Not exactly. Hazel never gave me a precise reason. But it was a perfectly natural thing to do. She had French relations after all.'

'Did she?' Billy was surprised. 'We had no idea.'

'They dated back to her grandfather. He married a Frenchwoman. Hazel was quite open about that.' Miss Dauncey smiled. 'He was a wine merchant and he married the daughter of his principal shipper, a Bordelaise. Hazel used to spend her holidays in France when she was a child. Her husband's death in the war upset her terribly and perhaps moving to another country – one she was familiar with and where she felt at home – was what she needed. In any event, she and Alma lived there for the next ten years and, according to Hazel, the only reason she came back was because she wanted to give her daughter an English education. It was purely by chance that she bought the house next to mine. But after she'd learned that I was a teacher she asked me for advice. I was working at St Mary's at the time, but it's only a day school and Alma had expressed a wish to go to boarding school. I was able to recommend one or two to Hazel. I tell you this so that you'll understand how we got to know each other. Up till then she had kept very much to herself.'

She smiled again.

'But after that we discovered we had a mutual passion for gardening and we began to spend more time with each other, pottering about. I found her a strange, shy person, but I became very fond of her in time; of them both in fact, she and Alma. I do miss them.'

She looked away.

'And before she went to France?' Billy had waited a moment. 'Did she tell you anything about her life then? We understand that she and her husband lived in Cornwall.'

'That's correct.' Sighing, their hostess turned back. 'But it's something I can't help you with. She never spoke about that time or mentioned any of the friends they must have had then. It was too painful for her. I don't know whether you're aware of it, but she had an extraordinary attachment to her husband. She never got over the loss of him. It was very sad.'

Billy hesitated. They had reached a critical point in the interview.

'Did it have anything to do with the way her husband died?' he asked casually.

'Very much so.' The promptness of her reply took both men by surprise. 'Although it was a long time before I heard the full story, but based on what I know now, I would say that a light went out of Hazel's life when he died, and she spent the rest of it in mourning.'

She studied her hands.

'I like to think it meant a lot to her that she had finally found a friend in me. But one thing I learned early on was not to pry into the myth she had built up around her husband, or to question it. I truly believe our friendship would not have survived it.'

Glancing at his old chief, Billy saw he was about to speak.

'I'm not sure I understand you.' Madden's frown was pronounced. 'What do you mean by a myth?'

'I felt she went too far, placing him on a pedestal; making him almost an object of worship. It wasn't healthy – not for her, or for Alma.'

Unaware of the effect her words were having on her listeners, she turned to look out of the window, though there was little to see there other than the grey morning light.

'A pedestal?' Madden echoed the word.

'Oh, Lord . . .' She turned back to them. 'Perhaps I shouldn't have said that. It seems disloyal now. But yes, a pedestal. There's no other word for it. I'm sure he was a brave man, and he died for his country. But so did many others. To hear Hazel tell it, you would have thought he was almost alone in having sacrificed his life . . . and his talent. She had a photograph of him in his army uniform, beautifully framed. It sat on a table in the corner of their living room with nothing but a bowl of fresh flowers beside it, and with James's medal in a velvet-lined case open in front of his picture. One couldn't help but be put in mind of a shrine. It made me feel uncomfortable.'

She looked down.

'I didn't realize he'd been decorated.' Madden had managed to hide his surprise.

'He was awarded the Military Medal for gallantry. It was Alma who told me that. Hazel was always very secretive on the subject. She didn't like to talk about it. But according to Alma, her father had taken part in an assault on a German position and when the officer leading them was killed, James had led a charge into the enemy trenches, where he was fatally wounded. She said her mother had been told the story by one of his comrades. She was so proud of him – Alma, I mean – and of course there was nothing wrong with that. I think we should all honour those who fall in battle. But life is for the living, and in time I began to think that Hazel had laid too heavy a burden on her daughter. Alma had been brought up to believe that the memory of her father was the most important thing in their lives and, although I never said so, I couldn't help feeling it was one of the reasons behind her decision to emigrate. I think subconsciously she wanted to free herself from the past . . . the weight of it.'

She put a hand to her head.

'Mind you, there may have been other reasons . . .'

In the silence that followed Billy again took the opportunity to glance at his old mentor. Madden's gaze had sharpened.

'Could you be more specific?' he asked.

'Must I?' She seemed to shrink from the question. 'It's really not something I want to talk about.'

But the glance she cast his way seemed to hold an appeal and, observing her reaction, Madden spoke again.

'I can see this is difficult for you.' He spoke gently. 'Let me try and explain our problem. Alma Ballard herself is an important element in this investigation. She must know more about her mother, and the people she had contact with, than anyone. It's not beyond question that both of them were acquainted with the couple the police are searching for. As Inspector Styles said earlier, these people are thought to be connected to James Ballard in some way, and the encounter, if it took place, could have been distressing.'

'Distressing?' Miss Dauncey faltered over the word.

'To Mrs Ballard in particular; but also to her daughter. If Alma had some reason for quitting England other than the one you mentioned, it would be best if you told us what it was. I know I speak for Mr Styles when I say that, provided it has no bearing on this investigation, whatever you tell us will go no further than this room.'

Madden sat back. He had said all he could.

Miss Dauncey stared at her clenched fists. It was clear from her expression that she was going through some inner struggle.

'An encounter, you say . . . a meeting?' She ran her fingers through her hair. The nervous gesture, together with her wavering voice, revealed her anxiety. 'Must I . . . must I really?' She made a final appeal.

Madden held her gaze.

'I think you should,' he said quietly.

'I'd like to make it clear at the outset that what I have to tell you is a *private* matter – Alma's personal business. Furthermore, I witnessed it under . . . peculiar circumstances, and have felt guilty about doing so ever since.'

Miss Dauncey flushed. A few minutes earlier, having interrupted the interview on the pretext of offering her visitors a cup of tea, she had disappeared into the kitchen, leaving Billy and Madden to wonder what it was that she was about to reveal to them.

'This is starting to bother me, sir.' As soon as they were alone Billy had spoken. 'All that stuff about Alma and her father, what she felt about him. What do you make of it?'

'It's hard to say.' Madden seemed stumped by his question. 'We need to know more.'

'Could she have fooled us about Canada? Could she be this woman we're looking for? But if so, who's the man?'

Instead of replying, Madden had put a hand to his lips and nodded in the direction of the kitchen. Better to wait, his gesture suggested, and at that moment their hostess reappeared with a tray in her hands.

'But I did find the occasion unsettling,' she went on now.

She had clearly used the time to compose herself. Seated before them again, busy pouring the tea, she spoke in measured tones.

'I still have no explanation for the *extreme* nature of Alma's reaction, and for this reason I'm prepared to share it with you, provided you stick to the assurance you gave me a few minutes ago. I don't wish to hear at some later stage that it has formed part of an official police report.'

'Again, you have our word.' Madden bowed his head.

'Then I'll start by telling you something about Alma herself, the kind of person she is . . . or was. I'm not saying it will help to explain the scene I witnessed, but at least it will give you some background against which to judge it.'

She broke off to pass a cup of tea to each of them. Her hand was steady.

'I first met her when she and her mother arrived to settle in Richmond. She must have been twelve or thirteen at the time, and although I was well used to dealing with young girls from my years at St Mary's, I had never met one quite like Alma. She was almost entirely without discipline, and I had the impression Hazel had let her run wild. Later on I heard she'd been the leader of a pack of children in the village where they lived, who were forever in trouble, though admittedly not in any serious way: stealing apples from orchards, climbing onto the church roof, that sort of thing. But I could tell that Alma had run Hazel ragged, and I wondered how she would settle into life in England. I didn't have long to wait.'

She smiled.

'Quite soon after they moved in next door, Hazel and I were in the garden planting some seedlings down near the river when we looked up and saw a canoe go speeding by, pursued by two men who were running along the bank after it, shouting furiously. It was Alma of course. She'd spotted the craft drawn up on the bank and decided to take it for a spin. Poor Hazel nearly had a fit.'

She shook her head.

'I have to say I was enormously drawn to Alma. She had the sort of daring we all hanker for. She made me regret my own youth and the chances for adventure that I felt I'd let pass by.

But that only increased the pleasure I took in her exploits. Soon after she went off to boarding school Hazel had a telephone call from the headmistress; it seemed that she herself had received a call only a few days earlier, purporting to be from Hazel with the sad news that Alma's grandmother had passed away suddenly. Would it be possible for Alma to attend the funeral in Guildford, the headmistress was asked; and after she had given her permission she was told that a taxi would call for Alma two days hence to take her into town for the service.'

She began to shake with laughter.

'The headmistress bought the story – hook, line and sinker – and only discovered the truth when she received another call on the day of the supposed service, from the manager of a cinema in Guildford who wondered whether one of her pupils might have gone AWOL. Alma had bought a ticket for the matinee, but unfortunately for her she was in her school uniform and the manager smelled a rat. She managed to see half of the film before the headmistress and another member of staff arrived to clap her in irons.'

'What was showing?' Billy couldn't help himself. He was grinning.

'*Animal Crackers.* Alma told me later that she'd read about the Marx Brothers in a magazine and wanted to see what all the fuss was about. That was typical of her. If she wanted to do something, she did it, and never mind the cost. What impressed me, though, other than the sheer inventiveness of the scheme, was the care she took putting it into effect. First she worked hard on imitating a grown-up's voice, lowering her own; and later, when she gave me a demonstration, I was quite bowled over by how well she managed it. She had also volunteered to work in the tuck shop, because she knew there was a telephone in the office behind it. She made her calls from there – to both the headmistress and the company that sent the taxi. She had spent just about all of her term's pocket money on the plan, and

Hazel quite rightly refused to give her another penny, but it didn't bother Alma. I think the pleasure of pulling it all off more than compensated for the loss of income.'

'She must have been punished for that.'

'Of course she was, in the rather petty ways that girls' schools favour. She spent hours in detention and was given all kinds of extra duties, but I doubt they had much effect. In any case, after two months and before the end of term Hazel was told that her daughter wasn't suited to the school, or the school to her, and that she would have to look for another. I was able to help at that stage and, after a bit of research, I pointed Hazel towards a more easy-going establishment in Dorset, one of those newfangled academies called "progressive", and by some miracle Alma managed to see out her schooldays there.'

Miss Dauncey bit her lip. It seemed that another thought had just occurred to her, and Billy waited impatiently for her to share it with them.

'It might be worth pointing out that initially I was surprised when I heard that Alma was set on going to boarding school. Given her spirit of independence, I would have thought she would have preferred the more relaxed regime she enjoyed at home. It was only later, after I had got to know them both a little better, that I realized she might have been seeking to escape from the rather claustrophobic atmosphere she'd grown up in.'

'You're referring to the status Hazel had conferred on her husband?' Madden's sudden intervention took Billy by surprise. His old chief had been sitting silent for some time, motionless on the sofa beside him. 'To the myth, as you called it, that she'd woven around him?'

'That's exactly it.' She seemed pleased to be understood. 'Hazel lived her life in hushed tones. She radiated a sense of loss and although, as I said, Alma was tremendously proud of her father, she had a spirit quite at odds with her mother's. I used to wonder if some of her antics weren't a rebellion against that, just as I thought her taste for adventure was related in some way to her father's heroics.'

'You felt she was trying to emulate him?'

'In some sense. She wanted to live up to him and, given the way Hazel glorified his memory, that wasn't surprising. Alma chose to view life as a challenge. She couldn't wait to come to grips with it. That was how I saw her, at any rate, and later on I was proved right; up to a point, at least.'

She frowned.

'But to get back to where I was: after Alma left school the question naturally came up of what she would do next. In spite of her sometimes erratic behaviour she'd performed well enough academically, particularly with regard to languages. But she had also shown some aptitude for art, and unfortunately that prompted Hazel to urge her to enrol at the Slade in London. She was sure Alma had inherited her father's talent.'

She sought Madden's eye.

'I say "unfortunately" because in point of fact Hazel was quite wrong on both counts. I had seen enough of James's paintings – her house was full of them – to know that his gift had been minor. He painted prettily enough, seascapes mostly, the sort that people buy, and I dare say he would have enjoyed a perfectly successful career as a commercial painter. But that was the sum of it; and Alma's talent, such as it was, was even slighter, something that she had to acknowledge in time and which I feel was painful for her. In her own mind she had always been her father's daughter. After she left the Slade she continued to live in London – she found a job in an advertising agency and was sharing a flat with two other girls – but she used to come down to Richmond to see her mother, and around that time I began to notice a change in her manner. I'd always thought of her as a cheerful soul, certainly an optimistic one, but now I began to notice a darker side to her nature: swings of mood that were quite extreme and would arrive without warning. I know Hazel was worried about her, and so was I. And there was something else that I, at any rate, found a little worrying.

'Despite the time she had spent in London and the fact that she appeared to be behaving the way young girls behaved – going to parties, and so on – there seemed to be no young man in her life, nothing even approximating a boyfriend. Now I've dealt with enough young girls to know that not all of them mature at the same rate. But Alma was in her twenties by now and not unattractive to the opposite sex, yet she seemed to hold herself aloof, or at least to keep her distance from any sort of emotional entanglement, and I wondered why.'

She hesitated.

'I don't claim any special insight – I'm not a psychologist – but I'd been able to observe Alma since early adolescence and I knew she was a romantic at heart. It's not uncommon with young girls, of course, but generally as they grow up and what we call real life begins to impose itself on them, they learn to modify their views and keep their dreams in perspective. But that change never occurred in Alma. She didn't grow up. That adventurous spirit I told you about, the image she had of her father, her willingness to break the rules – they all conspired to give her a picture of life that could never come up to her expectations. She'd become a fish out of water, poor girl, and I was starting to wonder where it would all end. She was still in that state, drifting and unhappy, when the war came.'

Miss Dauncey's voice had dropped as she spoke these last words and her visitors waited to see what the change of tone signified.

'Most of us can probably remember how we felt then – at the very start, I mean, when we heard Chamberlain's announcement on the wireless. But I doubt many of us reacted the way Alma did. To her it came as a clarion call. She couldn't wait to enlist. From the first she thought of it as a great adventure, the kind she had been waiting for, and nothing either her mother or I could say would dissuade her. I truly think she saw herself as following in her father's footsteps, living up to the example he had set. She joined the Women's Auxiliary Air Force at the first opportunity and I remember the day she came down to Richmond in her new uniform. She was so proud. She had gone to a professional photographer in London to have her picture taken and she gave me a copy. Would you like to see it?'

Without waiting for a response Miss Dauncey rose and went to a cabinet on the far side of the room. Billy used the brief pause to glance at Madden, but on this occasion failed to catch his eye. His old mentor's attention had been drawn to one of the paintings hanging on a wall, a portrait of a girl with long fair hair, in her early teens perhaps, sitting on a swing with a puppy cradled in her arms.

'Yes, that's Alma.' Returning with an album in her hands, their hostess had caught the direction of Madden's glance. 'I painted it when she was fourteen, but I didn't make a very good job of it. The puppy was a present from her mother. This will give you a better idea of how she looked.'

She opened the album at a place she had marked with her finger and handed it to Billy, who held it on his knees so that Madden could see the photograph mounted on the page. Clearly the work of a professional, it showed a young woman dressed in WAAF uniform sitting straight-backed with her fair hair, cut short now, neatly tucked under her cap. Neither plain nor pretty, Alma Ballard would have gone unnoticed in a crowd, Billy thought, were it not for her expression, which was animated, and for the eager smile that lit up her face.

'You can almost read her thoughts, can't you?' Miss Dauncey watched as they studied the picture. 'She was longing to spring into action. Heaven knows what she imagined she'd be doing. Flying Spitfires, I shouldn't wonder. Poor Alma! She was always running up against reality. Her languages proved to be her best asset. She spoke perfect French, of course – she'd grown up with it – and good German, too, which she'd learned at school. After basic training she was seconded to the Signals Corps and posted to a radio listening station at some godforsaken spot on the Norfolk coast. She used to come home for the odd weekend when she got leave, but it was as though all the life had been drained from her. I'd never seen her so miserable. Hazel was beside herself with worry. But then, just as we were beginning to despair, things changed for the better. Alma received a foreign posting; she was told she was being sent to the Middle East, and when she came down to Richmond to tell us the news I could see that the clouds had lifted. She was bubbling with excitement at the prospect. She couldn't wait to be on her way.'

Miss Dauncey reflected wryly on her words.

'Well, I don't know how much excitement there was in being a cipher clerk in Cairo, which is what she was, but at least it was abroad and exotic and a long way from dreary Norfolk. And although Alma couldn't say much about it – I'm sure you recall how strict censorship was during the war – she never complained in the letters Hazel used to receive, on that awful tissue-like paper with whole lines blacked out, because some fact deemed to be classified had somehow found its way into Alma's chatter. They were usually just about the weather and the camels and expeditions to see the pyramids, but reading between the lines, it was obvious that she was much happier than she had been. And although Hazel missed her dreadfully, she was relieved by the letters' tone – we both were, though later I had cause to wonder what Alma had *not* been telling us.'

She eyed them meaningfully.

'But to continue: she was away for more than a year. She left England towards the end of 1942 and came back a year and a half later. We had no advance word of her return. She simply telephoned one day from some camp on the outskirts of London – it was late summer – and told her mother she was back. A few days later she came down to Richmond . . .'

Miss Dauncey swallowed. She seemed to hesitate.

'Well, it was obvious to both Hazel and me that something had gone seriously wrong in her life. It wasn't that Alma was simply withdrawn: she seemed close to catatonic, almost unable to speak. She spent hours lying in bed in a darkened room and, when she did finally get up, she would either go off for long walks on her own or hire a rowing boat and drift down the river. I didn't dare say so to Hazel, but I began to fear for her state of mind – and her safety.'

She gnawed at her lip.

'One hates to say it of another person, but at one stage I feared for her life. She had always been a person of extremes, and I was afraid she might take some . . . drastic action to free herself from her misery. What made it worse was that I felt I couldn't share my fears with Hazel.'

'And yet you had no idea what was troubling her?' Madden's tone sounded a note of disbelief.

'If you mean, had she told us – then no.' She looked at him. 'But I had my suspicions. I was sure I knew what had brought poor Alma to this pass.'

'And what was that?'

'Why, a man of course.' Miss Dauncey spread her hands as though the answer was obvious. 'Nothing else made sense. I told you how she had been earlier, the difficulty she found with that side of life. She was quite . . . inexperienced, in every sense of the word, when she left for Egypt. She had no idea how the game was played: she took nothing lightly. Of course I had no concrete information to go on, but there was little doubt in my mind as to what had happened to her in Egypt.'

'And were you right?'

Again she hesitated.

'Let me finish my story first.' She spoke after a long moment. 'Then you can judge for yourselves.'

Watching her, Billy felt the tension rising in the room and saw from Madden's steady gaze, which was fixed unblinkingly on their hostess, that he too was waiting for the moment of truth to reveal itself.

'Since returning from Cairo Alma had been filling some desk job at an RAF depot in Epsom.' Their hostess had composed herself again. 'But early in 1945 she was demobilized and, instead of coming home to Richmond as Hazel had hoped, she took a flat in London and started looking for a job. Though I didn't dare say so, it looked to me as though she was drifting again – she seemed to have no purpose in life – and she still hadn't shaken off the black mood she had brought back with her from Egypt. Things went on like that for more than a year. Then, towards the end of last summer, she dropped her bombshell. She suddenly announced that she was going to emigrate to Canada, and when Hazel sought to change her mind, Alma said she didn't wish to live in England any longer; she was as blunt as that. "I hate this bloody country," she said, and I don't know which of us was more shocked, Hazel or I. It wasn't the sort of thing Alma would ever have said in the past.

'She began to plan her departure and started by consulting the Canadian High Commission about the procedures for immigration. There was no doubt that she was set on going, and her preparations were well advanced when Hazel fell ill. She had suffered for some years from heart trouble and when she finally went into hospital for a proper examination, it was found that she had occluded arteries: the blood supply to her heart was being blocked. Other than medication there was nothing the doctors could do: no operation was possible. It was by way of being a death-sentence, even if not an immediate one, and it fell to me to give Alma the sad news.'

Miss Dauncey sighed.

'I have to confess I was worried about how she might respond – it would mean giving up, or at least postponing, her own plans – but I should have given her more credit. Whatever problems Alma might have had growing up, and however oppressed she must have felt from time to time by the pall Hazel had cast over her own life, she loved her mother deeply and didn't hesitate. She returned to Richmond at once to look after her. She even managed to shrug off her own depression, or at least mask it so that she could devote herself to Hazel. There was hardly a moment when they weren't together, and Alma spent hours putting her mother's affairs in order so that there would be nothing to worry her. She took care of the garden, too, though she had never shown any interest in it before, and as a result she and I also spent time together and I was struck by how calm she had become. All that inner turmoil had evaporated. It seemed she had come to terms with whatever it was that had given her such pain, and was ready to face life again. I can tell you, I sent up a prayer of thanks when I saw it: I knew how much it would help to ease Hazel's last months.'

She looked away.

'She was starting to fail, poor dear. The simple act of breathing was becoming more and more difficult, and we had to keep an oxygen cylinder by her bed at all times. Alma had made up a bed in her mother's room. She wanted to be always on hand, but at the same time there was still some last-minute business of Hazel's to be sorted out – I'm afraid she was never a good administrator – and I can recall seeing Alma kneeling on the floor downstairs in their sitting room with piles of papers and documents around her, trying to make sense of them all. We both knew the moment was approaching – Hazel's doctor had told us it wouldn't be long – and, as people do in those circumstances, we kept ourselves as busy as possible. I had stopped teaching at St Mary's when the war ended, so I had plenty of free time to go over there and sit with Hazel so that Alma could get some rest. And then something strange happened, something that was never fully explained.'

She turned back to face them.

'I'd been out during the morning and, when I came home, I went over next door to see if there was anything I could do for Alma. There was no sign of her downstairs, only the usual untidy piles of letters and papers strewn around, so I went upstairs to the bedroom and found Hazel asleep. To my surprise she was alone in the house and I wondered where Alma was. It wasn't until I went to the window that I saw her. She was standing at the bottom of the garden quite near the bank of the river, gazing out over it. She had her arms folded, but more than that, they seemed wrapped around her, and I had the absurd thought that she was somehow trying to hold herself together, to stop herself from falling to pieces. I watched her for several minutes, but she didn't move a muscle. It was as if she'd been turned to stone. I wondered what had happened, what was going through her mind. Then Hazel started to struggle for breath behind me and I had to leave the window to fix the oxygen mask to her nose. When I went back to the window I saw Alma walking back up the garden to the house. I was planning to ask her if anything was wrong, but when she came into the bedroom and I saw her face, I changed my mind. Her eyes were quite dead. She hardly seemed aware of my presence. And when she did look at me, it was as though she was seeing a stranger.'

Miss Dauncey kneaded her forehead.

'I hardly slept that night. I knew something terrible had happened, but I had no idea what. Next morning I screwed up my courage and went over to see if there was any way I could get to the bottom of it. I found Alma tidying up in the sitting room, boxing papers. Before I had time to speak she said she had to go out to fetch some medicine for her mother from the chemist, and would I keep an eye on her while she was gone? The same dead look was on her face; she hardly seemed to know me. But I agreed, of course, and went upstairs. Hazel was asleep; she was breathing raggedly. I'd only been with her for a few minutes when the doorbell rang. I went downstairs to answer it and found a man I'd never seen before standing on the doorstep. He asked for Alma. "My name's Finch," he said. "Colin Finch. We're old friends."'

'Old friends?' Billy came to life with a start. He was transfixed by the story.

'That's what he said.' Miss Dauncey shrugged. 'But I didn't believe it for a moment. One look at him was enough. I guessed at once that he must be the man Alma had been involved with. And her strange behaviour the day before suddenly made sense. She must have had word that he was coming to see her. Perhaps he didn't know how much it would upset her. Or perhaps he didn't care. He was an attractive devil all right, but there was a hard look about him. He seemed to me one of those men who are at ease, no matter what the situation. He didn't show even a hint of embarrassment or discomfiture, no sign that he knew his presence might not be welcome. He seemed quite sure of himself.'

Her face had reddened while she was speaking.

'Can you describe him?' Billy leaned forward.

'Certainly. I've a good memory for faces. He was older than Alma, in his early forties I'd say, but younger than his years, lean and fit-looking, with dark hair cut quite short and a small scar on his left temple. What else . . . ?' She thought for a moment. 'Yes, he had brown eyes – I remember those – and sensitive hands. I wondered if he was an artist.'

'From his *hands*?'

'No, it was something else. He had one of those flat cases painters use to carry their drawings around in. I wondered if that was what had brought them together: whether he had used Alma's interest in art to get close to her. I'm not saying that's so; it was just a thought. But he did have interesting hands. His fingers were slender, but looked strong. It's the sort of thing I notice.' She flushed. 'So I can also tell you that he was married.'

'How did you know that?'

'From his wedding ring. He was playing with it as he spoke to me. I think that's what I found most offensive: how *brazen* he was.'

For the first time a note of anger sounded in her voice.

'Yes, but how can you be sure? I mean you can't be certain that he and . . .'

Billy struggled to find the right words. He wished Madden would speak. Having earlier played his part in the interview, his old chief had gone silent.

'Let me go on.' She quieted him with a gesture. 'You'll see what I mean in a moment.'

She paused.

'I felt I knew what effect his presence would have on Alma, and I wanted nothing better than to send him packing. But it was not my business to interfere, and I simply told him that she was out, but would be back in a while and in the meantime he could wait for her in the sitting room. I went back upstairs. I was already dreading what might happen when Alma found him there and half-thought of slipping out to warn her in advance. But I couldn't leave Hazel alone. She seemed restless in her sleep and she was sweating in the heat. It was the first week in June; we were having an unaccustomed heatwave. I went to the window to open it and, as I did so, I heard the front door open and realized Alma must be back. I stood there expecting to hear the sound of voices downstairs, but instead there was silence. Then I saw him – her visitor. He was down below on the terrace. He'd obviously wandered outside and was standing by the balustrade looking at the garden. I was about to turn away – I meant to go downstairs and alert Alma to his presence – when I heard her speak. Her voice came from below me on the terrace. She'd obviously seen him through the windows in the sitting room and had followed him outside. "*You!*" she said.'

'You?' Billy didn't understand.

'That was all she said. "*You!*"'

She stared at him.

'But it wasn't so much the word – it was the way she said it. I had never heard such anger in her voice, such . . . scorn, such *contempt*. As soon as she spoke he turned round, and I swear he went pale at the sight of her. I thought he was going to speak, but instead he simply held out his hands to her . . . like this.'

Amanda Dauncey extended her arms to their full length with her hands held open.

'I suppose he was making an appeal of some sort – that's what it looked like – but it cut no ice with Alma. I couldn't see her face, of course, only the top of her head, but I could see his and it was obvious he was shaken. "I might have known *you'd* appear," she said in that same terrible voice. "*Antoine . . .*"'

'Ant . . . ?' Billy was lost.

'Antoine. It's a French name.'

'But didn't he say his name was Colin?'

Miss Dauncey sighed. All at once she seemed exhausted.

'I can't explain that except to say that lovers do sometimes make up names for each other. But again, it wasn't the name, it was the way Alma said it. She made it sound like a curse. Perhaps I imagined it, but he seemed to sway on his feet, as if he'd been struck a blow. But then he recovered and, when he finally spoke, he sounded quite calm. "You must stop this," he said. "We need to talk." But Alma would have none of it. She was merciless. "No one asked you to come here," she said. "No one wants you." He gave her a long look then and, I have to say, he did seem sad at that moment, and regretful. "In that case I'd better go," he said. "Yes, you had," she spat back at him. "Before you do, though, there's something I want to show you." Without waiting for a reply she turned on her heel and went back inside. He followed her, and I heard nothing more until the front door shut a few minutes later and I realized that he must have left. When Alma came upstairs I began to explain about her visitor and how I had had to leave him on his own, but she cut me off. It was perfectly all right, she said. She had spoken to him and he had left. But there was no expression in her voice, no emotion in her eyes. It was as though she had shut me – and the world – out forever. Oh, Lord . . . !'

She wrung her hands.

'I did feel awful for having eavesdropped that way. I wished I hadn't. It was dreadful seeing Alma in such pain. I went home soon afterwards, but I kept thinking I ought to go back and explain what had happened. What stopped me was the thought that it would only make things worse. Then, before I had time to think any further on it, events overtook us. Hazel passed away during the night and when Alma rang me next morning to tell me, I decided there was only one thing I could do at that point and that was help her in any way I could. Whatever might have happened to her in the past, I felt no good could come of bringing it up. So I said nothing.'

She ran her fingers through her hair.

'The next few days and weeks were busy ones. I had thought Alma might want to stay in Richmond, at least for a while, but after the funeral she told me she was going ahead with her plan to emigrate and asked if I would help in clearing out the house. She wanted to put it up for sale as soon as possible, but would leave the business side of that in the hands of her mother's solicitor. So we got down to it, the pair of us, and before long we had sent whatever pieces and household items she wanted to keep to storage and the rest to an auctioneer. I don't know how Alma felt – she seemed to have shut her feelings away – but I know I didn't find it easy. There's something so sad about clearing up after a life, and in Hazel's case I found it especially poignant. We left the photograph of her husband, which had meant so much to her, where it was in the sitting room almost to the last and I put fresh flowers in the bowl every day. It was a sentimental gesture, I know, but I felt we owed it to Hazel. On the final day, when Alma left to go up to London, she packed it in her suitcase and somehow that seemed to mark the end of their time there – the last of them both.'

She sank back in her chair.

'So that's the story and, as I said before, I don't believe it's got anything to do with any police investigation. It was private to Alma, and to this day I don't know exactly what was behind it, except it was plain that somehow this man had hurt her very deeply. There's really nothing more I can tell you.'

Billy glanced at Madden again. He was used to his old chief's silences, but this one had been more protracted than usual. Madden was sitting with his chin cupped in his hand, seemingly lost in thought.

'Did you ever see him again?' Finally Billy himself spoke.

She shook her head. 'And, before you ask, Alma never mentioned him. Other than the name I gave you, I've no idea who he is or where he came from.'

'Did you keep in contact with her after she left?'

'We didn't lose touch. She still had her flat in London and she handled the rest of her preparations from there. She came down to Richmond on a few occasions to see Mr Royston – he was Hazel's solicitor – and we met briefly. But we weren't close, the way we once were, and it was clear to me that the wound she'd suffered hadn't healed. She had a steely look that I'd never seen before. I had the feeling that meeting that man again had brought it all back, and I could only hope that she would find peace of mind and a new life in Canada.'

'Have you heard from her at all?'

'A few times. She sailed from Liverpool at the end of July and I had a postcard from her soon afterwards and then a letter, both sent from Toronto. She didn't say much – only that she was finding her feet. She thanked me again for the help I'd given her, but formally, without any warmth, and I was afraid that in the end she would simply disappear from my life.

'But then I had a reprieve, if you can call it that.' Miss Dauncey smiled wanly. 'Three weeks ago I had another letter from her, which was a little warmer in tone. She was still in Toronto, but she wasn't intending to stay there. She wanted to see more of the country before she settled down, and planned to travel by train to Vancouver. She said she would write again once she got there.'

About to ask a further question, Billy paused. Beside him Madden had stirred at last.

'That remark she made about England – "this bloody country" – what do you think she meant by it?'

'I wish I knew. We both asked why she had said it, Hazel and I, but as I recall Alma gave no answer. I ought to say that we were treating her with kid gloves at the time. She seemed so fragile . . . in herself, I mean. We didn't want to upset her more.'

Madden pondered.

'And about this visitor she had – Colin Finch – do you know what it was she wanted to show him before he went?'

'I haven't the faintest idea, I'm afraid.' She shook her head hopelessly. 'I spent hours racking my brains over that.'

'You said he was hard-looking. What did you mean by that?'

'I'm really not sure . . . It was just something I felt.' She seemed disconcerted by the question. 'And it was only an impression – something to do with his eyes. He looked like a man who could handle any sort of situation. I felt he was probably unscrupulous, but that may have been because I realized how attractive he must have seemed to a young and inexperienced woman, and I had the feeling he had treated Alma badly.'

She shrugged.

'But I've no proof of that. There was really no reason for me to take against him. He wasn't here long; and while he was here, he behaved like a gentleman.'

23

'I DON'T KNOW ABOUT you, sir, but I'm finding it harder than ever to make sense of this. It's clear Alma worshipped her dad. But does that mean she's mixed up in this? True, she might have found some way of faking her trip to Canada, though I don't see how, but if we follow that line and we're wrong – if the Mounties tell us they've found her – we'll be back where we started with all that time wasted.'

Billy signalled his frustration with a sigh.

'And what about this bloke with the hard eyes? Where does he fit in? Is he the shooter we're looking for? Are the two of them in this together?'

He turned to see what effect, if any, his words had had on his companion. They were sitting in the back of the police car making their slow way back to London through the still foggy morning. Madden had been staring out of the window for some time, silent.

'Or could Alma be tied up with this in some way we haven't thought of yet?' Billy gnawed at his lip. 'Perhaps she knew what these two were going to do. Maybe that's why she took herself off to Canada. Because she didn't want to get mixed up in it. Was that what the scene Miss Dauncey overheard was all about? What do you think?'

Knowing his old chief's tendency to get lost in his thoughts,

Billy had kept his impatience in check for as long as he could. But finally he had to speak.

'Have you got an opinion, sir? You haven't said a word.'

His exasperated tone brought a smile to Madden's lips.

'I'm sorry, Billy . . .' He turned from the window. 'I was wool-gathering. No, I don't believe she went to Canada for that reason. It wasn't done on the spur of the moment. She was making plans to emigrate well before her mother fell ill – and before this man turned up. But as for the rest, I'm as confused as you are. Miss Dauncey assumed there'd been an affair between Alma and Finch. But would that have been enough to bring about the scene she witnessed?'

'Enough?'

It seemed to Billy his old chief had gone off on a tangent.

'What's the worst that could have happened to her – assuming Miss Dauncey is right in her diagnosis? Perhaps they had an affair and she got pregnant. Or he might have told her he was going to leave his wife and then gone back on his word. But would either have been enough to justify the fury Alma seemed to feel . . . the sense of betrayal? That was how I understood that encounter of theirs – at least as Miss Dauncey described it. Alma seemed to think she'd been let down.'

'Perhaps he didn't stand by her,' Billy suggested.

'If that was the case I wouldn't defend him. But could she really have expected their relationship to last? She was bound to find out in the end that he was married. I think there was more to it than that. I'm starting to wonder if there wasn't some other link between them.'

'Like what, sir?'

Madden shook his head.

'There's no point in guessing,' he said. 'We have to find out. It may be important: it could explain a lot of things. Since Alma's not available, we have to talk to this man Finch.'

'So you do think he is involved in some way?' At last they were getting somewhere, Billy thought.

'Involved . . . in these murders?' Madden frowned.

'He *could* be our shooter. Miss Dauncey seemed to think he was capable of anything.'

'So she did.'

Madden rubbed the scar on his brow. His frown had become a scowl.

'Look, I don't know where this is headed, Billy. I'm as much in the dark as you are. I'm trying to feel my way, but that meeting on the terrace that Miss Dauncey witnessed was too extraordinary – too *extreme*, to use her word – to ignore. We must get to the bottom of it. You *must* locate this man.'

'Oh, I agree.' Billy shrugged. 'And he shouldn't be too hard to find. Miss Dauncey thought he might be a painter. But then what? We can hardly go and ask him about some affair he might or might not have had with a young woman; and him a married man. Charlie wouldn't like it, that's for certain; Cradock would go spare. We'll have to find some evidence first that ties him to this case.'

'No, there's no time for that. The delay could be fatal.'

The sharpness of Madden's tone took Billy by surprise. For a moment he hesitated . . . but only for a moment.

'In that case I'll get on to it right away,' he said, smiling to himself as he said it. He realized he'd accepted the order without question, just as if he was still a green DC and Madden his superior. But habits were hard to break, he reminded himself. And it wasn't as though he'd ever had cause to doubt his former chief's judgement. 'Come to think of it, I wouldn't mind finding out a bit more about Mr Colin Finch.' He went on. 'For one thing, I'd like to know how he and Alma met – and where.'

Madden's nod concurred.

'Yes . . . and why she called him Antoine.'

'His name's Mickey Corder. No reason you should have heard of him. He's a small-time dealer, pond scum, one of the lower forms of life.'

Joe Grace's hatchet face was split by a smile.

'They know him well, down Wapping way. He hasn't got a business as such; he's more of a middleman. He'll get you what you need – a false ID card, or some dodgy petrol coupons – but he doesn't hold the stuff himself. He buys it off others and adds his commission to the price. That way he keeps his hands clean, or thinks he does. But this time he made a mistake.'

'Who gave you the tip?' Billy asked. He'd returned from Richmond a few minutes earlier to find Joe ensconced with the chief super in his office and both of them impatiently awaiting his arrival.

'Stan Barrow – remember him?'

'How could I forget? He was part of that old smash-and-grab gang we broke up before the war. You and I nicked him in '39. He used to be one of our snouts.'

'He still is, when the mood moves him.' Joe grinned. 'And he's still working as a cellar-man at the White Boar.'

'That den of thieves?' Billy chuckled. 'It's got a charmed life. The Jerries blew everything to buggery along the river down there during the war, yet somehow they managed to miss it. It made me wonder if there really was a God.'

He caught Chubb's eye. The chief super's brow was darkening.

'So what did Barrow have to say?'

'He rang me at home over the weekend, said he'd heard about the word I'd put out. He remembered Corder doing some kind of business deal with a woman weeks ago. She came to the Boar one evening and they met in a back room. He only got a quick look at her and he doesn't know what changed hands. But since Mickey traffics in forged or stolen cards, I thought it worth my while having a word with him. I picked him up at his lodgings in Whitechapel this morning and took him over to Wapping nick. He didn't want to say anything at first, but soon changed his mind.'

'Broke one of his fingers, did you?' Chubb glared.

'No, of course not, sir. I wouldn't do a thing like that.' Joe was offended. 'I just told him that unless he came clean, we'd be charging him as an accessory to murder. That got his attention.'

'I should hope so too.' Charlie's face brightened.

'Mickey told me he'd sold the woman two ID cards.'

'Horton and Oakes.' Billy scowled. 'How did she come to find him?'

'Mickey didn't know for sure. He's got a stall at one of those open-air markets. That's his front. She just turned up one day and told him what she wanted. Said she'd heard he could supply the goods. He fixed for them to meet next day at the Boar.'

'Did he give you a description of her?'

Grace nodded. 'It's a lot like the others we've got: dark-haired, ordinary-looking, no identifying marks. I showed him the sketches. He said the one with glasses could have been her.'

'Sounds like our lady. What do you reckon, sir?'

Billy turned to Chubb for his opinion and got a growl instead for his pains. The chief super seemed out of sorts today.

'I take it your visit to Richmond hasn't added to the sum of human knowledge, or you would have said so by now.' He glowered.

'Not at all, sir.' It was Billy's turn to look offended. 'In fact, I've got a story to tell you – one you may find hard to believe. It's about Alma Ballard and her father and some other bloke, and there's a good chance it connects to the case, though I can't tell you how just yet. Do you want to hear it?'

Chubb glanced at his watch.

'Not now. I have to see Cradock. Come back in an hour.'

'I heard on the wireless this morning this fog's here to stay for a while.'

Chubb stood by the window in his office peering out. The mist of morning still covered the city like a grey blanket. The air was still.

'A real pea-souper – that's what we're in for.'

The chief super spoke with gloomy relish. He turned to face Billy.

'So who is this Finch bloke? Do we really need to find him?'

'Mr Madden thinks so, and I reckon he's right.'

Billy smothered a yawn. Chubb had returned in even bleaker mood from his meeting with the assistant commissioner.

'That man's going to be the death of me. Now he wants a daily written report on the progress of the investigation. I know he's getting pressure from above, but I only have to mention the words "court martial" and he turns green. Luckily he'll be out of our hair for a couple of days . . . some conference in Manchester. Let's try and make the most of it.'

Billy had spent twenty minutes retelling the story that he and Madden had heard from Miss Dauncey's lips that morning. The chief super had listened to him in silence.

'She thought he might be an artist, but that was only a guess. I've told Poole to check with the Slade – Alma was a student there – and the Royal Academy too, in case they have a list of painters. There's also the London phone book. We'll check that as well, and see if we can find a Colin Finch who knows a Miss Ballard. But it's a common enough name, and we don't know if he even lives in London.'

'Yes, but *why*?' Chubb returned to his chair. 'Didn't Madden give you a reason? Does he think this chap is our shooter?'

'He didn't say so. But then he wouldn't, unless he was certain.'

'Well then?'

Billy shrugged. 'I don't think Mr Madden knows himself, not for sure. It's just a feeling he has. There was something about the story she told us, particularly the bit to do with Alma and this bloke Finch, that didn't seem right to him. He didn't buy the idea they'd been lovers. He reckoned it was something else. It's the sort of thing he used to pick up on, when I worked with him. You know as well as I do, sir, in a case like this you collect all sorts of facts, but only a few really matter, and Mr Madden had a gift for spotting them. Not that he always knew why: often it was just something he felt – a sort of instinct, I suppose – though he would have said it was simply a matter of paying attention. That's what he used to tell me.'

Billy chuckled.

'Antoine . . . He kept repeating that name in the car coming back, like it was supposed to mean something. Antoine.'

'That was what she called this bloke, right?'

Billy nodded. 'Miss Dauncey thought it might have been a special name, the kind lovers make up for each other, but like I say, Mr Madden had his doubts.'

'But he still doesn't know what it meant?'

'Not yet.' Billy grinned. 'But if you want to lay money on it, then I'm betting he soon will.'

24

'I've got nothing to report, sir. I just thought I'd give you a ring before I went home.'

Despite having spent the morning with his old chief, Billy had felt the need to talk to Madden again before the day was out. Just to keep in touch, he told himself. He had rung him at the house in St John's Wood, where the police car had dropped him on their return from Richmond.

'We still haven't located Finch. He wasn't either a student or a teacher at the Slade, and the Royal Academy has no record of him. We've been through the phone book too, and as far as we can tell he doesn't live in London. We'll have to spread our net wider.'

Madden had been down in the cellar when the phone rang, listening to the contractor, a man called Dakin, explain why they couldn't begin painting the back wall where the damp had been dug out and the wall rebricked. The plaster covering it was still too wet. He had insisted that Madden test it with his hand.

'It needs another day at least,' Dakin was saying, and the foreman in charge of the works, Milligan, had concurred.

'I was hoping we might start tomorrow, but Mr Dakin's right. We'll have to wait a bit longer.'

Earlier Madden had accompanied both men upstairs to inspect the rewiring under way in Aunt Maud's bedroom. Its aged occupant had been moved to her new temporary quarters without incident that afternoon, though the operation had called for the services of both Madden and Alice, each of whom had taken an elbow and supported the old lady as she moved with halting steps down the passage to the room prepared for her. Dakin had pronounced himself satisfied with the progress to date and promised they would be out of Miss Collingwood's hair by the end of the week.

He had arrived in the company of another man, whom he had introduced as an architect working for him on a separate project. And when he and Madden came back downstairs they had found this individual bent over an array of drawings spread out on the kitchen table.

'That's a new house we're building up in Blenheim Terrace.' Dakin had gestured at the plans as they passed through the kitchen on their way to the basement. 'The one that was hit by a buzz-bomb in '44 and taken out like a tooth – have you seen it? The houses on either side were hardly scratched.'

It had been a few minutes later, while he was crouching by the back wall obediently testing it with the tips of his fingers, that Madden had heard the phone in the hall start ringing. Shortly afterwards Alice's voice called from the kitchen to say it was the same gentleman from Scotland Yard phoning again.

'What about the Royal Artillery?' he asked Billy. 'Have you heard from them?'

'Not yet. The adjutant said it might take a while. Records of that kind – who was stationed where during the First World War – aren't stored at Woolwich. But he promised to track them down for me.'

'And nothing as yet on the woman?'

'We've had a couple of alerts. Two ladies called Horton recently moved into boarding houses – one in Putney, the other in Stockwell – but they're kosher. Police stations have been told to keep checking with hotels and boarding houses, and estate agents too. She could be on the move, shifting from place to place.'

Billy hesitated.

'Look, sir, I don't know what you feel about it, but it strikes me that whoever she is, she's altogether too comfortable doing what she's doing . . . buying those cards off Mickey Corder, changing names and identities.'

He had rung earlier in the afternoon to tell Madden about the arrest of the dealer.

'I'd assumed it was the man who had set her up. But if she's doing it herself, then I reckon she's bent. How else would she know about that world? So that raises a doubt again about Alma Ballard – about whether it could be her, I mean. Can you really see her behaving like a criminal? I can't. She wouldn't know how. If she is tied to this business, it must be in some other way.'

Billy waited, hoping for a comment. But all he got was a question.

'I take it you haven't heard back from the Mounties?'

'Not yet. But it's only been a day or two.'

'Then nothing's changed. The main thing is still to locate Finch. Keep trying, Billy.'

On his return to the kitchen Madden found Dakin drinking a cup of tea supplied by the thoughtful Alice.

'We'll be off in a moment, we're going up to Blenheim Terrace,' the contractor told him. 'Provided we can find our way, that is. Have you seen what it's like outside? Mark my words, we'll be fogged in by morning.'

He waited impatiently while his associate carefully folded his designs one at a time and slipped them back into the attaché case he had brought with him.

'I'll look in again on Wednesday to see how things are going. Will you be here, sir?'

'I'm sorry . . .'

Madden woke from his trance. He had lost track of time for a moment – and place.

'Yes . . . yes, most likely. I'll be staying until the work is finished.'

He accompanied their two visitors to the front door, bade them farewell and then watched as they strode off into the gloom.

'I'll be damned . . .' The words issued in a murmur from his lips.

Returning to the kitchen, he caught Alice's eye.

'Believe it or not, Alice, I've just had a moment of inspiration.'

'Have you really, sir?' Her motherly features glowed with pride.

'What I need now is your telephone book.'

Frustrating seconds were spent in a hunt for the object, but eventually it was unearthed beneath a pile of workmen's coats on a bench in the hallway. Having found the number he wanted, Madden dialled it and after only a brief delay was put through by the switchboard at the other end.

'I wonder if you could help me,' he said. 'I'm trying to get in touch with a Mr Colin Finch. I believe he's one of your members. Could you possibly check that and, if it's so, give me his telephone number and business address?'

He waited for more than a minute with the receiver pressed to his ear, tapping the pencil he had in his hand on a pad next to the phone.

'Yes, I quite understand.' He scribbled on the pad. 'That's very kind of you. Thank you.'

He replaced the receiver and dialled Billy's number at Scotland Yard.

'I've found him.'

'*Finch?*' Billy's yelp of surprise was reward enough. 'How the heck did you do that?'

'I remembered something Miss Dauncey told us. She said he was carrying a flat case when he called at the house, of the kind painters keep their sketches in. That's what made her think he was an artist. But she was wrong. He's an architect: they use the same sort of thing. I've just seen one.'

Billy whistled in appreciation.

'He's a member of the Royal Institute of British Architects: RIBA. His name's on their list. They wouldn't give me his home phone number – it's against their rules – but they let me have his business address. He works for a firm in London called Coulter & Stanhope. They've got offices on Piccadilly. It's too late to call on him now – he'll have gone home – but we can pay him a visit tomorrow.'

Madden paused.

'But we need to talk first, Billy, and I'd rather not do it on the phone. Can we meet first thing?'

'Yes, of course. But why? What for?'

Again Madden hesitated.

'Look, I've got an idea, but I'd rather not talk about it now. I want to think about it first. I've got a feeling Finch isn't what he seems to be . . . not from our point of view.'

'Do you mean he's not an architect?' Billy was baffled.

'No, he's that all right. It's his past I'm talking about – his and Alma's.'

'So you do think there was something between them . . . a relationship of some kind?'

'Yes, I suppose you could call it that.' Madden's voice was heavy with regret. 'But to tell the truth, I wish it weren't so.'

25

'MR FINCH? OH, DEAR, I'm really not sure if he's here yet.'

The well-permed lady at reception was in a dither. She had been in the midst of taking off her coat and hanging it on a peg on the wall behind her when Billy and Madden had entered the lobby and crossed the marble floor to her desk.

'I'm late myself this morning. It's this dreadful fog. The train from Leatherhead took forever. I don't know if Mr Finch is in yet. He lives out of London, too; in Abingdon. I imagine everyone's running late today. If you give me a moment I'll check and find out.'

Billy, for one, was glad of the delay. There was every prospect that the interview they were about to conduct would prove a bruising one and he wanted to be ready for it. Madden himself had made no bones about the challenge they faced when they had met earlier.

'My guess is he'll prove a tough nut to crack.'

His old chief had opened his mind to him when they'd conferred, and although Billy had guessed there was a surprise coming, he had not been prepared for the nature of it.

'I may be obliged to say some things that will startle you – and him, I hope. But better they come from me.'

They had met in a tea room off Jermyn Street soon after its

doors had opened. Walking down from Green Park tube station, Billy had found himself in a fog so dense it was hard to see more than a foot or two in any direction. Cars passing by in the street with headlights on had materialized out of the clammy greyness like undersea creatures and disappeared in a moment, their red rear lights blinking. With no clue at that stage as to what the older man had in mind, he had listened in wonder while Madden revealed the extent of his suspicions.

'As I said last night, I hope I'm wrong. But one way or another we have to find out.'

He had paused then, the tea room quiet around them. They had been the first customers of the day.

'I've had a night to think about this, Billy,' he said. 'I've realized I can do it alone.' He had peered at his companion. 'The worst that can happen is that he'll show me the door. Your situation's different. This could rebound on you and cause trouble at the Yard, particularly with Cradock. I don't want that to happen. It might be better if you stayed out of this.'

'No, sir.'

Billy's response had been immediate. As he told Chubb later, he wouldn't have been able to look himself in the eye if he'd allowed his old mentor to stick his neck out while he sat back.

'One way or another you're going to need official backing when you tackle Finch. He has to know it's serious.'

'So be it then.'

Nevertheless, experienced though he was, Billy had felt a flutter of nerves as they approached the headquarters of Coulter & Stanhope. A sleek structure dating from the thirties with a facade adorned with an Art Deco design of a woman dressed in flowing robes, it proved to be located some way down Piccadilly. Madden had led the way in through the glassed doors, and now they waited to see if the man they wanted to speak to had arrived yet.

'He is? Oh, that's good.' The lady behind the desk brightened. She looked up. 'I'm speaking to his secretary. She says could you tell her who you are, and why you want to see Mr Finch. He has no appointment scheduled for this morning.'

It was Billy who replied.

'My name is Styles. I'm a detective-inspector from Scotland Yard. This is Mr Madden. We need to speak urgently to Mr Finch.'

When her eyes widened in disbelief he took his warrant card out of his pocket and showed it to her.

She stared at it for a long moment. Then she spoke again into the phone, repeating what Billy had told her.

'I see.' She lowered the receiver. 'Miss Carter says she'll get back to me in a moment. Goodness . . .'

Breathless, she set about putting her desk in order.

When the phone rang again she snatched it up.

'Thank you, my dear.' She replaced the receiver. 'Mr Finch will see you now. Take the lift up to the third floor. Miss Carter will meet you there.'

'A visit from Scotland Yard! Well, this is a surprise. And I was just thinking how dull the day seemed, with all this fog.'

At ease and smiling, Colin Finch turned from the draughts-man's table where he was standing to greet his visitors. Dressed casually in an open-necked shirt, sweater and corduroy trousers, his glance took them in.

'And which of you is Inspector Styles?'

'That's me, sir,' Billy said.

'So you must be Mr Madden?'

He shook hands with them both.

'Give your coats to Miss Carter. She'll take care of them. And let's sit over there, shall we, and be comfortable?'

He pointed to a low table surrounded by easy chairs on the far side of the room. The office was spacious; besides the long draughtsman's table it also contained several cabinets and a desk that sat with its back to a large picture window, which in clear weather must have overlooked Piccadilly and the expanse of Green Park, but that day was darkened by the fog pressing close against the glass.

'And bring us some coffee, would you?' Finch spoke again to his secretary as he switched on a standard lamp.

Observing him, Billy thought that if he was unsettled by the sudden appearance at his place of business of an officer of the law, he certainly didn't show it. Lean and athletic-looking, Finch was just as Miss Dauncey had described him, right down to the small scar on his temple and the wedding band on his finger. And it was true – his hands did look sensitive, Billy thought, as Finch settled back in his chair opposite his guests and laced his fingers behind his head. What was lacking, though, was the hardness she had seen in his brown eyes. His gaze was neutral, and only mildly curious as he waited politely for one or the other of his visitors to begin.

'I'll get straight to the point, sir.' Billy was first to speak. They had decided that it would be best if he took the lead. 'One of the people we're seeking information about is a Miss Alma Ballard. I believe you're acquainted with her.'

'Yes, certainly.' Finch hesitated, but only momentarily, before replying. 'We met during the war.'

'Would that have been in the Middle East – in Cairo?'

'I see you're well informed, Inspector.' He smiled.

'Can you tell us when you saw her last?'

'Let me think . . . in June, it was. She was staying with her mother in Richmond. Would you mind telling me why you're asking these questions?'

The transition had been so smooth that for a moment Billy was thrown off-balance. He had to stop and collect himself, and during the brief interval that followed, Finch's secretary appeared carrying a tray with the coffee things on it, giving him further time to reflect.

'I'll get to that presently, sir.' He waited until the young woman had left the room. 'For now I'd be grateful if we could clear up a few points.'

Finch made a gesture with his hand: graceful, accepting. *Please continue*, it seemed to say. He leaned forward to pour their coffee.

'We're seeking information about Miss Ballard's past, including the time she spent in uniform. Sadly, with her mother dead, we've been forced to turn to other sources. Would you be in a position to help us?'

'Oh, I don't think so.' The architect shook his head. 'I only knew her for a short while.'

'Can you tell us why you went to see her?'

'There was no special reason.' Finch shrugged. 'It so happened my job took me to Richmond that day. I had some drawings to show to a client. I thought I'd look in on Alma. Someone had told me she was down there and I hadn't seen her for some time.'

'It was a casual call then?' Billy looked up.

'It was.'

'That's curious. Miss Dauncey, the lady who met you when you arrived, described your encounter with Alma Ballard in quite different terms. She happened to overhear your conversation from a room upstairs overlooking the terrace.'

'Did she indeed?' His eyes had narrowed, but only fractionally.

'Would you care to tell me the real reason you went to see her?'

As he put the question Billy felt the atmosphere change. This time the architect's pause was deliberate. He brought his hands from behind his head and laid them on his knees. Now, for the first time, Billy felt the effect of his gaze. The brown eyes had settled on his. They weren't smiling any longer.

'No, I don't think I would.' He spoke in the same quiet voice.

'I beg your pardon.'

'I can't tell you that. Or, rather, I won't. The subject of our meeting was private.'

The gauntlet had been thrown down, just as Madden had predicted.

'Mr Finch, this is a criminal investigation; a murder inquiry, in fact.'

'A murder inquiry . . . ?' He put a hand to his cheek and stroked it. Billy had the impression of a mind working rapidly. 'You should have said so.'

'You're required by law to help the police in any way you can.'

'I'm aware of that. But until you've said more – in particular how Miss Ballard could possibly be involved in a murder investigation – I don't feel obliged to answer any question that I feel is out of place.'

'And that would include any question about her?'

Billy had hoped the shot would go home – that he would at least get some reaction from it. But Finch was unruffled. His manner had changed in the last few seconds. He seemed a different person – cold, poised, very much on his guard. Billy pulled a notebook from his pocket. He needed a few seconds while he decided how best to proceed.

In the silence that ensued Finch turned to Madden.

'You're very silent,' he said. 'I assume you're not a detective, or you would have said so. But in that case, why are you here?'

'Yes, I ought to have explained.' Madden was apologetic. 'I used to be with the Metropolitan Police. Mr Styles and I are former colleagues. My name came up in this case he's investigating – it goes back many years – and he wondered if I could help him.'

'And can you?' His tone was challenging.

'I don't know. Let's see, shall we?'

Madden reached for his coffee cup. He took a sip and replaced it on its saucer. His movements were unhurried.

'At the conclusion of your visit to Richmond, Miss Ballard showed you something. Could you tell us what it was?'

'I've already made it clear I'm not prepared to discuss that meeting.'

'Did it have to do with her father?'

Finch offered no reply.

'Was it perhaps a letter from the War Office? I ask, because we happen to know that Miss Ballard was busy during her mother's last days going through all her papers, helping to get her life in order . . . before it ended. I'm sure she must have talked to you about her father. It was something she liked doing. She was very proud of him.'

'Indeed she was.' His expression was unchanged.

'Assuming it was such a letter, did it have anything to do with his death?'

Finch blinked. The reaction was momentary. But he had failed to hide his surprise. Nevertheless he maintained a calm exterior, running the tips of his fingers through his closely cut hair while he pondered his answer.

'I'm sorry, but that's something I'm not at liberty to discuss.'

'Not at liberty . . . ?' Madden weighed the reply. 'That's not quite the same thing as refusing, is it? Is that because she asked you not to reveal the letter's contents? Or are you just being discreet and tactful?'

'In contrast to you, Mr Madden – is that what you mean?' He glanced at his watch.

'So you do know that her father was convicted by a court martial in the First World War and executed?'

Finch looked down.

'I'm aware of it.' He spoke now in a different voice. 'Alma told me that day. She hadn't known about it before, and it had come as a terrible shock to her. All her life she had thought of him as a hero. She was extremely upset on the occasion you're referring to, desperately overwrought, which would explain the scene overheard by that lady. Alma had found the letter among Mrs Ballard's papers. God knows why her mother kept it. As I understood it, she had spent her whole life pretending it never happened. I felt enormous sympathy for her – for Alma, that is. I still do. But there was nothing I could do to help her, nothing I could say. I think she was in some kind of hell just then, and I could only pray that she would recover in the course of time.'

He looked up.

'There – is that what you wanted to hear? Perhaps you understand now why I was unwilling to discuss our meeting with you. It involved something deeply personal to Alma, deeply painful, and, quite frankly, none of your business. So unless you're prepared to be more open about this investigation that you say you are conducting, I suggest you both leave.'

Madden grunted. 'Yes, but that wasn't why you refused to say earlier why you went to Richmond, was it? You didn't know about the court martial until Alma told you. You had another reason for going to see her.'

Finch raised his eyes slowly. He gave his questioner a long look.

'Take care, Mr Madden.' His soft voice bore a hint of menace. 'You're on dangerous ground.'

'Am I?' Madden seemed unmoved by the threat. 'Or is it you who are treading on thin ice? It's clear from the brief exchange you and Alma had that, far from being merely "acquainted", you knew each other well – even if you weren't on the best of terms. I don't know what the cause of contention between you was; only that it had nothing to do with the death of her father. Whether you like it or not, you're obliged to reveal to Mr Styles anything you know about her. I have a feeling you're better informed on that subject than most. Of course you may think you're protected from doing so by the Official Secrets Act, but I believe you'll find those rules don't apply to a capital case.'

'I have absolutely no idea what you're talking about.' Finch stared at him.

'Haven't you? Then let me ask you another question, a simple one. It should be easy enough to answer. Why did she call you Antoine?' Madden waited, as though expecting an answer. When none was forthcoming he continued, 'And what did you call her? Sophie, Sylvie, Marianne, Giselle . . . ?'

'Have you lost your mind?'

'Because you both had names, didn't you: cover names? I imagine you were the circuit leader and she was – what? – your courier . . . your radio operator?'

Finch's gaze was stony.

'I'm talking about when you were in France together, Mr Finch: not the Middle East . . . not Cairo . . . When you were agents for SOE – the Secret Operations Executive. Because that's what you were. Am I right?'

Again he paused. Again there was no response.

'But what I don't understand is why you're so unwilling to talk about her. We've said nothing as yet to suggest we think she's implicated in this case. But the longer you stay silent, the more our suspicions will grow. Is there something in her past we should know about? What is it that you're hiding?'

Billy glanced at the still figure by the window. Hands on hips, Finch stood gazing out . . . at nothing, as far as Billy could see, except the fog that hung like a curtain on the other side of the glass, blocking all vision.

He looked at Madden; his raised eyebrows asked a question. Madden shook his head. *Leave him.*

Close on five minutes had passed since their last exchange, and Finch's only reaction so far had been to rise from his seat and walk to the window. Even this he had done unhurriedly and without any sign of the pressure he might have been under. Watching him, Billy could only wonder how often his nerve had been tested in the past; how often, indeed, his very life might have depended on his coolness.

The architect had said nothing so far in response to Madden's assertion. He had simply left them to wonder what was going through his mind.

Now, without warning, he turned on his heel.

'Very well.' He returned to his chair and sat down. 'Let's put our cards on the table. Before I say anything I want to know exactly what crime you are investigating and where it was committed. You've been very sparing with details up to now and unless you tell me everything, this conversation is over. In spite of what Mr Madden seems to think, I'm not obliged to speak to you. SOE operations are still classified, and while it's true I was employed by that organization during the war – as was Miss Ballard – I certainly won't discuss her past and what I may, or may not, know about her until I'm told what it is that you're after. For a start, I want to know on whose behalf you are carrying out this investigation, and what Mr Madden meant when he said it went back years?'

'On whose *behalf*?' Billy was momentarily lost for words. 'What do you mean, Mr Finch? This is an ordinary police inquiry. I'm responsible to my superiors – ultimately to the commissioner.'

'And no one else?'

Billy shook his head. 'If you think there's some other body behind this, I can assure you you're mistaken.'

'You've had no contact with the French authorities? You'll give me your word on that?' His eyes had hardened.

'The *French* authorities?'

Billy looked to Madden for enlightenment, but the older man could only shrug.

'Would you explain what you mean by that, sir?'

Finch jerked his head in emphatic refusal.

'Not at the moment; perhaps not at all. It depends. I told you: I want answers first. This murder you're investigating – when and where was it committed?'

Billy hesitated. He had a decision to make.

'I never said it was one murder, Mr Finch. In fact I'm investigating a series of killings. I imagine you have read about them in the newspapers. Four men have been shot dead in the past few weeks, and in different parts of the country, which answers your second question.'

He stopped. Finch was staring at him in astonishment.

'*Four* murders? *Those* four murders? Yes, of course I know about them. But what on earth have they got to do with Alma? Or me, come to that?'

'Sir, would you . . . ?' Billy caught Madden's eye.

He gave a nod of assent.

'When I said I used to be a police detective, that was true, but only part of the answer as to why I'm here. A more important reason is that I was present at James Ballard's court martial thirty years ago. He was in my company. Two of the men who've been shot sat on that court-martial board; a third was the medical officer who pronounced Ballard fit to stand trial; and the fourth was our corps commander, who approved the death-sentence.'

'God Almighty!' His stony exterior shattered, Finch stared at Madden in horror. 'That can't be true!'

'I'm afraid it is. Originally the police were searching for a man believed to be the killer of all four. Recently, however, information has reached them indicating that a woman yet to be identified is also involved, in what amounts to a plot to take the lives of those apparently held responsible for Ballard's death. In the circumstances, I'm sure you can understand how Alma's name came to their attention.'

'This is appalling.' Finch sprang to his feet. 'I can't believe it. I *won't*. No matter what you think, I can tell you from personal knowledge that Alma Ballard is a woman of extraordinary qualities and exceptional bravery. You have no idea how often she put her life at risk; of the dangers she confronted. I'm not exaggerating when I say I've never known anyone like her, and I doubt I ever will.'

Overcome by emotion, he turned away from them and stood with his head bowed. He was breathing heavily.

Madden put a hand to his brow. He, too, had been struck dumb; or so it seemed to Billy, as he watched his old chief struggle to find the words he sought.

'I have absolutely no doubt that what you say is true.'

On hearing Madden speak, Finch turned to look at him in wonder.

'In fact, when Miss Dauncey described her to us recently, I formed a picture of an extraordinary young person, unique in her way; but also quite unpredictable.'

Madden hesitated.

'Thirty years ago I witnessed a mockery of justice that I was helpless to prevent. It has haunted me ever since. I saw a sick man sent to his death for no other reason than it suited the demands of the military at the time. I would rather anything in the world than that James Ballard's daughter should have taken it on herself to right that wrong. But four men have already been killed and a fifth is in grave danger, and although as yet there's no evidence directly linking her to the murders, I believe she's the woman the police are seeking. All I ask is that you listen to what I have to say and make up your own mind. Either way, the question has to be answered.'

Seconds passed. The architect continued to stare at him. Finally, and without a word, he resumed his seat.

'Continue.' He spoke in a dead voice.

'Once the link between these murders was discovered, it was natural that the police would want to interview both Alma and her mother. However, they quickly learned that Mrs Ballard had died earlier this year and that shortly afterwards Alma emigrated to Canada.'

'It's the first I've heard of it.' Finch's gaze had narrowed. 'She never mentioned it to me. But if she's gone abroad, how can she be mixed up in this?'

'That's the question we've been asking ourselves. It was only after we had spoken to Miss Dauncey, and been given an account of your meeting with Alma, that Inspector Styles and I realized what an . . . unusual young woman she was. And I began to wonder if perhaps we'd been deceived by her – led by the nose. What if she'd returned from Canada secretly and set about taking her revenge on the men she held responsible for her father's execution? The question had to be asked.'

He stopped when he saw the architect was about to speak.

'I can already see a flaw in your theory.' Finch's voice had hardened. 'It's true Alma was distraught on learning the truth about her father. The pain of it was near unbearable to her. But what she couldn't know was whether or not the verdict was just.'

'Not when she spoke to you,' Madden agreed. 'But some time after she went to Canada the record of those proceedings was stolen from the Public Record Office in Chancery Lane and was never recovered. I was present at the court martial and can tell you it was a travesty of justice and the verdict a disgrace – facts that could well have been apparent from the record. The first murder took place towards the end of September, a month after the theft. The time-lag can be explained by the need to identify the prospective victims: to make sure that the right men were being killed. Let's suppose for a moment that Alma was party to the plot; even that it originated with her. What would she have needed to do? First lay a false trail. She had already announced her decision to emigrate before her mother fell ill, so that could have fitted in well with her plans. She booked her passage and sailed from Liverpool at the end of July. There's no doubt she went to Canada. But from that moment on, the only evidence we have that she remained there has come from Alma herself.'

'How did you arrive at that conclusion?'

'She wrote letters to her solicitor and to Miss Dauncey from Toronto, outlining a scheme she said she had to travel across the country by slow stages to Vancouver; the point being that if she wanted to muddy the water, and make her movements difficult to trace, that was the best way of doing it. The police here have asked the Mounties to help, but so far they haven't located her. If she is behind this plot, it's possible she returned to England soon after she reached Canada.'

'What about the letters she wrote?'

'Well, this, I admit, is pure speculation, but I remembered Miss Dauncey telling us that after her supposed posting to the Middle East, her mother continued to receive letters from her, which Alma must have written in advance and left behind in England for others to forward. It occurred to me she could have used the same device in Canada. All that was required was to find some person or agency that would post them for her at agreed intervals.'

He paused, perhaps expecting some further reaction from Finch; but the architect sat immobile, expressionless.

'If I'm right, she returned to England after a few weeks with a plan of action ready. First she stole the record – a daring act, but not as difficult to carry off as one might suppose. All it took was nerve. Now she had the names of her victims, but it took time for her to establish who they were and where they lived. In the meantime she set out to acquire some false identity cards.

This has been confirmed, by the way. The police have found the dealer in question; he admits selling the cards to a woman.'

'Has he been shown a photograph of Alma?'

'Not yet, sir.' It was Billy who answered. 'He was only picked up yesterday. But the woman we're looking for has been changing her appearance. She's described as a brunette by witnesses, but I noticed from a photo Miss Dauncey showed us that Alma was fair-haired. Even if this man doesn't recognize her from her picture, it won't rule her out as far as we're concerned.'

Finch grunted, but said nothing. Madden went on.

'She might have hoped the whole plan could be carried off without the motive for the murders being detected. The cause lay thirty years in the past after all, and there was no link whatsoever between the victims other than that single event: the court martial. But she was taking no chances. She stopped using her own name and, armed with the false identity cards, she went first to Ballater, in Scotland, where the doctor lived. He was shot towards the end of September. From there she went south, to Sussex. The second victim was a retired bank official in Lewes named Gibson. He was killed while out fishing, and the police have sufficient evidence to be able to place this same woman close to the murder site on the day in question. She had been using one of her aliases and had been in the area for a fortnight. It seems likely that she also called on Gibson on some pretext, in order to determine that he was the man she was seeking. Following that murder, and only a week later, the same woman called on the next victim, a retired schoolmaster in Oxford, posing as a collector for Remembrance Day, again in order to pin down his identity. He was killed a few days afterwards. The last man shot, Sir Horace Canning, was sufficiently well known not to need that kind of vetting.'

Madden paused to take stock.

'I haven't mentioned the gun that was used in these killings, but the police were able to establish quite quickly that the same weapon had been used in each case. And something else: the first three victims were all shot with iron-cored bullets, which according to experts here could only have been manufactured in Germany during the war, when they ran short of lead. Somehow these bullets found their way to England, most likely in a captured side-arm; a Luger in all probability. I mention this detail in the hope that it might mean something to you.'

Again he waited, hoping Finch would say something. The architect had paled slightly at his last words (or so it seemed to Billy, who was watching him closely). But he remained silent.

'Even before we spoke to Miss Dauncey, there was no escaping the fact that the woman the police were hunting was far from ordinary.'

Madden paused to give weight to his next words.

'Her ability to live in the shadows, to switch identities and change her appearance, to steal a court-martial record held under seal in a locked cupboard and leave no mark upon it, pointed to a person with experience well outside the norm: to someone used to living a clandestine life – to someone like Alma Ballard.'

At last the architect stirred. In the last few minutes he had shown signs that the tale he was hearing was having its effect, gnawing at his lip and at one stage putting a hand to his head. Now he sat forward.

'You make a strong case, Mr Madden.' His voice was calm, his tone even. 'But you're not being entirely truthful with me.'

'I'm sorry?'

'You neglected to mention the man you spoke of earlier: the one the police were searching for – the presumed killer. He played no part in your tale, I noticed. But then perhaps that's because you don't believe he exists.'

Billy glanced at his old chief. The look on Madden's face told its own story.

'You think Alma shot these men, don't you?'

Madden bowed his head in assent.

'I've never believed there were two people involved. I couldn't conceive of this being other than a solitary obsession, and since it's plain – to me at least – that Alma was the one who set the plot in motion, it must be her finger that was on the trigger. I would to God it were otherwise.'

His voice shook.

'The reason the police announced they were looking for a man was because a witness saw what he thought was a male figure approaching the second victim shortly before he was shot. The person was dressed like one, and the odd thing was that he knew he had been observed and seemed unworried by the fact. I believe that person was Alma, and she wanted to be seen dressed as she was. She had a knapsack with her and doubtless a change of clothes. When she walked back into Lewes later, it was as a woman.'

Finch sat like a statue, his face a mask.

'What do you want from me, Mr Madden?' He spoke at last. 'What do you expect me to say?'

'We need to understand how this came about. *I* need to understand. What drove her to it?'

His voice held a note of appeal. Then he pressed on.

'I can't believe the simple fact of her father's execution, however terrible, would have pushed her over the edge. There was something more, something from her past that helped lead her to make the choice she did. When she returned near the end of the war she was in deep depression. "Near catatonic" were the words Miss Dauncey used to describe her. Alma never revealed the cause of it; the only clue she gave was when she announced her decision to emigrate. She said, in effect, that she wanted nothing more to do with this country. We know how she felt about her father. But that wasn't the whole story, was it? What other pain was she carrying? What caused her to turn away from life? I think you know the answer.'

The morning had all but passed, but the day was no brighter. Dense fog still blanketed the wide picture window. A little earlier Finch's secretary had knocked on the door to remind him of a meeting of the firm's partners scheduled for noon, only to be told that he would not be attending it and she should alert the others to his absence.

As before, Finch had risen from the table following Madden's declaration, but this time, instead of going to the window, he had wandered about the office, hands in pockets and head bent, seemingly turning over in his mind what – if anything – he would say to them. At that moment he was standing in front of a framed drawing hanging on the wall above the draughtsman's desk. Turning, he caught the direction of Billy's glance.

'Palladio,' he remarked. 'Does the name mean anything to you, Inspector?'

'I'm afraid not, sir.'

'He was a sixteenth-century architect, probably the most influential in history. That's a house he designed near Venice.' He nodded at the drawing. 'His name is synonymous with harmony. When you see a Palladian villa you think: yes, of course, that's the only way it could be. He knew instinctively how to strike the right balance. Would to God Alma had been blessed with the same gift.'

Crossing the room to a cupboard, he returned with a bottle of wine and some glasses in his hands.

'Will either of you join me?' he asked.

'Thank you, sir. I'd better not.' Billy shook his head.

'I will.'

To Billy's surprise, he heard Madden accept. They watched as Finch opened the bottle and poured the wine.

'I met her first in the spring of 1943.' He resumed his seat. 'I was running a circuit in Orleans. And you were right, Mr Madden, my cover name was Antoine. Alma's was Chantal. She was sent over to be my wireless operator. It was a dangerous job; the Germans had good tracking equipment and they were relentless in chasing down radio signals. I had lost my last operator, also a woman. She had stayed on the air a little too long and, when the Germans burst in, she had shot it out with them rather than be captured. We all knew by then what lay in store for any agent who fell into their hands. Alma came with high recommendations. She was in the Signal Corps when she volunteered for SOE and was recruited mainly because of her French background. But she proved to be a natural. According to the people who trained her, she wasn't only intelligent and quick-witted; she had the capacity that was vital for our work of being able to assess a situation correctly and select the right course of action; all under pressure. Plus she was rated a crack shot.'

He caught Madden's eye.

'I soon realized I had a remarkable operative under my command. Alma slipped into her role at once. We already knew that women were generally better than men at assuming new identities; they seemed able to adapt to their new personas more easily; to live their lives more naturally outside the demands of their jobs. Alma was outstanding in that respect. She soon had a circle of acquaintances in Orleans who knew nothing about her clandestine activities, but provided the sort of camouflage needed to deflect suspicion. She was an expert WT operator, but even so I felt she was wasted in the role and I managed to persuade London to send me a replacement. Alma became my courier, and later on my second-in-command. She took over responsibility for organizing the reception of shipments of arms and ammunition sent over from London, usually by parachute drop. We were supplying two separate Maquis groups at the time, and she was my liaison officer. We were trying to get them to coordinate their operations – never an easy thing. The aim was to disrupt Nazi road and rail communications as much as possible, and Alma used to shuttle between them, offering advice and whatever else they were willing to accept in the way of encouragement. It was a job she proved adept at, not least because the men admired her. She was quite fearless. She used any excuse to join in their attacks on German convoys and emplacements, and before long the men were in awe of her; or so I was told. I don't know whether the connection between Orleans and Joan of Arc ever occurred to them, but it certainly did to me, and I warned her more than once to keep a rein on her thirst for battle. We were there to do a job, I told her, not to win medals, but even as I said it, I knew I was wasting my breath.'

His smile as he reached forward to refill their glasses was touched with sadness.

'The Nazis were never able to locate the Maquis camps – they kept shifting – but they knew what was going on and did their best to make movement in the area as difficult and dangerous as possible. God only knows how many times Alma was stopped and questioned, but she always managed to talk her way through the roadblocks, and the reason, I think, was because she was truly unafraid and the feeling communicated itself to the soldiers she encountered. Given how she was living and the risks she was taking, it was an extraordinary attitude of mind and something I've never really understood. Fear is natural, after all. It's part of what makes us human. But I never saw Alma show the slightest sign of it. However, I did get some insight into her when she told me about her father, how he had died a hero . . . the attack he was supposed to have led on the German trench . . . I expect you know the story – the one her mother told her?'

Madden nodded

'I never met her, the mother, but I wonder about her now. Just what did she think she was doing, creating that myth about a dead hero? What did she turn her daughter into? Some sort of throwback to the Middle Ages? I sensed Alma was somehow bent on living up to his example, and I warned her more than once against being reckless. But by now we were all working under intense pressure and there was nothing I could do but hope she would exercise good judgement. The invasion was in the offing, and we'd both been sent north to help with the efforts being made to disrupt the Nazi defences. We were dealing with a different lot of Maquisards and their commander had come to Le Mans, where I was setting up a new network with two of his men, to meet me.

'When they returned to their camp I sent Alma with them, travelling on her bicycle as she would need it later, while the men followed in a farm lorry. She was in the process of going through a German roadblock in the countryside as they came up behind her, and after she had passed the barrier she looked back and saw that they were in trouble. It turned out later that there had been a problem with one of the men's papers. In any event, it was enough for the officer who happened to be there inspecting the post – a lieutenant – to order the men to be detained, and as Alma watched from a little way down the road she saw all three of them being herded at rifle point into a nearby hut. I told you earlier how her gift for assessing a situation had been noted during her training. I'd had occasion to witness it in the past, along with her capacity for swift decision; and although I had recognized its value, I was also aware that if she had a weakness, it was this tendency to act on the instant, without reflection. At that moment, however, the gift stood her in good stead. She had realized at once that if the men ended up in the hands of the Gestapo, as was likely, it could prove fatal to the whole group, since one of the captured men was their leader. He would hold out under questioning for as long as he could – that went without saying – but in the end he would talk. Everyone did. There were four soldiers on duty at the roadblock, and the lieutenant made five. Alma was armed. She carried a pistol strapped to her thigh, on the theory that the average soldier wouldn't run his hands over that part of her body – he'd be too embarrassed – and she'd been proved right. She wheeled her bicycle back towards the roadblock.'

Finch drank from his glass.

'I received a full report of the incident later from Alma. London insisted on it. She made it sound quite simple. It was certainly over quickly. She retrieved her pistol and put it in a basket hanging from the bicycle's handlebars. By the time she got to the barrier the three detained men were inside the hut, with two of the soldiers guarding them. The other two challenged her as she came up to them, and Alma shot them without warning from close range and then gunned down the officer, who managed to draw his pistol, but got no further than that. The noise had brought one of the other two soldiers running out of the hut, but Alma killed him while he was still in the doorway. At that point, however, her pistol jammed; but just as the last soldier was raising his rifle to shoot her, he was tackled from behind by one of the men and, as they wrestled, Alma grabbed hold of the officer's pistol, which was lying on the ground, and finished the job.'

He drank from his glass.

'I still have trouble picturing the scene, and it took me a while to convince London that it had actually happened the way Alma described it. But in the end they reacted rather as you might expect. Although it couldn't be made public yet, Alma was awarded the highest decoration open to her, the George Cross; it was only granted for exceptional courage, for conspicuous bravery in circumstances of extreme danger. With the notification came a message from the King congratulating her. She was in tears when I told her. I knew she was thinking of her father.' He raised his glass to his lips.

Madden's gaze was thoughtful.

'That officer's pistol must have been a Luger – did she keep it?'

Finch nodded. 'It was better than the one she had, which had misfired anyway.'

'And I expect you had a certain amount of captured enemy ammunition at your disposal?'

Finch shrugged.

'Then that was how those iron-cored bullets ended up in England. She must have brought the gun back with her.' Madden brooded on the discovery. 'She returned in the summer of '44 Miss Dauncey told us, quite soon after the Normandy landings. Was there a reason for that?'

Finch studied the wine in his glass. He took his time replying.

'I don't imagine my answer will surprise you.' He spoke finally. 'It's what you came here to confirm.' His tone was bleak. 'As I said before, there was a side to Alma's character that had always given me concern. Unfortunately it was allied to what I most admired in her: her courage, her daring, her contempt for danger. But the speed with which she acted in a crisis, the confidence she had in her judgement, carried its own perils and I was aware that this certainty of hers, this lack of self-doubt, might one day lead to her undoing. Sadly I was proved right.'

He emptied the glass.

'The occasion came a few weeks after D-Day. The Allies had forced their way off the beaches, but the fighting was still intense. My particular organization was engaged in disrupting German communications wherever possible, cutting phone lines and mounting attacks on road and rail links. We were in action more or less continually, and Alma as usual was tireless. She had been due to meet with a sizeable group of Maquisards in the countryside south of Caen. We were expecting one of the biggest drops of the war, and Alma had been engaged in selecting and preparing a site to receive it. More than fifty canisters were going to be delivered and there had to be enough men on hand to deal with them. As it happened, Alma was late in reaching the rendezvous site – the Germans were scouring the countryside and the roads were more dangerous than ever – and just as she approached the place through a wood, she saw trucks filled with soldiers converging on it from all sides. There was nothing she could do but watch as battle was joined. It didn't last long. The Maquisards were outnumbered and a massacre followed. It was clear the men had been betrayed. They had walked into a trap.

'She managed to reach their camp later, but not before nightfall, and when she got there she found it in a state of chaos. One of the party at the drop zone had escaped the slaughter and found his way back. He was a recent recruit, the son of a prominent lawyer in Caen, and he'd been accused by the others of betraying the plan to the Germans. They had wanted to know how he alone had got away, when the rest had either been killed or captured. He had been badly beaten and, according to his accusers, had confessed to being an informer.'

Finch grimaced.

'One has to try to imagine the scene. For the moment no one seemed to be in control. The men were enraged: they had lost friends they'd fought side-by-side with for months. But at the same time it was clear to Alma that a more important question loomed. There was every likelihood that the traitor had given away the camp's location to the Germans. They had to move at once. There was no time to lose. Their captive was badly hurt, barely able to walk, but a solution was at hand. It was an unwritten law among the Maquis that they took no prisoners.'

Finch filled his glass again and drank from it.

'I expect you can guess what I'm about to tell you. Alma had always had this clarity of mind – the capacity to see what the situation called for and the courage to act on her conviction. The men knew what had to be done, but no one seemed ready to do it. Perhaps they had doubts about the informer's guilt. They continued to argue among themselves, but there was no more time to be lost. If they stayed there they might all be dead by morning. It was up to her to act on their behalf. She had the man they were holding dragged to his feet and taken a little way off. Then she carried out the execution herself.'

He buried his head in his hands.

'As soon as I heard about it I knew she had made a terrible mistake. Never mind the moral aspects of executing a man whose guilt was unproven. She had absolutely no right, even under the iron laws of the Resistance, to do what she'd done. Whatever punishment the man might have merited, it was up to his own people to deal with him. Our role had always been to support the French, to help them in any way we could; but we didn't control them and we certainly didn't have the right to dispense capital punishment where one of their nationals was concerned. What Alma had done could well be regarded as cold-blooded murder, and I knew there would be a price to pay. It didn't take long for the bill to be presented. That particular group of Maquisards were Free French, Gaullist, and the father of the boy who'd been shot by Alma – the lawyer I mentioned – was an important figure in the movement. The situation only worsened when doubts began to crop up about the alleged traitor's confession. It became clear that it had been beaten out of him; there was no corroborating proof.'

Finch put down his glass. He rubbed his face.

'I could see thunderclouds building up, and I wasn't surprised when I learned that Alma was being recalled to London. She was shocked when I told her. She was sure she had done the right thing and couldn't believe she'd be held to account for it. I put into her hands a detailed report I had written about the incident, which stressed the extreme urgency under which she had acted and pointed out that ultimately she had made the right decision, which was to get the men moving away from the camp site as soon as possible. I also sent a separate note to the head of our section pleading with him to stand by Alma and not forget her magnificent service record. I said we should do everything we could to support her, and offered to return to London myself if it was thought that would help at all.'

He stared at his hands.

'I don't know how much you know about our relations with the French, but they were never easy, and towards the end of the war they grew even worse. De Gaulle was determined that France should be an equal partner with this country and the United States, and he tended to take offence at any slight, real or imagined. It was Alma's bad luck to find she'd become a cause célèbre as far as the Gaullists were concerned. They were out for blood. They wanted her head. At first they demanded that she be arrested and charged with murder. The only concession they were willing to make was that the trial could wait until after the war, when it could be held in France. Our section head did his best. He fought hard, and in the end he got them to settle for her dismissal from the service. But she had to be disgraced; the French insisted on it. She was stripped of her George Cross and given a dishonourable discharge from the WAAF. When you arrived this morning and mentioned her name, my first thought was that the French authorities hadn't given up on the case and were trying to get her arrested and charged through the civilian courts. Needless to say, I had no intention of helping you.'

'Yet you and Alma seemed to have fallen out, when you went to see her at Richmond?'

Madden had waited for a few moments before putting the question.

'That's because she thought I had turned against her, along with everyone else. Apart from the report I sent to headquarters and the note I gave Alma, I wasn't permitted to play any part in what followed. The war was still going on, remember, and I heard about her only intermittently. The news of her disgrace didn't reach me until I had left France. I won't go into the details, but once the work of the Resistance began to peter out, I was transferred: first to Italy and then to the Balkans. All that is still top secret – the Reds had become the threat by then – but the upshot was that I didn't get back to England until early in 1946, when I tried at once to get in touch with Alma. I knew how wretched she must be feeling and I thought I might be able to comfort her. I couldn't have been more wrong. I found her living in a flat here in London, but when I called on her she simply refused to speak to me. She shut the door in my face. I wrote to her and tried to see her again after a few weeks, but with the same result. I realized then that she held me as much to blame as anyone – perhaps more so, since I had been her commanding officer – and she wouldn't listen when I tried to explain how I'd been posted to another theatre and had been literally out of touch for months. And that was how it continued. I never gave up. I made several attempts to see her and talk to her, but I was always rebuffed. Alma was, as I've said, and as others may have told you too, a person of extremes. She could never strike a balance.'

He stared into his glass.

'My visit to Richmond was the most recent attempt I made to see her, and you know the outcome. If anything, she seemed more disturbed than ever, and when she took me into the house I understood why. "Look at this," she said, and thrust that War Office letter into my hands. I must say my heart turned to lead as I read it: just a single paragraph notifying the recipient that Private James Ballard had been found guilty of desertion by a court martial and executed on such-and-such a date. "Like father like daughter," she said. Her voice was chilling. "But then we never know our true enemies, do we? Those we should really go in fear of?" And that was all. She refused to say another word. She simply stared me down until there was nothing I could do but pick up my things and leave.'

He got to his feet again and walked over to the window. As

before, he stood looking out at the grey curtain of fog. Almost motionless in the windless air, it seemed one with the silence that had fallen on them all.

'I can see now that she must always have been at odds with life. There was a part of her that was always separate, as if her real life was being lived in her imagination. To the men she fought with, it gave her a sort of aura. They saw her as different from themselves – almost as someone sacred. She formed no relationships, you know . . .'

He turned as if to make sure that his listeners had understood him.

'And although she was attractive enough – not beautiful, but with the sort of dash and courage that would have drawn men to her – they seemed to understand that she wasn't made of common stuff . . . that in a sense she was untouchable. And perhaps she preferred it that way.'

He shrugged.

'I valued her more than I can say, and loved her for what she was – free and without fear – but I did find myself wondering how she would cope with life after the war; how she could keep that wild spirit of hers uncaged. I thought it unlikely she would ever be at ease in the world.'

He drew a deep sigh.

'But I never dreamed she would turn her back on it.'

'Forgive me.'

Finch turned from the window at last and crossed the room to rejoin them. He had been standing there for long minutes, silent and immobile; when he approached they saw the grief written on his face.

'I've been thinking . . . I've just realized . . . This must be the saddest day of my life.'

He sat down.

'Will she hang?' he asked.

'That's not for me to say . . .' Billy began his reply, but then stopped. 'No, I'll be honest with you, sir. I don't see how she can avoid it, not unless she finds a clever lawyer and pleads insanity.'

'Insanity.' Finch's laugh was bitter. 'Well, I doubt anyone could claim she's in her right mind, but that won't make any difference. Alma would never stoop to ask for pity. What she's doing now is her duty by her father as she sees it, nothing more. Call it insane if you like, but she won't be deflected. It's not in her nature. She'll play the game to the finish.'

He sat silent, nursing his pain. Then he gathered himself.

'I would offer to help you if I could, but I doubt it would serve any purpose. Alma has turned her back on me. What I can offer you, though, is counsel. It sounds to me as though she has reverted to her time as an agent; she seems to be following the same rules, behaving as though she's living among the enemy. That means she won't be predictable. Look for her to surprise you. And one other thing: she'll have a bolthole, what we used to call a *cachette*. Most likely it will be a room somewhere that she only uses in emergencies. So even if you think you've got her on the run, she may still outwit you.' He looked at them. 'Have you any idea of her whereabouts?'

'Not really.' Billy shook his head. 'She may be in London: those identity cards were bought from a local dealer and, after Richmond, this is the place she knows best. But we can't be certain. It may depend on where her next target is.'

'You said there was a fifth man in danger?'

'He's the officer who conducted the court martial,' Madden said. 'I didn't make a note of his name at the time. It would be in the record, though.'

'Which only Alma has seen . . .' Finch nodded grimly. 'And by now she'll have tracked him down.' He was thoughtful. 'Aren't you surprised he isn't dead already? I would have thought he'd have been first on her list.'

'We've wondered about that.' Madden grunted. 'It may mean he's no longer alive. That would be a blessing, in more ways than one. But we can't count on it.'

Finch nodded in understanding. He glanced at his watch. It seemed he had said all he had to say, and Billy sought Madden's eye. It was time they were going.

'One last thing . . .' The architect collected himself. 'One final warning – and this is crucial. Remember you're dealing with a dangerous opponent, even a deadly one. Give her the chance to defend herself and you may regret it.'

'I appreciate that, sir.' Billy swallowed. 'I won't forget it.'

'I've already told you how swiftly she can react. It's unlikely even your most experienced officers will have come across anyone quite like her. The fact, too, that she's a woman may tend to give them a false sense of security. They had better not make that mistake.'

'I understand, sir.'

'I asked you if you thought she would hang for these crimes, but frankly I don't think that will happen.'

He paused then, as though to be sure that his words were fully grasped.

'You understand what I'm saying, don't you, Inspector?' He peered at Billy.

'Sir?'

'I'm saying I doubt you'll take her alive.'

26

'COME ON, LUV, TAKE another look. See if you can make up your mind. Is it her or isn't it?'

Joe Grace pointed at the copies of the sketches he and Lily had brought with them. They were lying side-by-side on the table in front of Hilda Carey.

'Get a picture of her face in your mind, first. Then look at these two drawings and think: does either one of them, or both, look anything like her?'

He caught Lily's eye and scowled. They were standing in the kitchen belonging to the boarding house Mrs Carey ran, a room still smelling of the breakfast she must have cooked for her tenants earlier that morning. Lily thought she could detect the smell of the sausages that might have sizzled in the large frying pan sitting on the stove, and heard her stomach rumble in sympathy. Their departure from the Yard had been hurried; she hadn't had time to slip up to the canteen for her usual bacon-and-dripping sandwich.

Only a hop and a skip away from Earls Court tube station, the boarding house was one of many such in that particular area of London. Indeed, they had arrived to find Mrs Carey enjoying a cup of tea with another landlady, one Edna Garfield, who had walked over from her own residential hotel (as she described it) nearby to enjoy a mid-morning chat with her friend, and who wasn't best pleased to have had it interrupted. She was sitting now at an angle to the table with her arms folded and a look of haughty disapproval on her angular face.

What had brought Grace and Lily hotfoot from the Yard – though that hardly described their halting progress in a police car through the fog-bound capital – was a message from Earls Court nick to the effect that a woman by the name of Emily Horton had, until recently, been one of Mrs Carey's tenants.

How recently?

Up until two days ago, it turned out when they reached the address given them and found two detectives waiting there, together with a uniformed officer. What Joe had demanded to know, with his usual bluntness, was why this Horton woman's recent presence in the boarding house had only been reported that morning, when the Yard's advisory about the two women's names had been sent to all police stations in the capital three days earlier.

'It's taking us a while to check all of them,' one of the detectives, the senior of the two, an ageing DC called Ringwood, had explained defensively when Joe had put the question to him. 'We're still not done. You wouldn't guess how many boarding houses and the like we've got around here. Not to mention the knocking shops that don't even register, but have to be checked just the same. Plus it was over the weekend and we were short-staffed.'

'She left on Saturday,' Mrs Carey had told them when they enquired. 'She only stayed a week. Said she was down from Birmingham looking for a job in cosmetics. Mind you, she wasn't one for a chat. Slipped out every morning quite early and only came back late in the evening. She didn't have a ration card – said she'd forgotten to bring it – but that didn't matter. She took her meals out.'

Asked to describe the woman, Mrs Carey had scratched her head.

'I'd call her ordinary-looking,' she had said, finally, smoothing the blonde locks she'd disturbed, which Lily could tell were dyed. 'Not pretty; quite plain, really. Her hair was a sort of brownish colour.'

'Sort of *brownish*?' Joe had been struggling to keep his temper. 'What does that mean?'

Lily had intervened.

'Do you reckon it was dyed?' she asked, and Mrs Carey's face had brightened at the question.

'I'd say so. Yes. It didn't look quite right; not her natural colour, if you know what I mean.' It had been clear from her expression that she didn't think her own tresses suffered from the same defect. 'To tell the truth, it looked a bit mousy.'

Joe had pulled out the sketches he had in his pocket then and showed them to her. Mrs Carey had looked at them for a long time; first at one, then the other, then back again.

'I don't know,' she'd said finally. 'I really don't. I mean it could be anyone.'

At that point Lily had imagined she could see steam coming out of Joe's ears.

Now they waited to see if the one last look that Joe had asked the landlady to take would bear any fruit. Mrs Carey bent closer to the table to study the drawings.

'I know 'er.'

The two detectives turned as one to see Edna Garfield pointing a bony finger. Mrs Carey's guest had been sitting silent for so long that they'd forgotten about her presence. Unable to keep her curiosity in check, she had quietly shifted her chair round so that she could look at the two drawings.

'That one there. She lodged with me a fortnight ago; she only stayed a week.'

She was indicating the sketch of the woman who had called on Mrs Singleton at Oxford.

'She had her hair done up in much the same way. Very smart she looked. Bit high-and-mighty, I thought. She never had time to stop for a word.'

'What was her name?' Lily asked before Joe could open his mouth. 'Do you remember?'

'No, I don't.' Edna Garfield was positive. 'It wasn't Horton, though.'

Her face lit up.

'But we can find out. It'll be in my register.'

Lily halted in her tracks. A howl of pain had just come from out of the fog in front of her.

'Bleeding Jesus!'

The voice was Joe's. By the sound of it he'd just walked into something, a lamp post most likely. Moments later Mrs Garfield could be heard offering supporting testimony, though the obstruction in question was not the one Lily had imagined.

'I'd forgotten about that postbox,' she said.

Moving forward cautiously, Lily came upon them. Joe was bent over, rubbing his knee.

'Cor, isn't it dreadful?' Edna Garfield regarded him with a sympathetic gaze. 'I've never seen the like of it. Twenty years and more I've been walking up and down this road, and I'm still not sure exactly where we are.'

Lily, too, had seen nothing to match it – the fog – though, like all Londoners, she'd experienced her share of pea-soupers. The newspapers said they were caused by the thousands of household fires: the smoke they sent up through the chimneys. That and what the weather experts called 'singular atmospheric conditions', which kept the air hanging motionless for days over the great urban sprawl. But whatever it was, as time went by the fog turned into something more like a clammy sponge. And the colour changed, too; it wasn't grey as before, but had patches of reddish-brown in it, streaks of ochre, and Lily reckoned it wasn't only the smoke from the fires that was trapped in it, but a lot of the soot as well. How else to explain the grime that you would find on the cuffs and collars of blouses and shirts at the end of each day?

'No, wait – there's Parson's.' Mrs Garfield had just spotted a grocery shop window beside them on the pavement. 'I know where we are. It's just a few steps further on.'

They had left Mrs Carey's and were accompanying her back to her own abode, which she had assured them was only a short walk away and which Lily, counting the streets they had crossed and the corners they had turned, calculated was no more than two and a half blocks distant from Earls Court Road. Earlier, before they had quit the boarding house, she and Joe had conferred.

'Sarge, I've got an idea,' Lily had said. 'If this is the same woman and if she's the one we're looking for, then maybe she's not straying far from Earls Court. All she really needs to do is keep changing her name and her appearance. It sounds as though she only moved a few streets to come here. Perhaps she's done the same thing again: maybe she's holed up somewhere nearby.'

Joe Grace had thought it over, his hatchet face set in a scowl. Lily had had some misgivings when she'd learned that he'd been added to their team and that she'd be working under him. He had the reputation of being a hard man – a right sod, to quote a detective she'd worked with on another case a couple of months earlier. But the bloke in question had been a lazy bugger, always ready to cut corners and never short of a sly dig at her expense, and she would say this for Joe (though she didn't call him that, not to his face): he was yet to make a reference to her sex or even hint that it might be a drawback. And if his manner was abrupt, which it was, and he made little effort to put himself out, at least he treated everyone else the same way, and Lily asked for no more than that.

'So what you're saying is that we ought to pull in more men and blanket the area, check every hotel and boarding house in a one-mile radius? And then hope we're not wrong?'

'Something like that, Sarge.' Lily wasn't sure how he was taking her suggestion.

Joe's eyes narrowed. When he smiled, his pockmarked face split into a grin that had more crocodile than man in it. (Or so Lily reckoned.)

'We'd have to check with the chief super first. We'd need his authority.'

There'd been no sign of their own guv'nor that morning. But shortly after Lily arrived at the office the switchboard had called to report that Inspector Styles had left a message with them to say he would be late getting in.

'It's not a bad idea.' Grace had thought it over. 'But I want to have a look at that register first.'

'Here we are,' their guide announced.

They followed her up a shallow flight of steps to a door with a sign affixed to the wall beside it, saying *Rooms to Rent*. Inside was a dimly lit hallway with a reception desk. Mrs Garfield slid behind it. She reached under the counter and came up with a hefty ledger, which she plonked on the desk and then opened at a place marked by a ribbon.

'Let me see now . . .'

The two detectives watched as she ran her finger up and down the pages.

'A week ago . . .'

The finger stopped. She bent lower.

'Yes, here we are. She checked out the Saturday before last.'

'What's her name, though?' Lily couldn't contain herself. 'What did she register under?'

Edna Garfield bent even closer to the page, a frown knotting her brow.

'Ooh, I can't read her writing – what's that she's written?'

'Here, let me see.' Joe's patience, never abundant, had expired. Reaching for the book, he spun it round and scanned the page. His finger moved . . . then stopped.

'Well, well.'

His eyes glittered; his grin was truly reptilian now, a crocodile poised to bite.

'Oakes . . .' he said, savouring the name. 'Mary Oakes.'

'Right? Everyone got that straight? Nobody touches her. Nobody looks at her. I don't know how long we'll have to wait inside, so any of you needs to relieve himself, he'd better do it now.'

Joe Grace glared at the four men standing in front of him – two of them were plain-clothes officers, the other two uniformed constables – not sure as yet that his words had been taken in and fully digested.

'If she spots any one of you before she reaches the hotel, she'll scarper and it's odds-on we'll lose her in this fog. So stay out of sight. That applies particularly to the uniforms. Keep your distance, but be ready to block the road and pavement in both directions if you hear a police whistle. Any questions?'

Standing at his shoulder, Lily couldn't help but feel pleased with herself. Her suggestion that they cast a net over all lodging houses and hotels in the vicinity had borne fruit even sooner than she had hoped. Little more than an hour had passed since Grace had received the chief super's sanction to put the plan into effect, and soon afterwards, before most of the police reinforcements summoned from surrounding districts had even got there, word was received at Earls Court police station that one of their own beat-bobbies had struck oil.

'He was checking the register at a ladies-only establishment called the Regal up near the Brompton Road,' Joe had told Lily after speaking on the phone to the officer involved. 'She's gone back to using the name Oakes again. It looks like she's switching from one to the other. She checked in on Saturday, soon after she left the boarding house. It's only a ten-minute walk up there.'

With Chubb's approval and the station commander's help, Joe had put a team together quickly. Besides the four men posted outside the hotel, he had enlisted the services of a senior detective he knew well, a sergeant named Braddock, and once they had got to the Regal and he'd seen the lie of the land, Joe had directed him to wait there in case their quarry turned up unexpectedly, while he distributed the rest of his forces. Now, having given them their instructions, he and Lily returned to the hotel, where he explained to her what her role would be.

'I want you to sit in the lobby,' he said. 'You can either be a new guest waiting to move into her room or a visitor come to pick up a friend. But look as though you just happen to be there.'

Joe himself had resolved to wait for the elusive Miss Oakes in her room, along with Braddock – a decision prompted by the single-sex nature of the establishment.

'If she comes in and sees two men sitting there in the lobby, chances are she won't stop to wonder who we are. She'll make a run for it.'

Initially, however, his plan had met with opposition from the manageress, a smartly dressed lady with well-coiffed grey hair named Mrs Holly.

'We simply don't permit men on the upper floors,' she had explained earnestly to Joe, whose look of sheer incredulity as he listened had almost caused Lily to split her sides; she had had to bite her tongue to stop herself from guffawing. 'They may call here for our young ladies, but they can only do so from the lobby.'

Having informed her, in somewhat brutal terms, that the only young lady they were there to call on was a person they had every intention of removing from the premises in hand-cuffs, Grace had eventually secured her reluctant agreement to his scheme. The two men would take up their positions in Miss Oakes's room on the second floor. Lily would remain in the lobby, cooling her heels. When their quarry returned, Lily would wait until she was on her way upstairs and then call Joe on the house phone to alert him.

Once again the thorny question of identification had arisen. Mrs Holly had peered long and hard at the two sketches, before announcing that she couldn't say for certain that either one was necessarily her guest.

'She does wear glasses, it's true,' she said. 'I suppose that one on the right could be her, but I wouldn't swear to it. Her hair looks different.'

Miss Oakes had made a reservation by telephone a few days before her arrival. She had given a home address in Ipswich, and although Mrs Holly admitted that she had not checked the details carefully – one didn't these days – it was doubtless the same as the one on the identity card that Miss Oakes had shown her. She had left the hotel soon after nine o'clock wearing a coat and hat.

'She said she was expecting a letter. She first asked me about it yesterday, and I had to tell her it hadn't arrived yet. But it came with the midday post. I have it here.'

Mrs Holly had pointed to an envelope lodged in one of the pigeonholes behind the reception desk.

'And before you ask, Sergeant Grace, I can't let you have it without authorization – a warrant or some such thing. What-ever she may have done, it still belongs to Miss Oakes.'

For a second Lily had thought Joe was going to make an issue of it. His gaze had hardened as he listened to the manageress and, knowing how unpleasant he could be when he chose, she had held her breath. But he'd surprised her by simply shrugging.

'That's fine by me. You can give it to her when she comes.'

Grace had taken Lily aside.

'We'll find out what's in it later,' he told her. 'This is starting to get interesting. I'm only sorry the guv'nor's not here. He ought to be in on this.'

Lily, too, had wondered what was keeping Styles that morning.

Left to her own devices now, she surveyed her surroundings. The lobby was small, but some effort had gone into its decoration. A pair of oil paintings – landscapes both – hung on the wall, and the floor was covered by a carpet that might have been Persian. The whole place had a genteel air that went with the well-cut skirt and blouse Mrs Holly wore and the string of pearls she was playing with nervously, as she watched Lily take her seat on one of two armchairs placed on either side of a small settee.

The manageress had hoped to absent herself from whatever was to follow. She had decided on her own initiative to post her secretary, a middle-aged lady named Miss Haynes, at the reception desk, while she herself sat in the office behind keeping an eye on developments through the window that separated them, but well out of the way of any unpleasantness that might occur. However, she had made the mistake of revealing this plan to Joe Grace before he went upstairs, and once he'd realized that she was the only person who could identify Mary Oakes – it seemed her secretary rarely emerged from the office – he had insisted that she remain on duty at the desk.

'We won't know it's her unless you tell us.'

She had paled as he pointed out the obvious.

'You've got to tip us the wink, luv.'

Lily looked up from the newspaper she was pretending to read. A young woman wearing a coat had come into the lobby, but she had reddish hair and wasn't wearing glasses. Mrs Holly greeted her by a name and handed her a key.

Lily glanced at her watch. She had been sitting there for close on an hour and had seen several women pass through the lobby, most of them young. Two had been new arrivals who had come laden with luggage. Others had entered and collected their keys from Mrs Holly, before taking the lift or the stairs to go up to their rooms. Tense at first, Lily had gradually settled into the routine, glancing up from the newspaper she was pretending to read at each new face, checking Mrs Holly's for any sign of recognition. Although she had impressed on the manageress the need to act normally, Lily knew from experience that you couldn't count on civilians to behave as though nothing was going on.

'Just give her the key and the letter when she comes,' Lily had said. 'We'll do the rest.'

But she had noticed, as the morning wore on, that Mrs Holly was becoming more agitated, rather than less so. She had already disappeared twice into the ladies' room at the back of the lobby, leaving Lily to wonder what would happen if Miss Oakes were suddenly to make an appearance. No doubt the secretary, Miss Haynes, would come through from the office to give her the room key. But it was unlikely she would greet her by name or hand her the letter. However, Lily knew what her room number was – 203 – and she could see the hook where it was hanging on a board behind the desk.

Not for the first time that morning the phone behind the reception desk rang. It was attached to a switchboard, and Lily had seen Mrs Holly connect several callers to rooms upstairs. This time, however, after a brief hushed conversation, she beckoned urgently to Lily.

'It's for you, Miss Poole.' She seemed to struggle for breath. 'It's Scotland Yard.'

Lily jumped to her feet. She crossed the lobby in a few steps and grabbed hold of the instrument.

'Poole here . . .'

'Chubb speaking. What's the situation there? Quickly now.'

Something was up. Lily could tell. The chief super's voice was fraught with tension.

'Sergeant Grace is waiting upstairs in her room with another detective. He's got four men outside in the street. I'm down in the lobby. When she arrives and collects her key from the desk I'm supposed to tip him off.'

'Can I speak to him . . . Grace?'

'I'll have you put through.'

'Wait. Listen. This woman is dangerous, do you understand?'

'Sir?'

'*Dangerous*, Detective. She's our shooter.'

'Jesus!'

Lily spoke before she could stop herself. She met Mrs Holly's glance. The manageress was standing on the other side of the reception counter, staring at her open-mouthed.

'Have you got that? She's a killer . . . and I'm not just talking about the men she's topped in the last few weeks. She's got a gun, and by God she knows how to use it.'

'But how do you—?'

'Never mind that now. Inspector Styles is on his way. He'll fill you in. Is there any way you can warn the men in the street?'

Lily thought. 'I could slip outside for a moment and tell one of them. He could pass the word to the others.'

'I take it none of you is armed?'

'Christ, sir . . . no, sir.'

'Then don't try to tackle her – not you, I mean. Let her pass through the lobby when she arrives. Now put me through to Grace.'

Lily tried to catch Mrs Holly's eye. But the manageress's gaze wasn't fixed on her any longer. She was looking over Lily's shoulder. Her mouth hung open.

'May I have my key, please?' The voice came from behind Lily's back. A woman came up beside her. Lily caught a glimpse out of the corner of her eye of a coat cuff and a gloved hand. 'And is that my letter there?'

The gloved hand was pointing at the pigeonhole.

Lily didn't dare look at her face. She kept the receiver pressed to her ear.

'Poole, are you there? I said put me through.' Chubb was getting testy.

'Er, no, I'm afraid I can't do that right now . . .'

'What?'

Mrs Holly had been standing as though paralysed behind the reception desk staring at the woman, whose face Lily hadn't seen yet. Now, like a robot coming to life, she reached stiffly for the envelope in the pigeonhole behind her and handed it over.

'I'm going to have to wait here a bit longer.' Lily fancied she could hear the false note in her own voice. 'We were supposed to meet, Annie and I, but she hasn't shown up yet.'

'Is she there?' Chubb had lowered his voice to a whisper.

'Yes, that's right.'

'Keep talking then, and stick to your plan. As soon as you get the chance, call Grace and warn him.'

The envelope had disappeared into the woman's coat pocket – Lily had been able to see that much out of the corner of her eye. She'd been holding her room key in her hand. But now she laid it on the counter.

'I've just remembered, there's something I have to do.' She spoke in a neutral voice. 'I'll be back in a few minutes.'

She turned without haste and made for the street door.

Lily stole a quick look over her shoulder. The woman had a small suitcase in her hand. She wasn't hurrying, but she knew all right – she had guessed – and Lily was as sure as she was of anything that if she let her go now, it would be the last they would see of her.

'Just a moment, Miss . . .'

Dropping the receiver onto the counter, she ran after her and at the same moment the woman spun on her heel. Lily just had time to note the athletic whirl of her body before she saw the case coming towards her and realized it was too late to duck. The corner caught her just above the eye and, as she went down, she heard Mrs Holly's scream.

Stunned, Lily found herself lying half-conscious on the carpet; she was flat on her back. The screaming had continued and, as though in a dream, she saw the back of the woman disappearing out of the door.

With an effort she managed to roll over and drag herself to her knees. Behind the desk Mrs Holly seemed rooted to the spot. She had stopped screaming, but now she was gasping, struggling to get air into her lungs. There was someone with her, Lily saw, and she supposed it must be Miss Haynes. Her own mind seemed to be operating like a tractor in slow gear, while her limbs felt leaden. Yet somehow she pulled herself to her feet.

She had one thought in mind now, and only one – to blow her whistle – and she stumbled across the floor to the street door and dragged it open. The cold air came as a shock and, as she stood wavering on the steps, a shadow moved in the swirling fog – it was a car passing by in the street – and she heard running footsteps away to her left. Unsteady on her feet and fearful of falling, she stumbled down the steps to the pavement, searching for her whistle in her bag, scrabbling about with her fingers until she found it. But as she put it to her lips she heard a shout. Then a shot rang out. It was followed by another, and all at once the foggy street was filled with noise. Men were shouting, a police whistle sounded; and then, louder than all the rest, she heard the metallic crash of a collision and the noise of breaking glass.

Lily started to run down the pavement in the direction of the disturbance, but the effort made her head reel and, when she put her hand to her brow, it came away bloody. One of her eyes had gone blind and she realized it must be from the blood that was flowing down her face. She tried to get her bearings, but the ground was tilting under her feet, and before she had time to grab at a nearby lamp post for support, her legs gave way and she passed out.

27

BILLY PAUSED AT THE door for a moment to watch as a detective from the Yard's forensic squad sprinkled powder on the glassed top of the dressing table. Even from where he was standing he could see the prints come up clearly on it. The men had been hard at work for the past half-hour lifting dabs, but whether they belonged to Alma Ballard was still anyone's guess, and Billy knew he wasn't alone in hoping that they would have run their quarry to earth long before that particular question was resolved.

'This fog won't last forever. She can't hide for much longer. Those ID cards are no use to her now. And if she uses her own name, which she may, we'll nab her.'

The view was Chubb's, and it had been forcefully expressed soon after the chief super's arrival from the Yard to inspect the scene. Billy had taken him up to Mary Oakes's room. It had already been searched from top to bottom, though with little result.

'She didn't have much with her,' Billy had told his superior. 'Just a couple of dresses in the wardrobe, and some underwear and what-have-you in the drawers. It looks as if she kept whatever was important to her in that case she was carrying.'

'The one she hit Poole with?'

Chubb had been fuming when he heard what had happened in the lobby.

'I told her *not* to tackle that woman. It was a direct order. She could have been shot.'

'Yes, but you've got to see it from her point of view, guv.' Surprisingly, to Billy at least, it had been Joe Grace who had sprung to Lily's defence. 'She knew the woman had twigged what was going on. It was that manageress's fault – that Mrs Holly. According to Poole, she was staring at Oakes as if she'd seen a ghost. When she took off – Oakes, that is – Poole went after her. I'd have done the same.'

'You would, would you?'

Billy saw that what Chubb was actually feeling was relief that none of his people had been seriously hurt; or, God forbid, shot dead. Shocked to hear from Billy on his return to the Yard what he and Madden had just learned, the chief super had rung the hotel at once, in order to warn Grace that the woman they were lying in wait for was also their shooter. Equally anxious, Billy had headed straight for the Regal in a police car with the bell ringing and, on his arrival, had learned from the sergeant's own lips how the trap set for Mary Oakes had turned into what he was pleased to call 'a complete bloody shambles'.

Hearing the shots in the room where he had been waiting, Joe had raced downstairs to find Lily lying on the pavement 'out cold', as he'd put it. As for the pair of coppers he'd posted at the end of the street, they still seemed confused as to what had happened. Both had heard running footsteps on the pavement coming towards them, and the detective had stepped out of the doorway where he was posted to intercept whoever it was. He had seen a woman approaching out of the fog, coming fast, but as he shouted to her to stop, she had fired a shot at him that struck the windscreen of a car a foot away, and then a second, which ricocheted off the pavement close to his feet.

'At which point the bugger did what seemed to him the sensible thing and hit the dirt while the woman went past him.'

While all that was happening, the second police officer posted there – but on the other side of the road – a uniformed constable, had tried to cross over, but instead had run in front of a car coming down the road that he hadn't seen, causing the driver to swerve violently and crash into a parked vehicle. The constable had managed to blow his whistle, but having taken his eye off the road, he had tripped on the kerb and ended up sprawled on the pavement alongside his colleague.

'I'm telling you, guv, the Keystone Kops had nothing on it.'

The woman, in the meantime, had disappeared in the fog. But Grace had rung the Yard at once and the alarm had been broadcast within minutes of the shots being fired.

'We got enough of a description: coat, hat, glasses and that case she whacked Poole with. There'll be coppers looking for her all over London.'

When Billy had briefed him on what they now knew about Alma Ballard, Joe had whistled in amazement.

'Crikey! If I'd known it was Annie Oakley we were after, I'd have paid a visit to the armoury first.'

Billy had asked to see Lily and was taken to the office behind the reception desk, where he found her lying on her back on a couch with a bloodstained handkerchief pressed to her head.

'I'm sorry, guv, I should have had her.' The young woman was mortified. 'I just never saw it coming.'

'Well, don't let it worry you.' Billy had tried to comfort her. 'You weren't the first to be caught napping by that lady. I'll tell you about her some other time. Just consider yourself lucky.'

Soon afterwards an ambulance, summoned by Grace, had arrived and in spite of Lily's protests she had been ordered aboard by Billy.

'It's just a precaution. I want to have you looked at.'

But her torments weren't over yet. Escorted out of the hotel by a woman police constable sent from Earls Court station, Lily had been ambushed by a press photographer. Tipped off about the goings-on at the hotel, he'd been lurking in the vicinity, mingling with the small crowd that had gathered outside. Lily's head had stopped bleeding, but a purplish bruise was already starting to spread over her eye and as she had walked on shaky legs to the back of the ambulance, the chap had darted forward out of the fog and got his shot.

'Well, what do you think? Do we put her name out?' The chief super glared at Billy. 'Should we give it to the press?'

'Alma Ballard's, you mean?' Billy weighed the question.

'I take it we can get a photograph of her from that woman you interviewed, what was her name, Miss Dauncey?'

Billy nodded. 'She'd want to know why, though. It might be better if we approached the WAAF first. They're bound to have a snapshot of Alma in their records.'

In search of privacy they had retired to the office, empty now that Mrs Holly had taken refuge in her private sitting room on the floor above, leaving her secretary to man the reception counter and explain to the guests as best she could why the lobby was milling with men, some of them uniformed police officers.

'Well?' The chief super pressed him.

'I've got a feeling that any photograph we publish won't look anything like those two sketches we have of her. If she's dyed her hair and changed her looks, it may only confuse people. But all the same we should put one out. There are people who knew her before the war – when she was a schoolgirl, and later when she came to London – who would recognize her. And as far as her name's concerned, I can't see any point in keeping it to ourselves. She'll know we tried to set a trap for her here, and she'll probably assume that we know about the connection to the court martial.'

The chief super grunted. He rubbed his chin thoughtfully.

'It won't make her life any easier, either. Those two names she's been using are dead letters now, and if we put out her name as well, she'll have difficulty finding a place to stay, even for a few nights. She'll still have to produce an ID card.'

Chubb saw the dubious look on Billy's face.

'What?'

'I was thinking of something that bloke Finch told us this morning. He said she was behaving like she used to in France, taking the same kind of precautions, and that most likely she'd have a bolthole, some place where she knows she'll be safe. He used a French word; it means a hiding place. Apparently they all had one, those agents.'

They sat brooding. Joe Grace stuck his head round the door.

'The press are getting restless.' He addressed Chubb. 'There's a fair crowd of them out in the street now. They want to know what's going on. Is there anything I can tell them?'

'Say I'll be making a statement shortly.'

Joe vanished. The chief super stretched, easing a muscle in his neck.

'It's a pity John isn't here,' he muttered. 'I wouldn't mind having his opinion on all this.'

'I'll ring him when we get back to the Yard,' Billy said. They had gone their separate ways following their meeting with Finch – Madden to return to St John's Wood. 'I promised to keep him informed.'

'Well, that's it then.' Chubb prepared to rise. 'Unless there's anything else you have to tell me before I meet the slavering pack.'

Billy hesitated.

'I've been wondering about the letter that came for her. I don't understand it. I mean, here she is moving about from place to place every few days, but she takes the trouble to give somebody one of the names she's been using and an address where she'll only be staying for a week.'

'You mean it could be important?'

'It might be. As far as we know, she still has unfinished business.'

'I take it you're referring to the fellow who ran that court martial?'

Billy nodded.

'I keep hoping we'll get a name from the Royal Artillery that Mr Madden will recognize. It might turn out that the bloke copped it later in the war, so we don't have to worry. But if so, why is Alma Ballard still hanging about? Why hasn't she gone back to Canada, or wherever? I won't feel easy until I know the answer.'

'And I won't feel easy as long as I know she's out there with a gun and ready to use it.' The chief super hauled himself to his feet. 'Which reminds me: the next time we get her in our sights, I want both you and Grace to be armed. If she thinks she can treat us like ducks in a shooting gallery, she's got a surprise coming.'

28

LENNY OPENED THE DESK drawer and took out the envelope. He weighed it in his hand.

It was as light as a feather. There couldn't be much inside.

He looked at the wax seal. There was some sort of impression on it, the kind that might be left by a signet ring. The envelope was also fastened with a thin red cord wound into a figure-of-eight around two metal attachments. It would be easy enough to undo. The wax he could scrape off with a knife. It wasn't as though anyone would complain. Least of all Lord Ackroyd.

'No, I'm afraid there's been some mistake,' his secretary had told Lenny in a hoity-toity voice when he'd rung her on Monday morning. His cockney accent had seemed to grate on her tender ears. 'If His Lordship had sent anything over to Sir Percival, I would have known about it.'

Which was just what Lenny had thought.

He was still ruminating on this interesting bit of information when the phone rang and he had Raikes in his ear.

'That young lady who was here on Friday evening – do you mind telling me what you did with her?'

'*Did* with her?'

'Only I'm responsible for people coming in and out of here,

and I never saw hide nor hair of her again, after she went up-stairs with that envelope. Did she stay up there with you?'

'What are you implying?'

'Was it something the pair of you had arranged in advance, with that story about her having to put the letter in your hands? Cos if you think just because Sir Percival's away you can pull the wool over my eyes—'

'Stop blathering, Raikes.' Lenny lost his rag. 'She left here just before half-past five. She took the stairs. I don't know what happened to her after that, but at a guess I'd say she went out with the typists as they were leaving, and you missed her.'

'I didn't miss her. She didn't go past me. I'm warning you, Loomis...'

Not caring to learn what fate might have in store for him, Lenny hung up. But Raikes had got him thinking. There had certainly been something strange about the woman – and her behaviour – and even though he didn't believe for a moment that she had stayed in the building all night after the staff went home (there'd be no point, there was nothing to steal), maybe she hadn't left by the lobby. Maybe she had gone out by the tradesmen's entrance. Kept locked most of the time, it was only opened for deliveries by the porter on duty there, another old sweat named Alf Simpson, who had lost a leg at the Battle of the Somme and spent his days sitting in a glassed-in cubicle. Lenny popped downstairs to have a word with him.

'Friday evening?' Alf had hobbled out of his den to greet him. 'Oh yes, I remember the lass. She knocked on my window and asked to be let out.'

Nothing like the obnoxious Raikes, Alf was a friendly soul, who made light of his disability and fun of the scowling presence in the lobby, with his ramrod-stiff back and his puffed-out chest of medals.

'Don't ask me where he got them,' he'd told Lenny once. 'But I doubt it was anywhere near the front. Raikes was Sir

Percival's batman in the war, and I know for a fact that His Nibs was a staff officer, so he must have been living soft in some chateau behind the lines, well out of harm's way.'

'Why did you let her out, Alf?' Lenny wondered. 'Why didn't you tell her to leave by the lobby, like everyone else?'

'She asked me nicely, that's why.' The old boy grinned. 'Said there was some bloke waiting for her in the street that she wanted to avoid. He'd been pestering her, she said.'

'And you believed her?'

'Why not?' He had shrugged. 'Anyway, what harm did it do? She slipped out, and that was that. Thanked me prettily, too.'

Lenny cocked an eye at him.

'I take it you thought she worked here?'

'You mean she doesn't?' Alf's jaw dropped, along with the penny. 'Blimey! I didn't know that. You won't mention it to anyone, will you?'

Lenny was quick to reassure him.

'Let's keep it our secret,' he said. 'And there's no need to tell Raikes, either, if he comes asking. Just play dumb.'

Then he had another thought.

'Let me out for a moment, would you, Alf? I want to have a look around. She was up to something, that young lady, but I don't know what.'

Saying he'd be back in a minute, he slipped out into the dank courtyard onto which the Apollo building backed and stood for a second, wondering what had prompted the woman to exit that way. Not far from Southwark Bridge, the office was in a part of the City threaded by narrow lanes and heavily bombed during the war. The only way out of the courtyard was an alleyway and Lenny strolled down it, hoping to find some inspiration – some hint as to why the woman had taken this route. The alley led to Friar's Lane, a narrow street running downhill towards the river. Though he could see no reason why the woman should have taken this route rather than leave by the front, Lenny walked down the cramped pavement, passing by the small shops and boarded-up bomb sites until he reached Thames Street, where he came to a halt.

There was no point going any further. Beyond there lay only a wasteland of damaged wharves and wrecked warehouses. Cloaked in fog at present, it was largely deserted, a part of the river between London Bridge and Southwark that had taken a particular pounding during the war and was said to harbour rats bigger than cats – not to mention other vermin of the two-legged variety. Lenny himself had always steered clear of it and he could think of no reason why his impromptu visitor should have felt any different.

So what *was* her game? He still had no answer to his question.

He kept staring at the envelope. He was itching to know what was inside it. Finally he couldn't resist the temptation any longer and took out his penknife. It proved easier than he'd thought to slip the narrow blade beneath the blob of wax and free it from the paper; as for the cord, it presented no problem at all. In less than a minute he had the flap undone.

Lifting it, he drew out the only item it contained and held it up to the light.

'Well, bugger me!'

It was a photograph of a young man in a private's uniform dating from the First World War. He was standing to attention, with a serious expression on his face. Nice-looking bloke too, Lenny thought.

Still, he couldn't pretend it wasn't a disappointment. He'd been hoping for something better – something juicy, incriminating even, or at least compromising: something that would bring the blood to Sir Percival's mottled cheeks. She was a young woman after all, and there was such a thing as blackmail.

But there was no point now in scratching his head. All he

could do was seal up the envelope and put it on the boss's desk along with the rest of the post. Blount's liner was due to dock at Southampton the following day and, unless he decided to take the rest of the week off, which was unlikely, knowing him, he'd be back in the office the day after that.

There was nothing Lenny could do now but wait and hope the mystery would be solved then.

29

'AH, THERE YOU ARE, sir.'

Billy looked up from his desk in relief at the sight of the tall figure standing in the doorway.

'Have they arrived yet?' Madden shed his coat and dumped his suitcase on the floor.

'Ten minutes ago. I'm just looking at them now.'

The long-awaited list of names had finally arrived. Less than an hour before, Billy had received a call from the Royal Artillery depot at Woolwich informing him that the package was on its way over to him at the Yard, and he had rung Madden at once to tell him.

'They're sending their service records as well, as you asked. A courier's bringing them.'

He had caught his old chief in the nick of time. With the work now completed in the house and Aunt Maud restored to her own room, Madden had been on the point of leaving to return home.

'There's nothing more I can do now,' he had told Billy when they had spoken on the phone the day before. 'I want to go home. Lucy will be back from Paris in a few days. I want to be there when she returns. And there's all the work at the farm I've been neglecting. I've been here long enough.'

Sensing that there was more to Madden's decision than he had revealed, Billy had said nothing. The release that day of Alma Ballard's name to the press, together with a photograph of the young woman obtained from the WAAF and dating from the time of her enlistment, had signalled the start of a critical phase in the investigation, one whose significance would not have escaped his former mentor. The hunt was nearing its end, and hitherto Billy had taken it for granted that Madden would want to delay his return home for a while at least, in the hope that he might see its conclusion.

He had been about to depart in a taxi when Billy had rung, and had agreed at once to call in at the Yard on his way to Waterloo so that he could cast his eye over the list.

'We've got the names of all the officers who commanded batteries in the Arras region in the summer of 1917 before and after the court martial: there are twelve in total.' Billy indicated the papers spread out on his desk. 'Three of them didn't make it through the war. It'd be a load off my mind if our chap was one of them, but that's probably too much to hope for. I've marked their names with a star. Here's the list.'

Madden took the single sheet of paper handed to him and scanned it.

'Alden, Benson, Blount.' He began to recite the names. 'Donald, Drake, Evans, Gregory, Palmer, Patterson, Roberts, Shepherd, Trimble.'

He shook his head.

'I'm sorry, Billy. None of them rings a bell. I did meet an artillery officer called Patterson once, but that was months before, and he certainly wasn't the same man who presided at the court martial. Mind you, I'm only guessing that he was stationed in the Arras sector.'

'Never mind, sir.' Billy managed to swallow his disappointment. 'Have a look at their service records while I slip downstairs. Charlie wants a word with me. He'll be glad to know you're here.'

'How's Poole, by the way?' Madden drew the sheaf of papers towards him. 'I saw that photograph of her in one of the papers yesterday, the *Mirror*, was it? It looked like a nasty bruise.'

'Oh, she's all right.' Billy grinned. 'Just angry. It was the headline: *Plucky policewoman collects a shiner.* She's not heard the end of it around here, I can tell you.'

'Where is she?' Madden had found the office empty apart from Billy. 'And where's Grace, come to that?'

'I've got more men working for me now. It's all the calls that are coming in. There's no space for them here, so I moved the operation to the detectives' room.'

'How is it going?'

'Better not ask, sir.' Billy stood at the door. 'You wouldn't believe how many times Alma Ballard's been "seen" since the chief super gave those two sketches and the photo to the papers. The phones never stop. She's got that kind of a face. She looks like a lot of women. Or they look like her.'

Lenny ran his eye over Blount's desktop. He straightened the blotter. It had been off-centre by a fraction. The pen-and-ink stand was where it ought to be, as was the new chrome-plated telephone that Sir Percival had had installed shortly before he had set sail for New York. Everything was in its place.

It had better be, too. As Lenny had learned by now, his employer liked to spray fear around him; fear and dismay. Although he hadn't shown up yet – it was ten o'clock, late for him, but then he might have slept in after the long drive up from Southampton yesterday, and the fog was still slowing the traffic – and his scowling presence hadn't yet made itself felt, you could sense the tension in the building. Staff had been a little quicker to get to their desks; the typists who generally chattered like birds when they arrived for work had crossed the marble floor of the lobby with lowered heads and sealed lips.

Raikes had been jubilant.

'Now we'll see,' he had said to Lenny, when he strolled into the lobby with a deliberately casual air, scanning the sporting pages of the *Daily Mail*. 'Now you'll find out what's what.'

'Are you feeling all right, Raikesy?' Lenny had affected concern. 'You seem a little off-colour.'

'You'll get what's coming to you, Loomis. Mark my words.'

Lenny had heard of people frothing at the mouth. Now he'd actually witnessed it. Raikes's spittle had carried over his desk as he spluttered, and Lenny had had to move smartly to get out of its way.

Also laid out neatly on Blount's desk now was the post that had arrived too late to be forwarded to New York. Lenny had opened the business letters as per instructions, and had left untouched anything that looked like personal mail. These last included the big envelope with the photograph inside, which he had closed up again, using Sir Percival's own stick of red sealing wax and the cord. It sat a little apart from the rest of the post, with the bold capitals PERSONAL and BY HAND catching the eye. He couldn't wait to see his employer's reaction when he opened it.

Who was the mysterious soldier pictured in the photograph?

Lenny had been racking his brains to come up with an answer. He'd reluctantly had to abandon the idea that it might be an illegitimate son of Blount's – one he didn't know about. Since the young man had obviously served in the First World War, he couldn't possibly have been fathered by Sir Percival, who wouldn't have been old enough. But that didn't mean there wasn't a mystery attached to it. Of that Lenny was sure. It was the sort of thing he had a nose for.

But however prescient his sixth sense was, it failed to alert him to the bombshell that Raikes dropped on him a few minutes later.

The commissionaire had standing orders to ring Lenny upstairs the moment the chairman walked into the lobby, but Lenny was still sitting at his ease behind his desk going through the racing results, when the lift doors opened and Sir Percival stepped out. Larger than life, bulky in his overcoat, he strode across the floor, his heels echoing like rifle shots on the polished parquet.

'I want a word with you, Loomis.'

Struck rigid by the sight of his employer, Lenny could only sit gaping as Blount's angry, inflamed visage hovered over him.

'What's this I hear about you and some woman?'

'Well, that went well.'

Charlie rubbed his hands with satisfaction.

'Properly penitent, I'd say. Now if we can only get him trained up, he might stop interfering and allow us to get on with our jobs.'

Responding to the chief super's summons earlier on, Billy had discovered it wasn't to have a word with him, as he'd thought, but to accompany him to the assistant commissioner's office, in order to acquaint their superior with the striking progress that had been made in the investigation during his brief absence in Manchester.

'It's good news, of course.' Charlie had been at his most unctuous. 'We know who we're after now. But there is one problem. You'll have seen the name that we've given out to the press . . . Alma Ballard?'

'Ballard? Yes? What about it?'

Eustace Cradock frowned. Not much to look at (or so Billy had always felt), the AC, Crime was on the short side, with thinning hair and specs that never seemed to sit straight on his nose. He had been largely unnoticed during his days in the budgetary and traffic departments – the sort of chap you would nod to in the corridor and then try to remember exactly who he was. Added to which he had one feature that could only be described as unfortunate: a sharply pointed nose, the tip of which had a way of turning red in moments of stress. Looking at Cradock as he struggled to place the name – it was clear he'd forgotten it – Billy was put in mind of a mole that he had dug up in his garden last summer.

'Well, she's got the same name as that soldier who was convicted and executed back in 1917 – the one I told you about.'

The chief super had paused at that point, his lugubrious face a picture of sympathy.

'You mean . . . ?' The tip of Cradock's nose had begun to glow. The penny had dropped.

'I'm afraid so, sir. Madden was right. It *is* all about the court martial. There's no doubt now. This woman is James Ballard's daughter.'

Chubb had allowed what seemed like a decent interval to pass in reflective silence. In reality he had been enjoying every moment of it.

'Now I know you'll want to make sure that the appropriate quarters are made aware of this' – the chief super's delicate allusion to the shadowy Whitehall figures who had leaned on their AC had made Billy smile – 'but what you can tell them is that it won't be made public straight away.'

'I'm sorry, Chief Superintendent. I don't quite . . .'

'We've given Miss Ballard's name to the papers, as I say, but that's all for now. We've made no mention of the court martial. However, it will all come out in the end – it'll have to – and it might be as well if those who feel this is a sensitive subject are made aware of that now. At least it will give them a breathing space, time to prepare their reaction. I'm sure you'd agree.'

Whether the AC did or not was never made clear, for Cradock had remained wordless. He had simply swallowed and, taking this as an invitation to continue, Chubb had treated him to a brief summary of the facts relating to the investigation.

'We've got police all over the capital looking for her, sir, and if she tries to leave the country we'll be waiting. I'd like to think that we'll arrest her soon, but it's only right to warn you there might be a problem with that. She is armed, as I've said, and there's some indication she might not give herself up. To be on the safe side I've issued a general order to all stations in the Metropolitan area that, in the event of her being cornered, she's not to be approached until armed officers are on the spot.'

Chubb had frowned.

'However, there is one aspect of the case that continues to worry us. Logically there should be one more name on her list of victims – the most important one in fact, the one she would clearly hold to be most guilty. I mean the officer who presided over the court martial of her father. Up till now we've been unable to learn his name, and while the fact that he hasn't been killed may have a simple explanation, I won't rest easy, and neither will Mr Styles, until this young woman is no longer a threat to him – or anyone else.'

Finding his tongue at last, the AC had muttered some words of encouragement and with that the meeting had ended and they had returned to Charlie's office, where he was presently enjoying his triumph with rather more satisfaction than Billy thought seemly.

'I'll have to leave you, sir,' he said. 'I've got Mr Madden here. He's looking at those names.'

'Wants to be in at the kill, does he?' Chubb rubbed his hands.

'Oh no, I don't think so.'

Billy shook his head. He had had some time to reflect on their conversation the day before and thought he knew what was in his old chief's mind. Having done all he could to help with the police investigation, Madden feared his only reward now would be to witness the unfolding of yet another tragedy thirty years after the first; and one he had been equally power-less to prevent.

'He heard what that fellow Finch said: that we wouldn't take her alive. If that's what it comes to, he won't want to be there.'

'I hadn't thought of that.' The chief super let out a sigh. 'But I can see his point.'

On the way back to his office Billy stopped off at the detec-tives' room and caught Grace's eye.

'Anything doing?'

'Not so far, guv.'

The room was crowded with desks, half of them occupied at that moment by the men he was using to deal with calls coming in from police stations all over London. None of the reported sightings of Alma Ballard had so far proved genuine, but Billy knew from experience that with this sort of operation you just had to plough on, in the hope that one of them would eventu-ally bear fruit. Meantime the phones kept ringing.

He noticed Lily Poole sitting at a desk in front of a notice-board fixed to the wall behind her. A copy of yesterday's *Daily Mirror* with Lily's photograph – black eye and all – occupying most of the front page was pinned to the felt above her head. In spite of her attempts to hide the disfiguring mark with face powder, the shiner was still much in evidence, Billy saw. When she looked up he beckoned to her.

'Come along,' he said. 'There are enough bodies in here. Let's see if we can find something useful for you to do.'

When he opened the door to his office he found Madden sitting where he had left him, with the dossier sent from Wool-wich spread out on the desk in front of him. He had a piece of paper in his hand, which he was studying with a thoughtful expression.

'I've been through their service records.' He glanced up. 'On the face of it they're no help: there's no indication that any of these officers ever served on a court-martial board. But one thing did catch my eye. It may not mean anything, but I thought I'd mention it. One of these men received a promotion around that time – a major. It came only two months after Ballard was found guilty and sentenced to death. He was made colonel.'

'Is that significant?' Billy asked.

'It might be.' Madden weighed the piece of paper in his hand. 'He wasn't only promoted; he was given a position on the General Staff. He was invited to join the brass. It could well have been a reward for services rendered.'

'For managing the court martial, you mean?'

Madden shrugged. 'I'm only guessing.'

'What's his name?' Billy came over.

'Blount.'

Madden handed him the piece of paper.

'Initials P.C.M.'

Blount studied the photograph for several seconds. Then he tossed it aside. He fixed his cold stare on Lenny.

'You're telling me she brought this?'

'That's right, sir. She turned up last Friday saying she'd been ordered to deliver the envelope to me.'

'To *you*?'

'To your personal assistant. She said her instructions came from Lord Ackroyd's secretary, but when I rang her later she denied it.'

'What made you do that?'

'As Raikes says, there *was* something funny about her behaviour.'

Lenny had recovered his composure. He was up on his toes now, doing a tap dance, dodging the accusations Raikes had filled their employer's ears with, making sure his own version of the story was told.

'Funny?'

'Strange, sir. I can't explain it. I just had the feeling she wasn't telling me the truth. I know Raikes thought I had kept her up here with me – he told me so – but the fact is she left in a hurry when she realized I was on to her. And as I told Raikes, it's odds-on she slipped out with the typists. They usually leave in a group and it was right at the end of the working day. In fact, now that I think of it, she may have chosen the time for that reason.'

Lenny had accompanied Sir Percival into his office and put the offending envelope in his hands. He had watched as his employer ripped it open and then listened while a string of oaths poured from his lips.

'Is this what all the bloody fuss is about?' Blount had glowered at the picture. 'Who was this woman? Raikes says he thinks you know her. Is that true?'

Lenny had had his explanation of the incident ready by then and he'd gone into it at length.

'After I'd spoken to Lord Ackroyd's secretary there was nothing more I could do.' He went on, 'I did think of opening the envelope, but since it was marked "Personal" I thought I'd better leave it for you.'

Blount made a threatening noise, a sort of growl that gathered in his throat. Lenny had heard it before.

'I go away for a few weeks and the place turns into a bloody madhouse. Get rid of this thing.'

He pushed the photograph towards Lenny.

'No, wait.'

Lenny's hand froze. Sir Percival drew the photograph back and slid it to one side of his desk.

'I'm going to get to the bottom of this.'

He glared down at the young face under the peaked cap. For just an instant he seemed to hesitate, as though a thought had struck him. Lenny watched, fascinated. Then Blount shrugged – angrily, it seemed.

'I want a meeting of department heads in the conference room in fifteen minutes. Tell them to bring their files . . . all current business. I want to know what's been going on.'

'Will you need me there, sir?'

'No. You can deal with this.' He pushed the pile of correspondence across the desk. 'Now buzz off.'

'Here he is, guv, I've got him.'

Lily lifted eager eyes from the copy of *Who's Who* she was poring over. One of the few reference books that Billy's office boasted, it rested on top of a cabinet filled with case files. Before either of the two men could move she had grabbed hold of the heavy volume and lugged it over to her desk.

'Percival Charles Martin Blount. He's a KBE. That means he's a "Sir", doesn't it?' She looked up. 'He was in the Royal Artillery all right – it says so. It gives his wife's name and his children's and his clubs . . . Oh, and it says he's chairman of something called Apollo Investments.'

Billy already had the phone book open.

'I've got his home number. He lives in Mayfair . . . Mount Street. But he'll be at the office now.' He flicked through the pages. 'Here we are: Apollo Investments. It's in Skinner's Lane – that's near Southwark Bridge.'

Madden and Lily watched as he dialled the number.

'Hello . . . yes, I'd like to speak to Sir Percival Blount, please. This is Detective-Inspector Styles of Scotland Yard.'

Billy covered the mouthpiece with his hand.

'I'm going to ask him straight out if he was the man who presided at that court martial.' He addressed the words to Madden. 'There's no point beating about the bush.'

He took his hand away.

'Yes, that's right, Scotland Yard . . . I see . . . No, there's no need to disturb him. But as soon as he comes out, tell him I called and ask him to ring me back. Say I need to speak to him urgently . . . Yes, I'm sure he's very busy, but this is important.'

Billy went silent. He was listening to what the other party was saying.

'You say he's been what?'

His brow darkened in a frown.

'He's been *where*?'

He stared at Madden.

'Now listen, Mr Loomis, and listen very carefully. The minute Sir Percival comes out of that meeting you're to tell him that I'm on my way over there, and I want him to stay in his office until I arrive. Impress on him that this is a serious matter. We think he may be in danger. Make sure he understands that. I'll be there soon to explain, but in the meantime other police officers will arrive. They're being sent as a precaution. No, I can't tell you what it's about. Just do as I say.'

Billy hung up.

'That was his personal assistant, a chap called Loomis. He says Blount's been in America. He only got back yesterday. I won't know for certain whether he's our man until I've spoken to him, but if he is, that could be why he hasn't been topped. Either way, we can't take a chance. He's in a meeting with his senior staff at the moment. I thought it safest to leave him there.'

He turned to Lily.

'Get hold of Grace. Make sure he's armed. The two of you get over to Skinner's Lane. Keep an eye on the lobby. There'll be more officers coming. If he's who I think he is, we'll have to give him round-the-clock protection. I'll be there shortly, just as soon as I've spoken to Mr Chubb, but if Blount has come out of that meeting he'll probably want a word with you. You can ask him about the court martial.'

Lily hurried from the room. Billy turned to Madden.

'It looks like we got his name in the nick of time.' He watched as his old chief donned his coat. 'I'll be having a word with

Blount shortly. You're welcome to come if you want to, sir. You might find it interesting to meet him again.'

'I very much doubt it, Billy.' Madden picked up his suitcase. 'Given how this whole business began, I'd just as soon never set eyes on him again. But let me know what he says, will you?'

'I will, sir.' Billy rose. He accompanied Madden to the door. 'Still, it's strange, isn't it?'

'Strange?'

'The way things work out. If anyone deserved a bullet in the head it was him – this Sir Percival. Now it looks like he'll escape without a scratch.'

The storm wasn't over yet. In fact it was still brewing. Blount's face was flushed. His features had thickened with anger. He glared at Lenny.

'Couldn't you at least have found out what this is about?'

'I did try, sir. But Inspector Styles said he'd explain it to you in person when he arrives. He shouldn't be long.'

'Scotland Yard, eh . . . Well, you'd better be telling the truth, Loomis.' Sir Percival's eyes had narrowed to slits. 'If this is another one of your little games . . .'

'Games, sir? I don't know what you mean.'

Lenny was starting to get anxious. He'd managed things well enough up to now. But this latest bombshell had knocked him sideways. He'd still been racking his brains, wondering what could be behind the inspector's call, when the doors to the conference room at the other end of the reception area had opened and the participants had begun leaving. Blount was the last to emerge, and Lenny had found that his knees were knocking when he'd got to his feet to intercept him.

'What about this photograph? You still haven't explained that.'

They had gone into Blount's wood-panelled office, lit by

lamps even at that hour, thanks to the fog that still clung to the windows, blocking out the daylight. Seated behind his desk now, Sir Percival jabbed his finger at the print, which lay where he had left it.

'There's something going on here and I don't like it.' He treated Lenny to a long, cold stare. It was his insect-under-the-microscope look. 'Raikes says you're up to no good. If that's the case, I'm warning you now: you're for the high jump. What did that inspector say exactly?'

Lenny swallowed. 'I was to warn you to stay in your office until he gets here: that you might be in danger. He didn't say how, or why. He was sending police officers over for your protection.'

'Christ Almighty! If he thinks I'm going to have a bunch of bluebottles cluttering up the lobby, he's got another think coming. I don't want them in the building. Is that clear?'

Lenny nodded.

'Now get out of here and leave me alone. And, Loomis . . .'

Lenny paused in the act of turning.

'Take care. I've got my eye on you.'

30

'CAN'T SEE A BLEEDING thing.'

Grace peered into the gloom. As its name suggested, Skinner's Lane was a cramped thoroughfare hardly wide enough for two cars to pass. Hampered by the fog, the driver who had brought them from the Yard had nosed his way carefully down it, finally coming to a halt in front of a solid-looking four-storey structure flanked on either side by bomb-damaged buildings boarded up, but not yet rebuilt. Glassed doors gave onto a lighted lobby. Lily could see a commissionaire sitting at a desk at the back of the hall. They hadn't gone inside yet. Joe had said he wanted to get the lie of the land. Well, good luck to him, she thought. Here, near the river, the fog was so thick you could hardly see your hand in front of your face.

They had arrived a few minutes earlier with the bell on their car ringing and their driver, egged on by Grace, chancing his arm with the traffic in a way that would probably have earned him a suspension if anyone had been there to observe it. Nor had there been any delay in their departure. Having repeated the instructions she'd been given, Lily had watched with a scowl as Joe had drawn a service revolver out of the drawer of his desk and slipped it into his jacket pocket. On the chief superintendent's orders, both he and Styles had paid a visit to the armoury the day before: they had been told to keep their weapons handy until the hunt for Alma Ballard was over. Acutely aware that she herself had been excluded from this precautionary order – despite the fact that she had passed the required firearms course with satisfactory marks – Lily had been chewing over this piece of blatant discrimination for the past twenty-four hours, but was yet to come up with any suitable response that would show her displeasure.

Didn't they realize she was primed for action? That she, more than anyone, had a score to settle with Alma Ballard? Lily felt she'd been hard done by. The blow she had received at the Regal Hotel had done more than lay her out – it had made her a laughing stock, and the subsequent mockery by her male colleagues had only served to rub salt into the wound. If anyone deserved a chance to lay their shooter by the heels, it was she, Lily Poole, and the fact that she'd been deprived of a weapon seemed to suggest there was a plot afoot (a male plot) to prevent her from being in at the kill.

As they stood there in front of the entrance another police car, a Flying Squad vehicle, drew up behind theirs, its aerial swaying back and forth. There were two uniformed officers inside. One of them climbed out.

'Grace, is it?' A thickset man, he wore a sergeant's stripes on his arm. 'Brady's the name. We got a message to get here as soon as possible. The dispatcher said it was to do with the shooter – this Ballard woman. Are you expecting her to show up?'

'Not necessarily.' Joe shrugged. 'But we reckon the head of this firm here could be on her list. This is DC Poole, by the way.' He gestured towards Lily and the sergeant's eyebrows went up in surprise. It was obvious he wasn't expecting to see a woman there. 'There'll be other officers arriving soon, but for the moment we're it. I don't suppose you're armed?' he added.

'Not a chance.' Brady grinned.

'Well, if you happen to run into her, remember that she is.' He reflected. 'I think you'd better stay in your car. You'll be less conspicuous there. But don't try to stop any women you might see entering the building. Leave them to us. We'll check their identities.'

Lenny sat down heavily behind his desk. He took a couple of deep breaths.

Christ! What next?

Watching Blount open the envelope was supposed to have been a lark. But it hadn't turned out that way. And now there was this call from Scotland Yard. What was that all about? He hadn't got a clue. But it smelled of trouble.

He was still trying to get his thoughts in order when the phone rang.

'There's a female police officer down here asking for you.' Raikes's grating voice set his jangled nerves on edge. 'She's a detective by the name of Poole. Are you in trouble with the law, Loomis?'

'I'll give you trouble, Raikes. What have you been saying about me behind my back?'

The commissionaire chortled.

'Got it in the neck, did you? And about time, too. What about this detective, then? Do you want to talk to her?'

'No, send her up.'

Lenny sat fuming. He'd have to think of some way of dealing with Ebenezer Raikes. The bastard was out to get him. But right now there were more immediate concerns to worry about. He watched as the lights over the lift flickered. The doors opened and a fair-haired young woman stepped out.

'Mr Loomis?'

'That's me.' Lenny rose to his feet. 'You must be Detective Poole?' He broke off, grinning. 'Didn't I see your picture in the paper yesterday? You're the plucky policewoman. That's a corker of an eye you've got there.'

'Thanks, Mr Loomis. I've heard all the jokes.'

She was a sight all right, with the liverish bruise blacking one eye like a cartoon character's. Her blonde hair was cut across her brow in a straight line and the jacket she wore gave her a mannish look.

'I need to see Sir Percival right away.'

'Yes, I know. I spoke to your Mr Styles.' Lenny paused. He nodded towards Blount's door. 'Listen, a word in your ear: he's in a filthy mood. Like as not you'll get the rough side of his tongue. I'm just warning you.' He came round the desk to join her. 'What's all this about, anyway? Is he really in danger?'

'I can't talk about it.' Her voice was tight. She seemed nervous. 'Just let him know I'm here. Tell him I have to speak to him.'

Lenny knocked on the door and put his head in.

'Sir?'

'What now?' Blount loured at him from behind his desk at the other end of the room.

'There's a police officer to see you, sir – a detective. Can I send her in?'

'Did you say *her*?'

'That's right, sir. Name of Poole. She says she needs to speak to you.'

'For God's sake, they sent a *woman* . . . all right, bring her in.'

He sat with folded arms as Lenny ushered his charge into the office and escorted her to Sir Percival's desk. About to take his leave, he paused. Blount was speaking.

'What's the matter with your eye?' he asked.

'Someone hit me, sir.'

'Christ Almighty!' Blount shook his head as though it was all too much. 'Show me your warrant card then.'

She took a piece of white pasteboard out of her jacket pocket and handed it to him. He examined it.

'What happened to your inspector . . . what was his name?'

'Styles.' It was Lenny who supplied the answer.

'Styles?'

'I'm acting for him, sir. I'm supposed to ask you a question.' The words tumbled from her lips, the urgency behind them palpable. 'It's something we *have* to know.'

'Well?' Blount scowled.

'Are you the man – he was a Major Blount – who presided over a court martial at the village of Saint-Bertrand, near Arras, in June 1917?'

Astounded by the question, he stared blankly at her.

'Are you out of your mind?'

'I'll explain why in a moment, but it's vital you tell us,' she pressed him.

'This is incredible.'

Furious, but unsure now exactly what was at stake – Lenny could read the uncertainty in his face – Blount flushed a deeper shade of red. Breathing heavily, he considered his reply.

'Very well.' His resentment was plain. 'Yes, I was the officer in question. Now would you tell me what bloody business it is of yours?'

His cold eyes bored into hers and for a moment she seemed to wilt. Her head went down; she seemed to sag on her feet. It was as if all the strain and tension she had exhibited moments before had drained from her in an instant. But she rallied quickly, straightening. Her hand went to her jacket pocket.

'Look at it.' She pointed to the photograph on the desk.

'I beg your pardon . . .' Blount was incredulous.

'*Look* at it.' Her voice was like a whiplash.

Lenny's glance had shifted to his employer and he saw his jaw drop. Blount wasn't looking at the photograph, though; he was staring at the woman. Lenny saw she had a gun in her hand. He wasn't more than a few feet from her, but for a second he couldn't move. He seemed stuck to the spot. Then he broke the spell, lurching towards her, but as he did so she turned and with a swift, scything motion struck him hard on the temple with the butt of her pistol. Stumbling, he fell heavily to the floor. Blood poured from the gash in his skin.

'Stay there. Don't move.'

As though in a dream, he saw her circle the desk until she was standing at Blount's side. She slid the photograph across the desk.

'Look at it,' she repeated.

'I'm damned if I will.' Blount all but choked on the words. But his voice carried a note of desperation. 'Who the devil are you?' He had paled.

'For the last time, look at it.'

She put the pistol to his temple, cocking it as she did so, and at the sound of the oiled click close to his ear he bent his head and peered at the photograph.

'I expect you've forgotten his name. It was James Ballard. He was twenty-three years old.'

She spoke in a monotone.

'You found him guilty of desertion in the face of the enemy. The verdict carried an automatic sentence of death, something you were well aware of. The proceedings lasted less than a day.'

Blount's mouth hung open. Lenny saw that he was trying to speak.

'Get up.'

She stepped back and after a moment he obeyed, using the desk to lever himself to his feet. She indicated with the barrel of her pistol the direction he was to take. As he moved haltingly around the desk the telephone rang. She reached for the cord and, with a sharp jerk of the wrist, tore it from its socket. Looking up, Lenny took her in properly for the first time and gasped.

'*You!*'

He was stunned by his failure to recognize her. True, she looked different from when she had brought the envelope; but he saw now who it was.

Blount had come to a halt. He was standing with his back to

the desk, watching the woman who had positioned herself to one side of him, out of reach, but with the gun steady in her hand. His eyes were glazed.

'Kneel down.'

Seemingly deaf to the command, he stayed standing.

'This is your last warning.' She levelled the gun at his head.

With a whimper Blount sank to his knees. Lenny saw the glint of tears in his eyes. The woman moved to a new position behind him. She spoke again.

'I expect they tied him to a post. Isn't that what usually happened?'

Even now her voice was without expression. There was something inhuman about it – the deadness in the tone. Lenny felt his blood turn to ice.

'They probably offered him a blindfold, but I don't think he would have wanted one. He was a painter; the visible world was what he loved, what he responded to, and I think he would have wanted to fill his eyes with it, with whatever was there to see, even if it was only the faces of the men he had served with before they shot him. Because that was the practice, wasn't it? You had to be killed by your own comrades-in-arms, so as to drive the lesson home.'

She was silent for a beat, as if wanting the image of the firing squad and the bound man to form in her listener's mind.

'But no matter . . . you can't answer these questions because you weren't there. You had done your part and it was left to others to finish the business. I won't ask if you ever thought of James Ballard in the years that followed, if you ever pictured what was left of him rotting in the earth. I won't ask if you ever felt guilty, because we are past that point now. You will think this unjust. Perhaps he felt the same. I am here to remind you that justice lies in the hands of those who dispense it.'

She moved, bringing her gun down to a point just behind Blount's neck.

'In your report on James Ballard's trial you said he gave no explanation for what he had done and, if we are to believe your account, no single word was spoken in his defence, or none that you thought worth recording. So be it. Let there be no word uttered on your behalf, either.'

'For the love of God . . .' The words seemed torn from the broken figure, slumped on his knees now, head bowed.

'I was coming to that. There is still time to make your peace with him.'

In the silence that followed, Lenny could only watch with horror as her finger tightened on the trigger. Some part of him still believed that she would relent in the end; that, having reduced her victim to a cowering heap, she would leave him to his shame and depart.

But then the shot rang out and Blount's figure jerked forward and collapsed like a doll, face-down on the carpet only inches from where Lenny was crouching. Smoke rose from the singed hairs at the back of the dead man's neck. The smell of burned flesh was in Lenny's nostrils.

Turning, the woman picked up the photograph off the desk. With the gun still in her hand, she looked down at him and he thought he saw his fate in her cold gaze. Like her voice, it had settled on him without expression.

He shut his eyes. There was nothing he could do. No prayer came to his lips. His mind was a void.

When he opened them again she had gone.

'Are you trying to pull my leg, young lady?' The commissionaire fixed Lily with a ferocious glare. '*What* did you say your name was?'

'Poole. Detective-Constable Poole. I told you.' She fumbled in her pocket and drew out her warrant card. 'See?' She showed it to him.

He'd been giving her a strange look, and that was even before she had reached his desk. Just a minute or so earlier, as she
and Joe Grace were about to enter the building, a police van had
arrived in the lane outside with a squad of uniformed officers
aboard and Joe had stayed behind to deal with them.

'You go ahead,' he had told Lily. 'I'll be with you in a
moment.'

She had crossed the marble floor to the back of the lobby,
aware that the commissionaire, an elderly bloke with close-
cropped grey hair and a spread of medals pinned to the pocket
of his funereal black suit, was observing her approach with
narrow-eyed suspicion.

'We're from Scotland Yard,' she had announced when she
got there. 'My colleague and me. Has your Mr Loomis told you
about us?'

'Loomis?' At the mention of the name, the old boy's face
turned purple. '*Loomis!* I might have guessed . . .'

Now he was glaring at her warrant card.

'Well, if you're really who you say you are, I've got some bad
news for you both – you and Mr Bleeding Loomis. I've just sent
a woman up to see Sir Percival Blount who said she was you.
What's more, she had a warrant card – and a black eye to go
with it.'

'Jesus Christ!' Lily was dumbstruck.

She saw his glance swivel away from her. He was pointing at
the lift.

'In fact, there she is now.'

31

As though paralysed, Lily watched as the woman walked across the lobby towards the entrance. Her heart was pounding, but she kept her head. Joe Grace was outside with a squad of police, and as long as Alma Ballard continued on her course she would walk straight into their hands. They would arrest her before she had a chance to run.

Her only fear was that she herself might alert the woman to the danger she was in. It only needed Alma to glance her way and she would probably remember Lily's face from the hotel; and even if she didn't, she could hardly miss her black eye. Obliged to look away, Lily was reduced to listening to the sound of the footsteps as they crossed the marble floor. It was only when they stopped that she turned her head to see what had happened.

Alma had come to a halt in the middle of the lobby. She was facing the entrance, and Lily saw that Joe had entered the building and was standing there just inside the glassed doors. He was staring back at Lily. She saw Alma's hand go to her pocket.

'Sarge, look out!'

She screamed the warning, but Joe already had his gun out and, when the shots sounded, they came so close together they might have been one. He staggered and went down. Alma turned and ran.

Lily sprang into life. She raced across the lobby to where Joe was lying. A spreading stain on one of his trouser legs showed where the bullet had struck home. He had managed to hoist himself up on one elbow and, as she reached him, he fired another shot after the fleeing figure. Lily dropped to her knees beside him.

'Never mind me.' His face was twisted in pain. 'Get after her.' He thrust his revolver into Lily's hand.

She hesitated.

'Go on!'

Lily scrambled to her feet and was in time to see the woman vanish through a doorway at the far end of the lobby beyond the lift and the stairs. Reassured by the mass of blue-uniformed bodies pouring into the lobby now – they would see to Joe – she set off in pursuit.

The door was open. Beyond it was a long corridor. There was no sign of Alma, but as Lily raced down the passage, figures appeared in front of her suddenly, men in shirtsleeves and young women who might have been secretaries. They had heard the shots and come out of their offices to see what was going on. Gun in hand, she forced her way through them and continued down the passage until she came to the back of the building, where she saw a door to the outside standing open. There was a glassed-in cubicle nearby. An elderly man was just emerging from it; he was limping.

'Did you see a woman go out of here?' Panting, Lily paused for a moment. He was staring open-mouthed at the gun in her hand. 'I'm with the police,' she told him.

'Opened the door herself, she did . . .' He found his tongue. 'Never seen her before in my life. Who . . . ?'

The rest of his question was lost as Lily sped through the open doorway and out into a small yard wreathed in fog. The only exit she could see was by an alleyway and she ran down it until she reached a cross-street, a narrow lane, where she paused to look both ways and caught a fleeting glimpse of a figure running away to her left. In the next moment it had vanished, swallowed up by the enveloping fog. Pocketing her revolver, she drew out her police whistle and blew a loud blast. Then she set off in pursuit.

The lane sloped downhill towards the river and Lily quickly abandoned the narrow pavement for the road. Here, near the river, the fog was rolling up off the water in dense billows and even the headlights of a car, which she saw ahead of her then and just managed to avoid, were only visible from a few feet off. She had lost sight of her quarry after that first glimpse, but there were no side streets Alma could have turned into, and if she had taken refuge in one of the boarded-up bomb sites Lily had spotted during her rapid passage, then she would be found when the area was searched, as it surely would be very soon.

Even as the thought entered her head she heard the clanging of a police car bell behind her and swerved off the road to avoid it. The car sped past. She was still running flat out, and when she came to the bottom of the lane she saw the car standing empty with one of the doors open. It had stopped at the very edge of the dockland area, now mostly a wasteland, at the mouth of an alley flanked by bomb-damaged warehouses. Gasping for breath, she blew her whistle again and heard an answering blast from somewhere down the fog-wreathed alley. She started down it, not running now, but picking her way carefully through the rubble strewn on the greasy cobblestones.

'Hello, Detective.'

A blue-uniformed figure had materialized out of the murk in front of her. He was wearing a cap rather than a helmet, and Lily recognized the Flying Squad sergeant to whom Joe Grace had spoken earlier: Brady was his name.

'You'll want to know how your sergeant is. He's on his way to hospital. He'll be all right. It was only a flesh wound.'

Another shape emerged from the fog behind him.

'This is Higgs.' Brady nodded at him. 'We saw you take off after Ballard and realized she might have come this way. We thought we saw someone running down this alley, but we couldn't be sure in the fog. By the way, she got Blount. Did you know?'

Lily shook her head.

'She shot him, like the others. It must have happened while we were out there in the street.' He wiped his face with a handkerchief. 'Will you look at that?' He held up the piece of dirtied cloth in his hand. 'God only knows what's in this fog.'

Lily tried to pierce the gloom behind him.

'Where does this alley go?' she asked.

'To the river. There's a wrought-iron gate at the end of it, locked; probably to keep the public out. She couldn't have gone that way.'

'What about these warehouses?' Lily gestured at the wrecked buildings on either side of them. 'Could she have slipped into one of them?'

'We saw a doorway as we came down.' Brady pointed back up the alley. 'We were just going back to have a look inside.'

While they were retracing their steps a police whistle sounded from the top of the alley. Brady turned to his colleague.

'Sounds like the cavalry's arrived. Hop along up there, Harry, and tell them this alley's no go, but we're checking the warehouse. Come back when you've delivered the message.'

They had reached the doorway. Lily stuck her head inside. It was just a shell now, she saw. Most of the roof had been destroyed and, although normally that would let in a flood of light, the blanketing fog above had created a twilight effect that reduced vision and blurred the outlines of the twisted metal and broken masonry scattered about the floor.

'What I wouldn't give for a couple of old-fashioned flares,' Brady muttered. He pushed past her into the building. 'I can't see any other doors,' he added. 'This looks like the only way out.'

Glancing over his shoulder, he saw that Lily had gone down on one knee.

'What is it?'

'I'm not sure,' she said. 'Have you got a match?'

He produced a box from his pocket and handed it to her. She struck a light and bent lower, touching the dusty floor with her fingertip and then holding it up with the burning match beside it.

'Look . . . blood.'

Brady whistled.

'Your sergeant must have winged her.' He looked about him. 'We're going to have to search this place.' He had dropped his voice, as though afraid his words might carry. 'But we'll have to get some men down here first. I'll send Higgs as soon as he gets back . . . What?'

He saw the questioning look on her face.

'You don't agree?'

Lily shook her head. 'I don't think she's hiding in here.'

'Why not?' He scowled.

'Because . . . because she's not that kind of person.' Lily struggled to explain. 'She had a plan coming here, she *must* have done. It hasn't come out yet, but she was one of our agents during the war. In France. She won a medal. The King wrote her a letter. She was a heroine.'

Lily couldn't believe she was saying these things about Alma Ballard.

'The Jerries tried hard to catch her, but they never could. She was too clever for them. And she had nerve, too – all the nerve in the world.'

'I see what you're saying.' He looked at her. 'But what's your point?'

'I don't believe she's lying curled up in here waiting to be caught. It's not in her to do that. She was always going to kill

Blount and she had plenty of time to scout the area while she was waiting for him to come back from America. She must have had an escape route planned. I think this is it.'

'So where is she now?'

'She was heading for the river. That means there has to be a way out of here onto the wharf – somewhere over there.'

Lily pointed to the end of the warehouse. Brady's frown had faded. He was grinning at her now.

'Then what are we waiting for, Detective?'

He set off across the warehouse. Lily followed.

Picking their way through the rubble, they came to a part of the floor that was less cluttered and covered with a thick carpeting of dust. It was Brady who spotted the footprints.

'There . . . going towards the corner.'

They followed the indentations, which were clearly marked in the dust covering the floor, and before they reached the end of them saw another bloodstain the size of a shilling beside the tracks. When they came to the corner they found a sheet of corrugated iron standing propped against the wall. Brady pulled it aside to reveal a flight of stone steps leading down. Lily bent to peer into the stairwell.

'I can see a door.'

'Just a moment.'

Brady looked back to see if Higgs had returned from his mission. The constable was just entering the warehouse through the doorway.

'Run back,' Brady called out to him. 'Tell whoever's in charge up there that she came this way. We think she's down on the wharf. Tell them to hurry.'

Too impatient to wait any longer, Lily was already descending the steps, which grew darker as she went down. Keeping her eye on the faint crack of light she had seen from above, she came to a door that was slightly ajar. When she pushed it open she saw the stone paving of the dockside in front of her and beyond it, though only for a moment – dense fog blocked out the sight almost at once – the dark, flowing water of the river.

'Here we are then.' Brady was at her shoulder. He spoke in a murmur. 'You go downstream, Poole. I'll go the other way. If you spot her, blow your whistle. I'll do the same.'

They parted and almost at once Brady's footsteps faded as he moved away. Alone in a silence unbroken except for the dismal hooting of foghorns out on the water, Lily went cautiously forward trying to pierce the mist in front of her, but keeping a weather eye on the river to her right. She could see it, but only in glimpses, and each time it disappeared from sight she slowed her pace, keeping her eyes fixed to the ground so as not to wander off-course and tumble into it. She had been moving forward at this slow, steady pace for several minutes when she heard the sound of men's voices behind her and stopped. These must be the officers alerted by Higgs, she thought, and for a moment she hesitated, thinking it might be better to wait until some of them had caught up with her. At that moment the bank of fog in front of her parted and she saw Alma Ballard.

She was standing on a pier jutting out into the river less than a dozen yards away. She had her back to Lily.

'Alma Ballard!' Lily dragged the revolver from her coat pocket. 'Stay where you are. Don't move.'

The woman turned slowly to face her. Lily saw she had a rope in her hand.

'Drop that!' Lily pointed the gun at her.

Alma stood motionless. For a long moment her gaze met Lily's. Then, as though indifferent to the order, she turned away, dropping to a crouch as she did so, and at the same instant the fog descended like a stage curtain and she vanished from sight.

Lily pulled the whistle from her pocket and blew a loud blast . . . then another.

'*Here!*' she shouted. '*She's here!*'

Still blinded by the fog, she ran along the wharf until she judged she had reached the jetty. Raised voices came from behind her, accompanied by the beat of hurrying feet. But they were drowned out by the sudden shock of a woman's scream.

It came from close at hand – from right in front of her now – and was followed by a loud splash.

Stumbling forward, Lily found the pier, but had hardly taken a step along it when she tripped over a lump of concrete and fell to her knees. Scrambling to her feet – and grabbing hold of the revolver, which had slipped from her grasp – she went on and saw a short flight of steps at the side of the pier. They went down to a landing stage. It was empty.

Another cry sounded – this time from further away downriver. A second later it was repeated. Then there was silence.

'*Lily . . . Lily . . .*'

The call came from behind her and, looking round, Lily caught a glimpse of Billy Styles's stocky figure. He was following in the wake of a pair of helmeted officers. He waved to her. She pointed downstream.

'She's in the water,' she shouted to them. 'She fell in. She's wounded.'

The two constables carried on down the wharf. Billy stopped at the jetty. Picking his way through the rubble, he joined her. Together they peered downstream, but there was nothing to see: only the fog that hung like a curtain before their eyes, motionless in the still air. Just then a foghorn sounded nearby on the river, then another and another . . .

'Like a dirge for the dead.' Billy muttered the words to himself.

'I had her in my sights.' Lily felt the weight of her failure. 'She was just a few feet away.' She showed Billy the revolver. 'I could have shot her.'

He studied her face. Then, after a moment, he put an arm around her shoulders.

'Don't fret, Lil,' he said. 'Maybe it's just as well.'

'But you don't understand, guv.' She was despairing. 'I couldn't do it. I couldn't pull the trigger.'

'And if you had, what then?'

He looked into her eyes. Lily shook her head. She didn't know what he meant.

'You'd have had to live with it.'

32

'IT'S FINISHED THEN? CASE closed?'

Secateurs poised, Angus Sinclair reached forward into the flower bed. Their summer splendour only a memory now, his rose bushes were ready for pruning.

'I would say so.'

Madden frowned. Aware of his former colleague's interest in the investigation – and grateful for the help and advice he had offered earlier – he had stopped off at the chief inspector's cottage on his way to the farm, to fill in the last pieces of the puzzle for him. And as though to mark the occasion the fog that had hung like a pall over much of the countryside as well as London had vanished, blown away overnight by a fresh westerly breeze. For the first time in days the sky above them was clear.

'They haven't found the body yet, but that's not unusual. Sometimes bodies wash up on the bank when the tide's out; at other times they sink, and then surface again a few days later. But the river police have picked up her rowing boat. They found it some distance downstream – past Wapping in fact. It was empty . . . drifting.'

He paused, as though to capture the image in his mind.

'Lily Poole heard her cry out. It seems Alma fell off the jetty as she was getting into the boat. She had been wounded. They found bloodstains. Grace must have winged her, Billy said. He rang me last night.'

The papers that morning, filled as they were with accounts of Blount's murder and the chase that followed, had also carried a brief statement by Detective Chief Superintendent Chubb to the effect that, with the presumed death by drowning of Alma Ballard, the police were no longer searching for anyone in connection with the shootings.

'Charlie knows he'll have to say more about her,' Billy had told Madden. 'But he's using the excuse that it wouldn't be proper until the body's been recovered and an inquest held. That won't stop the papers digging, though.'

Madden watched now as the chief inspector deftly decapitated a branch.

'Piecing it all together, they think she must have rowed upriver when the tide was flowing and left her boat moored to the jetty. That area of the docks is deserted these days, so it's unlikely anyone would have seen her. And the fog was on her side, of course. She could have forced the lock on the warehouse door earlier. She had plenty of time to plan the operation.'

'Indeed she did.' Sinclair stood back to admire his work. 'In fact it must have seemed quite like old times to her.'

'Old times? You're referring to her career as an agent?' Madden scowled.

'When she was in her element . . . yes. When she was most truly herself.'

The chief inspector glanced over his shoulder to see how his remark had been taken. Having more than an inkling of what his old friend must be feeling, he sought for the right words to ease Madden's mind.

'I know this has been painful for you, John,' he went on. 'But don't grieve too long or too hard for her. She wouldn't have wanted it.'

'Perhaps not.' Madden's face was a mask. He seemed unwilling to pursue the subject.

'How well do you remember the classics?'

'The classics?'

'Do you recall the Furies . . . the Erinyes? They were avenging spirits, the Greeks believed; and female, if I'm not mistaken. There was no escaping them. It might help if you thought of Miss Ballard in that light. She must always have known it would end this way.'

Not sure if he had struck the right note, Sinclair waited. Madden was regarding him with a quizzical look.

'That's a colourful way of putting it, Angus.' His smile came as a relief to the chief inspector. 'But I don't quarrel with it. Colin Finch had much the same idea. He thought she was a throwback to another age. What surprises me, though, is that she tried so hard to escape. Could she really have imagined that she had a future? Did she still think life had something to offer? She knew the police had caught up with her. I wonder she didn't shoot it out with them. Finch thought she would. He said as much.'

'Then perhaps it wasn't over for her yet.' Sinclair had pondered the question before replying. 'Perhaps there was something more she had to do.'

'Something more?' Madden frowned. 'That's possible, I suppose. But I can't imagine what.'

'I'll see you all on Monday.' Madden turned to wave.

Standing beneath the stableyard arch, as though posed for a photograph, George Burrows and his wife May raised their hands in response, while their daughter Belle, who stood beside them, cradled the newest member of the clan in her arms. Fred by name and all of ten days old, he had been born during Madden's absence in London.

'Lucy will be over here in no time,' he had assured Belle when the infant had been produced for his inspection earlier in the day. Plump and dark-haired, Belle had been a childhood friend of his daughter's and he still treasured the memory of them playing together in the stables while the work of the farm went on around them. 'She'll be back next week.'

With the outbreak of war the girls' paths had separated. Belle had enlisted in the ATS and had been stationed at Southampton. Lucy had joined the Wrens and, by means that had never been made clear to her parents, had contrived to get herself posted to the Admiralty where her career, though having little to do with the Royal Navy and much to do with London's nightlife, had threatened to give both of them grey hairs. Incapable of playing the stern father with his lovely daughter, Madden had nevertheless been rewarded by the discovery that, in spite of the more elevated social circles in which she now moved, Lucy had stayed loyal to old friendships and, having eagerly accepted her playmate's invitation to be a bridesmaid at her wedding to a Dorking carpenter two years previously, had continued to keep in touch with her. Indeed, her letters of late from Paris had been full of anxious enquiries as to Belle's condition.

As he set off down the road to the bottom of his land he found his thoughts straying to the past. Although his life had not been without its sorrows, he had come to think of himself as luckier than most. Married before he met Helen, he had lost both his first wife and the child they had to one of the great flu epidemics that had swept the world earlier in the century. Providence, though, had seen fit to grant him a second chance, preserving him from the slaughter of the trenches and bringing him not only a love that had grown stronger with the passing years, but a daughter to replace the one he had lost, whom he had watched grow into radiant womanhood.

No such blessing had been granted to James Ballard. And if indeed it was a curse from on high that had sent him to an early grave, it had lived on to bring his only child to an even sadder end. In the course of the day Madden had had time to reflect on the chief inspector's words and it seemed to him that the young woman whose loss he couldn't help but mourn – in spite of the bloody trail she had left behind her – was at one with the figures of ancient tragedy. Accepting her fate as she saw it, she had followed her doomed course to its bitter end. He would not forget her.

Still lost in his thoughts he came to the stream at the edge of his land and, before crossing it, looked back to assure himself that Hamish was following. In bad odour once again with his mistress – he had dug another hole in the garden the day before, this time in the lawn – the basset had blotted his copybook once too often.

'You must take him to the farm with you, John,' Helen had decided that morning. 'Wear him out. I want him too tired to even think of digging. Exhaust him.'

'Poor chap!' Madden had felt obliged to take the animal's side. 'He can't help it. Those paws were made for digging.'

'For digging up badgers perhaps.' Helen had been merciless. 'But not my flower beds. And he can use them for walking, from now on; or at least until further notice.'

Reflecting that his wife would be gratified by the sight of the weary-looking figure plodding some way behind him, he whistled.

'Come along, Hamish. It can't be as bad as that.'

He had intended to walk back through the woods, taking the higher path, but seeing the basset so woebegone, Madden decided to stick to the stream and follow the path that ran alongside it. It would be easier on the animal's tired legs, and in any case he was returning home later than he had planned. It was after four o'clock and the sun was fast declining. With the days growing shorter now, dusk fell quickly. Striding briskly along the leaf-strewn path, he soon reached Sinclair's cottage, where the only sign of life was a light burning in the sitting room. Not wishing to delay, he went past without stopping and soon afterwards felt a nudge on his ankle as Hamish – realizing that they were approaching home, and no doubt thinking of the dinner that awaited him – found a new spring in his step. Madden followed the stubby body with its waving tail until they had reached the gate at the bottom of the garden, where they both paused so that he could unlatch it.

Starting up the long lawn, he wasn't surprised to see the house in darkness. Helen would be late back. She had gone to Guildford to look in on some patients she had in the hospital there, and since their maid, Mary Morris, had the weekend off, she would be preparing their supper herself later on. In the meantime he could attend to some chores, and the first would be to feed Hamish, who was now making rapid progress up the side of the lawn towards the kitchen, where he knew his supper was kept. Before following him, however, Madden paused to scan the darkening sky and was rewarded by the sight of Venus low on the horizon glowing like a pearl in the gathering dusk.

Mary had left the dog's dinner – a tasty concoction of butcher's scraps – under a cloth in the pantry and, having retrieved it and placed it on the floor beside Hamish's water bowl, Madden went through to the corridor and on down to the entrance hall, switching on lights as he went.

Collecting his post from the silver salver lying on the hall table, he was about to take it into the drawing room when the phone rang in the study, so he continued down the passage to answer it.

'Hello, sir. I was hoping you might be home by now.'

There was no mistaking Billy's cheerful voice.

'I only got in this minute,' Madden said. 'What news?'

'We've found Alma's place . . . what did Finch call it?'

'Her *cachette*?'

'That's it. It was below Tower Bridge on the Surrey side, in

Bermondsey. The area's mostly a bomb site now – it took a pasting in the war – but the coppers down there were told that a woman had been seen moving about in it, so they had a good look round and came on a door in an abandoned house with a new padlock on it. They broke in and found it was a kind of storeroom full of women's clothes, tinned food, a first-aid kit, things you might need if you were going to hole up. We also found the warrant card she used to get in to see Blount, with Poole's name filled in on it. She could have done that after seeing Lily's picture in the newspaper and realizing she could pose as her and use the black eye as camouflage. We don't know who supplied her with the card. But I reckon it was in the letter she was waiting for at the Regal Hotel. She had arranged to have it sent to her there, because she knew Blount would be back in a day or two and she had to move fast. And that's not all.' Billy paused to lend drama to his next words. 'The court-martial record was there as well. It was in a suitcase along with some family stuff: snapshots . . . letters from her mother . . . that sort of thing.'

Madden was silent.

'She'd underlined all the names. Drummond, Gibson, Singleton, Canning, Blount. And yours, too.'

'Mine?'

'Plus the prosecutor's – some captain or other – and two chaps who gave evidence against Ballard: other soldiers, a sergeant and a private. Well, at least they don't have to worry now.'

Billy whistled.

'But the record was something to read. It was in his handwriting – Blount's – and it didn't leave much room for doubt. Ballard had deserted in the face of the enemy on such-and-such a date. He had left the line for the rear. The evidence was clear. The accused had offered no explanation for his actions. What Blount didn't say of course was that he'd gone mute, lost the power of speech. Just that he'd been examined by a doctor and found fit to stand trial. There was no word about any witnesses for the defence, either, or your statement in mitigation. Offhand, I'd say it was a fit-up.'

'I'm not surprised. My company commander said as much after he'd read it.'

'I told you they found her boat, didn't I?'

Madden grunted.

'There are some damaged wharves nearby. She probably kept it tied up there. The room itself was a ruin. Half the ceiling was gone. But she had some blankets along with the other stuff; she could have spent a night or two there at a pinch.' He sighed. 'And that about does it, I reckon. That covers everything. There's just her body to recover now, and my guess is it'll turn up tomorrow or the day after, at the latest.'

Billy was silent. He waited for Madden to speak.

'I always wondered how Oswald Gibson managed to remember my name when I couldn't remember his. It's obvious he got it from Alma.'

'When she called on him, do you mean? Before she shot him?'

'She must have gone through all the names in the record. Gibson remembered me saying I'd once been a detective, when I tried to tell Blount how trials should be run. That's why he considered writing to the commissioner. He thought I might be able to explain why such an ugly business was being resurrected after all these years. Still, as you say, it's over now.'

Madden sighed in turn.

'Oh, by the way, I know Helen wants to invite you and the family down for a weekend soon. She'll ring Elsie to fix it, but I hope you can come. Lucy will be here and she'd love to see you all.'

'We'll come. You can count on it. Especially when I tell the kids they'll be seeing Lucy. She always gets them going.' Billy chuckled. 'The same as she does with me.'

While he was speaking Madden had heard a muffled bark from Hamish out in the passage.

'I'd better go, Billy. It sounds like Helen's back. I'll tell her we talked.'

But when he went out into the hall there was no sign of his wife and he carried on along the corridor to the drawing room. With Mary off for the weekend, the house had been empty all afternoon and he needed to get a fire going. As he approached the room, however, he saw the back of Hamish. The dog was standing in the doorway. Only half of his long body was visible and, as Madden drew nearer, he heard him growl.

'What is it, boy?'

Madden bent to pat his head. He saw that the hairs on the basset's back had risen.

It was dark in the drawing room and he paused at the door to switch on one of the standard lamps. The dog growled again. Madden scanned the shadowy interior. The room was empty; or seemed to be. He wondered if a fox had got in. They could be surprisingly daring when the mood took them. More than one had been observed strolling the streets of Highfield late at night. He moved to the long table at the back of the sofa in front of the fireplace, where there were two lamps. But as he reached to switch on one of them, his eye was caught by something lying on the polished wooden surface. He couldn't make it out at first, but after he had turned on the lamp he saw it was a photograph of a young man in a private's uniform dating from the First World War. As he picked it up to hold it to the light, he heard a woman's voice.

'Look at it,' she said.

She had been standing motionless in a dark corner at the back of the unlit room near the empty fireplace, all but invisible at first. But now, as she moved forward, the light caught her face and Madden saw the pallid cheeks and wide, staring eyes.

'Is your name Madden?' she asked. 'J.H.T. Madden?'

'It is.' Madden eyed her carefully. She was wearing a shabby coat, stained with what looked like blood high up on her left arm. Her hair was covered by a plaid scarf. 'And you must be Alma Ballard.'

He saw the surprise flicker in her eyes. It was there only for a moment, however, and then the flat stare was back and he felt a cold hand settle on his heart.

'If you know who I am, then you know why I'm here.'

Her voice was hoarse. He could see the exhaustion written on her face.

'Quite the contrary.' He deliberately kept his voice calm. 'In fact, I'm curious to know what business you think you have with me.'

'You dare to say that?' Her gaze flared.

'Is it because I acted on behalf of your father? Because I was his defender and failed to save him?'

He knew it must be so. But he had to confront her. He must show her no fear. He kept an eye on her right hand. It was hanging at her side, empty for the moment, but near her coat pocket.

'His *defender*?' She spat out the word. 'You never raised your voice; you never said a word on his behalf.'

'And how would you know that? Were you there?'

When she was silent he went on.

'You've read a court-martial record that was compiled by a man who had only one purpose in mind: to see that your father was convicted. It seems you've called *him* to account and, if your conscience is untroubled by that murder and the others you've committed, so be it. But don't deceive yourself that your hands are clean. You've killed innocent people along with the guilty, men forced by circumstances beyond your comprehension to lend their names to a squalid act. Men who, for all you know, lived with that guilt for the rest of their lives.'

'My heart bleeds for them. As it will for you.'

Her eyes had gone blank again. She put her hand into her pocket and brought out a pistol.

'So you can't be reasoned with.'

Madden fought to keep a note of desperation from his voice. No plea for pity would move her. He could see that from her eyes, which registered no emotion. He measured the distance between them. He could get no nearer to her as long as the table separated them.

'The executioner has spoken. By now you must know what a cowardly business it is.'

He caught the sharp intake of breath.

'To shoot down men before they've even had time to reach for their rifles, the way you did at that German roadblock? To put a bullet in that poor French boy's head after he'd been beaten senseless?'

Two red spots bloomed on her ashen cheeks.

'Yes, I know all about you, Alma Ballard. You found that murder was simple, and you put the lessons you had learned into practice when you came back to England. A bullet in the neck was safest and quickest, but don't imagine you'll find it that easy with me.'

Madden had begun to circle the table towards her and, as he came nearer, she moved sideways onto the hearthrug, keeping a distance between them and raising her pistol at the same time.

'I'll kill you now, if I have to.'

He heard the tremor in her voice.

'Will you? I doubt it.' He halted. 'You want me down on my knees, like the others. That way you won't have to look at my face. Well, let me tell you something about myself, Miss Ballard. It's a secret, something I've never spoken of. When I was in the war – the same war your father fought in – I killed a German soldier with my bayonet. I ran him through and looked into his eyes while I did it. It was by far the worst thing I've ever had to do in my life, and I'll never forget it. If you want to shoot me now, then do it. But by God you'll look me in the eye when you pull the trigger.'

'Stop it!' Her voice rose. The hand holding the pistol had begun to waver.

'I knew your father. He was in my company. He was a fine soldier and a brave man, and what happened to him – what was done to him when the shelling robbed him of his senses and he couldn't speak – was wicked beyond measure. But if you can't see that what you have done is equally wrong, then you're no better than the men who put him before that firing squad. Now, either give me that gun or use it.'

He stepped forward, closing the space between them, and for a moment all hung in the balance as he saw Alma lift the pistol and steady it. But then her face seemed to crumple and it was she who fell to her knees. Bent into a ball, she clutched both hands to her stomach and, when Madden went down himself and tried to wrest the gun from her hand, she clung to it, turning the barrel towards her chest.

'No, child, no!'

He saw what she meant to do and, in desperation, felt for her wrist, meaning to wrench the pistol away from her body, but before he could get a grip of it, the gun went off and she convulsed. A sob came from her lips. The pistol slipped from her fingers and fell to the floor. As her body relaxed, Madden opened his arms and she fell into them. Her head came to rest on his shoulder and he looked into her blue eyes, still wide, but no longer staring. Already the life in them was beginning to fade.

'Hold on . . .' he whispered urgently in her ear. 'Stay with me . . .'

But he knew it was too late. Her coat had fallen open and the blood from her wound was all over her now, and him too.

She clutched at his arm. 'Don't leave me, please . . . don't—'

The words died on her lips. In the silence that followed Madden caught the faint sound of a car door slamming. Hamish's anxious bay echoed from the stone-flagged hallway, and the next moment the front door opened and footsteps sounded in the corridor.

'John? Oh, my God!'

Helen stood frozen in the doorway. She rushed to them.

'Oh, *no!*'

She had seen his blood-soaked front.

'It's all right . . . it's all right.' Madden found his tongue. 'It's hers, not mine.'

He kept the still form wrapped in his arms.

'I think she's gone,' he said.

Helen went down on her knees beside them. She reached out to touch the pale throat with her fingers.

'She's dead. Is it . . . ?'

She had already guessed. Madden nodded.

'She didn't drown after all. She shot herself – I made her do it.'

'John . . .' Helen took his hand in hers, grasping it firmly. She could see the shock in his face; his eyes were unnaturally bright, the pupils dilated.

'I told her things she couldn't bear to hear.'

The pain in his voice found an echo in her heart and she touched his face.

'My darling . . . Let me take care of this.'

'No, it's all right.' He insisted. 'It's all right. But I must ring Billy.'

He saw the concern in her eyes. She still held his hand in hers, and he pressed it in response.

'Don't worry. I just need a moment.'

But he stayed where he was, still on his knees, with the body held tightly in his arms until Helen, sensing that he needed help, kissed him on the cheek.

'John?'

'Yes . . . yes, of course.'

Coming to himself at last, he carefully laid the body on the hearthrug. Buttoning the shabby coat, he loosened the scarf around Alma Ballard's fair hair and drew it off. He saw her face fully then for the first time. Empty of all life now, the blue eyes were still open and, with a soft touch, he brushed them shut.

'Poor child,' he murmured. 'Poor lost soul.'

EPILOGUE

'Depraved, dissolute, decadent ... Those were the words he used. It was at the Labour Party conference in 1945. He was talking about the upper classes, of course, and I can remember thinking at the time: Oh dear, if only I could be *one* of those, but I never get the chance. He's probably a minister by now. I wish I could remember his name.'

Violet Tremayne bathed the Maddens' luncheon guests in her smile. Her glance alighted on Billy.

'But do tell me, Mr Styles, are you a supporter of this government? Do you agree with their ideas? Do you believe that people can actually be made better – in the same way, say, that a lawnmower can be improved? I've tried asking Helen the same question, but I can't get a sensible answer from her.'

'Well, I didn't vote for them myself.' Billy grinned. He caught Lucy's eye. The Maddens' daughter had returned from Paris with her beauty unimpaired, in spite of a new hairstyle. Gone were the long tresses he had always admired. In their place was a dashing new cut that fitted her head like a golden cap. 'But my wife did – Elsie, that is. She thinks they'll bring better schools, better healthcare, better housing ...'

'A socialist paradise, in other words?' Violet's eyes glowed with sympathy. 'The poor dear. You must tell her to be brave. She's in for a grave disappointment.'

'Lady Violet has been living in Moscow for two years,' Helen explained. 'She says she's seen the future, and it doesn't work.'

'Oh, very droll, Helen. I know you like to make fun of me, but one of these days you'll realize the error of your ways – only by then it'll be too late. Your communist friends will have taken over, and John will find he's managing a collective farm.'

Billy glanced down the table to where Madden was sitting and saw him smile for a moment, and then, as though distracted by some other thought, look away through the windows of the dining room out over the garden to the wooded ridge beyond. Three weeks had passed since Alma Ballard had breathed her last, and Billy himself had hurried down to Highfield to over-see the removal of her body to Guildford mortuary and to take a brief statement from his former mentor. Later Madden had given evidence at the inquest, also held in Guildford, and had appeared side-by-side with Billy and Chubb to answer questions at a crowded press conference. At his insistence, his own part in the investigation had not been disclosed, and he had been presented as someone whose advice had been sought after it was learned of his connection to the court martial.

That same week Alma had been buried beside her mother in a Richmond cemetery.

Madden had travelled up to London with his wife for the funeral, the arrangements for which had been left in Amanda Dauncey's hands. Word of the ceremony had been withheld from both press and public, and the only other mourner present had been Colin Finch. On learning from Billy about the part he had played in Alma's life, Miss Dauncey had invited the archi-tect to be present, and before the coffin had been lowered into the grave he had placed on the casket a medal bearing the image of St George slaying the dragon.

'It's the one that was awarded to her,' he had told the others afterwards. 'I'm not alone in thinking she was cruelly treated in being stripped of it. Our section head got hold of it somehow. This is where it belongs.'

It had originally been planned for Billy to bring his whole family to Highfield – Helen had invited them all down for the weekend – but an outbreak of measles in the Styles household had led to the visit being postponed to a later date, and only Billy had come down from London that Sunday for lunch with his friends. Though warmly welcomed by his old chief, he had found Madden quieter than usual, more withdrawn and, sensing that the time was not yet ripe to close the door finally on the mystery that had once surrounded Alma Ballard, Billy had resolved not to bring up the matter that day.

His instinct had been confirmed by Sinclair, when he arrived for lunch.

'He doesn't want to talk about it now,' he told Billy. 'He still blames himself for what she did – how she took her own life. But what else was left to her? John's words had struck home. She might even have believed by the end that what she had done was wrong. All the future held for her was the hangman's noose, and who can blame her for wanting to avoid that? We'll have a word together after lunch. You can tell me then whatever John might wish to know later. I'll pass it on to him when the time's right.'

Meanwhile the debate at the luncheon table had continued.

'My *communist* friends?' Helen was incredulous. 'I don't know any communists.'

'That's what you think. But they're all around us. Isn't that so, Mr Sinclair?' Violet rounded on him.

'I'm really not sure.' Cornered, the chief inspector cunningly passed the ball on. 'But Lucy can tell us. She's just spent three months in Paris. According to what I've read in the newspapers, France is full of communists.'

'Is it?' Taken equally by surprise, the Maddens' daughter

blinked. 'I'm not sure I actually *met* any. I mean, people don't just come up to you in the street and say: "*Bonjour*, I'm a communist."'

'Exactly my point.' Lady Violet was triumphant.

'Mind you, I did see Jean-Paul Sartre in a nightclub once.' Lucy brightened. '*He's* a communist.'

'I hope you treated him with disdain.'

'I didn't get the chance.' She giggled. 'There were too many people around him.'

'What were you doing in a nightclub?' Helen asked. 'You were supposed to be learning French.'

'Oh, Mother!'

Prior to lunch they had been treated to a fashion display laid on for Billy's benefit. Disappearing upstairs for a minute, Lucy had returned to the drawing room dressed in a garment the like of which he had never seen before. Cobalt-blue in colour, pleated and stretching almost to her ankles, the dress had billowed out like a sail as she pirouetted before them.

'It's the latest thing from Paris, the New Look. You must have heard of it.'

Indeed he had. The subject had even been debated in Parliament, where the new fashion had been dismissed by a large lady of leftist sympathies as 'the ridiculous whim of idle people' and a waste of scarce material.

'Now, just to put you in the picture,' Lucy had said, 'Mummy and Lady Violet think it's lovely, Angus is in two minds and Daddy simply scowls.'

'Daddy scowls because Daddy is still wondering where you got the money to buy that, and all the other clothes you brought back with you.' Sitting beside Sinclair on a settee, Madden had displayed a broad smile that seemed to suggest a different reaction. 'Especially since you kept telling us you were penniless.'

'I've explained all that. I was living on a tiny budget. I practically starved.'

'Yet you seem well fed.'

'Don't listen to him, Billy. Just tell me what you think.' She had positioned herself in front of him. 'I know I can count on you. How do I look?'

Under the spell of her smile – he'd succumbed to it years ago, when she was still a child – Billy hadn't needed to search for an answer. The word was already on his lips.

'Wonderful!' he said.

'So Alma was wounded in London? It's something I haven't liked to ask John.'

Sinclair studied the lawn at his feet.

'She was hit in the arm,' Billy replied. They had left the others after lunch and gone for a walk in the garden. 'It wasn't a serious wound, and when her body was examined it was found that she had disinfected and bandaged it. But she must have lost a lot of blood before she got back to that room of hers. I think she was pretty well played out by the time she arrived here. We found a conductor on the line from Waterloo who remembered seeing a woman slumped asleep in her seat. He had to wake her to tell her the train had reached Highfield. She stopped at the butcher's in the village to ask the way to the Maddens' house. The lad she spoke to said she looked ill.'

'But how did she get downriver?' The chief inspector was frowning. 'Was it in the boat? I thought it was seen drifting empty?'

'It was. Or rather, it looked empty,' Billy explained. 'We reckon she was lying down flat on the bottom and just letting it drift with the current. The constable who saw it from the bank only got a glimpse of it. Then the fog closed in. Once she was out of sight, she could have rowed down to Bermondsey, come ashore and then let the boat float on.'

'I thought Poole heard her go into the water.'

'She heard a splash all right. But there were lumps of rock and concrete littering the jetty where Alma had her boat moored, and I think she just rolled one of them into the water. You had to be there to see how thick the fog was, sir. I don't fault Poole at all. In fact, I've put her down for a commendation, and the chief super's approved it.'

'That's capital news.' Sinclair beamed.

'It'll make up for her getting that shiner, I reckon.' Billy smiled. 'She took that hard. She had to put up with a lot of ribbing over it, especially from Joe Grace. But she got her own back. When she went to see him in hospital she took him a big bunch of flowers. Joe nearly had a fit.'

Sinclair chuckled. 'I always knew she'd turn into a first-rate copper. Keep an eye on her, Billy.' He looked at his watch. 'I must be getting back. Will Stackpole is coming over this afternoon to chop wood for me for the winter.'

Will was the village bobby and an old friend of Billy's.

'He feels he's been left out of this whole Ballard business. He thinks he ought to have had a hand in it.' Sinclair smiled. 'He tells me he'll be retiring in a year or two. He'll be the last of his kind, at least as far as Highfield is concerned. They won't send us another bobby after he's gone, more's the pity.'

Billy grunted in sympathy.

'Everything's changing now. It's all patrol cars and fewer feet on the beat. I hope they know what they're doing.'

He remembered then.

'By the way, Charlie sends his regards. He and his missus are coming down to spend a weekend with the Maddens quite soon, he tells me. He said he was counting on seeing you again.'

'He didn't happen to mention King Lear, did he?'

Billy grinned. 'I seem to remember him saying something about that to Mr Madden, but I wasn't sure what he meant.'

'Were you not indeed?' The chief inspector's eyes glittered. 'I was only surprised to learn that the two of them were acquainted. You can tell him I look forward to seeing him and hope he and his lady will favour me with a visit. I might even offer them a cup of tea.'

He glanced over to a distant corner of the garden, where Madden and Helen were engaged in discussion.

'They're debating the fate of that old beech tree,' he said. 'I don't want to interrupt them. Will you thank them for me, Billy? Say I had to be on my way. I'll see you again soon, I hope.'

'But it's such a lovely old tree,' Madden was saying. 'I'd hate to lose it.'

'So would I. But it's dying, poor thing. There's nothing we can do about it.'

'Let's cut it back again.'

'We did that last year, and look at the result.'

The tree in question, a weeping beech, had spread its branches like a great tent over the corner of the garden for generations. Still in its prime when they had first met, its green leaves slowly turning to russet as autumn advanced had formed an impenetrable curtain, offering cool shade even on the hottest of days. But lately the leaves had grown sparser and now its bare, drooping branches presented a sad spectacle.

'But . . . but it's part of our history.'

Madden slipped an arm around his wife's waist. Laughing, she caught his eye.

'Are you trying to make me blush, John Madden?'

Years ago they had sought shelter from a rainstorm under the tree's sheltering limbs. Not yet married, they had hurried home from a walk in the woods hoping to find the house empty, only to discover that Helen's father had returned earlier than expected. Seeing the lights in the house switched on, they had parted the curtain of branches and found the privacy they wanted under the great dome of leaves.

Looking up at her husband's face, Helen felt her heart lighten. The shadow that had lain there was slowly fading. She knew he would continue to go over the events of the past weeks in his mind for a while yet. He would look to see where he had failed. But in time he would come to accept what she already knew – that he had done all he could, and could have done no more – and when that day came, and it would be soon now, the ghost of Alma Ballard would finally be laid.

'You're right,' she said. 'It's a lovely tree. A lovely *old* tree. Let's give it another year.'

Author's Note

In November 2006 Parliament passed a law pardoning men of the British and Commonwealth armies convicted by court martial and executed during the First World War. In the course of the debate the Defence Secretary, Des Browne, said: 'I believe it is better to acknowledge that injustices were clearly done in some cases – even if we cannot say which – and to acknowledge that all these men were victims of war. I hope that pardoning them will finally remove the stigma with which their families have lived for years.'

However, the law did not overturn the sentences, which remain in effect.

AVAILABLE FROM PENGUIN

River of Darkness

This *New York Times* Notable Book introduces Inspector John Madden who, in the years following World War I, is sent to investigate a gruesome attack in a small village.

The Blood-Dimmed Tide

Set in 1932, Madden discovers a young girl's mutilated corpse near his home in rural England, bringing him out of retirement to chase a killer whose horrific crime could have implications far afield in a Europe threatened by Hitler's rise.

The Dead of Winter

Set in 1944, Madden pushes the investigation of the murder of young Polish refugee and former employee Rosa Novak, uncovering her connection to a murdered Parisian furrier, a member of the Resistance, and a stolen cache of diamonds.

**PENGUIN
BOOKS**